EVAN'S

SUNSET

ANGEL

Believe in
Love!
Jeni

EVAN'S SUNSET ANGEL

Written by Jeni ©

Bare Tree Publishing LLC SC

COPYRIGHT

Evan's Sunset Angel
Copyright © 2019 by Jeni

Published by Bare Tree Publishing LLC

ISBN: 978-0-9970951-8-0

Cover Design by Deeds Publishing

First Edition 2019

Acknowledgements

My cheerleaders: for their encouraging words.

My grammar editor, Jill for her dedication and the vast amount of time she spent through the grammatical aspects of the book.

My critique editor, Ann, for her dedication and the extensive hours we spent with those "nit-pick" finds.

My first read editor, Heath. Thank you for your support, and so much more!

TYG…

Also by Jeni

Kellan's Sweet Angel

Dirk's Angel of Destiny

The Angel Series

BOOK THREE

Chapter One

An eerie blackness surrounded Callie. She was being held captive in some kind of shipping crate. It was dark and hot. Since the kidnapping, she hadn't seen a speck of daylight and had lost touch with time. She didn't know if it was morning or night, or how many days had passed. Callie hated not being able to see anything and would often trick her mind into not panicking, by closing her eyes.

Leaning against the shipping crate's cold wall, she missed the noisy activity that had occupied the other side. The sounds of men shouting, fork lifts beeping, their engines humming, and tires squealing on the floor as they moved other crates. Each time a crate was moved its metal bottom scraped across the concrete floor, and she heard the frightening shrieks from the women inside them. Both sounds shivered deeply into her bones.

With all the bustling going on outside her crate…hers stayed motionless. She had been thankful for this, but now she was cursed with the deafening hush.

Before everything went quiet she'd been given a loaf of bread and bottles of cold water. She had dripped the condensation on her sweaty face and preserved the liquid by taking only necessary sips.

The stuffy air lasted longer than the food and water. Despair fell on her, and she prayed for help to arrive.

She was awakened by the shrill sound of the crate door opening. She didn't have time to cover her ears because a light shined right in her eyes, blinding her. She couldn't see the faces of the men approaching her but their arrogant voices frightened her.

They grabbed her arms, and feeling afraid she kicked her assailants. They caught one of her legs and tugged. She screamed and her arms were let go. Free, she shot her hands forward and they collided with a hard object. She continued yelling and fighting them, praying they'd go away. Finally they did and she was left alone in the dark.

They came back. This time they wore masks and again, she couldn't see their faces. It was hard to trust them especially when their impatient tones assured her she was safe but they were liars! The bearded man told her she was safe, but he didn't let her go. Instead he kept her in this crate and left her. Why should she believe these men who verbalized they were nice but roughly handled her? Again, she fought them by kicking, hitting, and screaming. They left and returned with angrier voices and brighter lights. She curled her body into a small ball making it harder for them to get her, and she was extremely grateful when they finally left, leaving her alone for a longer time.

Callie fell asleep and was awakened by the same shrill sound of the crate door opening again. Tucking her face into her knees, she covered her head with her arms and inhaled a fearful breath anticipating the pawing hands and unsettling voices that would soon reach her.

She waited but nothing happened. No one touched her. No one spoke to her. It was quiet, but she sensed a presence. Raising her head, a shimmering light illuminated the crate with a golden hue. A tall silhouette of an angel appeared. Its aura radiated kindness as it knelt before her with an outstretched hand that didn't force her or touch her. Its aura was different than all the others who had come in. A peaceful feeling washed over her, and Callie knew her worst fear had come true…she had died and this angel was here to take her home.

The angel invited her to go with him and promised to keep her safe.

"Yes," she mumbled.

Trusting the angel, she took his hand and his wide wings gently and warmly embraced her. His earthy scent made her feel safe, safer than she'd ever been. Wrapped in this angel's love is where she wanted to spend eternity.

The angel's caressing voice said, "Let's go home."

Knowing the angel would get her home safely; she closed her eyes and quietly stated, "To heaven…"

Chapter Two

Evan prayed Dexter was able to hold his promise and not drug Callie. His phone conversation with the FBI agent earlier today raced through his mind. It was torture hearing Dexter say, "Callie isn't letting any of the rescue teams near her. They want to drug her."

"Please don't let them drug her before I get there!" he begged then negotiated. "If I can't get her out, then they can but not before I try!"

Dexter agreed to this.

Immediately following his phone call with Dexter, he had contacted his brother, Eric, who was a licensed pilot and had his own helicopter. He was grateful for the air ride here; a lot less travel time than by road.

Eric lowered them towards the ground.

Evan's sky view of the rescue crews below was insane! Fire trucks, police cars, vans, and ambulances scattered the area. Why did they need all these people to rescue one person? Landing safely on the ground, Evan thanked Eric, exited, and joined Dexter.

The two men shook hands.

"Any luck on getting Callie out?" Evan asked.

Dexter sadly shook his head. "None *and*," he held up his hand, "I made sure she wasn't injected with any drugs."

Relief showed on Evan's face and Dexter didn't bother to tell him that no one's tried to get her out since their phone conversation and that for them the next step was an injection.

Off to the side, Evan saw a paramedic holding a small black case. He knew it was the drug man, on standby, ready to inject Callie with a calming drug. If it hadn't been for his protests she would have already been injected. The thought of her being drugged was unbearable! He had to succeed!

"I'll get her out," he said confidently.

"Let's go." Dexter motioned his hand for Evan to follow and led him to the shipping crate.

"I can't believe no one's been able to get her out," he remarked off-handedly and swung the screeching door wide open. A shiver shot down his spine.

"Stop!" a voice behind them called out. "You can't go in!"

Turning, Dexter and Evan saw a man running towards them frantically waving his hands.

"You cannot go in without safety gear," the man said, breathlessly.

Evan gave him a ridiculous look, but the man shook his head and gave him a pair of earplugs. "Mister, you're going to need these. The wild woman has screaming fits."

Evan's jaw twitched. "Wild woman?" he inquired.

"Yes, sir," the man said, "and we suggest you wear these."

Another man stepped forward with an armor long sleeved jacket and mask.

"Why?" Evan expressed uncertainty.

The first man spoke up. "When we went in to take her, she tried clawing us."

The second man piped in explaining that the mask would protect his face from her fists.

"Fists?" he repeated.

Both men nodded.

He shook his head saying, "I'll take my chances."

"But, sir," they protested and tried telling him about the statistics of using the gear.

Evan wouldn't budge. All of it was too heavy and too impersonal, especially the mask! That thing was scary, and he understood why Callie didn't trust them. How did they expect people to trust them looking like crazed aliens? If he had any chance of being successful, he needed Callie to personally touch him and know she was safe.

Evan gave them a hellish glare and declared, "I am not wearing any of this crazy shit."

He folded his arms across his chest taking a defiant stance.

The two men from the rescue team shook their heads and let him pass taking side bets on how long he'd last without protection.

Feeling everyone's eyes preying on his back, Evan held his head high and confidently entered the crate. They thought he was insane for going in to fetch the "wild woman" without armored clothes, but he didn't care. He was determined to get Callie out of the crate and safely in his arms. Holding her was all that mattered.

The front of the crate shined with daylight, but Callie was in the back where it was dark. She wasn't tied up, but she stayed huddled in the corner. Seeing her so unfocused broke his heart. He cautiously moved towards her. In a calm tone he recited her name. He spotted the bottles of water and plate; both empty. *How long has she been without food and water? Did the bearded man take her and abandon her right away?*

Though he had no proof about who kidnapped her, he had his suspicions, and right now all of his haunting questions were answerless with no foreseeable future of having any answers.

He crouched to her level so she could face him evenly instead of looking up and feeling defensive. So far, she hadn't screamed. He took this as a good sign and believed she was listening and trusting *his* words that she was safe. He opened his arms inviting her into them and prayed she'd willingly accept. She did by leaning towards him and his heart glowed. Rising to their feet she stumbled. He caught her and folded her into his arms.

"I've got you, you're safe," he reassured. "It's time to go home."

She nodded and agreed she was ready to go to heaven. *What!* His heart raced. *Oh, my, God! She thinks she's dead!*

She lay limp in his arms, and he began to panic. "No! Sweetheart, wake up!" he begged fiercely.

Callie heard the angel's pleas, but she was so tired...*I just want to sleep.*

Her hand skimmed the angel's whiskered jaw, reminding her of Evan and when she slapped him. Her memory walked backwards to that day.

Like always, he came up from behind and scared her, but he also tickled her sides and pulled her backwards. His lips grazed her ear as she fell into his arms. Her body tingled everywhere. She was flustered but then her defending instincts kicked in, and she turned sliding her free hand across his unshaven face.

His first initial reaction was shock, but he quickly recovered and flashed a playful smile, daring her to do it again.

While she debated this, his voice dipped low, and he whispered a husky warning. "Slap me again, and I'll kiss you."

Mischievous eyes tempted her. If his lips on her ear sparked heat, what would happen if their mouths touched?

The stitches on his temple softened her abrasive gaze, and she extended her hand towards the injury, but he pushed it away.

"Don't," he said, curtly.

She was devastated, assuming the reason he stopped her was because he thought she was going to hurt him. Quietly, she said, "I wasn't going to."

"I know," he replied harshly. "Safe travels, Callie Cat. See ya when you return."

She grumbled a sassy remark to his retreating ass. He didn't acknowledge that he had heard her, but she was convinced he had.

Coming back to the present, she recited the sassy words she had spoken. "No, I'll see you."

"Yes, sweetheart, open your eyes and see me."

"No. Let me sleep," she protested, tossing her head side to side.

Determined to wake her, Evan demanded, "Callie Cat, wake up!"

She thought *why is the angel calling me Callie Cat? Evan's the only one who calls me this.*

"Callie Cat."

The angel's voice seeped into her brain, and she became aware of the patting on her face.

She moaned, "Evan."

"Yes, honey, I'm right here. Open your eyes," he stressed, rubbing her temples.

She tried but the light was overwhelming and whimpered it was too bright.

He shielded her eyes with his hand. "Callie, look at me."

Her eyes fluttered several times while she comprehended the angel's identity. "Evan?"

"Yes!"

She squinted, and he saw her skepticism. "Show me your scar."

He thought it was an odd request, but he turned his head for her. Watching her recognize him solely by his skinned blemish was soul binding.

"Oh, my God, Evan!" she cried. "It is you! You found me!"

Tears flowed like a river down her face.

"Yes, Callie Cat, I found you." His voice cracked with relief, because she was alive and in his arms. *Finally!*

"I knew you would!"

Her confidence in him of finding her was overwhelming. Tearful emotions surfaced and trickled down his cheeks. *I am finally holding her!*

Callie swung her arms around his neck. Too many hours had passed of not knowing when she would hear his voice again and now here they were holding each other! Their first official hug! It was better than when they danced at the wedding. *That dance* had been the beginning of something, and she hoped the kidnapping hadn't squashed any of those plans.

They tightly embraced.

"Don't let me go."

"I won't," he promised.

All the '*what if*' days that had passed made him feel old, but in the last few minutes time shifted, and he felt ten years younger!

"We're going home, Callie."

"What about Sunbird?" she asked about her beloved semi tractor.

He smiled. "The two of you will be staying with me for awhile."

"For how long?" she asked.

"For as long as you want."

She sighed with relief and laid her head on his shoulder.

"That's my girl," he whispered, unaware she wanted to be his girl.

Both were hopeful that their relationship could be picked up where it was left.

Callie settled into his safe embrace as he carried her out of the crate leaving behind the hellish ordeal she'd been through.

Exiting the cargo crate a medical team rushed over to them and tried taking Callie. She screamed and refused to let go of Evan's neck.

"Stay away," he hissed to the team.

Displeased, they backed off, sensing his need to protect the "wild woman" he held so dearly. He had become a contradicting giant; gentle with the woman and roaring at the forces trying to pull her away.

One of the paramedics, Jamie heaved a heavy sigh. It was a sticky situation. The two weren't going to let go of each other and before the woman could be released, she had to be examined. But she didn't trust the medical team, and Jamie knew she wouldn't willingly go with them. Nor did he think the man would allow her out of his sight.

Evan scolded himself for not calling Chase and seeing if the traveling doctor was available. If he had been within their flight path, he and Eric could have picked him up in the helicopter. In his defense, his main focus had been on Callie and getting here. Not once had he ever considered the possibility of the horrible state they'd find her in! He hadn't ever seen anyone so distraught, and it frightened him.

Glancing at the paramedic approaching them, Evan gave a fair warning. "She's not going anywhere without me."

"Yes, I understand. Would you be willing to hold her while I examine her?"

"Yes, I would."

"Great!" Jamie smiled, extended his hand and introduced himself.

Stating their names, Evan firmly shook hands with him. "I appreciate you working with us instead of against," he stated gratefully.

"You're welcome." Jamie said. Keeping eye contact with both of them he began explaining, "I'll do a short examination such as check your pulse, heart rate, and temperature, if you agree to get checked out with a local physician within twenty four hours."

"I will make sure she does," Evan promised. "Our doctor can send you a copy of the report."

Jamie shook his head. "It won't be necessary. I trust your word."

"Thank you," Evan sincerely said.

Jamie's eyes met Callie's as he said, "If you're ready I'm going to begin."

Callie nodded.

Jamie swiftly finished and handed Evan the discharge papers stating Callie was in good health.

Evan folded and tucked them in his back pocket.

"My information and cell number is there. If your personal physician has any questions, he can get in touch with me," Jamie said.

"Appreciate it and thanks again for working with us," Evan stated gratefully.

"You're welcome. Good luck."

Evan didn't let Callie go until they arrived home, and he laid her on the bed in the upstairs guest room. It would be her room while she stayed here through her recovery.

Tucking the blankets around her, he tenderly whispered, "Sweet dreams, Callie Cat."

Chapter Three

Dexter was leaving the shipping dock with extra money in his wallet. He had placed his lone bet for Evan's success in retrieving Callie aka the wild woman. The rescue crews had given her this nickname when they had failed on their second rescue attempt. They had sorely underestimated Evan's determination of getting Callie out.
None of them believed he had any chance of walking out of the crate unharmed *and* with her. Especially dressed in jeans and scruffy boots versus the heavy jacket they threw at him.

Dexter patiently waited outside the crate. The longer Evan stayed in was one more rescue worker's ego sliding to its knees. When Evan finally exited the crate carrying a subdued Callie, Dexter loved their stunned reactions. *Priceless!*

Renaming them in his mind, the *rescue jerks.* They had become too accustomed with their expensive equipment in getting the job done. It was nice to bear witness in that humanity hadn't been lost in this high tech world. It made throwing his authoritative weight in supporting Evan ten times better, and the money he had won was icing on the cake.

Leaning against the side of the SUV, Dexter sent his two agents a coded message: **Smart girl is safe.** He knew they'd understand it meant Callie had been rescued. One of the agents quickly responded with a thumbs up sign. Jack, the other agent, responded several hours later, surprising him with a phone call.

"Hello," Dexter greeted. "I didn't expect to hear from you so soon."

Jack understood what he meant. Due to this undercover assignment often it was days or weeks before he surfaced. "Yeah, I have a few minutes. So the rescue plan for Callie went as planned?"

Telling a white lie, Dexter said, "Yes." There was no need to tell him the delayed details. The important thing was Callie was home safe and besides Jack couldn't do anything about it now anyway.

"Where's Kara?" Jack asked.

"She's safe."

Jack didn't like Dexter's short reply and wished he could have questioned his partner for a more exact location. But as it was, he was pressured with time and had to make good use of it.

"Where is Iguana?"

"Trailing the hound," Dexter replied.

"Is he having any luck?"

"Some. How's Humphrey?"

"Can't wait for it to be over," Jack grunted. Humphrey was the last person he wanted to talk about. He wanted more information than Dexter was willing to give and wondered why his partner was being evasive.

Dexter asked, "Any news on your end?"

"There's buzz of a meeting coming together soon about the shipment," Jack informed.

"It's what we need."

"No shit! Listen, I gotta go, but I'll keep you posted on what I find out."

"Be careful."

"Thanks." Jack ended the call and clipped the phone to his belt.

Locking the car he went inside to pay for the gas and flirted a little with the cashier. Saying, her eyes were as pretty as a blue sky made her blush. Thinning his lips into a smile he was careful not to show her his ugly teeth. The crooked dentures he wore were part of his undercover disguise along with the long, hot, itchy beard. It all made for an unflattering appearance. If only, he could count the days left of wearing it but currently there was no end in sight. Some days he thought he might be close, only in the end, to be disappointed. The information he gave Dexter sounded promising, but Jack also knew he shouldn't get his hopes up.

Driving back to the compound where he and Abel were laying low, his thoughts drifted to Kara. He was glad she was safe and wondered how she was adjusting to her new surroundings. *Where was she? Was she making new friends?*

His jaw tensed thinking about the men she was meeting. He was pessimistic about her choices, especially since her last lover had been the jack of all asses. Had she learned her lesson?

The security guard waved him through the gates, and he drove the curvy concrete mile leading to the house. The compound sat on ten acres of woods with a two story house and a three car garage. Inside had the traditional kitchen, dining room, living room, and bedrooms. There were several bedrooms upstairs and some on the main floor. All were filled with bunk beds; designed to accommodate many outlaws. The living room had couches and recliners and a large flat screen TV had been mounted on the wall over the fireplace.

Abel, his crime boss, was already outside waiting for him. Jack put the car in park and Abel got in hinting he was late elaborating the length of time it should take to put gas in the car. Having proven his loyalty to the man many times, it irritated Jack that Abel still got antsy if he ran a few minutes behind.

Luckily, the answer easily rolled out of Jack's mouth. "Yeah, sorry, I got carried away flirting with the cashier. She was a pretty little thing. I wanted more time with her but," he paused. "I didn't want to worry you."

Just as Jack had hoped, Abel looked him in the eye and made amends. "I'm sorry, Humphrey. It's my nature to be suspicious, but I shouldn't be with you. You're the most loyal man I've ever had. In a few days, we're going to find out about the shipment that's coming in. Soon after, I'll be making my move to disappear. You still interested in coming to work for me?"

"Yes!" Jack said, excitedly, because saying no would be putting his life in extreme danger. He'd come this far, he wasn't giving up now.

"Good!" Abel's face beamed relief. "Take a left at the end of the driveway."

"Where we going?" he asked, turning.

"You'll see," Abel said mysteriously.

Jack nodded and kept his eyes on the road while Abel talked. "Humphrey, my family is gonna love you."

"I'm loveable," he said, grinning, and this time he showed his crooked ugly teeth.

Chapter Four

Slamming the front door shut Kara screamed at the top of her lungs. Angry at the world she threw her purse across the room. It hit the floor, skidded across it, spilling the contents from the unzipped pocket. She walked over to it and kicked it into the kitchen before exiting out the back door. *I hate this place!*

Outside she picked up a rock and whipped it through the air. It hit the side of the garage making a menacing sound. She needed to hear it again. Picking up another rock she threw it against the building. Her evil marksmanship knotted another round of frustration in the pit of her stomach. After several more throws her arm became tired, but it hadn't lessened the storm raging inside. She stomped back in the house. In the mirror she glared at her reflection.

"This place sucks!" she raged. She had been dumped into a "safe place" and was having a crappy time adjusting to a new area, name, faces, job, and no friends!

Friends...well she didn't have many friends where she came from but at least she had familiar faces. Guilt ripped through her thinking about the best friendship she ever had, ruining it with several stupid decisions.

Name...Holly Belles was her new name. After answering to Kara for twenty some years it was hard answering to a new name. She hated the name, but people loved it because it reminded them of Christmas. She despised being a person that didn't exist.

Job...Out of ten fingers, six had bandages on them and there were several burns on her hands and arms. The steam burns were the worst. She still hadn't got the hang of the steamer oven. Her new job was a prep cook at a catering company in town. She enjoyed cooking but wasn't sure cooking in bulk was her calling.

New town...The town of Purlieu was a surprisingly good size. It had a grocery store everyone flocked to, a few convenience stores, churches, gyms, and family owned restaurants. It lacked a real commercial district but Junction City had all of this and was less than an hour's drive, but it required a little more planning. In fifteen minutes she could be on the other side of town. And three minutes from her house she could be on a deserted road.

Deserted road...This is what she needed! Adrenaline pumped through her veins while her foot pressed the gas pedal of the compact car she drove these days. She raced out of town at a harrowing speed. She was alone on the straight open road. The car accelerated gaining speed past eighty and still climbing. It was exhilarating! The same as when the speed boat zoomed across the open sea freeing her from the sheds.

Images of Greg, her former boss and lover, flashed across her windshield. She was tormented by the statement love is blind. The truth of this was Greg never loved her and accepting this was what hurt the most. *He's an asshole and the reason I'm here!* Greg's face changed into Jack, the FBI Agent, and his harsh cynicism showing her the pictures of Greg with another woman proving she was only a pawn in his life.

Tears welled in her eyes and the road ahead became blurry. It forced her to slow down, pull over onto the shoulder of the road and park the car. She leaned her head on the steering wheel and sorrowfully cried for all the reckless decisions she had made from the New Year's Eve party through today. She'd been so stupid and driving like a mad woman just now had been dumb, too. What if she had lost control of the car and had a fatal car crash? Getting killed was not an option. She couldn't let Greg get away with what he did!

A harsh knock on her door halted her misery. A man wearing a faded red shirt and overalls stood outside her window. The bill on his cap shaded his eyes, but she noticed the grease smudges on his face and clothes. He obviously needed help and she hand rolled the window down and came face to face with an angry man.

"Lady! What the hell!" he yelled. "You're driving like a maniac!"

"Um…" she stammered, but he cut her off.

"Are you trying to kill others or just yourself?"

"There's no one else out here," she feebly defended.

"Do I look like nobody?" he fumed.

"No." She shook her head. "I'm sorry."

"If I ever see you speeding like this again I'll take your license away," he threatened.

Kara's eyes widened, fearing the threat of having this freedom taken away.

"Do you understand?" he bellowed.

She nodded her head emphatically and tried apologizing, but he wouldn't listen.

"I don't want your damn apology! I want you to obey the damn speed limit! Now get out of here!"

He crossed the road back towards his house, and she drove straight home and didn't exceed the speed limit; not even one mile per hour over.

Iguana watched the young lady drive off at a turtle's pace. Yelling away his stress had felt damn good! This new assignment was keeping him on his toes. He was cranky due to the lack of sleep. The punching bag had not diminished his shitty attitude. The speeding car had only heightened his temper. He jumped the ditch and ran over to the car envisioning a fist fight with the driver. The last thing he expected to see was a sobbing woman. Disappointed because he couldn't physically fight, he verbally lashed out.

Hours later, sweat dripped from Iguana's temple as he pounded his fists into the punching bag hanging from the barn rafters. The woman's face haunted him. He was not proud of the way he reacted. *What the hell is wrong with me? I acted like a mad man...didn't even ask if she was okay. She looked terrible, defeated, and lonely. Had she been trying to kill herself?*

If she had, he might have just helped her complete the job with his irrational shouting. Regret passed through him. *I shouldn't have lost my temper and yelled at the woman especially when she had been crying. Maybe I should find her and apologize?*

Or just leave it alone, because I have enough things going on and don't need anymore distractions.

Chapter Five

Gazing out the second story bedroom window Callie had a glorious view of Evan's one ton dually leaving the driveway. The stormy gray was a beautiful sight! Its Duramax 6.6 L turbo-diesel engine thundered down the road with its upgraded bigger tires and a 6 inch lift. The truck's height was no problem for Evan's six foot four inches. Though she had never driven Evan's truck she had sat in the driver's seat. One time Evan goaded her to climb up, and she easily did. She couldn't tell if he was amused or haunted by the fact she didn't ask for his help. The cushiony seat conformed to her body. Instantly, she felt at home; the same as she did in Sunbird. It was strange thinking she could be comfortable behind another truck's steering column. For one crazy second, a part of her felt like she was betraying Sunbird.

Callie envied Evan's juggled schedule of working in the fields and managing the operations at Maslund Trucking. She missed her busy driving schedule. It was a hard leap from having deadlines to having nowhere to be.

On her second day here, Dirk called saying, "Cal, you've accumulated a lot of paid time off. Enjoy yourself."

"Are you forcing me not to work?" she had accused.

He sighed, "Highly encouraging you, because you deserve a vacation."

"For how long?" she inquired.

"How long do you need?"

"I'll let you know."

After a few days of lounging by the pool and reading books, she was bored. She joined a book club at the library but it didn't give her any sense of accomplishment like her job did, such as safely delivering loads on time. It was true, all these years she hadn't taken time off. Her job was a vacation! Traveling the country east to west and north to south *and* getting paid was awesome!

Her favorite view had always been from Sunbird's driver's seat. At the end of the day she loved the proud feeling that she had contributed something to the world. Now all she had to contribute was helping Evan with chores around the house but this didn't occupy enough of her time. Nor did it help with getting back to the routine of her first week here. Always an early riser, she discovered Evan rose earlier than her. As she poured her first cup of coffee, he was heading out the door but paused, taking the time to ask how she was.

These brief encounters were semi formal opposite of their comfortable phone conversations. She felt shy having to face him. It was a lot like their first dance when she struggled to stay calm; her insides bouncing all over the place as the sentences running through her head were stuck on her tied tongue. In both instances, Evan eased her tension with his charming smile and friendly glib, and like the dance, she really wanted to be in his arms.

Callie didn't see Evan the rest of the day since he came home late in the evening when she was getting ready for bed. From the bottom of the stairs he'd shout, "Hey, I'm home!"

She'd appear at the top of the stairs listening to him recite his busy day. Never did she descend from the top two steps, nor did he ascend past the bottom two. They chit chatted until the first yawn; it was a race to see who could hold out the longest.

Then Evan would say, "All right, time for bed. Sweet dreams, Callie Cat."

"You, too, and don't let the bedbugs bite," she'd wish.

He'd laugh adding, "You either."

Unfortunately, their stairwell conversations came to an end. Callie was plagued by horrible nightmares. She'd wake up sweating, tangled in the sheets from fighting with her captors. Evan, awakened by her terrifying screams always sat on the bed's edge while she retold the images in her head.

One night, she woke up and was lying face down on the bed. Her arms were extended forward and Evan was holding them.

"What happened?" she had asked.

He had sadly said, "When I walked in you were standing on the bed. Your eyes raged into mine. Like a cat you sprang off the bed and attacked me."

"But, I remember hitting and kicking my attacker," she recalled and Evan's pained expression told her she had targeted him.

Horrified, she gasped, "No!"

He had pulled her into his arms and reassured her it was okay.

"Hurting you is not okay!" she said tearfully.

"Shhh," he hushed and his calming voice lulled her back to sleep.

The erratic sleep pattern caused her to wake up late, and she missed seeing Evan in the mornings. Throughout the day she'd nap; catching up on the previous night's loss of sleep. At first, the dreams didn't appear in her naps but then they did, and she was haunted by the trembling images her eyelids displayed.

During the night she was thankful for Evan helping her versus the daylight when she was alone while he was working. She had to find a solution to break this horrible cycle. Unfortunately, she had not come up with any ideas to solve this dilemma. All she knew was that the menial house chores weren't keeping her mind occupied. She had to find something that did before the nightmares drove her to insanity.

****

In the rearview mirror Evan glanced back at the house. More specifically his eyes searched for movement in the window of the bedroom Callie occupied. Was she sleeping or awake and staying hidden? Two nights ago he had to pin her body between him and the bed just to keep her from hurting him. He hated doing it, but he needed to get her calm and awake. Night after night she was tortured with nightmares. He suffered, too, as an observer; it was painful. He always stayed with her until she fell asleep. At least she had solace in the day and didn't have to deal with the horrible images plaguing her nights.

His watch alarm chimed, and he frowned, because it reminded him of the time he arrived home late. Hearing her scream, he rushed up the stairs to help her. She had been on the verge of waking up from the dream, but then his watch alarm beeped and it tail spun her into the mire again.

Digging her fingernails in his arm, she shrieked, "You're not Evan!"

He had released her, and she fled the room, seeking refuge in the hall closet. It had taken quite a long time to coax her out. She cried in his arms and voiced her guilt.

"The kidnapping, it's all my fault. I should have been paying better attention. I should have known it was a trap and the minute I saw *his* boots, I knew I had fallen prey to the predator. I thought about running into the corn field, but he said he'd find me."

"Shhh, it's not your fault!" He tried reassuring her.

She insisted, "It is! My head wasn't in the game. I was thinking about you and couldn't wait to see you."

His own guilt surfaced. "I distracted you," he spoke remorsefully.

But she had been adamant and refused to let him take the blame. "No, Evan, it wasn't your fault. I'm the one responsible for the lapse of my safety and placing myself in a vulnerable position. Believe me! I've had plenty of time to beat myself up over this."

There was no way he was going to let her accept all of the responsibility for the kidnapping. It was his fault, too, and he told her this.

"Callie, I'm to blame, too. All the days you were gone I pounded myself with regret. I knew you were shaken up by what had happened at the fuel stop. I should've met you on the road instead of letting you come alone."

She had sweetly placed her finger on his lips and reasoned, "If I can't take the blame, neither can you."

"Correct. We need to stop blaming ourselves. The simple truth is it happened. *He* wanted you and *he* was going to get you no matter what."

Their eyes mirrored the tremendous guilt they had. Sharing the blame helped ease the pain.

Evan had softly taken her hand in his and gave it a gentle caress.

In return, she had tightly squeezed his fingers and then said, "Evan, I never blamed you. The kidnapping wasn't your fault, so please forgive yourself."

He felt compelled to share the same message. "Callie Cat, it wasn't yours either, so you need to forgive yourself."

"Okay," she yawned.

"I mean it," he reiterated as he tucked the sheet around her. "Sleep tight."

She yawned again and mumbled, "Don't let the bedbugs bite."

He pulled the door toward the frame, leaving it open about an inch. The last sentence reminded him of a happier time. They had bantered back and forth through texts, and he had said, "Don't let the bedbugs bite."

Her retorted reply had been, "do let the bedbugs bite."

Their texting was a pleasant memory that was dear to his heart, and he longed to hear laughter in her voice again. Hell, he'd settle to hear amusement in it. Right now, even a small speck would be a bushel of hope.

Chapter Six

Callie's eyes focused on Kylee unloading the cleaning supplies from her truck and carrying them to the front door. Then she heard the door open as Kylee came in.

"Hello! Anyone here?" Kylee called.

"Yes! Hello!" Callie greeted from the top step. A part of her wished she had snuck out the back door.

"Mind if I start in your bathroom?" Kylee asked from the foyer.

"No. Go ahead."

Kylee started up the stairs. "Hey, how are you?"

She shrugged. "Good. What about you?"

"Staying busy," Kylee answered. "I feel like I need time to unwind."

"Would you like some of mine?" she laughed. "I have more than I need!"

Kylee smiled. "How about giving me an extra hour at the end of the day?"

"Just one hour?" she joked and the two of them laughed.

"Would you like me to clean your room?" Kylee asked

Callie shook her head. "Naw, I cleaned it the other day."

"Okay, but don't tell Evan you did. He might dock my pay for the *one* room I didn't do," Kylee laughed.

Callie giggled and watched her friend spray the shower, sinks and toilet with a foaming liquid. It was her cue to leave and she headed downstairs to tidy up each room before Kylee cleaned it. Circling back to the kitchen, she washed and dried the dishes Evan had used that morning. Stepping into the laundry room, she folded their clothes separating them into two baskets; his and hers.

Kylee poked her head in the doorway and announced she was leaving.

Callie walked her to the door and gave her a hug good-bye. "Thanks for cleaning."

"You're welcome. Have a good day, I'll see you later."

After closing the door, Callie picked up the laundry basket and ventured down the hallway leading into Evan's bedroom. She placed his clothes on the dresser because putting them in the drawers made her feel like she was invading his privacy. On the wall opposite of the dresser was a king size bed. Compared to Sunbird's, this bed was massive!

Strolling into the bathroom she smelled Evan's scent of vanilla and almond. Glancing into the shower, she laughed at its enormous size. There were two shower heads and it looked as though ten people could fit in it! The sleek white marble counter beneath her hand bridged his and her sinks. His scent led her into the luxurious walk in closet. She twirled twice through it and then pressed her nose into the fabric of a long sleeve shirt inhaling his delicious scent. In the corner on the floor were his shoes. They ranged from all kinds of boots: cowboy, steel toe, snow and other heavy work boots to sneakers, a pair of dress shoes, and closed toed sandals. A pair of flip flops had her laughing because she'd never seen him wear anything but boots and was having a hard time picturing them on his feet. Khaki pants, pressed jeans, shirts with collars, and business suits hung on hangars. Other jeans, t-shirts, boxer shorts and socks were neatly folded on the shelves.

Evan's master suite gave her an idea of how dwarf her living quarters were. Why did one man need so much room? There was no way he could ever live in Sunbird's tiny space. The guest room she was staying in was bigger than Sunbird's cab. *Will I be able to adjust to the small cab after having a bigger space?* She loved the double bed and stretching her whole body limb to limb without touching the wall in the cab. Then there was the closet! She loved hanging her clothes versus keeping them folded on Sunbird's two shelves. The bedroom closet was hardly full and it teased her to go shopping for more than five days worth of clothes. The thing she loved the most and highly appreciated was having the washer and dryer at her fingertips. She didn't miss going to the Laundromat. She used to hate having to wait in line for a washer and dryer. Not having to wait was the best!

The house was quiet and from Evan's room she was able to hear the dishwasher beep signaling it was done. It amazed her how quickly she had adjusted to the quieter side of life versus the constant purr of diesel engines on the road; from Sunbird to the neighboring trucks at the rest areas and truck stops.

She passed through the dining room. Twelve chairs surrounded an enormous table! Its dark wood was polished matching the china hutch. Both pieces looked like they could be heirlooms. This, too, suited Evan and again she wondered, why one man needed such a large dining room set? Did he host family Christmas dinners? Was the table or Sunbird's cab bigger? She giggled while pondering this.

Callie unloaded the dishwasher. She had gotten fairly familiar with his kitchen and knew where most of the dishes went. On the things she didn't know where they went, she'd write a question mark on adhesive paper and stick it to the item, leaving it sit on the counter. Evan put them away, but she wished he left the answers to where they went. This way she'd learn and wouldn't bother him.

She had never seen dishware like Evan's. It was a setting for ten with two different plate sizes; dinner and salad along with bowls and mugs. They were unique because they had tractors painted on them in an array of five colors: red, green, yellow, orange, and blue; two of each color. Their design was a replica of the man himself; practical and adorable. She guessed that he probably wouldn't want to be referred to as adorable, but he was. Her gaze lingered on the ten mugs neatly lined in a row.

She giggled thinking about how civilized she felt using ceramic dishes versus the paper plates she used on the road. Of course, she couldn't use anything but throwaway dishes, because she had no way of washing them. The only "real" utensil she carried was a pocket knife and it was rare she used it, to eat with.

Growing up her family had a place setting for twenty with three sets of forks for each person. By the time she was out of elementary school, she knew what courses each of those forks were used for. Her parents loved hosting parties for her father's clients and employees. Having always been surrounded by people this might've been another reason she was more than happy to welcome the life of a trucker with the solitude, a different city, and no attachments.

Mid afternoon she strolled out to visit Sunbird parked behind the barns. Sliding into the driver's seat, she patted the dash saying, "Hey, girl, how are you?"

She didn't stay in the seat long before scooting onto the bed. Leaning against the propped pillows, she clasped her hands behind her head, reminiscing happier times. A year ago, if she had been away from the road for this amount of time she would have gone insane; wishing on every star to be back on the road. These days, this wasn't her wish.

Callie wasn't sure when or if she would be ready for the road again. *Do I want to?*

It was time to investigate what kind of changes she needed to make in her life. *What do I really want?*

After Kellan and Kylee's wedding the normalcy of her life had started to change; stopped making sense. When she and Dirk had left Purlieu, he had said there was an office position available. Had the spot been filled? Dirk also said she'd always have a job with Maslund Trucking whether it was driving or something else. *Am I ready to hang up my keys for something else? Am I ready for a desk job? Sitting behind a desk would be a lot less confining than behind the steering wheel.*

Callie yawned. Taking a nap would be divine, but she couldn't! She had to stay awake tonight. She was determined not to fall asleep before Evan came home. Leaving Sunbird she took a walk through the fields bordering the property line. In several places her feet sunk in mud, and she feared being stuck there all night. Evan would never look for her out here.

At the back door, she removed her dirty shoes and went upstairs to take a shower. Washing her hair she noticed the shampoo was getting low and made a mental note to write it on the shopping list hanging on the refrigerator door. She thought it was an ingenious place; centrally located in a high traffic area of the house. She dried herself with an oversized fluffy towel. It was so soft she kept her body wrapped in it as she headed to her room. She yelped in surprise when Evan's cat, Owen, stood in the middle of the hallway meowing. Bending, she petted his head and cooed, "Hey boy. Are you hungry?"

He purred while rubbing his body against her legs. "All right, let me get dressed and I'll feed you."

Owen followed her and jumped on the bed. Callie put on a shirt with a pair of cotton shorts. She sat next to him, and he moved into her lap. She laughed, unsure if the cat was hungry or just wanted company. She lay down on her left side and curled her arm under her head. Owen stretched out beside her, his stomach exposed waiting for her to rub it. Her hand glided through silky soft fur listening to him purr. It was relaxing, and her eyelids dropped. *Just for a minute* she thought, confident the cat was hungry and wouldn't let her snooze, but she was wrong.

Minutes slid to hours, and her drifting peaceful slumber turned treacherous. She twisted between the blankets as images of the smelly man and his hefty arms shoved her down. He was on top of her, maliciously laughing saying she couldn't get away.

She shouted, "Let me go! Get away!"

Finally the man was thrown off her and the bearded man was next to her. He dragged his hands over her body and stopped at her waistline.

She raised her knee and pleaded, "Don't."

He pushed it aside saying he wasn't going to hurt her, but she didn't believe him.

"Tell Evan…"

Then…it was quiet, and she was alone…blinded by the dark. Crawling on her hands and knees she swept the floor in front of her and found where the floor and wall met. Standing on her knees she pressed her ear against the cold metal shouting for help. She heard voices but they didn't hear her, and she beat her hands on the wall. No one came, but she didn't give up. Instead, she hit harder and yelled louder.

Chapter Seven

Evan rolled over, groaning. Hearing the coyote's cry sent an eerie shiver down his spine. It sounded so much like a woman screaming. He heard it again. Sitting up, his mind joggled awake. *Callie!*

Swinging his legs over the side of the bed he pulled on a pair of boxers, ran down the hall, and then sprinted upstairs to her room. Every ruthless dream she had was about the kidnapping and the time she spent in the shipping crate he rescued her from. His understanding was she had been kept in this crate. Each rendition she told of the sounds she had heard gave him an image that she'd been in a warehouse. She had heard other women screaming, diesel engines from semi rigs, trailer doors shutting, and men shouting in different languages. All he could surmise is the warehouse they used was a central transport location.

Lately, the nightmares had grown more violent and due to the bruises he had from past assaults he stopped trying to wake her. Not once did he ever blame her. Evan knew she was lost in the dream fighting off her captors.

Approaching the doorway to her room, he was tortured by the sight of her standing in the corner beating her fists on the wall. It brought him so much pain hearing her chanting sob, "Let me out."

In this stage of the dream he often was able to awake her by calmly repeating, "Callie, honey, it's me, Evan, you're home and you're safe."

Tonight, his repeated coaxing wasn't working, but he didn't give up and neither did her begging pleas to be free. By morning, he doubted she'd remember this, but the bruises would tell her something had. The last thing he wanted to do was interfere, but he couldn't let her continue hurting herself. He reached for one of her hands. As he expected, as soon as he touched her, she turned and attacked him, throwing her powerful fists towards him. His hands expanded wide, and his palms blocked her punches. His fingers enclosed her smaller hands, pushing them down.

"Callie, stop! It's Evan. Wake up!"

Trying to free herself from his grasp, she twisted her body. Fearful of breaking her arm, he released her, and her fist drove straight towards his face. Moving his head sideways, he escaped the hit, and her hand sliced through the air. Grabbing her arm, he spun her so that they stood in a spooning position; him behind her. Before he could capture her other free hand, she scraped her fingernails along his arm.

"Ow!" Evan bellowed, managing to keep her arm clamped under his. The scratching was the last fighting mechanism she used, and he was extremely grateful she didn't try biting him.

Trying to get away from the bearded man, Callie continued fighting. She screamed in his ear, twisted her body, but her arm was pinned in his. It wasn't fair! She had to get away! She had to find Evan! One more try! Digging her heel into the floor she used the remaining strength she had to push her body into *him!* The arms around her tightened, pulling her, and she gave in to the backward freefall.

Evan's back hit the wall hard. Using the wall to his advantage he slid them both to the floor and swiftly crisscrossed his longer legs over hers.

"Let me go!" She struggled beneath his strong hold but with less vigor.

"Callie, wake up, you're safe."

"Don't let me die in here, don't let me, don't…"

"I won't," he reassured, unsure of how to wake her.

Callie began to cry. "Evan. Tell Evan."

"Tell me now. I'm right here," he soothed feeling her strength weaken. Helplessly, he mumbled, "Callie Cat."

Through the haze she heard Evan calling her name but then his voice started fading away. "Evan! Don't go! Come back! I'm in here."

Her head swayed side to side. "Evan! Wait!"

"Callie Cat, I'm right here," he pleaded, and she *finally* heard him!

She opened one eye then the other and surveyed her surroundings. Moonlight shined through the dark, and she felt the soft grass.

"I'm not in the metal box," she told herself.

"No," he answered.

She turned her head and saw Evan; concern etched in his face.

"Evan, are you for real?"

"As real, as I can be." Hesitantly, he touched the top of her head. "Are you awake?"

"How'd we get outside?" she asked, disoriented and squeezed her fingers on the soft and hard surfaces beneath her hands. "Wait. We're not outside."

He chuckled, "No."

"I thought the carpet was grass," she admitted, ruefully. "And your leg was a log and damn it. I had another nightmare, didn't I?"

"Yes."

"I am so sorry!" she cried.

"Don't apologize. It's not your fault."

She hissed angrily, "It's *HIS!* I hate *him!*"

Evan clenched his teeth, because he knew who she was referring to. It was the bearded lawman. The kidnapping should have never happened. There should have been another way to appease the undercover boss. Hatred for the lawman ran deep in his veins. Badge or not, Evan knew if he ever came face to face with him he'd senselessly knock his ass to the ground. "I know, I do, too."

"In the dream, I saw you, but I couldn't reach you."

"Do you remember anything else?" he asked, hopefully.

She shook her head commenting on how her hands hurt. He placed her hands in his and gingerly rubbed them, saying nothing in regards to why they hurt.

"Time for you to go back to bed," he encouraged.

She yawned. "Please stay with me until I fall asleep."

"Yes, I will." His sincerity made her heart spiral.

"Evan."

"What?"

"The never ending hours of silence in the dark I think that was the worst."

He hugged her tighter. "You're not alone anymore. Know that I'm always here for you, day or night."

Callie processed his words. Did he know about her daytime troubles? *I should tell him. Right now, go—*

She opened her mouth but nothing came out. She didn't exactly know what to say and instead let her emotions do the talking.

He sensed her tension but was at a loss of how to help relieve it. Feeling the warm trickle of tears on his chest distracted him.

"Callie Cat," he softly consoled. "It's going to be okay." He swept his fingers through her golden hair and was fairly sure he had touched every curly strand on her head.

"Evan, do you have any regrets about bringing me here?"

"No." His hand tenderly slid down her neck.

"Even with the nightmares, you don't regret it?"

"Even more so with them," he said, giving her shoulder a reassuring squeeze.

"I don't know what I would have done if I was by myself out on the road and had to deal with these nightmares."

"You would have called me and this time I would have had Eric fly me to you even if it was in the middle of the night."

"This time I would've let you." She pulled him closer. "I wouldn't have been so stubborn."

"I'm not so sure about that. Sometimes you can be very stubborn." He lightly teased and held her dearly. So many women would be envious of Callie right now wishing it was them in his arms and not her. But for him, Callie was always the woman he wanted and it seemed surreal that she was here in his arms.

He breathed in her refreshing scent and loved that she hadn't made any attempt to move away from him. In fact, she had done the opposite. She wrapped him tighter, and he gently placed a kiss on her head. She became quiet, and he thought she might have fallen asleep. He was a bit startled when she reached up touching his bristled jaw.

"Evan. Thanks for being here."

He nodded, wishing he could speak, but her caressing fingers erased that ability. He stood, lifting her with him. He wanted to stay with her through the night, in case she needed him, but joining her on the bed wasn't a good idea. It would be too easy to curl up with her. She needed rest instead of having his masculine body lying next to her.

He opted for the big chair beside the bed and sat down with her in his arms. She shivered, and he pulled the giant homemade quilt that had been made by the women in his family generations ago off the bed, covering them both. He loved holding her, and it was even better than what his imagination had conjured.

"It's good to have you home with me," he said softly.

Her body curved nicely with his reminding him of their dance at Kellan and Kylee's wedding. What a magical moment it had been! Her sparkling smile had danced into his heart. It had changed him, deciding it was time to show her a kinder side; a side she wanted to know. When they danced he had wanted the moment to last forever. It was the same wish he had when they had talked via the phone, and this moment right now, holding her. He wanted it to last forever.

She stirred and whimpered. He huskily whispered, "Shhh, baby girl, you're safe. I've got you."

Her hand moved lazily over his chest, and he inhaled sharply at the strong emotion he had for her…his *Callie Cat*. She was his. While she recovered, this was the time to show her how much she meant to him. He wasn't going to hide the feelings he had for her anymore, but he had to do it without scaring her or risk losing her forever.

****

Callie sat on the top step listening to Evan prepare breakfast. For the first time in a long time food smelled good. Kiddingly, she was afraid she might be turning into a vampire. She was pale and had lost weight from no appetite. Her eyes were bloodshot from the lack of sleep, and she could feel herself verging depression, which was even more depressing, because this isn't what she was striving for.

She needed to tell Evan what was going on with her. Ask him for help, see him, talk with him, but her body didn't budge. She didn't want to be any more of a burden than she already was. Everybody thought she and Sunbird would have been back on the road by now, but they weren't. The nightmares had wreaked havoc on their lives. It had been weeks since he brought her home, and she wasn't any closer in her recovery than her first day here. But his plans had been messed up, too. None of what she was going through is what he had expected would happen.

How sad her life had become. She lacked the confidence needed, wishing she wasn't so shy about having a face to face conversation with him. Versus the ear to ear ones they used to have before she was kidnapped. There were a lot of things she used *to be* before the kidnapping happened. She used to not be afraid of things. Looking Evan in the eye would have been one of them. Now the only time she faced him was in the middle of the night after one of her tormenting nightmares. Although, burying her face in his chest really shouldn't count as seeing him.

This morning, she had the perfect ice breaker. Asking him why her hands hurt, guessing it had to do with the nightmares she kept having of fighting with the kidnappers, screaming and trying to escape the cargo crate, and almost rape. She tried not to dwell on the lonely fear that had crept into her life. If only she had the courage to speak with Evan, sharing her turmoil.

She tried encouraging herself to tell Evan she couldn't sleep, she was afraid to close her eyes, and she missed him. *Say it!* She goaded.

While contemplating on whether to talk with Evan, she heard him leave. With the missed opportunity she went to take a shower then began another challenging day of how to stay awake.

Chapter Eight

Evan had one foot in the truck when he heard Kylee calling his name. Turning around he saw her enthusiastic wave.

Catching up to him she said, "Hey, Evan. Since you're not eating the noon meal with us today, I made you a sandwich to take with you."

"Thank you," he graciously accepted it. "How's the cleaning business going?"

"Booming!" she exclaimed. "Every week I'm adding new clients. I'm hiring more housekeepers, so if you know anyone who might be interested. Let me know."

"I'll keep my ears open."

"Hey, got a minute."

He grinned. "Three."

"How is Callie?" she asked. "Is she eating?"

Evan gave her a guilty stare, and she continued, "The other day when I was there I noticed the dark circles under her eyes, her skin is pale, and she looks really thin."

"I'm guessing she eats, but I'm not sure." He blew out a frustrated breath and unloaded. "To tell you the truth, I hardly see Callie. In the middle of the night she's plagued with nightmares. Night after night, I'm her hero rescuing her from the damn crate. Afterwards, she cries in my arms."

He conveniently left out the violent parts of her nightmares. "All I can think about is how terrifying it had been. The despair she must have experienced of not knowing what was going to happen or if she was going to survive." He agonized.

Kylee experienced the sorrow in Evan's eyes. It was so heart breaking!

"In the mornings, she doesn't come downstairs to see me before I leave. At night she stays in her room," he retorted bitterly. "It's been almost a month since I brought her home and she hasn't improved. I don't know what else to do!"

Kylee was heartbroken witnessing the pain in his eyes.

"I really thought by now she would have been back on the road. Not that I want her gone, but if she was, it would mean she was healed."

Evan didn't realize until just now how much he missed Callie's exuberant spirit. "I'm tired of seeing the empty existence of her in the house. Don't get me wrong, I don't regret bringing her home, but I just wish…"

"Things were different?" Kylee suggested.

Evan shrugged. "I miss Callie. I miss talking with her! I want to see joy in her eyes again!"

Kylee's eyes held sorrow. She stepped closer and placed her hand on his arm. "I'm sorry things aren't going the way you thought they would."

"Thanks," he mumbled.

Kylee asked, "Have you tried talking with her on the phone throughout the day? Isn't there a game you two used to play while she was away?"

Remembering, he said, "Yeah, duh, why didn't I think of this?"

"It might be a good way to bring her out of her shell."

"Great idea, thanks!"

"You're welcome. It's much easier to see things when you're outside of the box." She giggled. "Where does Callie go during the day?"

He shook his head. "Other than visiting Sunbird, I don't know."

"Where is Sunbird? I didn't see it anywhere in the driveway."

"I've got her parked out back behind the machinery shed." He frowned. "Maybe, I should park her closer to the house."

"Not a bad idea. It could help if she could see Sunbird out the window."

"Yeah, thanks," he said.

Kylee saw a glimmer of hope in his smile.

"Remember, Callie's strong willed and isn't one to readily ask for help," she gently reminded him.

He nodded. "True."

Yet before the kidnapping he felt as though Callie had started letting him into the tall stockade built around her heart. His watch chimed the hour. "I need to go."

"Good luck and don't give up on her."

Evan climbed in the truck. Sticking his head out the window he said, "Thanks for listening."

"You're welcome."

Driving off he waved his hand out the window. In his rearview mirror he saw her waving back. From K-man's driveway, he turned left towards his parent's house. Five minutes later he was pulling into their driveway. His mom's trunk was open and in it were tons of grocery bags. He helped her unload them. Filling his sturdy arms with several bags she bubbled with laughter over his good timing. The phone in his back pocket vibrated. When the last load was brought in and set on the counter only then did he reach for the phone.

"Is it work?" Mrs. Nichols asked, watching the frown pull on her son's face when he read the messages.

"Yeah," he answered, "Trouble with a driver."

"Not Callie, right? She's still with you at home?" His mom asked, and he confirmed yes.

"How is she?"

He shrugged. "She's all right."

"The poor girl and all she went through. Oh, it's just terrible! I can't imagine what it was like for her. How scary it must have been. Evan, my precious boy, you are very kind for taking her in." She pinched his cheek. "But then I wouldn't have expected any less from you, because I raised you right." She beamed.

"Thanks mom. You're the best." He hugged her, and she reciprocated. From toddler to adults she never took one single hug from her children for granted; cherishing each hug.

"I can't believe she was taken by the same people who had tried kidnapping The Taylor's niece. By the way have you heard from Dirk? How are they?"

"Yeah, I talked with him the other day. They're having fun and are planning on coming home soon."

"Speaking of having fun, when is your date with Janie Baker?" she asked.

Evan scowled, hating the way she just eased the other girl into their conversation. Nor did he miss the twinkle in her eye. Between her and his sisters they have set him up with just about every available female in town. He appreciated their efforts, but he wasn't interested in their matchmaking, and he hadn't found a gentle way to tell them no more. Nor was he up for the messy elaboration of why.

"Hmm," he rolled one shoulder.

"Evan. A shrug isn't an answer. Besides, what other plans do you have? What will it hurt if you just go out with her? One date," his mom hinted.

Evan looked up from his phone into his mom's persuasive eyes. His mind screamed *I have plans that don't include Janie. Going out with her will hurt. One date is too many. Crap! It'll just be easier to appease her.*

In defeat, he sighed, "Fine, I will."

She clapped her hands together. "Splendid! I'll give her a call right now and let her know you'll pick her up at six."

"No five."

She enthused, "Five it is. Thank you!" She gave her son a big hug, grateful to get Janie off her back. The girl was relentless in her pursuit of dating her son. Carol often felt as though the girl stalked her just to get a chance to ask about Evan. It was a crazy thought, and she hoped this wasn't the case. She didn't want her son marrying the wrong woman. One of her other children had chosen the wrong mate and was currently working through the emotional side effects of it. Carol sadly shook her head. Why couldn't people just be happy? Why were there so many people who wanted to tear others down? Just so they could feel better about themselves.

Evan piped up. "Oh. Wait. I can't this week."

"That's fine. I'll pick another week and let you know when."

Evan nodded feeling weird about having his mom schedule the date. He was a grown man. He should be doing it, yet talking to Janie was the last thing he wanted. The less he had to socialize with the girl, the better. At least, he wouldn't have to do it this week. He was off the hook for at least another week and wondered how long he could avoid it.

Glancing at the clock on the stove he said, "I gotta go, Mom."

"Don't forget the pork chops. I just took them out of the freezer. There should be enough for you and Callie for a couple of meals. Have her put them in the oven on 350 for about an hour."

"Okay, thanks." He gave her another big hug. "I love you."

"Love you, too," she said and then in a more grateful voice she added, "Thanks again for agreeing to the date with Janie."

He grunted, and she felt the need to explain why it was important to her. "Honey, I just want you to be happy."

"Who says I'm not?" he countered.

"You are, but you aren't," she stated, confusingly.

"I am," he reassured and gave her a hug. "Mom, thanks for worrying about me but it's all good. One day the right woman will be ready for me."

From the drivers seat Evan tossed the bag of chops into the other seat. His mom assumed Callie knew how to cook, and he wasn't sure if she did. He took for granted that she did know how. Come to think of it he hadn't noticed a dent in his food supply. So if she wasn't cooking, what was his house guest eating?

Through the window, Carol watched her son drive off in his big pick-up truck. *Oh, dear, what if he takes that big truck on his date? He should borrow Eric's car.* She began putting groceries away while his comment about the right woman being ready for him threw her off. *What did he mean? Who is he referring to? All the bachelorettes within a fifty mile radius were ready for him. It seems he's not ready for them! Why? Maybe this date with Janie will change his mind. Maybe it's time I stop interfering with his love life. He's a grown man and can make his own decisions. His father and I did teach him to think for himself. Yes, after*

Janie no more match making for Evan. Now Eric on the other hand could use some help.

Leaving his mom's house Evan glanced at the frozen food and decided to take it home before going to the office. There was a chance he would return late this evening due to the driver issue that had erupted. Stopping now also gave him the chance to check on Callie.

At the intersection he turned right. His foot pressed harder on the foot pedal. The torque fired up, colliding with the engine gaining speed on the straight road. There were two curves coming up that he hunkered around, driving as though he was in a sports car versus his lifted dually. He was very familiar with these roads since he'd been driving them a long time; a tractor at an early age and a truck when he turned sixteen and got his driver's license. On the tractor he was going the mach speed of slow, reasoning this is the reason he was impatient behind the wheel of a street vehicle; he just wanted to drive fast.

Stepping inside the back door, he hung his hat on the peg, raked his fingers through his matted hair but kept his boots on. He placed the chops in the fridge then wandered the house looking for Callie and found her in his home office. She was stooped over the 1000 piece puzzle that had kept him occupied through many sleepless nights worrying about her, alone on the road.

Sure, she could take care of herself! After all, she was the one who had taught Dirk the ways of life on the road. However, knowing this hadn't lessened his concerns especially in the days to follow when his heart had started swaying her way. It played a small part in having a tracking device placed on Sunbird. He remembered how pissed she was when he and Dirk approached her about it. At first, she didn't believe all the semi tractors at Maslund Trucking were having this safety feature added. Her sharp eyes had dug into his, not Dirk's, believing she was being singled out. He supposed she was sort of right since Sunbird was the first one they had done.

Callie sensed she was being watched as the scent of almond vanilla surrounded her, electrifying the air. She whipped her head around to see Evan quietly staring at her. Sometimes his intense gaze made her feel skittish but not at this moment. Right now her heart flipped in all sorts of directions. Along the way his teasing remarks had turned tender, his snickering smiles had turned sexy, and he had this magical way of being able to see deep into her soul. It left her feeling exposed and a bit tongue tied.

"Hey," she greeted shyly.

"Hey, yourself," he said, grinning.

"I hope you don't mind that I'm working on your puzzle."

Evan shrugged. "I don't. I'll take all the help I can get with it, but I've gotta warn you."

On his pause, she analyzed the humor glowing in his eyes.

He snickered, "It can be quite puzzling."

A giggle rippled out of her, and then it evolved into a bigger laugh with him joining in.

"Sorry, I couldn't resist," he said, humorously.

She gasped, "Oh, gosh. It felt good to laugh."

"Overall how are you doing?" he gently asked.

"When I'm not bothered by the nightmares –" she stopped and gave a small laugh. "It's so quiet here."

"Does the quiet bother you?"

She frowned. "It's not that it bothers me, it's just hard to get used to. For so long, I've been surrounded by diesel engines and it was kind of comforting. Make sense?"

Evan gave a short nod. "Would my beauty like me to fire up Sunbird and park her outside your window so you can sleep?"

Callie laughed harder this time but glancing at his somber expression she realized he would actually *do* this for her. His genuine gesture made her feel important!

Smiling, she said, "Thanks, but I think I can get used to the quiet."

"Let me know if you change your mind," he said. Remembering his conversation with Kylee, he added, "Hey, instead of having Sunbird behind the barns, how about bringing her up to the house?"

"Why?"

"She needs to be closer."

Callie gave him a curious look but didn't question him further. "Thank you," she said gratefully and joyfully.

"You're welcome." His heart kicked, because she was happy with this idea.

An awkward silence settled in and he watched her bite the corner of her thumbnail. It wasn't the first time he noticed her do this.

"I make you nervous," he stated.

"No." She shook her head. "I'm not used to being around people."

"Bullshit. It's not people. It's me," he harassed.

She shook her head again. "Not true. I hide from Kylee, too, when she comes to clean. If I had known she was coming the other day I would have hidden in Sunbird."

He smirked and felt better knowing it wasn't just him. "So you're not avoiding me."

"No. Why would you think this?"

"Because you don't come down in the mornings nor do you greet me in the evenings. I miss it," he suddenly confessed.

She gave him a wide stare. Swallowing nervously, Callie agreed she missed it, too.

"Then why have you been avoiding me?"

"I haven't been avoiding you," she said looking down at the puzzle but felt the sting of his stare. It was time to tell him the truth.

He gave a frustrating groan. "Bullshit." He grabbed her by the shoulders. "You can't even look me in the eye and tell the damn truth!"

She swung him a confusing glance. "It has nothing to do with you."

"Oh, I've heard the, it's not you it's me line before. In fact, I've used it before. I just didn't think you'd be the one using it on me. Damn it." He released her and started walking away.

She followed him. "Wait, Evan. I'm not lying."

He turned around and she expected to see anger on his face but instead it was sorrow. Heartache ripped through her. This is what the nightmares had done with their relationship. Correction, this is what the bearded man had done to their relationship! An unsettling rage prompted her to speak the truth.

"No, Evan, don't go! I'll tell you the truth." Her pleas had his hand paused on the door handle. "What is the truth?" He faced her.

"It's the nightmares. I can't sleep."

He gave her a ridiculous look. "You're telling me you can't sleep because of the nightmares? Duh, Callie, I already know that!" he snapped, exiting the house.

She ran after him. "No, Evan. You don't understand."

"Go back in the house," he retorted, bitterly. "I'd say we could talk tonight but I'll be home *very* late so you and your nightmares will have to sleeplessly wander around the house without me."

He backed his truck into an easy Y turn and left her standing helplessly in the driveway. She was stunned over his reaction. She tried telling him the truth about how bad the nightmares were but he didn't even listen; didn't want to. Could she blame him? This isn't what he signed up for. *Maybe I should just pack up my stuff and leave. Maybe getting back on the road is exactly what I need!*

She shuffled back inside the house with misty eyes and his sharp tone ringing in her memory. *Does he want me gone?*

Picking up her cell phone she sent him a message. It was something she hadn't done in a long time and it felt good. Her message read: **Evan. I don't want to leave but if you want me to, I'll understand. I'll quietly leave with no hard feelings. Maybe one day, we can pick up where**

we left things; on a good note before all this crap got in the way. I want you
to know I wasn't lying about the nightmares. There's more to it than you
think. It's time you know the truth of what's really going on with me. I'm
ready to tell you when you're ready to listen.

Callie Cat.

She turned on the television and thought about what Evan had said
in regards to him coming home late tonight. Was it work? Did he have a
date? No matter what, this was the least of her worries. Without Evan
here, how was she going to cope with the nightmares? Tonight will be her
first test of coping with them by herself.

*If I can find a way to deal with the nightmares without any help, then
perhaps Sunbird and I can finally get back on the road. It would be nice
having a normal routine again.*

As Callie lay on the couch, Owen jumped up beside her.
Stretching her arms above her head, she remembered Evan telling her
about bringing Sunbird closer to the house. She yawned thinking *I'll do it
after the movie is over.*

****

Callie woke up to brightness shining in her eyes. She inhaled a
deep breath and pushed the panic down. Looking up she realized it wasn't
a light at the end of the tunnel. It was the television screen. Breathing
easier she muted the set. The house was quiet...too quiet. Where was
Owen? Last thing she remembered was petting the cat's fluffy fur while
he curled against her belly.

Where was Evan? Passing the clock in the den it was one o'clock
in the morning. Was he home? Her bare feet quietly padded down the
hallway to his bedroom. About to enter she stopped when she heard
talking and cringed thinking he had a girl with him. Turning away, she
halted, hearing his urgent voice. He was the only one speaking. Pushing
the door open she saw Evan tossing and turning and was relieved he truly
was alone.

"Don't go. It's too dangerous," he mumbled.

She knelt beside the bed. Softly she touched his shoulder saying
his name. His eyes jerked open, and he flinched from her touch. Sitting
up the sheet fell exposing the hard lines of his chest. She wanted to touch
the massive muscles but didn't dare to if he was still sleeping.

In a startled voice he demanded, "What-what're you doing here?"

He couldn't stand to see her eyes full of concern.

It was her turn to ask, "Evan, are you awake?"

"I-I don't know." He rolled over revealing his bare ass, and she
became very aware of the fact that he slept nude.

She sat down on the edge of the bed. "Where are you?"

"In my bed, apparently with you unless I'm dreaming that you're really here," he snapped as he turned his head toward her.

"You said, don't go. It's too dangerous. Who were you talking to?" she asked.

He grunted but didn't answer right away. With an irritated sigh he said, "You."

"Oh."

"Are you sure you're really here and not a figment of my imagination?" he asked not believing it.

"I'm really here." She held her hand out, and he squeezed it.

"If you are here, don't go away." On a whim, he pulled her over his hip laying her next to him. "To tell you the truth, I think this is a dream."

His whispered words tickled Callie's ear sending sensual shivers throughout her entire body. His rock hard body; all of it pressed into her back. His arms glided around her, his hands holding hers as he cuddled her.

Reassuring him, she said, "Evan, I'm really here."

"Stay with me, Callie Cat. Don't go. It's too dangerous," he said, sleepily.

Hearing Evan's heavy steady breath told her he had fallen asleep, and she speculated if he had fully awakened at all. It was possible she had been a part of his dream. *What will he think when he wakes up in the morning and sees me in bed with him? I should go.*

She tried moving away, but he held on tighter. She easily gave up and accepted she was staying here the remainder of the night. Snuggling next to him felt good. There had been too many lonely nights where she had dreamed of being held like this. Her dreams had started changing. She wanted a man to love. In return she wanted a man to love her for who she was. Believing in happy endings she fell asleep and slept soundly.

Chapter Nine

Evan opened one eye and was a bit disoriented seeing Callie next to him. It might have felt like the morning of a one night stand of not remembering how they got here but *he did* remember last night's events except for how she got into his bed. Those images were a little fuzzy. It was innocent since she was fully clothed unless she took advantage of him, but he knew she wouldn't have done that.

"What happened? Did you have a dream?" he asked.

"No. You did," she replied.

"I thought you were a dream."

"I'm for real!" She quoted the same words he had spoken after one of her nightmares.

He frowned. "You heard me from your room?"

She shook her head. "I fell asleep on the couch."

"You did?" he said, perplexed.

"Yeah, I went to see if you were home and heard talking. I thought you brought a girl home." She blushed.

"Why would you think that?"

"Because you said you'd be home late."

"And you just assumed I had a date?" he grumbled.

"Yes."

"FYA, I was working late at Maslund." He threw her an irritated glance.

"FYA?" she questioned.

"For your assumption," he said, adding, "Besides, you're the only girl who has slept in this house."

"Yeah right," she muttered sarcastically. "All the girls in town want to be in your bed."

He tsked. "There's a difference between wanting to be in my bed and actually *being* in my bed."

"Okay, correction. None of them *slept* in your bed," she protested.

"Or in the house," he corrected.

"It doesn't mean you didn't have *sex* with them *in* your house or *bed*. It just means you kicked them out before they had a chance to fall asleep."

Leaning against the headboard he shot her an annoyed look. She was so far off from the truth with her statement, but he didn't give her the satisfaction of furthering the argument. He let her keep the small triumphant smile plastered on her jealous face and averted the conversation back to last night.

"So you heard me talking. What did I say?"

"Mainly, you begged me not to go, saying it was too dangerous."

"Hmm," he absently mumbled.

"What did you mean by it?" she asked, but he didn't answer right away. Feeling fidgety she began biting the corner of her thumbnail.

Evan was lost in her stunning tan eyes. He wanted to wake up seeing them every morning. Even when she and Sunbird were back on the road, Callie could be the first one he saw in the morning. Thanks to technology they could use their cell phones for face conversations. It could be the best of both worlds: a loving relationship in Purlieu and out on the road. He didn't care that she was a truck driver; he never did and had no intention of changing her, ever! It was in her blood. Sunbird's drivers' seat is where she was most happy! He, and so many had expected her to be back on the road driving again but something was stopping her. Since there wasn't anything physically wrong with her, he suspected it had to do with her mental emotions. The nightmares made her relive the kidnapping and the things that had happened during that time.

He finally spoke in a calm voice. "Callie, I read your message. I don't want you to leave but when you're ready you will. Though, I'm not sure I'll be able to let you go. Maybe you'll see you don't have to leave the way you have in the past."

She gave him a confused look. There was so much he wasn't saying and yet so much he was. She couldn't comprehend it all.

"That's a loaded explanation," she remarked.

"Yeah," he nodded, trailing his finger down her cheek.

She took a chance. "What if I'm never ready to get back on the road?"

His brows furrowed. "You will."

"How do you know? This might not be what I want anymore."

"It is. It's who you are. Give it time, Cal. You'll come around to what you know you've always wanted." He heavily sighed.

Her brain blurted. *You and Sunbird is what I want!* This revelation stunned her, and she wasn't able to conceal it.

He saw the faint astonishment flicker across her face and interpreted it as her need and want of getting back on the road. "See. Your subconscious already knows what the rest of you, is afraid to admit."

She shook her head. "I'm not sure you're ready to hear what I have to say."

"Maybe not," he agreed, assuming what she was going to say had something to do with her leaving. "Maybe one day, you'll see you don't have to choose."

Is he saying what I think he's saying? Her hand clutched his wrist. "Wait, are you —"

She stopped midsentence because she felt scratches on his skin. Glancing down she saw the red lines.

"What happened to your arm?" she asked in alarm.

Evan shrugged and removed his arm from her grasp. "It doesn't matter."

"Was it the berry bushes in the outer field?"

"You've been back there?" he asked sharply.

"Yeah, on my walk the other day," she informed.

"I noticed your muddy shoes on the mat but didn't think you'd venture so far."

She was happy he had noticed, but also sad, because they hadn't a chance to talk. They talked more when she was on the road than they did now. Well, of course, it was because of the nightmares throwing her schedule off, *and* she wasn't communicating her problems with him.

"Remind me to get you a pair of knee high boots for you to wear in the fields. They'll protect you from any snakes should you encounter any, and I'll give you a stick to carry just in case."

His concern turned her heart to mush.

"No more field walking until you've got the proper gear," he forewarned.

"I'll go into town tomorrow and buy some boots at the Discount General."

He shook his head. "No. I know a better place where you'll get good quality and a reasonable price."

"We can go together?" she asked.

"Sounds good," he said with a happy smile.

He sat up forgetting about the marks marring the rest of his body. Unfortunately, the falling sheet revealed the rest to her.

"Evan!" she gasped. "What happened? You look like you walked through a patch of thorns!"

He froze. "What?"

"Your body is full of scratches!"

"Ah, it's no big deal," he said.

Evan quickly exited the bed and was completely unaware of the salivating view he was giving her. The last thing he wanted was to leave her alone in his bed; wishing he could strip away her clothes and lie between her legs showing her how much he cared. But then she noticed the damn scratches, and he was stuck between two hard places. Either he told her the truth or he avoided the subject altogether. He chose the latter, because he wasn't ready to tell Callie the scratches had come from her. He couldn't! It would break her! So, he and his erection crossed the room into the bathroom. He closed the door but didn't bother locking it.

Having the doors inside the house locked bothered him for some reason. He chalked it up as another one of his odd pet peeves as was sharing his food, changing his radio station, and tardiness to name a few. Stepping into the shower, he welcomed the cold water on his head as it cascaded over his body.

Callie watched Evan cross the room. She enjoyed seeing his bare back and ass. Sturdy muscles wrapped his shoulders and lined his spine, buttocks and legs. *Magnificent!* Callie bit her lip; refraining the urge of dragging her hungry mouth across the vast area. A tensing heat slid in as she wished he'd turn and show her his frontal view; no doubt it was just as impressive. Provocative images swarmed her brain. She, clamping her legs around his lean waist and firm thighs as he thundered her cunt. Frustrated for not being able to play out her fantasy she rolled her face into the pillow and groaned.

Callie thought about joining him in the two headed shower. It would be a bold and sexy move. Sure, there'd be plenty of room for her, but she wouldn't be in there to stay on one side. The fantasy hazed her vagina, swelling it with a convulsing need of wanting, but she wouldn't allow herself to give in. Reluctantly, she dragged her feet up the stairs.

She paused in the doorway of her room and was struck with an image of pounding her fists against the wall. Turning her hand over, she viewed the yellow bruises along the edge. She bent her fingers forward and stared at her nails and recently remembered a nightmare of digging them into her captor's flesh…but…it wasn't a dream! It was real! The ugly red marks on Evan's body flashed in front of her!

"Oh no!" she wailed. It wasn't the kidnappers she had hurt! It was Evan! The marks on his body were from her!

"They're from me!" she shouted. Her hands flew into her hair, pulling it. "Oh, shit, oh, shit, oh shit."

Her despair turned to anger because Evan side stepped the truth! He purposely let her think his injuries were due to thorns versus telling her the truth. How dare he lie to her! She sprinted towards his room. He was sitting on the bed putting his socks on when she barreled in. He didn't hear her come in, and her stern voice startled him.

With her hands on her hips she glared at him and shouted, "I can't believe you lied to me. Just so you know, I'm a big girl and can handle the truth!"

"Truth about what?" he asked. "And what did I lie about?"

"Show me your body," she demanded. "I know I've been hurting you. Now show me the fucking scratches!"

Pushing his chest, she pushed his back onto the bed and started tugging the long sleeve covering his arm.

Her eyes raged with conflicting emotions; among them was concern but it still didn't mean Evan wanted the truth to hurt her. He grabbed her wrist, ordering her to stop, but she didn't.

She twisted free from his grasp and insisted, "I want to see what I've done to you."

"You haven't done anything to me."

"I have!" she screeched. "Quit fighting me and show me, damn it!"

She pushed the sleeve up, and he pushed it down.

"Stop it right now," he said, roughly, but she didn't listen.

In an attempt to block her pursuit, his hand moved downward and collided with hers. Clutching the fabric she pulled hard, ripping the seams apart. The material gave way and exposed the injured skin. Unprepared for the awful sight she shrieked.

"Oh my God! I did this?! No!" she cried in horror.

His pissed eyes told her yes.

"Let me see the rest of it!" she commanded.

Evan knew she'd fight him again if he didn't, so he shed the shirt letting her see the gouging red marks on his arms, shoulders, and all the ones on his chest.

Callie was sickened by what her nightmarish nails had done to his beautiful body! She let out a mournful cry.

Witnessing her despair devastated him. This is what he had wanted her to avoid seeing and feeling. He didn't want her to experience the heartache and guilt that was vividly visible.

"What gives you the right to keep this from me?" She traced a long crimson line on his chest.

He grabbed her hands and pushed them away. "I have that right!" he fired. "What gives you the right to attack me?"

Callie hadn't ever seen him this furious and now second guessed her wild actions. Suddenly she was confused. *What is wrong with me? I am not acting like the calm level headed person that I am.* She retreated from him. "I-I'm sorry."

"Don't be." He spatted.

"What do you mean don't be? I am!"

"Are you?" he retorted. "If you were sorry, you'd be down in the mornings apologizing. Instead, you're not! You stay in your room all day, avoiding me! The only time I see you, is in the middle of the fucking night!"

"I know – we need to talk. If—"

"If you know, then why don't you stop avoiding me?" he shouted.

"I'm not the only one doing the avoiding! You are too! You always come home late."

"Un-fucking believable!" he yelled and gave a disgruntled groan. "I work all day – oh hell! If I did come home early, it's not like you'd be awake to welcome me."

"Fuck you!" Her eyes whipped, as did her hand; right across his cheek.

Instantly, his eyes darkened and rage flashed in them. The air between them felt dangerous. He took a step towards her, but she quickly lunged sideways and ran upstairs to her room. She slammed the door shut; locking it. Shocked by her behavior and fearful of his reaction, she paced near the door. *Will he leave the house or try talking with me?*

A few minutes later, there was a sharp rap on the door, and she cried out in surprise. The door handle jingled. On the other side he cursed loudly. She heard the lock click and half a second later the door swung open. She had to jump back; otherwise it would have hit her. A fuming Evan stepped in, but he didn't stop.

He advanced towards her, his anger cutting into her. She kept retreating until she backed into the dresser. Grabbing beneath her arm pits, he lifted and set her on top of it with his eyes blazing.

She swallowed nervously. "I-I'm sorry. I didn't meant to..." she trailed off feeling the fury radiating from him.

"Don't you ever lock a door on me again," he said through clenched teeth. "And the last time you slapped me, I told you...if it happened again I'd kiss you."

Before she could utter a word he clamped his hand on the back of her neck and pulled her towards him. He swiftly lowered his mouth and slipped his agitation in her hot mouth. His tongue commanded a response, but she didn't need much coaxing.

She ran her fingers through his blonde strands as the kiss intensified and she tasted his anger, hurt, and frustration. She wanted more of his heat penetrating her body. Every inch of her was tight and hot. She was addicted to his daunting passion and she wrapped her legs around him. The needed want she had for him scorched through her like a wildfire. Its heat ricocheted between them. She felt his fury dissipating, and tasted his tenderness.

Abruptly he released her. Spinning on his heel, he left her speechless and breathless. His boots stomping on the stairs and the door slamming shut announced his departure. An eerie shadowy feeling covered her; she felt cold and empty. *He can't go! We need to talk!*

She slid off the dresser and ran after him, but as she stepped out the front door he was already turning onto the road. The windows in the old farm truck were rolled down, and she yelled out for him to stop. He kept going, and she wasn't sure if he had heard her or chose not to. *Shoes! I need shoes!*

Running back inside, she slipped on a pair of sneakers, tying them fast. Halfway through the kitchen she remembered her purse and went back to get it. No way was she driving without a license. Standing in the driveway she contemplated which vehicle to take; Evan's good truck or Sunbird.

Chapter Ten

Kellan honked his horn and frantically waved his hands trying to get Evan's attention. With a disgruntled grunt, he used his cell phone. Hearing Evan's hello he frantically said, "Dude! I've been trying to get your attention."

Hearing K-man's rushed tone alerted him. "Why? What's wrong?"

Kellan shouted in his ear. "What is she doing?"

"Who?"

"Callie! Look!"

In the combine, Evan turned to see Sunbird at the field entrance. "Shit!"

There was no way he would reach her in time. It was like watching a movie play in slow motion. If she kept driving forward Sunbird was going to sink into the mud. Cursing, he threw the tractor in park, turned off the engine, and hastily climbed down. His truck wasn't parked anywhere nearby so he sprinted across the field. By the time he reached her she was standing on the ground. He was out of breath but had enough to scold her as he stepped into her space.

"Callie, what the fuck are you doing? You can't drive Sunbird into the field! She'll get stuck!"

"I know duh," she said, sassily. "I parked her on the edge."

He gritted his teeth and ferociously lashed out, "That is the field!" He glared at her and pointed a finger at Sunbird commanding, "Get in. Slowly back her up and get all tires on the hard surface."

"No." She refused, folding her arms across her chest, framing her breasts. It was an electrifying sight. "I need to talk to you."

He sighed heavily, and then bitterly retorted, "Well, you picked one hell of a place to do it."

"Sorry, but you didn't give me any choice. You just stormed out!"

He leaned in. "You have something to say?"

"Yes." She spatted with determined eyes.

"It's about damn time you do," he said harshly.

She lifted her hair on the left side of her head and held it on top of her head exposing her sexy neck. If there wasn't a fifty ton semi tractor threatening to be stuck, he would have laid his mouth on it. He was physically twisted just thinking about it. Then she tipped her head back, lifting her lips. All he could think about was the kiss they shared earlier. The way her lips wrapped elegantly with his, he just wanted to sink his tongue amidst their softness again. *Soft and sink...* These two words brought him back to the present problem; Sunbird sinking in the mud.

"Callie," he spoke gentler this time, but he still towered over her.

She was powerless against the rock eyes that sunk into hers, questioning her knowledge. The mud looked a lot firmer than it really was. If she had known it wasn't safe she wouldn't have jeopardized getting Sunbird stuck. She had been on the verge of telling him this when her neck tingled below her ear. The same spot his fiery eyes had fixated on. It fired her up.

He proposed a deal. "Let's get Sunbird out of danger and then I'll give you my attention."

She nodded, agreeing but wondered what he truly meant. Would he be lending her his lips or ear? She wouldn't mind the first option. Back in the driver's seat, she powered the window down.

Evan was a charming sight; starting with the dusty cap shading his brooding eyes moving to the shirt stretching across his rippled abdomen to the faded jeans hugging his firm ass. Even the heavy boots on his feet helped his rugged appeal. He was divine! *Scrumptious!* She threw him a ravenous smile.

For a moment, Evan didn't move. He was too busy fighting down the urges to say the hell with Sunbird, open her door and ravage hungry kisses *all* over her body. *Delicious!* Less than an hour ago he had stormed into her room kissing away his frustration. A deep yearning sparked within him, an arousing need awakened. Gazing at her now hadn't diminished any of it.

Sunbird's engine roared in his ears. Instead of turning his throat hoarse he hopped on the yellow beast's second step holding on to the edge of the open window. His head was at the height of her shoulder, a perfect view of her sexy neck.

"Don't be nervous," he said when she brought her left thumb up to her mouth.

In a haughty tone, she replied, "Why would you think I'm nervous?"

He shook his head. "I don't think. I know."

Her irritated eyes asked how he knew.

Pointing his finger he said, "You're biting the corner of your nail again. That's what you do when you're feeling skittish, and you always do it a lot when I'm around."

She was about to protest then stopped because he was right. However, him calling her out on it didn't stop her agitation. Sensing this, he rubbed her shoulder and gently reassured, "Its okay. You'll get used to me."

"Will I?" she challenged.

"Yes."

"And how do you know?"

"Because you like me, Callie Cat, now let's focus on the task at hand."

Ugh! It irritated her that he knew so much about her. At times it felt he knew more about her than she did. Yes, she did like him, a lot, but since arriving in Purlieu things hadn't gone the way she had wanted them to go.

"Callie Cat, do you trust me?"

Without hesitation she confidently answered, "Yes."

Hearing the definite trust in her voice gripped his emotions.

Patiently, he instructed, "Okay, give her a little gas and slowly creep her out."

"Is there anyone behind me?" she innocently asked, but her question caused all sorts of tumultuous viewings in his mind.

He swallowed hard before he stammered, "Uh…no…not yet, anyway."

She gave him a sharp look. "Why do I get the feeling you're talking about something else."

His voice dropped an octave into a sultry husk. "You'd know if someone was behind you."

She dared, "Are you that someone?"

His grinning reply was playfully wicked. In his gaze she saw fortuitous images of them and a riveting heat rushed in.

She inhaled deeply. "Damn."

The cursing strengthened his desire. "You have a trucker's mouth."

She spat, "Damn straight, I do." Then forewarned, "And don't think you can change me."

"Wouldn't dream of it, besides…you're perfect just the way you are."

"You wouldn't? I am?" she questioned with a frazzled expression, and he nodded.

Giving the foot pedal a small push, she confessed, "You know, I don't hate Callie Cat like I used to."

"What changed?" he asked, feeling Sunbird retracting.

Callie focused her view on the dashboard and whispered, "The kidnapping."

Her vision blurred. "Alone in the crate, so many times I wished and prayed there'd be a day when I'd hear you call me Callie Cat…just one more time."

Evan brushed away the few tears that had fallen on her face. "Damn, sweetheart."

"I know it's crazy, right?" she sniffed.

His thumb stroked her cheek, and his finger lifted her chin forcing her to look at him. His solace gaze drove away the sadness replacing it with a strengthening cheer.

He renewed her humor when he said, "All right, I'll start calling you my Crazy Callie Cat, how's that?"

She giggled, and her smile lifted his heart.

Callie steered the conversation back to Sunbird noting two wheels were on the blacktop. Evan encouraged her to maintain the slower speed, keeping the wheels straight, and don't worry about taking up the whole road. Trusting him she didn't waver from his instructions, and he was proud of her for following them versus arguing with him. When all of Sunbird's tires were back on the hard surface Callie slumped with relief hanging her head down. "Don't worry I won't make the same mistake twice."

"Good," Evan said firmly.

"I'm not dumb about mud, but I really thought the ground was firmer than it was," she said, defensively and leaned back in the seat.

His eyes immediately were drawn to her breasts, their peaks visible through the thin shirt. Every cell in his body was tight.

In a strained voice he said, "It's hard to tell with mud. It's similar to a woman's breast except opposite."

"What?" she asked, bewildered. Her body responded lustfully beneath his sharp gaze. Raising his view, his eyes flickered with a sensuous heat, heightening the attraction she had for him.

He began talking in a low wispy tone. "Mud goes hard to soft. A nipple…" he paused, his voice seductive, "soft to firm."

Callie uttered his name on an oscillating breath, and his searing tone groaned her name. Their electrified gazes met. She ran her tongue across her bottom lip, driving him wild. Evan was caught between kissing the passion out of her, here in the middle of the road, and sending her home.

He had to choose the second choice, because once he kissed her it would be hard to stop; as he found out this morning. Besides, it was time they talk. Clear the air on the misunderstandings between them.

"Callie," he stated with a resigning sigh. "Go home and put a bra on. Then we'll talk."

"What?" she said, saddened by his sudden mood swing and envied his ability to easily downshift his sexual provoking. She'd need to remember this the next time their passions tangoed.

"You wanted to talk to me right?" he reminded her, and she slowly nodded her head. *Yeah, talk.*

"Okay then. Go home and put a bra on," he instructed.

Callie's eyes were wide with question, and his held warning. "I can't talk to you without one on."

"What if I don't want to?" she asked provocatively.

"I can't give you a straight answer on that one." He hopped to the ground, glancing at his watch. "I'll be home in thirty minutes to give you the attention I promised you. It's up to you to decide which one you want from me."

Her eyes bugged, *really?*

"You'll either be wearing one or you won't be," he hinted. "See you soon."

"Which do you prefer?" she shouted out the window but all she got in return was a wave. His way of saying, you choose.

All the way home she struggled with the answer. Walking into the house she struggled with it and in her room holding the bra she still struggled with the answer. Being heard or being sexually satisfied; both were two great options.

****

Thirty minutes later Evan walked through the back door eager to find out the answer. He wasn't in the room ten seconds, and he was confused. She had her hair tied back. It rested between her shoulder blades, exposing her sexy neck, tempting him to lay his mouth on it, nuzzling it until she came undone. Then there was the bra issue. Oh she had one on but it was thin! Her stiff nipples pressed through both sets of fabric. His jeans were very tight.

He groaned, "Sweetheart. What the hell? I thought I made my intentions clear if you chose not to wear a bra."

"I am wearing one."

"Not a very good one," he commented, closing the distance.

Before she had a chance to exhale her deep breath, he was next to her. She noted how much taller he was than her five feet eight inches. Standing beside him she felt small. The dance they shared, she hardly noticed his height or where her head had landed on his chest. All she remembered was the snug fit of their bodies and the safe haven of his arms. He reached behind her, tugging on her hair band. She started to protest but stopped when he redid it, placing it higher on her head explaining the tail needed to be higher.

"Why?"

"So I could do this." His husky voice careened delight into her belly. His mouth plummeted to her neck; suckling it. Shivers shot down her spine and a stimulating desire swept in.

Sinking with pleasure she murmured, "Catch me."

Catching her, he pulled her close liking the way she curved into him. His mouth swiftly sought hers. Enjoying her divine sweetness, his tongue delved deeper, and he realized he could easily become addicted to her.

A frenzy passion exploded between them. A spirited energy fueled power into them. He lifted her closer, and her legs circled his waist. Fiery gasps and tingling sensations passed between them.

Evan's panted breath was hot on her cheek and hers on his. It sent a hurried desire into his groin. He unfastened his pants granting his erection the space it requested. The garments that covered their lower extremities fell to the floor. Feeling his hardened penis against her abdomen, she positioned her vagina closer, giving Evan a clear sign of what she wanted; he too wanted sex now, and talk later.

"Keep your legs and arms around me," he instructed coyly as his fingers fumbled with the tiny foil packet.

Hearing the noisy packaging she immediately knew what he was doing and asked, "Do you always use one?"

"Yes," he firmly confirmed. "You?"

"Always," she said solemnly, and he believed her but didn't understand the quiet questioning in her eyes.

"What else?" he prompted.

"I'm on birth control." She read *so* in his eyes. "Do we need a condom?"

Surprise crossed his face, then caution.

"Evan, I want to feel *you* inside me." She stated.

He gave her a thoughtful glance, and she begged, "Make me feel alive."

Never had he had such an inviting offer. Only with her would he do this and tossed the condom aside. "Damn, sweetheart," he rasped. "I can make you feel alive."

Desire consumed both of them.

Steadying her body against the wall, he entered her hard, and swiftly reached her moist core.

"Yes," she gasped passionately and begged for more. Her fingers clutched his ass; squeezing it. Every time she did, he penetrated deeper inside her; sharing his energy with her and making her feel alive. Her grunted yeses pleased and teased him.

With no condom between them, he experienced more of the raw richness a woman's body offered. Or was it just her? She was a perfect fit for his abundant size, and he easily glided through her wet layers.

Together, they shared generous pleasure. Their bodies united and rhythmically moved as one. He felt her core muscles tighten and clench as she showered him with velvety sensations, and she felt his body shudder as the waves of his orgasm rolled in. Their breathless cries were the last sound they made and together they sank to the floor.

Chapter Eleven

Evan stepped out of the shower, wrapped a towel around his waist and gave Callie a cheerful greeting. "Good morning, sleepy head."

He said morning but surely he was teasing. She rolled over and glanced out the window. The sunlight didn't look right for evening.

"What time is it?"

"Almost seven," he said.

"In the morning?" she said incredibly.

He chuckled, "Yeah."

"What? No way did I sleep the whole night!"

He laughed and sat his half naked body next to her on the bed. "Yes way! You did and the rest of yesterday, too, and no nightmares."

Her jaw dropped in disbelief. "The last thing I remember is collapsing in your lap."

He smoothed his palm over hers. "You fell asleep, and I brought you in my room."

"How do you know I didn't have any nightmares after you left for work?" She clasped their fingers together.

"I didn't leave the house. I stayed with you."

Her eyes expressed sweet appreciation.

"No one's ever..." She started, but Evan already knew and finished the sentence by stating, "Taken care of you."

She glanced up at him in surprise because he knew this!

He placed his other hand on her cheek. "Cal, I know your parents weren't the greatest of nurturers."

"True." She nodded. "And, I know it's their loss but..."

Seeing her pain was heart breaking. "It's your loss, too," he hushed.

Callie was shocked hearing him verbalize the words she often thought. *He knows my pain and understands the betrayal I feel!*

"They didn't even think about me or my feelings. It was all about them. They didn't ask or try to understand what I wanted. They were more concerned about their reputations."

"I know, honey." His fingers rubbed her cheek. "What they did wasn't fair to you. It was selfish. Maybe one day they'll see things differently."

"It hasn't happened yet." She sadly remarked.

"C'mere." He opened his arms, inviting her in, and she willingly accepted. He kissed the top of her head. "Let me take care of you, Callie Cat."

"You know, I can take care of myself."

"I do know, but isn't it nice to be taken care of every now and then?"

"I suppose."

"Let me. I want to."

His adoring tone wrapped sunshine around her heart. She believed him, and the feel good feeling she had was indescribable!

Her fingers traced the edges of his mouth, skimming his lips. He nipped at her fingers and then one by one he sucked them. Coyly, she trailed her moist fingers down his throat, chest, belly, and stopped at the towel. Dipping her hand beneath the towel she wrapped her fingers around his penis and stroked his hardy length.

She swept her breasts against his mouth, and he took turns suckling them while her hand pleasured him. He moaned as she wisped his name across her wanton breath.

They were caught in the sexy haze surrounding them and the giving and receiving of intense passion. Their bodies flamed with desire, and it was up to them to extinguish the fiery passion consuming them.

He laid her on the bed, and in her eyes, he saw how much she wanted him in her. Using her feet, she skillfully removed his towel while he positioned himself between her slender legs.

He entered her and started out with long slow thrusts. Lifting her bottom he deepened his strokes, and his thrusts increased speed.

"Closer," she begged, and he pushed harder.

Wrapped in a strong hold of her legs around his thighs, and her arms around his neck; their bodies rocked with a perfect rhythm.

"Yes!" she cried.

Their bodies quivered, shuddered, and shared tumultuous sensations. Together, they floated on a climatic cloud, their cries; breathless and satisfied.

"Don't let me go," she murmured, and he held her.

Twice, she slept in his bed, and he loved it! Sending her back to the guest room was going to be hard. Let alone when the day came and she and Sunbird went back to work. Then there would be all the overnight stays she would be having out on the road.

"I'm not going anywhere," he stated, hugging her tight.

His statement felt heavy. She felt he was insinuating the fact that he wasn't going anywhere but that she was; because it was her career that took her away. *Is this what he means? I should probably have him clarify exactly what he means.*

She ran her hands up and down his arm over the scratches, and she felt him tense; reminding them both of yesterday's forgotten conversation.

"Why did you come out to the field yesterday?" he asked.

"To talk," she said. "I couldn't let another night pass and take a chance on physically hurting you again. But another night did pass."

"And, you didn't harm me," he said.

"Evan, you're the last person on earth I'd ever want to hurt."

He rubbed her arm. "I know."

The depths of his eyes held true belief and it warmed her soul. "I wish you wouldn't have kept it from me."

"Callie," he sighed. "I didn't keep it from you. We just haven't seen each other. You don't come out of your room. The only time I do see you, is at night…"

"…rescuing me from my fucking nightmares," she stated.

"Pretty much," he said solemnly. "Are you sorry I brought you here?"

"No!" she cried. "I'm not! I love being here!"

Hearing her say this made him happy. "Then why have you been avoiding me?"

Her eyes saddened, and she touched his shoulder. "I'm sorry you feel I've been avoiding you, but I haven't."

He turned away and rolled to the other side of the bed but not before she saw the rejection in his eyes. *Oh, I should have told him sooner.*

"Evan."

His injured prideful eyes screamed *what?*

"I haven't been sleeping."

He ridiculed, "Duh! I know! The nightmares are waking you up."

"They've gotten worse. They're not just at night!" she wailed. "They're during the day, too! Every day I try and stay awake until you get home, but I can't. I'm so tired of trying to stay awake," she snapped angrily.

"That's because you need rest to get better," he said.

"No! You're not listening!" she shrieked.

"I am!"

She shook her head. "But you're not understanding or comprehending."

"Then help me," he cried in anguish.

Frustrated, she slapped her hand on the mattress. "I can't sleep without having nightmares!"

He narrowed his eyes and studied her.

"You know about the night terrors," she said, and then continued after he nodded. "Well, I've been getting them during the day when I take naps."

A small dawning appeared in his eyes.

"This is why you don't see me in the morning. I sleep late and wake up after you leave for work. I roam the house all day trying hard to stay awake, but by late afternoon I'm so tired!" She shouted harshly. "I end up falling asleep before you get home, and then…" she trailed off.

"The vicious cycle starts all over again," he said, understanding this is what she was holding back the other night.

Her eyes held defeat.

He moved closer and wrapped his arms around her. "Callie, I had no idea."

She mumbled, "I know. I should've told you."

"Why didn't you?"

"I didn't want to be a burden."

He sighed. "You'll never be a burden. If I'd known, I could have been helping you cope with it."

She gave him an apologetic smile. "I'm sorry."

"Sweetheart, you forgot about my proposal."

Her thoughts jumped to conclusions *marriage?*

Unaware of what she was thinking, he covered her body with his and gazed softly into her eyes. "I told you I'm here for you morning, noon, and night."

"Oh, yeah, and I have definitely taken advantage of your in the middle of the night offer, more than once."

"Yes, and that's okay," he gently reminded her.

She frowned, and he cupped her cheek. "No don't be sad. I *want* to be the one helping you. I just wish you would have told me sooner about your sleepless habits," he said, regretfully.

His injured eyes swept heartache into her.

With her eyes focused solely on him, he took this opportunity to recite the changes that were going to be made. "In the mornings, I will make sure you're awake before I leave the house. After every nap, you'll send me a message to let me know you're awake. Understand?"

She was speechless beneath his piercing gaze. All she could do was nod her head.

"Throughout the day, we will keep in touch. If you'd like we can play the word game again."

Her eyes brightened. "I'd love to! Gosh, I've missed it."

"I've missed you," he said spontaneously, and then witnessed how much joy his words brought to her.

His eyes reflected her happiness, and he couldn't help feeling they were headed in the right direction towards her recovery.

Her stomach growled.

He laughed. "I guess you're hungry?"

She smiled. "It appears so."

He bent and kissed her belly. "Don't worry little tummy. I'll make you the best egg sandwich you've ever had."

"It's perfectly happy with the eggs it's been having." She defended.

He made a disgusted face. "That's because it doesn't know anything different. After today you won't be able to look at another square egg again."

She rolled her eyes. "Whatever."

"You'll see."

She was about to leave, but he caught her hand, pulling her back into his arms. "Hey, you can't leave without a kiss."

His lips glided over hers and his almond taste sent a glowing sensation through her. Her fingers clenched the muscles rippling across his broad shoulders, and she pulled him closer indulging in the merriment of their zesty kiss. The thought of having too many miles distancing them from each other weighed heavy on her heart. She didn't want one single day to pass and not be able to touch him!

"Scrumptious," he murmured and kissed her again.

Callie's surrender weakened him to the point that all he wanted was to make love with her, cherishing every gaze and touch; taking nothing for granted. While entertaining his pondering thoughts, both their stomachs riled angrily.

He bowed his head and gave a resigning sigh, "You go get ready while I make breakfast."

"Do you want me to help?"

"Nope, I'll be fine." He grinned and ushered her up the stairs, and then went back to his bedroom to finish dressing before heading to the kitchen.

Standing at the stove, he heard her feet coming down the stairs. Then he heard her voice. Turning, he saw her and was positive his heart stopped beating. Her hair lay loose around her shoulders, and her sparkling tan eyes complimented the blue blouse she wore. The solid print was kind to her curvy breasts. Though he couldn't see past the padded bra, he was familiar with what was behind the scenes and didn't bother hiding his smiling pleasure.

"I smell bacon!" she exclaimed.

"It's almost ready. Go ahead and sit. Would you like tea or coffee?" he asked.

"Coffee please," she answered, sitting at the rectangle table.

Behind her was the odd sitting nook. Though it was quaint, it also appeared out of sync with the rest of the room. The fireplace centered the exterior wall and had a window on each side of it. An oak coffee table sat in front of the fireplace. It was the centerpiece for two winged back chairs and the couch. The couch divided the room, because sitting on it, you faced the fireplace, and then your back was to the rest of the kitchen. She supposed there was a logical reason for the unique set up.

The three pieces of furniture were upholstered in a plaid design consisting of green, yellow and blue pastels. The lighter colors were uplifting matching Evan's happy go lucky attitude when he whistled, laughed, or teased her.

"What's going on in that pretty little head of yours?" he asked, setting the coffee in front of her. He didn't let go of the cup until she safely clamped her hands around it. The last thing he wanted was for her to spill the hot liquid on her shorts and burn her pretty legs.

"Thank you. Oh, and you put it in my favorite mug with the yellow tractor on it!" she said delightfully.

"Of course," he said nonchalantly and kissed her.

She felt the tingling heat all the way to her toes. "It's silly thoughts."

"Silly or not, I want to hear all of them."

"The fireplace nook," she told him. "It's a strange area."

"I agree. Originally the whole house was only that area and the kitchen. The fireplace is the original placing. My many greats grandfather did his cooking in a black kettle hanging on a hook over an open fire. In fact," Evan walked over to the mantel and picked up a black kettle. "This is the original one he used."

Her eyebrows rose. "Wow!"

"Doesn't look like much, but I think it was fairly big for one man."

"It's bigger than Sunbird's cab," she observed.

Evan chuckled.

Callie added, "Your many great grandfathers ago wouldn't know what to do with this size of a house. Hell, there are days I don't know what to do with it myself." She threw up her hands.

"Are you making fun of me and the size of my house?"

"Evan! Your bathroom is bigger than what I live in when I'm on the road."

"Shit, Callie. A hotel room is bigger." He chuckled.

She shrugged and grinned. "True. So your house and farm has been in your family for generations?"

He nodded.

"Must be nice," she remarked, feeling strange because never before did she ever think having roots was important. She ran from her heritage years ago and never wanted any part of it. Establishing roots used to scare her but building something like this with Evan wasn't so scary. She placed her hand on his and was thrilled when he placed his other hand over hers sandwiching it.

"Hmm, yeah, it is kind of nice knowing the Nichols' name has been in this area a long time."

Gently he released her hand, stepped over to the stove, plated their food and brought it back to the table. Between two pieces of toast was scrambled eggs piled high along with onions, peppers, mushrooms and cheese with three strips of bacon on the side. Her taste buds watered. Picking up the sandwich she innocently stated, "It's huge!"

Her words made his groin tighten. Watching her pull the sandwich into her mouth his cock danced wishing her luscious lips were taking him in. Unable to keep his eyes off her, he observed the awe inspiring expression float across her face, and his jaw slightly dropped, and heat raced through him.

"This is delicious!" she raved.

The excitement in her voice sexually exalted him. "It's so flavorful. It's the best thing I've —"

Evan interrupted her mid sentence with a kiss. His tongue slid in, catching hers.

Breathless, she corrected, "Okay, make that the second thing."

"Good." His eyes shined satisfaction. "My food can't be the best thing you've had in your mouth," he teased. "So, how's the sandwich?"

Shyly, she admitted, "You were right. It's better than anything I've ever eaten."

"Yeah?" he asked, and she nodded.

Coming from a country club family, and then being tossed into the fast food world and truck stop diners for so long, he realized her taste buds probably hadn't had the privilege of dining with the best homemade food in the country. The countrified meals he was raised on was better than any rich fancy food she might have grown up with and definitely a whole lot better than the greasy diners she had learned to live with.

Evan chuckled, "Thanks."

Seeing his happy smile spread joy through her.

"You're welcome," she said.

Evan finished first and sipped his coffee while she ate the rest of hers. He liked that she wasn't embarrassed to eat in front of him *and* that she didn't hide her hungry appetite from him.

"Thank you Evan. This was wonderful," she complimented. With a neighing laugh she said, "Funny how the scrambled egg in the sandwich feels appropriate."

His interested eyes were filled with question, and she answered, "I feel emotionally scrambled."

Evan gave a slow nod and rose taking their plates to the sink. He rinsed them before putting them in the dishwasher. Then he picked up the wash cloth from the sink and began washing the stove top.

"Callie, I'm not going to pretend I know anything about how it was for you. Other than scary, heart wrenching, desperate, lonely, and worried that you weren't going to be found."

Everything he described was what he had experienced. Suddenly he felt her arms around his waist. He twisted, and she melted into his embrace.

"Evan, you know exactly how it was. How do you?"

"It's everything I was feeling," he said with heartache.

"You're wrong about one thing. I knew you were going to find me."

"I *had* to find you!" he claimed, desperately.

"As soon as I saw the boots with the embroidered snake by the driver's door I knew it was the *bearded man*. I let my guard down," she said devastated. "I was so stupid and couldn't believe I had done that!"

Evan wouldn't allow her to take the blame. "Stop blaming yourself. It happened. *He* wanted you, and *he* was going to get you no matter what!"

Then he shifted the blame onto himself. "I should have met you on the road instead of letting you come alone. I knew you were shaken up by what had just happened at the gas station. I should've –"

Callie placed her finger on his lips. His guilt weighed heavy on her heart. "No, Evan. If I can't take the blame, neither can you."

Their eyes mirrored the insurmountable guilt they had. Sharing this blame somehow helped them to forgive themselves.

With remorseful eyes, Evan took her hand and held it tightly.

Gently, but firmly she said, "Evan, I never blamed you. It wasn't your fault, so please forgive yourself."

"Only if you do the same," he reasoned.

She gave him a disheartening look, but he shook his head. "No, Callie Cat, I mean it. We may blame ourselves, but together we can forgive. Besides, I'm proud of the way you helped us find you!"

"You mean when I removed the GPS chip from the phone and stuck it in my pocket?"

He nodded. "Yes, and when you wedged the phone into the floorboards. It verified you were in the vehicle. I've never been prouder," he complimented, and she felt his pride.

"Thanks." She shyly accepted. "When I woke up in the van with all those other girls, I knew I was in trouble and had to do whatever I could to leave a clue; praying you'd find it."

"I did." His eyes smiled as he lifted her hand to his mouth and delicately kissed the back of it.

Powerful emotions tingled through her all the way to her toes.

"I really do hate *him*," she commented.

"Me, too," he said.

"Have you heard if they found him? Sage had said the bearded man, and the man with the scar helped her at the restaurant."

"Uh-yeah," he said, realizing there was a lot she didn't know. "We need to talk about everything we found out during the days you were missing. Do you have time?"

Callie rolled her eyes. "You're the one working not me. Do *you* have time?"

"Callie Cat." He caressed her cheek. "I always have time for you."

His soft sincerity floated over her like a warm breeze. She liked it when Evan tangled his hand with hers and led her over to the sofa, easing her into his lap. She sat sideways with her lower back against the arm of the couch, and his arm supported the middle of her back. She tingled inside and out when his other hand rested on her shin, and his fingers drew circles on her bare skin.

Callie's eyes expressed interest because she wanted to know what had happened in her absence. She squeezed his hand and said, "I'm listening."

Evan's eyes gleamed mysteriously. "I guess I'll start with the big news of when Dirk and Sage arrived and who was following them."

"Tell me," she insisted excitedly.

Chapter Twelve

Evan began by asking, "Do you remember Hank, the man posing as a vacuum cleaner salesman here in town?"

"The sleaze-ball wanted by the FBI?"

He nodded as his hand infiltrated under her shirt and up her back. "Hank got away before the Feds could catch him."

Callie liked his thumb tracing her spine. "That's right. I remember hearing about it before we left."

"Mm-hmm," Evan murmured lazily. He was addicted to holding her, breathing her scent, and touching her silky skin.

"The federal agent in charge of that investigation was Dexter," he commented.

Callie's eyes flickered with recognition. "Dexter, he's the one who helped you find me," she stated.

"Yes. Well, he also ended up following Dirk and Sage here to Purlieu."

"Ooh, the plot thickens."

Evan gave a grim laugh. "It thickens a lot."

"How?" she asked, and his fingers tightened on her back.

"The bearded man," he began then paused and gently took her hand. "He is an FBI agent on an undercover assignment."

"What!" Callie hissed her surprise. "Then how did, no, why did…"

"Why did he take you, I know," he finished harshly and hated seeing her depleted look. "I've been asking myself the same question."

Evan continued. "He's working with the top dogs in the human trafficking ring, and he had a hand in kidnapping Sage."

"What!" Callie exclaimed, clutching his hand.

Evan nodded and went on. "The two men you and Dirk pummeled had reported to the bearded man and his crime boss that two men in a yellow rig took Sage from them."

"We didn't take her, we rescued her," Callie spat hotly.

"Correct." He rubbed her leg, calming her as the rest of the sentence sank in.

She smirked. "So everybody was looking for two men in a yellow rig?"

Evan chuckled, "Yeah, but then they realized the two of you separated and didn't know which one of you had Sage. Dexter followed Dirk, and the bearded man was ordered by his crime boss, Abel, to follow you."

"Who is Abel?"

"He's the man you saw at the truck stop with the bearded man."

Callie gasped, "The one with the scar? The same one Kylee described as the delivery man?"

Evan nodded. "Uh-huh."

"Yikes." Callie whistled. "If the bearded man is an FBI Agent, does he know Dexter?"

"Yes. He's part of Dexter's team," Evan answered. "Here's something else you don't know. Dexter and the bearded man came up with the plan to kidnap and rescue Sage from the men in the car, but instead, you and Dirk rescued her before they could."

"Whoa! Are you serious?" she stated unbelievably.

"Yeah," Evan confirmed.

"Kind of weird," she whispered. "How it all played out."

"Almost like destiny had its hand in everything." Evan commented.

"Yeah," she agreed as an odd shiver shot through her. "So the bearded man is one of the good guys?"

Evan's jaw clenched. "Dexter seems to think so, but if he is good I don't understand why he kidnapped you. He told you he was done following you. He lied."

Callie shook her head. "I accused him of the same thing, but he told me he hadn't lied. His plans were changed when I recognized his boss' facial scar and asked how I was familiar with it."

"What did you say?" Evan inquired.

"I didn't tell him anything. He asked a few other times, but I never told him how I knew. Eventually, he gave up and quit asking."

"We thought the reason why you were taken, was because the traffickers wanted to send you overseas but certain things didn't add up," Evan said.

"Like what?" she inquired.

"The day you went missing. The signal on your phone's GPS chip stayed on for a long time leading us to a warehouse. I have no idea if us finding the warehouse was planned or by mistake, because the signal vanished soon after we found the warehouse."

"Oh, Evan, you must've been so worried," she sadly stated.

"I was." He rubbed her back again. "Then Dexter shows up and promises to help find you. His team and all their fancy equipment found the van you were transported in along with your phone that you stuck in the floorboards. Jack, another agent from Dexter's team, brought us your phone. He seemed nice but didn't say much. In fact, here's another thing I found odd. Dexter had to coerce Jack into finding Sage's friend who went missing."

"Why did her friend need to be found?" Callie asked.

"Evidently, the same day Sage was kidnapped, her friend went missing, and Sage was the number one suspect in her disappearance. Witnesses verified Sage was the last person to see her friend."

"What! That's ridiculous! Anyone who knows Sage knows she'd never harm anyone," Callie said vehemently.

"I know." Evan pursed his lips. "There was an odd tension between the two agents in regards to finding Sage's friend. Jack seemed apprehensive about finding the friend, but he finally agreed."

"Hmm, interesting," she murmured.

"It was weird. My gut tells me something felt off."

Callie agreed it was odd, making him feel good that he wasn't crazy for having these thoughts.

"Did they find Sage's friend?" she asked.

"Yep, and her written statement verified Sage had nothing to do with her kidnapping; freeing Sage to join Dirk on his harvest run."

"That's right, you asked me to help with that."

Evan grunted. "I found another driver to help. And besides, I wasn't sure I was going to be ready to send you back out on the road. If I did, I would have definitely gone with you."

Their eyes merrily met, because they both knew, she would have objected to being grounded or babysat.

Callie questioned, "So how did you find me?"

"It was crazy." He shook his head. "As quickly as the signal had disappeared, the signal on your GPS chip reappeared," he snapped his finger, "just like that."

Her eyes widened. "It did?"

He nodded. "Uh-huh."

"So, you think the plan for me wasn't ever to go into human trafficking?"

"Correct. Though, I have no proof. All I have is my gut saying so."

She slowly nodded her head. "Ev, I trust your instincts. Do you have any idea why I was taken?"

He sighed heavily. "No. None."

"So…do you think the bearded man is good or bad?"

He shrugged. "I'm still on the fence about it."

"Right! Hard to tell because if he *is* good why did he take me?"

"You see my point."

"It's crystal clear," she said, breathing him in, feeling safe.

He repositioned their bodies; laying them side by side; him in the middle between the sofa and her. Nestling her close, he rested one arm beneath her head and draped the other one over her midsection. Together, they enjoyed each other's warmth.

"We fit nicely together," she stated, squirming closer.

He leaned forward and wickedly whispered, "In other ways, too."

She playfully swatted his arm. "You're talking about sex."

"Yes." He nuzzled his nose in her neck then hinted, "But I'd like to think here, too." He placed his hand over her heart.

She turned over to look at him, and he loved the way her eyes danced with happiness. "No one's ever indicated this before."

"Good." Keeping his eyes locked with hers, he glided his hand into her shining hair. "I love running my fingers through your hair. I could do it all day long."

"I'd let you." Thoughts of having him do this for the rest of the day seemed hopeful.

"Evan, I am happy to be sharing this moment with you versus…" she didn't need to finish the sentence; they both knew the horrible outcome of the other for instance.

"I'm sorry for breaking the mood."

"Callie, honey, you haven't." The endearment easily rolled out of his mouth making it sound like she was his. Then he captured her in a possessive kiss making her feel that she *was* his.

He caressed the side of her face and shakily said, "I, too, am happy to be with you. Not once did I ever give up on seeing you again. I couldn't!"

"Remember the argument we had?" she inquired. "You were mad at me for being stubborn."

Misty eyed, he nodded, and she continued, "I was mad at myself, too, for being stubborn. But, I wasn't going to admit this to you or me. I wasn't going to let a man tell me what to do."

A chuckle rumbled deep in his chest. "I was frustrated because I *knew* I couldn't tell you what to do. Not that I'd ever want to."

"You wouldn't?"

His derisive laugh was a compliment. "No, baby girl," he said, "Telling you what to do would break your spirit. And why in the hell would anyone want to do that?"

"So many have wanted to," she said, and his affectionate eyes stormed her soul.

"Well, I don't. Your spirit is beautiful."

"You think so?"

"Yes."

"Evan," she said, teary- eyed. "You have a wonderful way with words."

"Only for you," he mumbled, caressing her cheek and chin.

"And I was afraid you wouldn't want me in your life."

"Silly girl, I do and have for a long time."

She touched his bristled jaw. "I worried that if you didn't find me you would've blamed yourself."

"I would have and people would have spent the rest of their lives trying to convince me otherwise."

"Yeah," she said wistfully. "I know how you feel. Dirk and I blamed ourselves for what happened to Sage, though it was no one's fault."

He wrapped his arm around her. "Callie, I *had* to find you. Life wouldn't have been the same without you in it."

She placed her hand on his chest. "In my heart, I knew you would. I just prayed it didn't take a lifetime. When I thought the angel was taking me to heaven, all I wanted was to see you one last time to tell you your search was over, and I was safe and you were free to live your life."

"Oh, sweetheart," he fiercely stated, "my heart never would have been free. I would have forever loved you."

Instead of protesting the dreamy statement of loving her forever, she accepted it, and snuggled into his protecting embrace.

Chapter Thirteen

Callie shivered and twisted. She opened her eyes and saw Evan's smile.

"I was hoping I wouldn't wake you," he said.

"I was so comfortable."

He chuckled, "You were snoring."

"Oh. What an awful sound that must have been. No wonder you woke me up."

He laughed again. "It was kind of cute."

She groaned. "I doubt it."

Evan carried her up the stairs, and she said, "You know I can walk."

Smiling, he replied, "I know."

"Sage speculated that the man with the scar was after her. Do you know if he is still after her?" Callie asked him, as he set her on the bed.

Evan loved her a little more because she was concerned for her friend. Shaking his head, he said, "According to Dexter, Abel was told that Sage wasn't the girl they were looking for."

"Who told him?" she probed.

Evan shrugged. "I just assumed the bearded man told Abel, per the information he received from Jack, who I think is their middle man."

Callie's eyes produced confusion. "He's what?"

Evan sat down on the bed next to her. Giving her a lopsided grin, he explained, "The middle man, meaning he works between Dexter and the bearded man. It's too risky for their undercover agent to contact them so they've placed another agent in the field with him."

"Huh, interesting theory," she said.

"I think Jack has a low key position in the undercover operation. A job that is less conspicuous."

Callie suggested, "Something that lets him move more freely within the operation."

"Exactly," Evan said. Watching her frown, he asked, "What are you thinking?"

"What if...one of them is a double agent?" she voiced.

Evan whistled. "Damn, Callie Cat, that's an interesting twist."

She shrugged. "If he has a low key position within the undercover operation, it would give him the mobility to have access with both sides."

"Therefore both sides trust him," he remarked.

"Yes!" she said excitedly. "If he's diabolical he could manipulate both sides."

Evan hissed through his teeth. "Scary."

"Yeah, and if the bearded man kidnapped me, is he evil and pretending to be a good guy?" she said.

Evan winced, "Maybe."

Callie inhaled sharply and clutched his arm. "Oh! Could this be why the bearded man stopped asking me questions about his boss' facial scar?"

His eyes quizzed hers, and she continued, "Evan, after Jack's visit in your office with you, Kellan, Dirk and Sage, could he have told the bearded man we're friends with Kylee and this is the reason why I'm familiar with the scar?"

"Meaning, you'd know about the scar from when Abel had posed as a delivery man?" Evan inquired.

"Yes," she confirmed.

"Whoa," Evan whooshed. "If this is true, then…" Anger flashed in his eyes.

"What?" she inquired.

"Jack knew I was looking for you. Son of a bitch," he cursed bitterly. "When Jack was here, did he know where you were? And didn't say anything?" Evan's jaw twitched.

"Or couldn't?" Callie questioned. "Could this have been the tension between him and Dexter?"

"Damn," he muttered.

Evan's stunned look broke Callie's heart. Attempting to ease his mind she suggested, "If Jack is working with the bearded man, and if he knew where I was, maybe he did help me, get back to you."

"Yeah, maybe," he said with a frown. "Right now we aren't going to worry about it. It's time for you to rest. I'll be downstairs when you wake up."

"Are you babysitting me?" she accused.

"No," he said softly. "I'm behind on a lot of paperwork and there's too much distraction at the office."

"You're not working in the fields today?"

"No. Past few nights its rained making the ground too wet," he explained and then teased, "We don't want to get any tractors stuck now do we?"

"Ha-ha." She tossed him a lopsided smile.

"Sorry, I couldn't resist," he grinned and gently caressed her cheek with his knuckle while his eyes tenderly scanned her face.

Lying on her back she was able to look him in the eye. Love swirled inside of her, but she didn't dare speak her heart. She felt as though they might be at the spot where they were before the kidnapping happened but was afraid to jeopardize it by saying words he wasn't ready to hear.

Evan wanted to tell her how much she had his heart but didn't want to scare her into making a run for the sunset. Covering her with the blanket he wished her sweet dreams before he left the room.

"You always wish me this but so far they haven't been sweet."

"One day they will," he said confidently, and then left.

Feeling spoiled Callie fell asleep. Unfortunately, her peaceful dreams turned evil. She was being chased, and then grabby hands held her hostage. Shouting, she kicked her assailant and finally escaped! Free, she ran away and screamed for help!

The minute Evan heard Callie screaming he jumped out the chair and headed towards her room. He met her at the bottom of the stairs as she collided into him.

"Evan!" she said, frantically. "Help me!" Her hands clamped his shoulders.

"Callie, what is it?" Evan gripped her sides and felt her panic.

"The bearded man…he…he was chasing me…but then I was back in the crate, and-and got away," she recalled, adding, "After he took my boots off another man came in trying to…"

Her fingers clutched the fabric of his shirt, and Evan cringed fearing the end of the sentence. "Shhh, breathe."

Callie inhaled, relaxed, and he asked what happened next, and she said, "Humphrey came back and pulled him off me."

Evan was confused because she'd never mentioned the name Humphrey before.

"Humphrey?" he repeated the name.

"Yes."

"What did Humphrey do?" Evan questioned.

"He took my boots off."

"Why?" Evan inquired.

She spoke in a distant tone. "He suspected I had a tracking device on me."

"He never checked you for it before?" Evan asked.

"Correct," she verified.

"What happened after Humphrey removed your boots?"

"He took them; left the crate and the other man came in and started harassing me." She shuddered, setting Evan on edge. "He put his hand over my mouth so I couldn't scream, but I fought with him, and he finally let go. That's when I screamed."

"Callie Cat," he whispered affectionately and rubbed her arms.

Her eyes were emotionless as she recounted the nightmare that had awakened her. Evan realized she had dreamt about an incident that occurred while she had been kidnapped. He tried paying close attention to the details, but he was lost trying to separate the roles between the bearded man and the new fellow, Humphrey. Somewhere along the way Humphrey had replaced the bearded man, adding a new confusing twist.

Callie continued, "Everyone there feared Humphrey, because after he beat up the man who tried hurting me, he made it clear to everyone that I was his and off limits. He threatened them with their life if anyone ever tried messing with me again. I felt relatively safe after his announcement. What I didn't know is, was I safe from him?"

Evan swallowed his concerning anger.

"I kicked Humphrey when he tried putting my boots back on. He sat on my legs and his hand skimmed my body. But it was strategic not sexual."

"Like he was looking for something?" Evan asked.

She nodded. "Yeah, he was."

"The GPS chip?" Evan guessed.

"Yes, and he found it in my pants pocket, but he didn't remove it."

He gaped at her. "What?"

She nodded. "All he said was, 'Shhh, don't tell anyone.'"

"Whoa." Stunned, his jaw dropped. "That's a little strange."

Agreeing, she nodded.

Needing reassurance, he asked, "You're sure this Humphrey guy didn't hurt you in any way?"

Catching his meaning, she rolled her hand into his and confidently reassured him. "No, he didn't. I truly believe the last thing he wanted was for me to get hurt. When he wasn't there he had another man watch over me. I sensed they both were concerned about my safety."

Evan was skeptical. "No one else messed with you?"

"No." Her eyes and tone were firm.

"Thank God," he whispered with such meaning.

"I know."

Her eyes bloomed with curiosity.

"What?" he asked.

"Why do you think the bearded man, I mean Humphrey, let me keep the GPS chip?"

He cocked his head to the side. "Wait. Humphrey and the bearded man, are the same person?"

She nodded. "I believe so, because the bearded man responded to the name Humphrey many times."

An eerie shiver ran down his spine. *Fuck!*

"Callie, tell me about the other man who protected you."

"Not much to tell. He had a goatee and always wore a hat."

"What kind of hat?"

"A ball cap and he always had the bill pulled down making it hard to see his face."

"Do you know his name?"

She squinted, trying to remember. "I can't remember what it is. Other than it was a very unusual name. Not the average Joe, John or Bob. I'm sorry."

He rubbed the back of her hand. "It's all right. You'll probably remember it when you least expect it."

"Like when I'm in the shower?" she teased.

The image of her in the shower was picturesque, and he smiled. Taking his focus off his sexy thoughts he asked, "Are you ready to go back to bed?"

"Hmm, not really," she murmured. "I'm afraid of the nightmares returning and having to wake up alone again."

"I've got an idea." In one swift move, he lifted and carried her to his room. Unfolding the sheet, he laid her in the middle of the king sized bed. "You can sleep with me. If you have anymore nightmares I'm right here."

Feeling tiny in the luxurious bed she laughed.

"Lay down," he instructed, and she scooted down into the softest sheets she'd ever felt. Her eyes lit up and met his smiling face.

"Were you still working?" she asked.

He nodded. "As much as you needed to sleep, I needed to work."

"I guess we helped each other out."

"Good night." Evan kissed her forehead then turned his back to her.

She snuggled closer against him and all he wanted was to wrap his arms around her, but he didn't dare. He was too afraid of how his body would respond. He was aching for her but tonight she needed emotional support. Perhaps a part of him needed this, too.

"Evan?"

"Hmm,"

"If the bearded man let me keep the GPS chip, and if he truly was protecting me, do you think this means he could be one of the good guys?"

"I don't know, maybe." Evan rolled onto his back opening the invitation of having her roll into his side. He could feel her perky breasts through the thin material of her camisole. Before he had a chance to put distance between them, she slung her arm across his torso and nestled her head in the crook of his arm. He didn't fight fate as he threw his arm around her.

"Evan." She gathered courage to continue. "A lot of nights after we talked I'd lay in the dark hugging my pillow pretending it was you. Wondering how it would really feel lying next to you...like this."

Her truth was astounding, and he dared, asking, "And how is it?"

"Wonderful." She shyly stated.

"I like it, too," he softly said.

"Evan, I...have another confession."

He held his breath.

"My feelings for you go beyond friendship."

He prayed she couldn't hear the beating of his ecstatic heart. Acting on instincts he did exactly what he wanted to do. He rolled them over on their sides and wrapped her in a cherishing embrace. If she became aware of his hardening penis so be it. He was a virile male, and she was a sexy woman.

"Callie Cat, I feel the same about you," he soothed. "And have for awhile."

"Really?" she said surprised.

"Yeah," he said ruefully. "It's why I've been a jerk to you. I had to annoy you. I couldn't take a chance on having you see how much I liked you."

She gasped. "Oh my gosh. All this time you've liked me?"

He gave a low chuckle.

"Why tell me now?"

"The timing is right. After we danced at the wedding, all I could think about was how I had wasted too much time taunting you. I should have been trying to make you laugh. I decided to change my ways. The next morning my heart was heavy having to watch you and Dirk leave. I couldn't bring myself to say good-bye to you in person. Days later, when I heard your voice on the other end, I was so relieved you were okay, but after hearing your tale I was really nervous about your safety."

She nodded her head. "Good thing you didn't tell me about your worries. I would've freaked out."

"Don't I know it," he said dryly. "You needed a friend, not a parent. I also knew I had to be a better friend for you. So I stopped hiding and started showing you a nicer side of me."

"I'm ready now."

"Good," he said happily.

"Crazy how one dance changed us so much," she said yawning.

"Hey, beauty queen, it's time for sleeping. If you don't I'll send you back upstairs." He gently warned with a smile, but since she couldn't see it, she took his threat seriously.

"Don't make me go upstairs," she pouted.

"Shhh, sleep," he encouraged.

There had been too many lonely nights, lying awake wondering how it would be having her here. Feeling the quiet rise and fall of her sleeping beside him was extravagant! He would have enjoyed it more if his thoughts hadn't been so jumbled. They had him staring in the dark. His gut instinct still suspected her kidnapping had nothing to do with human trafficking.

Humphrey. He finally had a name for the bearded man who kidnapped Callie. Was this his real name or an assumed identity? His thoughts slid to Jack.

Which agent knew the truth about all his other silent questions, such as, how did Humphrey know to look for the GPS chip? And why *that* particular day, instead of on the day he took her? The only conclusion Evan came up with was no one suspected she had it. So, again…what happened that made Humphrey think Callie might have a tracking device?

Who helped Callie get home safely? He was fairly sure someone had orchestrated the use of her GPS chip to signal him to her whereabouts. In regards, to protecting Callie, did Humphrey act alone, or was it a request from Jack?

Evan's thoughts backtracked to Humphrey. He had questioned Callie more than once on why she was familiar with Abel's scar and then he stopped asking. *Why?*

Pressing his thumb and finger on his temples, Evan quietly groaned as his memory jumped to the day when Jack had brought them Callie's phone. This is when he, Kellan, Dirk, Sage and Dexter had discovered the GPS chip had been removed from her phone.

Evan's eyes widened. *Shit! We openly discussed our speculation about Callie having the chip in her possession!*

He shivered. *Jack…is he the connecting link? He was there soaking up all the information we were so innocently giving!*

His gut twisted. *Did Jack already know about Callie's predicament? He must have been the one to tell Humphrey about the GPS chip. Could he have known her location and didn't tell us?!*

Dread drifted through him. *Son of a…*

Chapter Fourteen

Jack cradled her in his arms as he browsed the dock for the deep sea fishing boat named Maria. He had made arrangements for them to be stowed back to U.S. soil. Rapidly he spoke in the captain's language verifying the details of the original deal they struck. Relying on his instincts, Jack knew they were in trusted hands and boarded the ship. The captain mumbled obscenities after seeing the physical abuse on Kara's face and limbs. Hating the sight over the suffering she had endured, Jack hated himself and was unable to stop the cracking of his heart.

The captain barked an order to one of his men then led him down a stairwell, through a small hallway and into a tiny room. Before he was allowed in, a mattress was placed on the floor. He surmised it was probably pulled from one of the bunk beds and he felt sorry for the mate who had to go without, and yet he was extremely grateful for the cushioned comfort given to them.

"Gracias," he had generously thanked the captain. The captain patted his back telling him he was a good man for rescuing the girl, but Jack knew better. He wasn't good. A better man wouldn't have put her into this situation to begin with. He should've blown his cover and taken her far, far away from the clutches of men like Hank and Abel.

He was given several bottles of water and was promised more if they needed it. He thanked the captain again, closed the door and set Kara on the mattress.

Immediately, she rolled her body into a ball, protecting herself. He knelt beside her and gently touched her arm. She flinched and guilt swam through him because she had learned to distrust a touch. He hushed kind tones near her ear telling her she was safe, and he wasn't going to hurt her. It took awhile before she believed him.

Finally she rolled over and looked at him with a stunned expression. He feared she might scream and hoped to God she didn't. If she did, he'd have to force his hand over her mouth and then she'd be wary of his good intentions.

In a miraculous tone, she stammered, "H-Hum...phrey."

Delight swam through him. "Brave Angel, you remember me?" he said incredibly.

She nodded. "I said your name to the others." Her voice croaked because her throat was dry.

"Good job," he praised, petting the top of her head. "Here, drink some water." He held the bottle to her lips, helping her drink.

She thirstily drank. When she was done she pushed the bottle towards him. Their fingers collided and a bolt of electricity shot through him. She gave him an alarming look, and he was fairly sure she felt the same jolt.

"It tastes so good." Her voice was smoother this time since the water had coated her throat.

His eyes filled with regret. It was because of him that she had to live with little water.

"I was so scared," she admitted helplessly.

"My brave angel," he soothed, and he continuously smoothed her neck and shoulder with his hand. A cramp rolled into her legs wracking her with horrendous pain. She hissed and tried bending her legs, but he wouldn't let her. Her soured expression hurt him, too. This, too, was his fault. It probably had been a long time since she'd been able to stretch her legs and wondered if she remembered how to. His strong hands kneaded the tight muscles and slowly stretched her legs, encouraging her to relax. Finally she uncurled her legs, and he praised her again.

She asked where they were and he said, "Inter-coastal waters."

Kara curled her nose and said, "It smells like fish."

Amused, he said, "Yes, we're on a fishing boat."

"You've kidnapped me again?"

"Yes."

"Are you taking me to another bad place?"

"No," he reassured.

"So you rescued me?"

"Yes." He placed his hands on her shoulders and looked directly into her blue eyes. "Kara, you're going home."

Watching her process what he said was like viewing a television show. First she displayed disbelief that this was the truth. Second was hope that it was the truth. Third she believed it was the truth. Seeing her glossy eyes turned his heart to a mushy mess. Giving her good news was heavenly. His heart pranced with joy. He'd never experienced such emotions before.

"Thank you," she whispered.

The exhilarating relief on her face was untouchable. Her eyes swam with tears and she fought hard not to cry, but after everything she'd been through a good cry is what she needed! Of all the females he'd ever known they would've already been a blubbering mess. All of a sudden, he realized his brave angel didn't want to cry in front of him. Pride for her rippled through him and with everything she'd been through, he couldn't let her deny herself the right to cry.

Impulsively, he gathered her into his lap. Wrapping his arms around her, he soothed, "It's okay to cry, brave angel."

The tears came, her body shook, and she cried hard into his chest. He absorbed all the fear and desperation she had starting with the day he had put her in the van through to this evening's rescue. Brushing the hair off her tear stained face, his fingers raked through the rest of the tangled strands, and he was deeply burdened with how long it had been since she last brushed it.

Though she thanked him, he wondered, *will she ever forgive me for what I did to her? What does it matter? I'll never see her again. Once I drop her off with Dexter, she'll confess her friend had nothing to do with her kidnapping and go back to her old life, and I'll go on with mine.*

****

"Humphrey, wake up." Abel kicked his partner's foot.

Jack rolled his head to the side. His crime boss stared down at him, and he wished for the day he didn't have any bosses to report to. *One day,* he vowed silently. Though he had no idea when, because the end was nowhere in sight. He had become too good at his job that none of his bureau bosses wanted to give him any kind of leave. They feared he wouldn't come back to the job, and he couldn't confirm if he would return to this line of work once he had distance from it. He wanted and needed to be out of this current undercover position. It was taking a toll on him; physically and mentally. He just hoped when it came time to leave it wasn't in a body bag but often he feared this might be the only way he was getting out.

"Yeah, man, I'm awake."

"Were you dreaming about those models on television again?" Abel asked.

"Huh?"

"You were mumbling about angels."

Fuck! Often; like a movie. Images of Kara's rescue displayed themselves behind his closed eyelids. *I hope I didn't say anything incriminating!*

Hiding his panic, he guffawed, "Shit, it's probably the last commercial I saw before I fell asleep."

Abel cackled. "Well, if you're not *too* up, get dressed and let's go."

Catching his meaning, Jack gave him a cocky grin. "Where're we going?"

"I've got a surprise for you." Abel hinted.

Abel's smirk had Jack feeling edgy. Yet...Abel's body language radiated calm, and Jack didn't think he had said anything incriminating while he slept. Jumping off the top bunk, he felt comfortable asking, "What is it?"

Abel announced, "I'm introducing you to Hank. There's an important meeting happening today, and as my right hand man, I want you to be there."

Jack stared at him and truly hoped Abel wasn't leading him to his death.

"Is this the meeting you've been waiting for?" Jack inquired.

Abel grinned. "Yes it is! After today we'll know everything about the shipment and then we'll know how to establish our own plan for ditching this place."

Jack patted Abel's shoulder and appreciatively said, "Thank you so much for including me."

Abel glanced around them. Seeing that no one was around, his eyes showed compassion and Jack knew he had convinced him of his sincerity. "Humphrey, there's no other man I want by my side."

"Thank you, Sir. It's an honor." Jack said as a part of him truly did feel dangerously honored by the drug lord's middle man.

    "Now when I introduce you to Hank, shake his hand, say a short hello, and then leave the talking to me."

"Got it! I'll just stand over in the corner like I always do."

"Perfect." Abel slapped his shoulder.

****

Hank walked in the room with three massive bodyguards in tow. They were tall with the widest shoulders Jack had ever seen. He wouldn't have wanted to tangle with them for anything in the world and thought for sure one of their hands could flatten a grapefruit. No telling what they could do to a man's head. *How many bullets would it take just to injure them?*

Abel introduced Hank to Humphrey.

Jack was beyond thrilled with being able to shake hands with the biggest crime lord ever! He met Hank's scrupulous eyes. It was chilling, and he could've sworn he might've just met the devil. The man's voice was smooth; flawless, and he understood why so many unsuspecting women fell for his charm. He could tell Hank was a man used to getting what he wanted. He wasn't a man to trifle with but one to be reckoned with. He commanded respect and promptly received it.

Hank sat down in the chair behind the desk his keen eyes on the seven elite men invited to attend. Hank laid his arms on the desk and clasped his hands. Clearing his throat, he began talking.

"Men, thank you for joining me today. I'm going to get right to the point." His voice thundered with authority. "There are three loads I'm most concerned about. We're trucking two of them to the sea ports; one to Louisiana and the other to Florida. The third will arrive in Memphis and will be sent down the river on a barge to the sea. All should be arriving soon."

A fellow wearing a red bandana tied around his forehead voiced a question. "Sir, why are we breaking them up?"

Hank snapped, "It'll be easier, less suspicious."

"What if the mission is compromised?" The man asked, alarming Hank.

"Compromised?" Hank sneered and slowly stood up. With his hands flat on the desk and his arms supporting the weight of his body, he leaned forward giving the man a scrutinized glare. "Now why on earth would it be compromised?"

From where he stood, Jack had a good view of the man's Adam's apple pulsing. *This isn't going to end well.* Jack shifted slightly to the left, farther away from the splatter of blood that was coming.

The man stuttered, "N-no reason, just c-covering the b-bases."

"Well, its dumb fucking luck you even asked! Who hired you?" Hank roared. His hand shot out and grabbed the man's shirt collar, twisting and lifting it as the man gasped for a breath. A foul smell filled the room. Jack stared in quiet fascination. Several times in his life he had heard the saying "scared the shit right out of him", but he had never witnessed it until now.

"Leroy," the man wheezed.

Stunned! Jack thought, *damn it! Memphis is compromised!*

Hank released his grip and pushed him backwards. An evil laugh rumbled out of him. "Leroy. He was a dumb son of a bitch too! Well, tell him hello for me."

Hank swiftly removed the gun from his hip holster, aimed it at the man and squeezed the trigger. The deafening boom of the bullet shot forward straight into the man's heart. Blood ricochet and the man dropped to the floor his eyes wide open.

Hank pointed in Jack's direction saying, "Humphrey."

Jack stepped forward, honored that the crime lord remembered his name. "Yes sir."

"Dispose of his body."

"Yes sir," he said again as he slid his hands into a pair of black leather gloves he kept on him at all times. It came in handy for jobs like this. Grabbing the feet, he dragged the body out the door, agitated that he wouldn't be able to hear the rest of the conversation. He'd have to rely on Abel to fill him in on the details.

Ugh! He had been so close! Then this idiot came in ruining everything! Jack emptied the dead man's pockets, cut his boots, and stripped his clothes, leaving his underwear on. No way was he getting into *that* shitty mess!

Jack didn't find any listening devices which meant he wasn't working with any law enforcement but who did send him? Who supplied him Leroy's name? He removed the cash from the man's wallet and tucked it into the inside pocket of his boot. Then he placed the wallet next to the body. He struck a match burning the pile of discarded clothes and then stacked some crates in front of the body. Making sure he was alone and that no one followed him out the door, he dialed Dexter's number. Hearing his partner's voice he briefly explained the scenario. Hanging up, he went back inside only to discover the meeting was ending. *Damn my luck today.*

* * * * * * * *

In a lightning move, the other man grabbed Jack by the waist and pushed him to the floor. His cheek lay flat on the cold dirty tile and his arms were forced behind him as handcuffs were snapped on his wrists. Then he was roughly hauled to his feet.

What a fucking day!

He and Abel stopped at a diner on their way out of town. Waiting for their food to arrive Abel filled him in on what he had missed at the meeting. Things were moving forward with the other loads and the Memphis load would be re-routed.

Apparently, Hank told Abel he'd be contacted closer to the date as to where the new destination will be. Hank said this load could still be sent down the Mississippi River but the point of entry onto the river would be north of Memphis. Hank was also taking precautionary steps by changing the destinations of the other sea ports but not too far from the original destinations. This information had Jack silently jumping for joy.

"Hank's not worried about the authorities watching the river?" Jack asked.

Abel shook his head, confiding Hank wasn't concerned since the law men wouldn't know when or where they were accessing the river.

Playing his part with Abel, he mentioned, "Maybe we can throw the feds off with a fake location of where they're entering the river."

"Hey, I like that idea."

Jack also informed him the dead man wasn't wearing any tracking, or listening devices.

"For now we'll leave this information between us. It's odd the man threw out Leroy's name," Abel said.

Jack didn't think his crime boss had anything to do with sending the man and was just as stupefied as he was.

Throughout their meal they flirted with the waitress but Abel's hands became frisky. His rubbing hand slid from the girl's arm to her ass, squeezing it. A man loomed over their table warning Abel to remove his hand.

"Why?" Abel asked.

The man informed them that the waitress was his girlfriend.

Abel verbally provoked him. "If you don't want to watch me flirt with your girl then you should leave."

The man grabbed Abel by the shirt. Jack leaped to his defense and hit the man in the jaw completely unaware he was a police officer until the man flashed his badge.

"You son of a bitch," Jack cursed. "You damn cops think you can push people around and then hide behind the badge at the first punch. Ya'll are a bunch of sissies!" Jack hissed and spit in the officer's face.

"Shut your damn mouth," the officer shouted and backhanded Jack across the face.

Outside on the sidewalk, he and Abel's eyes met with the usual understanding that the person arrested will call once they're released from jail.

Jack was practically thrown into the backseat of the car. Hunching against the door, he tasted the blood from his split lip and refused to answer any of the officer's stupid routine questions.

"Smart guy, huh?" The officer said and slammed the door shut.

The booming sound of the door reminded him of when Hank shot the man wearing the red bandana. *Who sent that man to the meeting?*

At the precinct, they took away Jack's weapons and cell phone but left him with his jacket, and he used it now to cover up with. He hadn't been allowed to make a phone call and had been put into an enclosed cell with cemented walls and no windows. There were two bunks, but he was alone. Jack yawned, stretched his legs on the shorter cot, sort of welcoming the lumpy mattress. He was so tired. Maybe, he'd be allowed a phone call later. Unable to fight it, his eyelids closed, and he slept.

His dreams picked up where they left off this morning before Abel awakened him. He was Humphrey again back on the fishing boat in the tiny room consoling Kara. She confused him, because he didn't understand why she let him comfort her? Why didn't she hate him as much as he hated himself?

Many times Jack wished he could go back in time and never put her in *that* van. He spent many hours trying to reassure his self, *he* didn't; *Humphrey* did. Of course, he was the one who had to live with the decisions that Humphrey made and *this* decision haunted him daily.

Jack had never felt so close to heaven as he had that day holding her, feeling her arms contract tightly and trustingly around his torso. He'll never forget the warmth and strength she spread through him.

Kara had asked, "Is rescuing me part of your job?"

"Yes," he answered, stating the half truth. Taking her away from the sheds was part of his job but the magnetic connection between them wasn't. Also, not part of his job description was the possessive feeling that washed over him when he held her, or that the trust he felt in her hug, made his heart sing.

She sobbed, "Thank you."

Jack didn't understand why she thanked him. She should have been yelling at him for taking her in the first place. Again, she should hate him, yet he didn't sense this emotion from her. *Why?* Surely, in time Kara would grow to hate him, but in the meantime, he cherished the moment.

Jack woke up and was startled to see Dexter occupying the other bunk. Groggy, he said, "Have you been arrested, too?"

Dexter chuckled. "No, but they want to. They're not appreciative of my tight lipped explanation of why they can't press charges against you."

Jack smirked. "I'm sure you were your usual charming self."

Dexter nodded. "I finally convinced them to put you in a solo cell until I arrived."

Jack moaned, "How long did I sleep?"

Dexter chortled, "Took me ten hours to get here."

"Boy, I needed the rest. Thank you," he said appreciatively.

"Tell me what happened at the meeting," Dexter encouraged.

"What a fiasco!" Jack huffed and filled him in on everything that happened. "So with me out of the room I had no idea what was being said. Luckily, Abel filled me in."

"And, you believe Abel's telling you the truth?" Dexter asked.

"Yeah, I think so," Jack said confidently and provided him the information about the other loads going to the different nearby sea ports and the part about accessing the river north of Memphis. "We need to find out where the other sea ports are. We've got to stop the loads. It'll be too late if the ships make it into international seas."

"I'll get the team working on it." Dexter promised.

"So did you find the body?" Jack asked.

Dexter nodded. "Yeah, but he was a no name. No previous records but the man lived thirty miles from Purlieu."

"Wilma's hometown," Jack said. "What if the man was purposely sent to destroy the Memphis plan?"

"You think he was sent to warn Hank?"

Jack cocked his head to one side. "Or did Wilma sacrifice the man making it "look" like Memphis was compromised. When in reality it never was, but if Hank thinks it is, he'll send the load someplace else."

"Like to Purlieu?" Dexter hinted.

Jack snapped his fingers. "Yes! That's it!"

"Why there?" Dexter asked curiously.

Jack placed his hand over his eyes. "Ugh, how did I not see this?"

"See what?"

"Abel told me that Frank wants to take over the business from his uncle."

"Hank's as evil as they come. He'll never give up his reign. Frank will have to kill him," Dexter said.

Jack nodded. "Yes, and he can do it on his own turf." Logic fell into place, and his eyes widened. "Wilma's loyalties aren't with Hank, they're with Frank! She's been helping Frank sabotage things for Hank!"

Dexter whistled through his teeth. "Yikes! This is getting even more dangerous. There's going to be crossfire."

"Yeah, but I might be able to use it to Humphrey's advantage," Jack remarked.

"Do you think Abel knows anything about Wilma and Frank's plan?"

Jack shook his head, "I don't think so. From what I've gathered his loyalty is with Hank. He fears Hank more than Frank."

"What about you?"

"I haven't met Frank. I get things ready for him," Jack grimaced. "Then I'm sent away on another errand. I never see the man. Only the dark tinted windows driving by after his visits."

"So, the man, who got killed, was sent as a guinea pig?" Dexter mused.

"I believe so. With the man dead, it guaranteed that Hank wouldn't find out who had willingly compromised the meeting. I saw the frightened look on the guy's face. He had no clue he was being sacrificed until it was too late. Saying Leroy's name was the death ticket. It was a brilliant plan. More than likely it was Wilma's plan."

"Smart."

"Ruthless." Jack shivered. "She's almost like a female version of Hank. Frank's lucky she's on his side."

"You think they're bed buddies?" Dexter inquired.

"Uh, I'm not sure," Jack answered carefully. "I'm not entirely sure Wilma's interested in men."

Dexter's brows lifted in surprise. "Oh, wow, okay."

"Yeah," Jack muttered.

"Be careful," Dexter fretted. "I need you alive for the next case."

"Kara. You said she's safe. Has that changed?" Jack voiced concern.

"She is."

"But you're not going to tell me where she is?"

"No." Dexter confirmed.

Changing the subject Jack said, "I'll contact Iguana and fill him in on what we just discussed."

Dexter nodded. "All right, sounds good."

"So when can I get out of here?"

"Anytime."

Feeling rested and restless Jack said, "I'm ready."

Chapter Fifteen

The lady's hand clamped Kara's chin. It hurt, but she didn't dare move. The last girl who had tried fighting the lady was punched in the stomach and dragged away. Kara didn't want the same fate so she didn't move and breathed the lady's wretched perfume while she manhandled Kara. Through the rough palming Kara remained still.

"Oh, I like you. You can be a star in…" The lady purred filthy things in her ear, and she didn't show any facial expressions.

Finally the lady released her and selected her choices. "Abel, here are the girls I want to keep."

The man with a scarred face leaped forward and abided the request. She and several other girls were led to a dilapidated shed. A giant door screeched on its rails as it was being opened. They were pushed forward, and she saw several girls already inside; their hands bound with thick rope. She sat in the dirt watching the sunlight disappear as the door banged shut. Days passed before she saw the full light of day again and was able to catch rays of sunshine and raindrops through the Swiss cheese holes lining the shed's walls. At night, she wished on the diamonds in the sky for her nightmare to end.

The doors opened for two reasons: to be fed and to be chosen. Of the girls chosen, some returned to the sheds. The tortured screams of those that didn't return were heart wrenching for all still alive. Kara had learned to scoot her way into the depths of the shed's grimy shadows knowing one day her luck would run out, and she'd be *chosen.* Until this happened, she managed to avoid the fate of becoming the lady's star and prayed for the option she believed was her only escape from this pathetic place; a quiet death…

Kara tumbled in the sheets. Her dreams were not kind tonight; taking her back to the sheds. She heard the eerie screech of the door slowly sliding open. A shadowy figure filled the cracked entrance. It was a man. She smelled his perspired scent as he approached her. A small ray of hope sparkled through her desolate heart.

Above her, his deep voice hushed in the dark. "Brave angel, I found you."

She knew *him* but couldn't speak his name because he immediately put tape over her mouth. He didn't know her throat was too dry, inhibiting her ability to talk.

Kara's subconscious spun her to the tall stalks of grass scraping her face. It wasn't fun being draped over him like a gunny sack as he ran through the field. His fingers gripped her legs but the rest of her body bounced against his back. Securing herself to him, her arms circled his waist, but it was still uncomfortable! She squirmed, and he swatted her butt telling her to be calm. He was fierce, yet she understood he didn't want to be caught, because she didn't either.

The salty air and waves crashing surrounded her senses and she noticed he was wading into the water. He moved her off his shoulder when he was waist deep. Setting her down, her bare feet touched sand, but she hardly felt it, because her lower limbs were numb. She started sinking, but he caught and lifted her, pressing her against him. Leaning on his solid chest she began marching her legs in place trying to get the blood circulating again.

He spoke. "We have to swim out to the boat. Don't get lost in the water. Understand?"

She did but panicked because his strength exceeded hers by a football field. How will she keep up with him? Standing free in the water she amazed herself by not wanting to get away from him. Of course she didn't know where to go in the dark. She also had no clue where the hell they were, and she certainly didn't want to go back to the sheds. Was this a rescue? Or had her situation jumped her out of the frying pan and into the fire. Turning her around, he held one finger to his lips indicating he wanted her to stay quiet. She nodded. If this was a rescue she didn't want to be the one to jeopardize her chance at freedom. Slowly, he removed the tape from her mouth. Tears stung her eyes because it stuck hard to her skin. It was more painful than any bandage she ever had.

"Don't lose me," she whimpered.

He promised he wouldn't and ushered her into the black ocean. They waded until the water was up to her neck and then he whispered, "Here we go."

Placing his hand on her waist, he leaned them into the water. He kept his arm around her mid section as they swam out to the boat. At the boat, he instructed her to tread water while he removed flippers from his feet. The waves constantly rolled into her face leaving salt on her lips. Using every ounce of strength she had, Kara kicked harder determined to get her head farther above the water. It worked but then her legs weakened, and she began descending. Without warning a big wave washed over her head, pushing her under, and her arms sliced through the water. Rising to the surface, she gasped for air but swallowed another wave. Strong hands gripped her arm pits and lifted her into the boat. Hunched over, she choked on the waves she had just drunk.

Gently, he patted her back and asked, "Are you okay?"

"Yes," she sputtered and clutched his shirt. "Humphrey…"

He didn't answer. She called his name again, louder this time and again he didn't answer. He wasn't there. He had disappeared, and she was alone in the dark. *Where'd he go?* She closed her eyes for three seconds, and then opened them. She was home…in bed and by herself. Kara placed a hand over her fast beating heart. Her dream had been about the rescue! Such vivid images!

"Will these dreams ever stop?" she whined in the dark, wondering when her dreams would be normal again, and she wouldn't be tormented by her tortured past.

Everything that had happened after Humphrey dropped her off in Dexter's care; she wasn't convinced she hadn't jumped into another fire. She rolled over touching her stomach where it had laid on Humphrey's sturdy shoulder. She touched her ear remembering how his whispered breath had made her insides tingle.

Kara tossed and turned but sleep did not find her.

Thirty minutes before sunrise she got out of bed, showered and went to the kitchen to make coffee. Curled in a chair she drank three cups of coffee while watching the sun rise as her thoughts drifted to the interrogation room.

It was the beginning of her journey for revenge. The two FBI agents told her she was free to go back home to Arkansas but there was nothing for her to go home to. She had survived through the perils of hell only to find out that Greg, the man she thought who loved her, had used her! And, he was the one who sent her to the devil!

With her heart ripped out of her chest she was consumed with rage! Hell bent on making Greg Nell pay for what he did to her! Looking at the two FBI agents on the other side of the table she verbalized she had a lot more to tell about her former boss's shady deals and the millions he had embezzled. The agents' mouths dropped and their eyes bugged. *Priceless!*

She packed books into her library bag. Gathering her purse and keys she headed out the door to her car. Often Kara wondered if she shouldn't have just kept her mouth shut, but she had been crazed over what Greg had done. At one time she would have walked through fire for him. She let out a dry laugh. Ironically, without being asked, she kind of already did.

Greg had fled the country with some blonde floozy, trading her life for an impossible debt he had. Hurt by his betrayal she silently vowed to get even with him and planned on using his own greed to take him down. She suspected he had sacrificed her only because she was his best secretary. Having worked closely with him, she was well aware of his shady characteristics, plans and actions. Why else would he have gotten rid of her? But he had clearly underestimated her!

He had no clue about the information she had on him! He wouldn't see her revenge coming at all! Especially, since he wrote her out of his life forever. She was the last person in the whole world he would ever suspect on taking him down! But she was going to do it, if it was the last thing she did! Every day was a reminder of why she had been rescued and why she was here; to seek revenge on Greg Nell!

She lived for the day when he was in handcuffs on his way to prison. Sort of similar to the way she was living these days. Not entirely, but she had no idea what was required of her when she agreed to this. It wasn't fair *that* she had to change cities, jobs, and her name!

In the beginning, it was chaotic, but since being here she took notice of the changes within herself. Her bitterness had turned to gratitude. She was thankful to be alive and living in the real world again. She appreciated the sun! Seeing it and feeling its warmth! She loved staring into the sky wishing she could paint all the shades of blue. Dipping into her childhood she made shapes out of clouds again. Even on dreary days she found something positive in the day. She never wanted to go back to the sheds and knew she'd never miss: the putrid smells, the humidity, signs of daylight through the cracks in the walls, drippy roofs, and always…always having fear.

These days when she glanced in the mirror she liked the girl staring back at her. She wasn't spoiled, rude, or felt like the world owed her something. She was less bitchy and condescending. Instead of cutting people down she raised them with a compliment. Revenge was still her goal but now she tried to enjoy the little things in life she had missed before. Example, of this was the red gravel path she took leading to the library. She squished her nose into the colorful flowers along the way.

In the past, she would have breezed past them not caring about their beauty. The library had become one of her favorite places whereas where she used to live she hadn't ever set foot inside one. She was too busy being busy. Reading books had become a favorite pastime. She crouched for another flower and breathed in its sweet nectar, imagining its succulent taste on her tongue.

Nearby, she heard ladies laughing and their high heels clicking on the concrete. She rose to stand as the smell of perfume wafted through the air but for Kara it hovered like a rain cloud pouring on her. It made her dizzy, and she fell, scraping her hands on the ground. She felt the sting but this was the least of her concern. The air was stuffy and she was finding it difficult to breathe.

****

Iguana watched the girl sniff the roses one by one. Her eyes dazzled with joy and she expressed appreciation, acting like it was her first time smelling flowers. If it had been any other girl or any other situation he might have found her attractive, but he wasn't here for love. He had a specific assignment; a tedious task holding no room for fun. When this specific job was done he hoped to squeeze in some R and R. Continuing to watch her, he gasped with shock when she staggered and fell. He left his post and ran over to help her. She was choking for a breath. Recognizing the signs of a panic attack he quickly pulled her up on her feet, ignoring her flinches and calmly instructed her to breathe in and out.

Kara felt strong hands clutching her armpits lifting her to cleaner air. Instinctively, she tried drawing away but the grip wouldn't let go. She couldn't help the memories of being grabbed this way while in route to the sheds. But then she heard a kind voice telling her to breathe, and she forced the bad memories away. She was pretty sure this voice was here to help her. The man told her to breathe in, exhale slowly, and she listened.

"There you go." He said when she was breathing normal.

Courageously, Kara opened her eyes. *Crap! It's the guy who yelled at me. Eek!*

Her mind reversed to her demon of a day, speeding down the road determined to drive her troubles away. No such luck. After this man had threatened to take her license away she had driven home and collapsed on the bed. She had cried hard for her new pathetic life as if her last one hadn't been pathetic enough. Somewhere between feeling sorry for herself and blaming Greg she had fallen asleep.

In the morning, she had awakened with a new outlook. It was still Greg's fault but for the first time she took responsibility for the decisions she had made. No one had twisted her arm or held a gun to her head. At the time, it was her decision and hers alone in taking the risky steps leading to her demise or downfall. From that day on she was watchful of the speed limit signs. There was no way she was going to have her license taken away. In order to get to work she'd have to rely on co-workers. Eventually, it would grow tiresome. Plus she'd have no way of getting around town, running errands, and there was a good chance she'd go insane if she couldn't get out and drive.

Now, eager to be away from him, she lifted her foot and lost her balance. Her body rocked sideways, and she gripped his hard arms.

"Hey, are you okay?" he asked worriedly.

Kara shook her head. "No. Not really. One minute I was in the process of standing, the next minute I was dizzy and on the ground unable to breathe."

"It was a panic attack," he said in a matter of fact tone.

"You're a doctor?"

His eyes twinkled with humor. "No. Not a doctor."

Annoyed, she snapped, "You're not a doctor but, yet you can diagnose me?"

He chuckled, "My, my, you are spunky. But then what else would I expect from a girl who drives like a maniac."

"Oh. So you do remember me." She frowned.

"How could I forget you almost running over me?"

"I didn't come anywhere close to hitting you. You weren't even on the road," she protested.

"How would you know? You were going too fast to see anything," he harassed. Though they exchanged barbs Iguana was proud of his current behavior versus the yelling he did that day. The minute he lifted her off the ground he recognized her and wondered if she'd remember him. She did.

Kara opened her mouth but said nothing. Compared to that day, right now he looked a lot less intimidating. In fact, beneath his grin, he looked concerned.

"Are you sure you're okay?" he asked.

"Yes, I think so," she said, hesitantly, and he released his hold on her noticing she awkwardly put space between them.

Trying to ease her discomfort he extended his hand and introduced himself. "Hi, my name's Iggy."

Iguana wished he didn't have to alter his name but it was too dangerous if he didn't. He had to keep his true identity hidden from certain people in this town.

Kara's eyes questioned first; then her voice. "Like piggy without the p?"

He laughed, "Yes, Ma'am."

After a few seconds when she didn't say anything he said, "This is usually when the cute girl tells me her name."

"Ah, yeah…sorry…" She paused while her mind fumbled, *shit he needs my name.* She swallowed and stated her faux name. "My name's Holly."

"Like Holy only with two L's?"

Kara rolled her eyes. "I'm far from worthy of having one L in my name."

"Ah, not the way you drive," he teased.

"Ha. Ha. I get it. Holy shit," she said derisively.

"Exactly," he chuckled. "And if you choose to go out with me Friday night I'll be the one driving us."

It took her a moment to understand what he was saying. Her eyes registered surprise. "Are you asking me out?"

"Last time I checked 'go out with me' meant that." His wide grin covered up any sarcasm she might have heard. "Well?"

"So you're not mad at me?" she questioned.

"How about we call it a draw? I'm pretty sure I made you mad, too. I'm really sorry for yelling at you. I was having a frustrating day and took it out on you. It wasn't fair of me," he sincerely apologized.

"I was having a frustrating day, as well," she said.

He added, "And seeing you try to kill yourself didn't help."

"Yeah," she mumbled.

It worried him that she didn't deny trying to kill herself. Maybe this was his second chance to be nice to her. It wouldn't hurt having a friend while he was here. In fact, hanging out with a local girl will help him blend in; a good disguise for the real reason he was here. "Well, are we on for Friday?"

Smiling she said yes.

"Great, I'll pick you up at six o'clock. What's your address?"

She supplied him the information. Before they parted he asked if she was all right, and she reassured him she was. Browsing through the library Kara began doubting her Friday night plans. *Is dating allowed for protected witnesses? Should I really go? How do I answer the getting to know you questions? Oh, why did I say yes? I should cancel.* But she didn't want to. Eventually she chased away the doubts because getting out is exactly what she needed.

****

Iguana's fingers pressed the numbers on his cell phone. Holding the receiver against his ear, he waited for Jack to answer. Hearing Jack's curt hello Iguana said, "Hey, man, I wasn't sure you'd pick up."

"Ig! Oh, man, it's good to hear from you. What's up?"

"You know who I'm following right?" Iguana asked.

"Yep, Dexter told me. How's it going?"

"It's frustrating. At first, I thought he was looking for more, uh, product but this doesn't seem to be the case," Iguana said.

"What is he doing?" Jack asked.

"He's following certain people. One in particular and I hope to have information soon as to why. In the meantime, I found a local girl to hang out with around town. It'll help me blend in better."

"A girl, nice," Jack prided. "At least one of us will get some action."

"It's not like that. She's cute but she reminds me of…" His voice broke, and Jack now understood the underlying reason for Iguana's call.

"Ah, Ig, I'm sorry."

Embarrassed, Iguana cleared his throat. "Yeah, thanks."

With his friend's focus slightly altered, Jack didn't bother updating him on the recent conversation he had with Dexter and decided to send him a text later on about it.

"Keep me posted on the progress," Jack encouraged.

"Yes, I will," Iguana promised.

Chapter Sixteen

Kara paced by the front door ten minutes before Iggy's arrival. *Will he be on time? Will he stand me up?* In the mirror, she gave herself another nervous glance liking the tan Capri pants and white blouse with pink flowers she had chose to wear. It was casual and comfortable. She had slipped her feet into a pair of white sandals. They were simple, and they showed off her latest pedicure.

A knock on the door had nervous wings spanning in her stomach. *It's time!* She peered through the peephole just to make sure it was Iggy and hated that she was so mistrusting. Opening the door she giggled when she saw his attire.

He was wearing white jeans, a dark blue shirt and black cowboy boots. He looked ridiculous and adorable all at the same time. If he was her boyfriend she might have persuaded him to wear dark color jeans, but he wasn't hers nor was she interested in having him be one. Adding a boyfriend into her mixed up life would complicate things. She had to keep her focus on her main goal; *revenge.*

Iguana tried gauging her reaction. He knew how silly his outfit was, but he wasn't here to impress her. When she opened the door he half expected her to come up with an excuse for being seen in public with him. But her quick giggle and stepping out the door left a good impression.

"Would you prefer going to a restaurant or a movie?" he asked, guessing she'd want to hide him in the dark.

Kara chose restaurant because sitting in the dark with a man terrified her.

Iguana masked his surprise but was pleased that she wasn't embarrassed by his appearance.

At the restaurant, he brushed up on his gentleman skills of opening doors for her, pulling her chair out, and keeping his focus on her while also scanning the room for danger. They ordered soft drinks, and after glancing over the menu they placed their order with the waiter.

Kara glanced around uneasily remembering the last time she was in a sit down restaurant. It had been with Sage. *I was upset and acted childish...and then I was taken out the back door unaware of what was happening until it was too late.*

Iguana noticed her nervous eyes. He spoke her name, but she didn't seem to hear him until the third time when his tone was sharper. "Holly."

Her eyes innocently drew to his. "What?"

"You were a million miles away."

"Uh, yeah, sorry, I was thinking about…things," she replied lamely.

He gave her a careful glance. A part of him wanted to ask what things but another part of him sensed she wouldn't have said much. Besides it was none of his business. What did it matter? He wasn't here to find out about her past. It would lead to something other than friendship. Heck, at this moment, he wasn't even sure if they should be friends. The main objective for this date was to help his identity blend in around town.

He kept the conversation casual, such as: favorite foods, colors, flowers, movies, television shows, and books she liked to read. He appreciated it when she reciprocated the questions back to him.

They didn't have a lot in common. In her spare time she liked reading, and he tinkered with engines, stating in college he studied mechanical engineering. His favorite food was steak, and she loved most foods as well as exploring different dishes to cook, mentioning the culinary position she had with the food catering company in town. As the conversation kept flowing, they discovered even their morning rituals didn't align. When she woke up, she turned on the TV for the daily news and a weather report, and Iggy began his day with an exercise routine.

"Good thing we didn't go to the movies," she said after finding out he preferred spooky and gory films whereas, she didn't, and liked romantic comedy the best.

He asked, "What's your favorite flower? Don't bother telling me you don't have one, because I think girls have to know this before graduating high school," he teased.

"Well, I have more than one." She smirked.

"And they are?"

"The sweetest smelling ones," she grinned, giggling.

An unexpected laugh erupted out of him, because her answer threw him off. "What about your favorite color?"

She rested her chin in her hand and gave him a thoughtful stare.

Is it purple?" he pointed above her eyes.

Her hand lifted to her head. *Holly's* hair was stick straight short just below the ears, and the color was royal purple with blonde roots.

"You don't like it?"

"I like it. It's cute. It suits you," he complimented, watching her blush.

"Thanks," she said, shyly. "I appreciate all the colors. Even gray, but maybe if I had to choose, I might lean towards the bright pastels."

He steered the conversation back to the day they met. "Was everything all right with you?"

"I had a really bad week and just needed a break. I needed to feel alive and in control of my own life."

"Even if it meant there was a chance of killing yourself?" he asked. *Uh, who am I to talk? I take risky chances all the time!* Then he reasoned *I do this for a living!*

"At the time I didn't care."

She didn't care, what the heck? What could possibly be so bad in her life, for her not to care about living?

Iguana reached over and patted her hand. She jumped at the sudden contact, and he thought her reaction was strange. However, he didn't comment on it.

Instead, in a kind voice he said, "Holly, it'd be a shame not having you around. If you ever need a friend to talk with, please consider me as one." *What am I doing? I'm not here to make friends.*

"Uh, thanks," she said in a strange voice. "Since moving here—"

He interjected. "Wait, you're not from here?"

She shook her head, and then felt nervous for opening this door. Since she had, she moved forward. "I haven't had much chance to make friends."

"How come?"

"I stay busy with my job. I'm usually pushing past forty hours a week and I guess it stands to reason we're so busy because we're the only caterer in town."

"Did the catering job bring you here?"

She shrugged. "It was a good place to start over."

"What are you starting over from?" He hadn't meant to get so personal but her statement easily led him here.

For a brief moment her direct stare flickered unsteadily. Then it was gone and a peculiar feeling gripped his insides.

"From the bad decisions I've made," she stated, and he hadn't ever heard such a powerful testimony filled with animosity and certain finality. It was honest and heart wrenching all at the same time. He wanted to know more but didn't know how to pursue it.

On a lighter note, he changed the direction of their conversation. "I'm guessing your parents loved Christmas."

"Why?"

"Because they named you Holly," he pointed out.

"Oh, yes." Kara smiled and decided that telling him a little bit about her childhood was okay. "It was my mom's favorite holiday."

"Oh, yeah?" he mused.

She let out a teasing laugh, "It was a sin if the house wasn't all decorated inside and out by December 1st and presents wrapped under the tree by the 15th!"

"Sounds like a festive household."

"It was!" She laughed as her eyes lit up with fond memories.

He wanted to ask more, but their food arrived and they ate in silence. When the bill came he took it and handed the waitress a credit card.

Kara insisted on paying for her meal, but he wouldn't let her. Thanking him, she excused herself to the ladies room. Exiting the restroom, she found him waiting for her in the lobby with a warm smile and an offering arm to walk out together.

This is nice. Greg never walked with me. Yeah, I thought he was being a gentleman by bringing the car around so I wouldn't have to walk. It never occurred to me that every time I got in the car he was ending a call saying it was work, but it was his mistress. Then all those times when he dropped me off saying he had a meeting...it was to go see HER! Oh, I am so stupid for believing him!

"Quarter for your thoughts," Iggy's voice interrupted.

"The reality of hindsight," she smirked, enjoying his perplexed look.

"Such a broad subject," he chuckled.

She held out her hand. "I'll take my quarter."

He opened the car door for her, and then closed it after she got in. Sliding in behind the wheel he handed her the coin. "A quarter won't get you very far these days."

"Maybe not one but a whole bunch will."

"A saver, are you?"

"These days, I am."

He found her remark odd and guessed maybe she had bad spending habits. He was having mixed feelings about wanting to know more of her. She was a mystery he couldn't afford getting tangled with. His time in Purlieu consisted of serious business. There was no room for error or making friends despite his earlier offer of it. On the drive home they listened to the radio. It played a variety of music from hip hop, classic rock, and country music. She tried to cover a yawn but failed.

With a rueful grin, he said, "You're either truly tired or I'm boring."

"Oh! I am not bored!" she reassured him.

"Good. Perhaps we can do this again."

"That would be nice."

Staying true to his gentleman ways, he walked her to the unlit front door. "You should turn your outside lights on before you leave the house. This way you won't have to walk in the dark."

"They're burnt out, and I haven't had a chance to call the landlord," she stated nervously. *Is this where the gentleman ends, and he turns into an asshole, trying to take advantage of me in the dark?* She reached inside her purse for her keys, and fingered the most pointed one. *If I have to, I'll stab him.*

Iggy noted the slight terror and agitation in her eyes. He took a few steps backwards and saw her relax.

"Holly," he began, curious with the way her eyes wavered when he spoke her name. "I've had a great evening. Thank you for spending it with me."

"You're welcome and thank you for asking." The end of the evening had arrived. She wasn't an idiot, remembering a kiss was expected, but she wasn't ready to kiss anyone! She clasped her fingers and swung them below her waist.

"Holly, can I see your hands?" he asked, eyeing her white knuckled grip.

She gave them to him.

"If it's all right with you, I'd like to give you a gentleman's kiss."

Her expression was full of apprehension, and he could tell she thought he meant a quick kiss on the lips. Smiling, he lifted her hands, kissing the back of them, instantly relaxing her. She tossed him a relieved smile, thanked him again, stepped inside and locked the door behind her. It had been a good first date.

Dressing into her pajamas her mind stayed on their date. Iggy had been a good start in getting her feet wet in the dating department. Not once did she ever feel threatened into doing something she was uncomfortable with. Unlike Greg who always pressured her into doing things outside her comfort zone. *Foolishly, I believed he loved me. Look where that got me…in trouble!*

Iggy seemed to be kind-hearted, but she wondered if his demeanor would change the longer they knew each other. *Will I even be here long enough to see that happen?*

Pulling the blankets over her head she closed her eyes. Falling asleep, her thoughts were heavy. *Men…they are peculiar creatures, but so are women. Greg taught me how selfish a man can be, putting his needs before anyone else's. I wonder if the woman in the picture knows how much of a sleaze he is. Or is she as naïve as I was? Who is she? How many other women does Greg have?*

****

Iggy arrived on her doorstep the next day with a toolbox and a cheerful good morning.

In surprise, she asked him what he was doing here, and he said, "I'm here to fix your front porch light."

It was kind of him to do this without being asked, and she told him so. He shrugged and asked her to lead him to a ladder. He began working outside and she headed inside. She began mixing ingredients for a pie thinking lately she was just like the front porch lights; she too was burnt out.

The choices she made with Greg were the start of her life's light burning out progressing to the kidnapping, the sheds, and learning the truth about Greg. Since arriving here her life had become a little brighter. Last night's date had been an awakening. Having been in the company of a good soul was refreshing.

Within the last eighteen hours her life's light was burning happier. Iggy's gentleman actions made her feel important, worthy, and respected. She liked the polite kiss on her hand. It was old-fashioned, but she didn't mind at all. A kind touch is what she needed.

Greg was a strange man. He never liked kissing and the few times they did, it wasn't good. Sex was *always* on his mind and *always* on his terms; when, where, and how he wanted it. It was odd but so were his moods; drastically changing without warning. However, she had become fairly good with identifying the swings. It helped her become his number one secretary but the truth was she had just been a glorified high paid slut. Reflecting on it made her ill especially when sex had played a part in negotiating her salary. Kara had no idea what she was getting herself into. Having been forced away from it she now saw the damage that had been done; mostly to herself.

From the board room to the bedroom Greg needed to be in control. He thrived on the adrenaline rushes over the sinister deals he made with clients. He was consumed with nervous energy and frustration exhuming this relief through rough sex. He had created fake companies for his clients to invest in, took their money and deposited it solely into his accounts. This is why he fled the country and sent her away. He had maneuvered the fall of the investment firm as he walked away with millions and no paper trail to tie him to any of it. Or so he thought.

Greg hadn't anticipated on her lying to him, but she did. A month before he left, he asked her to stay late and shred all the files in the two drawer filing cabinet he stored in the corner of his office. After this was done he wanted the maintenance department to dispose of the cabinet. Her instincts nagged her and instead of shredding the documents she scanned them to a file on her computer and saved them under an undetected file name. She also saved them on several portable data drives and stuck them in her purse. The original documents she put in manila folders and the next morning before work she opened a safe deposit box at a local bank. The documents Greg wanted destroyed contained the fake agreements of the companies he had created, the contracts he had his client's sign, emails he initiated, and of course, his signature on the falsified paperwork.

Privately, in his office while biting her back, he asked, "Did you get everything done last night?"

She answered yes, reasoning there was a thousand things she got done and not once did he say thank you.

Blessedly, she had been rescued and now she was working with the FBI on burning Greg with this paper trail. It was a confusing time for her. While she was grateful to be rid of Greg she hated the journey that was forced on her. Yet she was thankful for life but also aggravated because revenge was so far away. She was determined not to give up. If she did it would mean Greg won, and she wasn't about to let him win! *Never!* No matter how hard the journey was…she couldn't let him get away with what he had done! He was going to pay for what he did to her!

The oven timer buzzed, signaling the pie was done. She removed it from the oven. Carrying the pie through the back door she went to find Iggy and found him in the garage.

"Hey, there," he greeted. "All I have left is the back porch light."

"Thank you," she said, smiling and set the pie on the work bench in front of him. "I made this for you as a way of showing you my gratitude."

"Oh. You didn't have to do that," he said awkwardly, worrying she might have misunderstood his helpful intention.

"Oh. I know," she reassured. "It's just that I wanted to thank you for helping me and saying the words didn't feel like enough. I needed to keep my hands busy and thought why not show you how much I appreciate not having to look at the burnt out lights. It'll be nice not being reminded with how I feel," she babbled.

"How you feel? What do you mean?" he asked worriedly.

Understanding she just voiced her thoughts, she twirled nervously in a circle and backed away. Then she turned and headed out of the garage. *Crap, crap, crap!*

"Holly, wait." He grabbed her elbow, but she twisted and hit him in the shoulder with her free arm.

For a split second she was lost as to where she was and shouted, "Let me go!"

He did and immediately stepped backwards holding his palms up. "Shhh, easy, I'm not going to hurt you."

Kara snapped her attention back to the present and saw Iggy's astonishment. Horrified with her behavior she held her arms out. "Oh, I'm sorry, Iggy. I'm so sorry. I didn't mean to hit you. Or make you afraid of me."

"It's okay. I'm not," he said, noting how horribly lost and confused she looked. "Holly, it's okay. C'mon, we'll go inside."

She shook her head. "No. Not inside," she said in a hallowed voice, and he clearly saw she was somewhere else.

"Holly?"

"No. I'm –" On the verge of telling the truth, she stopped. She couldn't! She was bound by law to keep her secrets safe. But she was tired of bearing this burden alone! She wanted a friend. Iggy could be one, but she still couldn't tell him anything! She covered her mouth holding in the sob but it only instigated tears.

"Holly." He was concerned, because she looked like a caged animal needing to flee. Extending his hand, he negotiated, "Don't run. Stay here and talk with me."

He stepped towards her, but she darted to the side out of his reach. In his eyes, she saw how he truly believed if she talked, it would make everything better. She knew he wanted to help solve whatever problem she had. Wishing she could confide in him, but if she did it could put him in danger. She had hurt enough people along the way and couldn't take a chance in hurting a new friend. No this was her cross to bear.

Shaking her head, she said, "Iggy, I've made my bed."

In four hops she was in the grass, and then she turned and ran to the lot line as Iggy called behind her for a girl who didn't exist.

Iguana watched her sprint farther away. He shouted her name, but she didn't stop or turn around, seeming as though she hadn't heard him. Sensing she needed this he didn't bother going after her as he pondered about her making the bed comment. This girl was becoming more of a mystery to him; more than he had bargained for and more than he should want to know.

Chapter Seventeen

Nearing the end of the yard, Kara jumped into the field of yellow grass running until her lungs hurt. At the far edge of the field she darted into the woods and slowed to a jog after stumbling. Then her foot caught on a weed, pitching her forward towards the ground. Her hand fell on a jagged rock, jarring her with a frightening thought, *what if I trip, fall and break my neck? No one would know where I was, who I really am, or where to look for me.*

Iggy would have scoured the field but many seasons could have passed before anyone found her body in the woods. How awful it would be!

"Iggy…" she muttered. He was only trying to help. *I'll call him.* Reaching inside her pocket she discovered her phone wasn't there. *Crap! It's on the kitchen counter.*

A rain drop landed on her arm. Glancing up she saw dark clouds lining the sky behind her. Thunder rumbled. In order to stay ahead of the storm she forged on, following the dirt trail out of the woods into a clearing. A weathered barn came into view. She ran for its shelter as rain dropped hard on her head. Reaching the open doors a wild gust of wind pushed her in and rain pelted her legs. To get away from the whipping rain she began climbing the ladder into the loft. Nearing the top, nature angrily bit her backside with a forcing wind. Scampering into the loft, the ladder swayed sideways, and her foot almost got caught in the wrung. Relief filled her as she was well aware that if she hadn't been able to get her foot out in time the ladder's weight would have pulled her from the loft onto the barn floor below!

It was the second time in the last thirty minutes she escaped an accidental death. Freaked out, she huddled into the deep hay bales away from the edge. The cold rain, the gusty wind, and her heart pounding ferociously reminded her of the rescue boat and the memories of the wave trying to drown her. Maybe it would have been better if she had drowned in the ocean.

Kara curled into a ball, sitting the same as when she was in the sheds with all the other girls. Her thoughts tumbled backwards to after Humphrey pulled her out of the water. He set her in the passenger seat, and then sat behind the wheel on the opposite side and drove the high powered boat through the dark night at a fast speed. She was amazed that he knew which way to go. She kept watching for the enemy to appear from behind, but he assured her no one was following them.

The boat bounced over the water throwing waves over the window and onto her; soaking her. Then the boat veered to the right changing the wind's course as it blew coldness directly into her; chilling her. Sensing her discomfort Humphrey pulled her from the seat and tucked her into the small space on the floor beneath the steering wheel by his feet. The ride had been rougher but a lot drier, and she huddled against the side of the boat feeling every bump.

Currently, she leaned on the dry hay bales listening to the rain on the roof. Lightning flashed across the sky as the storm thundered on.

Her mind strayed back to Humphrey. He confused her, because she didn't know what to think about him. Kidnapping her certainly had put him on her bad list, but then he also had protected her, insisting she use his name with the other men. His encouraging words to be brave traveled with her through her darkest fears and helped her cope with the rough men sniffing, pawing, and grabbing her.

Through her days in hell she cursed Humphrey for putting her there and revered him for making her know his name. She wanted to believe he was a good man.

Presently, Kara cowered into the safety of the hay bales. She certainly didn't feel safe with the storm raging outside. She thought of Iggy and prayed he wasn't out in this weather trying to look for her. Closing her eyes she dozed off and woke up after the rain stopped. Without a ladder or phone she began worrying how she was going to get down from the loft. Then all of a sudden she heard voices approaching; a man and woman. *They can help me get down!* Excitement coursed her veins. Kara was on the verge of alerting them that she was there, but heard their angry voices and instead stayed quiet.

"Uncle, I still don't understand why you let her go," the woman pouted.

"Sister, you left me no choice," he shouted. "I was cleaning up your mess. You shouldn't have kidnapped the woman trucker. The owners of Maslund Trucking had federal agents helping them search for her. Keeping her wasn't worth the risk of having the authorities on our trail. We've worked too hard to have the whole operation ruined. You need to forget about her."

"Whatever," she huffed.

The uncle yelled, "No. Not whatever. You will."

"I'm not promising anything, and you'll just have to live with it," she sassed.

"Damn, girl, you need a good fuck." His voice boomed a humorless chuckle.

High in the loft, Kara cringed. The uncle's laugh was eerie and bone chilling as its tuba tone shivered déjà vu through her. She was struck with an uncanny sense that this voice was familiar but didn't know how or where. Strangely, at the time of hearing it, wherever it was, she knew she never wanted to hear the evil voice again, and now she was! Kara continued listening to them argue.

The sister spat, "There's only one fuck I want but it isn't being reciprocated."

"This is why you're seeking revenge?"

"Yes."

"Let it go. Find someone else," he ordered.

The sister said nothing, and he continued. "Listen. The reason for this meeting is to let you know the Memphis load has been breeched."

"What? How?" she asked.

"One man was acting suspicious. He spoke out of turn, asked stupid questions, and then said Leroy had sent him." The uncle snorted. "Dumb son of a bitch had to be taken care of."

"Unbelievable!" the sister gasped. "What's the plan now?"

"I don't know," the uncle grumbled.

"What about having the load routed here to this abandoned barn?" the sister suggested.

"Routed here?" the uncle mulled it over. "I like it!"

"So what happened to the man?" the sister asked.

"I shot him right between the eyes. I had Abel's right hand man dispose of the body. I believe his name's Humphrey. That boy has promising talent," the uncle declared.

Mixed emotions ran through Kara. She was devastated hearing Humphrey's name associated with these awful people, horrified because the uncle admitted to shooting a man in cold blood, and frightened because she knew without a doubt everything she had just heard was dangerous information!

Below, Kara heard the uncle say, "One more thing, I've heard you been taste testing."

"Yes," she openly admitted. "You're not the only one who gets to decide if the product is top notch."

"Well, don't get carried away with it," he warned. "It's addicting."

Kara suspected it was drugs they were taste testing. She had watched enough detective shows on television to know the drug lords always sampled the products. This had to be what was in the breeched load. Lying on her stomach Kara became prey to a pounce and counted four feet padding on her back. *Please don't be a mouse!* Forcing herself to remain calm she held her breath, staying still. There was no way she could let them know she was here! They wouldn't be receptive at all to the things she had heard! They would kill her too! She had to keep her presence a secret!

A gray cat passed by her, mewed and swished its furry tail in her face. The animal sat on the edge of the loft making its presence known with another meow.

The uncle said, "What is that?"

Irritated, the sister answered, "It's a cat."

"Good. I'd hate to find out that someone is here."

She scoffed, "This place has been abandoned for years. Every now and then teenagers make their way out here to party but they're easy to run off. Other than that, it's very private."

"Excellent. It's a great place to deliver the load."

"No one will suspect a thing," the sister replied.

"Good and I like how my GPS didn't even acknowledge this as a road."

A sinister snicker rumbled out of the sister. "It is the perfect place for *everything*."

Then the uncle said, "I need to go. I'll contact you again soon."

Kara heard their voices moving away. Next she heard car doors closing and two different car engines starting. Then silence. Lifting her head she didn't see anyone and started constructing a plan to get out of here. She began sliding hay bales across the loft and pushed them over the edge onto the floor. It was a crazy idea but it was the only one she had. It took awhile, but she finally had bales stacked high enough for her to safely jump into. She was truly sorry for the person who had to put them back into the loft.

Anxious to be away from this place and the scary conversation she heard, she ran out of the barn, walked through the woods and then jogged in the dark through the grassy field all the way to her yard. Three feet from the back door the porch light turned on. She half expected to see Iggy's face appear, but he didn't, and she realized he had installed motion lights. *Nice!* His thoughtfulness had a warm glow passing through her heart. Maybe he didn't hate her after all.

Kara did her nightly routine of locking all the doors before heading into the bedroom and changing into pajamas. The ensemble consisted of cotton shorts and a camisole. Much different than the silk nightgowns she used to wear before her life turned upside down. She had to admit she didn't mind the change.

Since being Holly Belles there were a lot of changes she had made in her life. She had gotten rid of the expensive lacy bras and panties, the designer clothes, shoes, and fancy car. Settling for the clearance racks filled with jeans and cotton shirts. This new way of life certainly wasn't what she had ever envisioned. But it was a welcomed switch from the one she had been leading. She looked at it as a way of putting herself in time out.

Having distance from her former life she saw her past self and what a bitch she had been. Nowadays, she liked the new and improved person she was becoming; feeling the growth within. She had *almost* forgiven herself for *most* of the bad decisions she had made this last year. Who knew this small town would have such a big affect on her?

Tucked safely in her bed Kara thought about the barn conversation. It was odd how the man and woman addressed each other. She called him uncle, and he called her sister. Were they code names? The uncle's voice sounded older than hers. Kara wondered about the woman the sister wanted gone. Why and who was she? What did it mean when the uncle said keeping the woman would have jeopardized their operation? Their operation had to be drugs. Kara's memory replayed the uncle's evil laugh and it shot another shiver up her spine.

Her mind swung back to *Humphrey*. A rock dropped in her stomach. *Humphrey can't be bad! If he is, why did he deliver me to Agent Dexter? But the uncle knows him.*

Just when she was starting to believe Humphrey could be a good man, he ends up being associated with these horrible people! She hated thinking the worst of him especially when he was so kind to her through the rescue. He was sympathetic and had hugged her while she cried, telling her how brave she had been. Crazily, she refused to believe Humphrey was a full blown bad guy. He couldn't actually be associated with these evil people. He just couldn't!

Was he Dexter's informant? When writing her testimony, freeing Sage from any responsibility, the Agent had insisted she leave Humphrey's name out of her statement in regards to the kidnapping and rescue. It made her believe he was one of the good guys, but after what she heard in the barn this afternoon…if he is bad, it shouldn't surprise her because she had a knack for attracting the wrong kind of men.

****

Kara opened the front door and screamed. Iggy was standing there with his knuckles poised in mid-air ready to knock on the door. Immediately, he apologized for scaring her.

"It's all right. I just wasn't expecting anyone to be on my door step. What's up?"

"I wanted to stop by and see how you're doing. Are you heading out somewhere?"

Smiling she said, "Out to the mailbox."

"Mind if I escort you?" He fell in step beside her.

She mumbled, "Hey, I'm sorry for running out on you the other day."

Breaking the ice, he chuckled, "Yes, you literally ran out."

She gave him a rueful smile. "Yeah. Sorry."

He shrugged. "It's no biggie. Though the way you took off. It seemed as though you were trying to outrun something. Kind of the same as when you were speeding down the road?" he observed.

She tossed her head to one side and gave him a thoughtful look. "You could be right."

"Anything you want to talk about?" he asked, taking the mail from the box and handing it to her.

She gave him a helpless look. More than anything in the world she wanted to tell this kind caring man who *she* was. Tell him everything about her! Why she was here, how she got here, and everything about her horrible life. She had a crazy feeling he would understand.

Iggy followed her into the house and guessed, "You want to, but you can't."

She dropped the pile of letters on the coffee table and flopped on the couch. He joined her, sitting close and slid his arm along the top of the sofa behind her head.

Kara eased backwards. He was intimately close. It made her nervous. In the past, she would have welcomed this kind of pursuit, but not now. She wasn't emotionally ready for a physical relationship. Since her life went askew she needed to focus all her attention on being a better person. So far she was happy with the results of the progress she was making and loved facing the woman in the mirror with a cheery response.

Sensing her hesitation he smiled. "Holly."

It took a few seconds before she lifted her gaze to his, and he wondered why she responded slower to her name than most people did. "I just want you to know I am offering you friendship. At this time in my life, I'm not looking for a serious relationship."

"You are? You're not?" she said dumbfounded. "Most men want at least sex."

He chuckled. "I suppose. I'll be honest with you. I don't need a girlfriend. I need friendship," he said grinning.

Her relief was prevalent and immediately she relaxed releasing a giggle. "Me, too," she said. "I have a lot of personal things going on, and

I don't need the distraction of a boyfriend-girlfriend relationship, but I could definitely use a friend."

He extended his hand saying, "Friends?"

She readily accepted agreeing, "Yes, friends."

"Great!" He beamed then changed the subject. "Hey, I'm teaching a self-defense class. I think you should take it, it would be good for you."

"Me? Why?"

"Have you ever taken a class?"

She shook her head.

"That's why."

"I guess I could."

"Great! You can sign up online. If you want I can help you register right now." He took the initiative of pulling her laptop from the coffee table. Opening the lid he pulled up the search engine revealing the last thing she had researched.

"Why are you looking at trucking companies in the area?" he curiously asked.

"Um, yeah," she hemmed and hawed. "I was seeing what other businesses were in town."

"Why a trucking company?" he asked, his voice more direct.

Kara said the first thing that came to her mind. "I was wondering if any of them had moving trucks to rent."

Her answer sounded legit, but he couldn't help being suspicious. "Are you planning on moving anytime soon?"

She shrugged. "Not planning on it, but I don't know what the future will bring."

Iguana was troubled by her statement. Most people when talking about the future said it mysteriously, but she said it with a hint of doom. His instincts threw up a warning flag. Then he remembered what she said about lying in the bed she had made. Leaving it alone for now, he shrugged and said, "True." And lightly added, "Well, don't leave town without saying good-bye."

"Okay, I won't." She smiled, but crossed her fingers behind her back thinking *unless I'm rushed out of here.*

Iggy helped her register for the class. He stayed for supper, appreciative of the roast beef sandwiches she made. She rolled her eyes, down playing his compliment reminding him he could get a better and bigger sandwich at the drive-thru down the street, but he insisted homemade was a lot healthier.

"When do you work again?" he asked.

"Saturday afternoon. We're catering a child's birthday party. We're making lots of peanut butter and jelly sandwiches and cupcakes."

Iggy grinned. "Ah, yes the staple food for kids."

"Don't forget macaroni and cheese."

"Yeah," he sighed. "Those were the days."

"Innocent days," she commented sadly.

Unable to stop his curiosity he dropped a bombshell of a question. "So where did you live before you moved here?"

He was upset when she didn't answer right away. Her gaze bounced everywhere, except on his. She seemed to be searching for the right answer. All he needed was the truth, but judging her rigid body, he realized his innocent question wasn't so innocent for Holly. Another red flag flew up.

"Was it Mars?" he teased, needing her back on the offense.

She forced a laugh, hating her poor reaction to his unsuspecting question and wished she could tell him about the dark, dark place she came from. Telling this truth would only raise more suspicion and worry.

"It wasn't Mars but it's something I don't want to talk about."

By the way her body relaxed, Iggy knew this was the truth. He searched her quiet face and wondered if she'd ever confide in him. For now he was honored with the little bit she had told him. It was a small start. "I can respect that," he replied.

If only he could tell her his truth about what he did for a living. It might help her trust in his ability to help with her secretive past. But if he did, it would only raise questions leading to dangerous answers. He couldn't put her life in jeopardy. Maybe after his job was done he could come back and help her.

"Thank you," she said appreciatively.

"You're welcome. That's what friends are for," he said with a sincere smile.

Iggy got up to help clear the table. After everything was put away, Iggy thanked her for the meal and left.

Kara's thoughts wandered through trails of questions. *Is Humphrey an agent or an informant? What if he's playing both sides? Is Agent Dexter's team in danger? Jack...should I warn him? Will he laugh at me like he did on the first day we met?*

Kara's memory traveled back to the interrogation room; after Humphrey rescued her and before she met Jack. Agent Dexter had been questioning her and was expecting her full cooperation, but she refused, because of her loyalty to Greg.

Suddenly, the door flung open and bounced off the wall. In walked Agent Jack with a cocky smile. Her naïve attitude made him laugh. He had flung heart wrenching photos of Greg with another woman in front of her. After accepting the painful truth, she shared the ugly truth with the agents about her former boss.

Hours later, their smirking glances had changed to astonishment with all the secretive information she had about Greg. They asked if she had any concrete evidence supporting her accusations.

Kara negotiated, "Yes, I do. However, I will not be able to provide you with the location of these documents until after papers have been signed assuring my safety."

By signing the witness protection forms, Kara was on her way to a new life of revenge and starting over. Though, life here in Purlieu had her doing more starting over and less with revenge.

After signing the documents, Jack escorted her down the hallway to the back door where they waited for an SUV to pick her up and take her to the hotel.

Jack showed her a hint of compassion and possible understanding when he discreetly slid a compact phone into her palm, telling her his private number was programmed into it. His strict instructions had been for her to call if she was in danger.

"If you do call, for safety reasons don't use your name. I'll know it's you, because you're the only one who has this phone." He forewarned. "This journey you're on. Trust your instincts."

She nodded as his dark eyes poured confidence into her.

As she went out the door he softly recited two familiar words. "Be brave." She turned around half expecting to see Humphrey behind her, but he wasn't and neither was Jack. Odd how two men could sound the same, unless they were brothers? She had asked Jack earlier that day if he had a brother. He said he didn't, but it could have been part of his cover?

Swinging back to the present, Kara decided it would be best to let Jack know what had happened. She reached inside the black duffel bag with the green trim and pulled out the emergency phone. Under contacts she saw Jack's name and pressed her finger on the key and it rolled into dialing the number. She inhaled a deep breath then held it. She waited, listened, and thought for sure her heart was going to jump out of her chest. She heard his voice but it was his voice mail. Swallowing nervously, she cleared her throat, her head pounded and somehow she found her voice.

"Hey, it's me," she began shakily. "Uh, um, this may not be anything important but I thought." She paused. *What do I think?*

"I overheard a conversation I shouldn't have between some bad people. They were talking about a shipment of drugs and how one of them kidnapped a woman trucker. Luckily, they didn't know I was there; otherwise I would probably be in a body bag by now. Well…I just

thought you should know this in case something happens to me, uh, bye."
She ended the call and shoved the phone into the duffel bag, then scooted
it to the back of the closet. Her hands were shaking, and she hoped Jack
didn't think she was too stupid for giving him the message.

Later in the day, she regretted having called Jack. What if he
called asking for more details? He'd be disappointed because she didn't
have any. She had no knowledge about when or where the shipment was
going. In regards to the lady trucker she didn't know the trucker's name
or any other information about the kidnapping. *Plus, according to the
uncle, they let the lady trucker go.* Now, Kara doubted that she might not
have heard everything correctly. By nightfall, she was sound with her
decision of leaving him the message. It may be nothing but what if it was
something?

****

Jack removed the gas nozzle from its cradle and placed it into the
tank. He took this solo time to check his personal phone messages and the
secret phone he kept hidden. His heart pounded heavily in his chest when
he saw a familiar number. *Kara.* She was the last person he ever thought
he'd hear from. Even when he discreetly gave her the burner phone, he
didn't think she'd use it, but seeing she called, instantly provoked worry;
surfacing other feelings he had forced himself to forget.

Just like he had instructed she didn't state her name, she said,
"Hey, it's me." She paused, and then continued in a wobbly voice. Her
message left him speechless. Stunned, he covered his face with his hand.
Unsure of how she heard any of it, he was concerned with the key factors:
bad people, a shipment of drugs, the kidnapping of a woman trucker, and
to top it off she could've been killed if she'd been discovered. A quirky
feeling tugged on his instincts. *The only female trucker I know of is
Callie.* He dismissed the idea of there being any possible chance Callie
and Kara's paths had crossed.

Jack never expected her to run across trouble but now that she had,
he was extremely grateful he had given her the phone. If he hadn't, who
would she have trusted?

Chapter Eighteen

Callie stepped into Evan's home office. The room was between the front door and the short hallway connecting to his bedroom. Across the room her eyes honed in on the picture she had saved from Kylee's trash pile. She had instantly fallen in love with the sunrise photo as it represented her favorite time of day; early morning and its tranquility before the day's hustle and bustle began. Though, lately it represented something different. The promised rising of a new day. Something she oddly needed to be reminded of.

Since her home had been Sunbird's cab there wasn't room for the large picture. Evan promised to keep it for her until she had a place of her own. He had stated, "I have the perfect place for it."

It was the first glimpse she ever had of his caring side. However, it didn't last long, because a few minutes later he had been back to teasing and annoying her. Viewing the picture on the wall she had to agree it was in a great spot! It looked really good in this room! While she was here she could enjoy the picture she saved. Her thoughts ran to her involvement of saving its photographer, too.

Is it a small world or destiny's world?

What is my destiny? Is it to stay here and never go back on the road? There were moments when she wished this house and Evan could be hers, too. Then the picture could stay right where it was.

Callie ran her hand along the desk's smooth surface. It was made of oak with a caramel finish. Four strong legs supported a thick flat top that was six feet long and four feet wide. It was an impressive piece of furniture holding Evan's weight as she has witnessed him sitting on the desk's edge. Behind the desk sat a swivel chair with a high back and heavy duty caster wheels that glided across the hardwood floor. She loved the chair! It was comfortable and in it she felt knowledgeable and confident. If only her driver's seat could be this comfortable. *There are a lot of comforts outside of Sunbird's cab that I will miss. Seeing Evan everyday is one of them and hearing him whistle.*

This was the longest off the road stay she'd ever done. Her normal routine was taking a few days off and then gone again. She was enjoying the longer stay in Purlieu. She was safe here. On the road, her brain never shut off. She was thinking about everything and wary of danger, but here she had become lax.

One of them, for example, was when she almost got Sunbird stuck in the mud. She was convinced her brain had turned to mud, because she hadn't been thinking! Instead, she had been feeling and on the road this was a dangerous commodity. Another example was the afternoon when she let Evan sneak in. She didn't hear him because she'd been in her own little world! It was scary realizing how easily she'd become accustomed to living with her guard down. *I can't live like this on the road! If I do, I'll fall prey to predators.*

Just then Kylee breezed in and startled her. *Ugh! What is wrong with me?*

"Callie!" Kylee came to stand beside her. "Saving *that* picture was fate! I am so thankful you did! After finding out who the photographer is, I would have forever felt horrible!"

"You didn't know," Callie said.

Kylee dusted the square table between the two winged back chairs; a favorite chair style of Evan's.

Hunter green was the main color as it circled the room from the drapes to the chairs to the French doors entering the room. The throw pillows were accented in maroon complimenting the plush golden maize carpet.

"When Evan asked me to help redecorate this room I wasn't sure about his choice of color for the carpet. But he insisted this was the color he wanted." Kylee frowned. "It looks like corn. I guess it fits a farmer."

"I think it looks like a sandy beach," Callie said, holding back Evan's comment he had made one evening.

Miles apart, his tired voice had wisped, "My new carpet reminds me of your tan eyes."

His compliment found its way into her heart. She left hints of seeing it, and he had promised to show her the next time she was in town.

"Kellan said Evan's been coming home for dinner. Does this mean the two of you are eating together?" Kylee casually asked.

"We do if he has time. Some days he packs a lunch and goes straight from the field to the office so he can be home earlier in the evenings," she answered.

"You don't pack his lunch?"

"No. Why would I?"

Kylee shrugged.

Callie took offense to it and pursued. "Why would I pack his lunch? He's a big boy and can do it himself."

"He is." Kylee agreed and sensed she might have overstepped her friend's boundary.

Callie wasn't about to let it go. "There's something you're not saying, so say it."

"It's what we women do to help out around the house."

"I *do* help with the chores so Evan *has* time to pack his lunch." Callie replied with a smirk.

"Well, okay then," Kylee snuffed. "Men like it when women do nice things for them."

"Women like it too," she countered. "Isn't it a two-way street?"

"Yes it is." Kylee smiled. "Are you and Evan going to Charlie's tonight?"

"Uh, I don't know. He hasn't said anything."

"Charlie's making a new margarita flavor. Kellan and I are going, so if you guys go, let me know."

"I'll ask him and let you know."

****

"Callie!" Evan hollered. "Are you home?"

"Upstairs! I'll be down in a minute!"

Callie breezed into the kitchen with a radiant smile bouncing off her face. As she passed him, he caught her wrist and spun her into his arms. First he teased her with a light brush of his mouth, and then slipped his tongue between her parted lips. She reciprocated, sharing her fire with him. Their moans mingled together. His hand cupped the side of her face, and his eyes stared tenderly into hers.

"Callie, you're a treasured beauty."

Her heart leaped, but her gaze shyly averted to the side.

"Look at me," he whispered, gently pressing his fingers on her scalp. "It's true."

"It's intimate."

"Yes." He hugged her. "Have you eaten?"

Her answer was muffled against his shoulder, but he felt the shake of her head.

"How about I make us some eggs?"

She leaned back and grinned. "Sure."

Peering into the fridge his eyes rummaged the shelves. Shutting the door he sadly said, "The only thing I don't have is bacon."

"I'll get some when I'm at the store today."

He nodded his approval. "Today's egg choice will be sunny side up for my sunny girl."

She rolled her eyes. "I'm not sure I'm as sunny as you think I am."

"You are." He reassured.

Callie watched Evan move through the kitchen with an easy confidence. He cracked eggs into the frying pan, then shuffled to the toaster lowering four pieces of bread into it and then gracefully slid his socked feet over to the refrigerator removing the butter and jelly. When the toast popped up she snuck in behind him placing the slices on their plates.

"Hey, what're you doing?" he moved sideways to avoid stepping on her bare feet.

"Helping," she giggled.

"All right, you can butter the toast." He reached over her shoulder and placed the container in front of her. With her hair piled on top of her head, he couldn't resist nuzzling her collarbone.

"Delicious," he murmured, loving her moaning sigh. "You know, I like your hair up."

"Why?"

"So I can see your neck."

She gave him a look of wonderment. "Most men prefer it when women wear their hair down."

"Must be to hide their ugly necks," he joked, and she laughed. "Honey, yours is very sexy." His breath tickled her skin. "Don't hide it from me."

She gave him a baffled expression. No one had ever indicated this part of her body was sexy. Yes, her ass and eyes but never her neck. "You really like it?"

"God, yes," he stated firmly.

Then he confirmed it by kissing a certain spot on her neck. Shivers shot down her spine and into her toes. His mouth stayed on the satiny surface, carousing behind it to the other side. Her lifting hand applied pressure on the back of his head, and her fingers curled his scruff, hanging on while he relentlessly fueled her passion.

"Oh, baby," she fanned breathlessly.

"Does it answer your question?" he whispered.

"Yes. If I wasn't so hungry I'd let you continue."

Evan chuckled and reluctantly focused his attention to the eggs. They worked well together. She set the table while he finished. Evan sat at the head of the table viewing the fields, and she sat on his left with a good view of the driveway and part of the front yard.

Callie had never had eggs like this. She daintily used her fork to cut through the white part deciding to leave the yellow yolk for last. Out of the corner of her eye she watched the way Evan ate his. He mashed and peppered the eggs, and then scooped the gooey mess onto his toast eating it opened faced.

"Is it better that way?" she asked.

"I think so." Amused, he watched her copy him and then after her second bite he asked, "Well?"

She nodded then blushed as egg dripped down her chin. Before she could catch it with a napkin, his finger swiped the dribble, presenting it to her with a mischievous grin.

His eyes dared her and watching her contemplate his offer quickened his heart rate. Her timid tongue divided her lips then touched his finger; tasting the egg.

Evan froze as lust rushed in.

She ran her tongue along the ridge of his index finger.

His penis hardened.

She sucked his fingertip.

He sharply inhaled.

Seeing the heavy rise of his chest, Callie knew her bold move had the same effect on him as it did her. The flickering of her tongue across his roughened skin and licking the egg off of it stirred her desire and ardor appetite. The dark predatory gaze he burned into her had her thirsting for his passionate kisses. Her mouth advanced towards his just as one of their phones signaled the arrival of a message breaking the sultry trance between them.

Callie slowly sat back in her chair reaching for her phone as Evan pushed away from the table, stretching his legs under it.

A war broke out between his two heads. The lower one wanted to carry Callie into the bedroom and finish what they started. The upper head that made most of his sound decisions showed him the right now to do list and taking Callie to bed was not on it! On the list was helping Kellan in the fields, afternoon meeting with the mayor, helping his dad mend a fence, and maybe taking her out tonight.

Viewing the apprehension on her face, he pointed to her phone and asked, "What's up?"

"Kylee's asking if I want to go with them to Charlie's tonight," she said in a perplexed tone.

"Why not go with me?" he inquired.

"She says you have plans."

The muscle in his jaw twitched, and he looked puzzled.

"I do?" he said, wishing he could remember what the rest of the world already knew.

Together they stood taking their dirty dishes to the sink. Evan rinsed the plates then put them in the dishwasher while she put items in the refrigerator.

He would love to take Callie to Charlie's! He hadn't been there for awhile and it would be nice for them to get out on a date…wait a second. *Do I have a date tonight?*

Uh-oh! He spun around. "Hey, which Friday of the month is it?"

"Uh," she groaned, unsure what he was asking.

He pulled his phone out of his back pocket and searched the calendar. There in capital letters were his evening plans. The date for his mom! *Shit!* Devastation swept in as he pinched the bridge of his nose.

Callie interrupted his thoughts by saying, "You promised your mom something."

"What?" he said.

Callie smiled. "The look on your face is the one you get when you forget to do something for your mom."

He gave her a stunned look. Yet, he was impressed with her ability with recognizing this particular expression. He was caught in the fact she, too, had watched him over the years.

Not denying it he said, "Yes. I promised to do something for her and forgot all about it until just now."

"What is it?"

"Ahh," he faltered, not wanting to tell her but knowing he had to.

His eyes danced nervously, and she took a sensing guess. "You have a hot date, tonight, don't you?"

"Sort of," he cowered. "And I wouldn't go so far to say she's hot."

Her heart sank. "How can you sort of have a date?"

"I promised my mom," he said lamely, gritting his teeth knowing how pathetic this sounded.

She glanced at the table then back at him. Evan saw a devastating embarrassment reflected in her oval pools. *No! I can't let her discard the vibrant emotions that had just transpired between us. Or let her think it all meant nothing to me, because for the first time ever with a woman; it meant something!*

He cupped her shoulders. "No, Callie. It's not like that. Just now at the table, I felt it too. I'm not using you. I—"

She shook her head and reasoned. "No. You're a virile male."

I have to make her understand! "No. Listen. You need to know I agreed to this date before things got heated up with us."

"Cancel it then."

"I can't. My mom—" His hesitant eyes flicked remorse. *What am I? Five? Saying I have to please my mom? I sound ridiculous! Because I am! This whole situation is fucked up! I am pleasing my family first instead of myself. And now I'm putting Callie in last place. This isn't what I want!*

She wiggled from his grasp and held up her palm. "Please stop. You were always telling me how women lined up at your front door."

"Metaphoric," he responded.

"Well, I'm sure me being here has stopped their pursuit."

"It hasn't."

"See. I'm ruining your social life."

You're not stuck to the roof of his mouth.

Though it hurt, she forced a smile. "Don't worry about me."

I'm going to.

"It's not like I should expect there's more between us than sex," she said, trying to down play all the loving moments they've recently shared.

"No, Callie you're–"

She interjected. "Right, I know."

She didn't know!

"Here's what I do know. One, you're making your mom happy. Two, you won't cancel the date. Three, you're not ready to tell the world about us." She used her fingers to count her points.

Losing ground he argued, "You're wrong."

"I'm not." She gave him a pondering stare. "You know what. The day is young. I bet I could find someone to take me out."

"For tonight?" he asked unsteadily.

"Or any night for that matter," she threatened. "There are plenty of men in town who would be proud to take me out."

The clenching of his jaw did not go unnoticed by her, and her smug smile did not go unnoticed by him.

She's teasing me. God, I hope so. Callie on a date with another man twisted his gut. The thought of another man holding her hand or kissing her did not sit well with him. *Maybe I should cancel tonight's date. If I did then there would be no need for Callie to go on one, too, opening the door for us to go out. Of course, my mom will sorely remind me that once a commitment is made it shouldn't be broken unless I'm on my deathbed.*

Callie didn't mean to upset Evan by saying she, too, could go on a date. She just didn't want him feeling guilty for going. However, after stating this, she entertained the idea of getting out of the house this evening. She gave him a reassuring pat on the hand.

"Go. Have fun. Don't worry about me."

"It sounds like you're trying to get rid of me," he said wounded, following her down the hall.

"I'm not." She kept walking. "Don't feel guilty for living your life. I'll survive."

His arm snaked around her pulling her hard against his taut frame.

Possessive eyes swayed into hers as it triggered a dangerous excitement within her. In her past relationships if the guy started showing their zealous side she found it repulsive, but with Evan it was different. She found herself gravitating towards it and him.

"It's not fair of me to say this, but I'm jealous as hell thinking about you with another man." He tugged hard on her ponytail yanking it out of the band.

"Make sure you wear your hair down," he commanded.

"You're right it isn't fair," she seethed as her eyes blazed wildly into his. Her hand snaked behind his head, and her nails dug into the flesh. "I'm jealous, too."

Her catty expression dominated his sexual desires. "Callie, you're turning me on."

She hissed. "Good! Think of me when you're with *her!* Who is the lucky lady?"

"Janie," he winced.

"*Baker?*"

"Yeah," he confirmed, watching her jaw drop.

She stomped her heel on his foot and shouted, "Un...fucking believable!"

"Ouch!"

She twisted away from him and raged, "I'll wear my hair however I damn well please! No man will tell me what to do!"

He let her flee up the stairs. "I guess this means you don't want to join us?"

Halfway up she grabbed the railing and turned around glaring. "As if!" she harrumphed. Callie slammed the bedroom door closing off the sound of his obnoxious laughter that had followed her up the stairs.

Chapter Nineteen

The afternoon had started off so promising. Between the nuzzling kisses and licking his finger it had created all kinds of havoc with her emotions. Now, hearing his date was with *Janie* had her flustered and mad!

Hearing the closing of the automatic garage door and the roar of Evan's truck engine indicated he had left. *Obviously he's taking his truck to impress her! What woman wouldn't love that truck!*

If she found a date for tonight, there was a good chance they would end up at Charlie's, also. She'd have to see Evan and Janie together, holding hands, dancing…would they kiss? *Ugh!* These thoughts made her tummy squeamish and a disgusted jealousy seeped in. The flip side was if she did go to the party she could fight for Evan. The scary part about this was she didn't trust herself not to act like a crazy person. And what she knew of jealousy is…it wasn't pretty on anyone. It was probably best if she stayed away from Charlie's and let Evan enjoy his time with Janie.

She moved forward with her trip to the grocery store by making a list. It occupied her troubling thoughts but it was a temporary solution. Trying to locate her purse preoccupied her mind again. It was lying on Evan's desk next to a stack of papers. The header on the top page read Maslund Trucking Employee Schedule. Rifling through the pages she observed several blue and red pen scribbles. If she stayed in this evening, maybe she could take a look at this. Already she was excited for the opportunity of helping Evan with a work project. Not only would it occupy her time and thoughts it would challenge her brain as well.

At the grocery store, Callie parked Sunbird in a stall away from all the other cars. Through the gossip, she was aware of how the towns' people barely tolerated her driving Sunbird in town, and wished she'd drive a smaller vehicle. She definitely knew they wouldn't appreciate Sunbird parked beside them at the grocery store.

She retrieved a cart from the rack; then pushed it through the aisles removing her wanted items from the shelves and to the cart. She came to the bacon section and stopped. There were so many choices: maple, apple wood, hickory smoked, low salt…

She had a smirking thought. This is where she was in her life; choosing bacon. It should have been a lot easier than the tougher decisions she made on the road, such as, changing lanes safely or calculating the last drops of fuel without running out of it. Yet it wasn't.

"I'd go with hickory smoked or maple."

Callie's gaze followed the voice giving her recommendation. It belonged to Francesca Wilmington. Forcing a smile she said, "Hey, Francesca, I haven't seen you in a long time."

"Hi, yourself," Francesca said. "At first, I wasn't sure it was you. I heard you had a mishap out on the road. Are you doing okay?"

Francesca moved into Callie's space and touched her arm.

"I'm working through things," Callie answered. "How are you? Last I heard you were working in the office at the canning factory."

"Yes, but now I'm at the office in Junction City."

"It's not too far to drive everyday?"

"Not really. Once the highway is done it'll be a lot faster," Francesca remarked. "Have you seen the progress they've made on it?"

Callie shook her head. "Uh-uh."

"It's impressive. If you'd like, we can take a drive out there and look at it."

Callie gave a non-committal shrug.

"I hear Charlie's making a new margarita flavor tonight. Are you going?" Francesca asked.

"Uh-um, I'm not sure. I know Evan's got a date and—"

Francesca interrupted. "—oh, yes, with Janie Baker. Well, you should go. You shouldn't have to spend the night alone. Callie, we are the new generation of women! We certainly don't need a man to accompany us to a party." Her eyes flashed excitedly. "In fact, if you'd like we can go together."

Callie gave a light laugh but it didn't reach her eyes.

"I'll think about it and let you know. Is your number still this?" Callie rattled the number off.

Francesca laughed gaily saying, "Here's my new number."

Thanking her, Callie tried stepping away, but Francesca squeezed her arm.

"Callie, I'd love to see you. I hope you change your mind about tonight."

Francesca sashayed towards the produce. She needed to go there, too, but wanted space from the other woman. There was something about Francesca that always made her feel weird. Never could she place her finger on what it was exactly and today was no different.

Callie steered the cart down the canned soup aisle looking for potato soup. It was an easy meal she could make in the microwave and wouldn't have to rely on Evan. Placing the cans in the cart and without looking over her shoulder, she hastily swung the cart around and just missed crashing the cart into another shopper. Luckily, she didn't hit him.

"Oh! My! I am so sorry!" She quickly apologized but the man wouldn't listen.

Bitter black eyes pierced her like a spear. It was bone chilling, and he viciously raged, "Watch it, girly-girl!"

Callie retreated backwards and looped into the next aisle eager to be away from him. There was a young woman crouched on the floor, but since people knelt for items on the bottom shelf, she thought nothing of it. Passing her, Callie heard her choking on shallow breaths. Recognizing the signs of a panic attack she immediately jumped to the woman's aid.

Callie calmly spoke, "Shhh, slowly breathe in…then out."

She repeated and breathed with the stranger.

"Good," Callie said and was happy when the woman followed the instructions. They breathed together a few times and the woman's breathing became normal. Callie took this as a good sign she was going to be okay.

The woman gripped her arm and thanked her.

"You're welcome," Callie said.

"Holly! What happened?" A man appeared beside them.

Friendly eyes filled with concern questioned Callie. She calmly informed him. "I don't know. I found her on the floor choking."

Helping Holly up, he said, "Thank you for helping her. My name's Iggy and this is Holly."

Callie shook hands with the couple.

Kara hated that she had to be introduced as Holly and wished she could tell people her real name.

"Here lean on my cart." Callie offered.

"Thank you," she said.

"Tell me what happened again?" Iggy inquired.

Callie listened to Holly say, "I'm not sure. One minute I was standing. Next, I was on the floor and couldn't breathe."

"I'm glad you're okay," Callie said sincerely.

"Me, too, thanks again for your help," Kara said gratefully.

"You're welcome. Have a good evening," Callie wished before walking away.

****

Iguana's eyes were full of concern. "Holly, are you sure you're okay?"

"I am now," she replied.

"I'll stay with you while you shop in case you have anymore issues."

"Actually, I'm done. I just have to check out."

"All right, I'll walk you out to your car."

Noticing he didn't carry any bags she said, "You didn't buy groceries."

"No worries. I'll come back later." He was unable to tell her the real reason he was there. His assignment led him here, and he had been ninety percent sure who was being followed but seeing Holly wavered his hunch. This wasn't the first time his assignment and Holly had been in the same location; at least two other times. Red flags flared in his brain. He didn't want to believe it but sadly he had to consider the possibility.

"I really like Callie," she stated.

He picked up on Holly's matter of fact tone. "You know her?"

"I've seen her at the library. I don't think she recognized me but every time we've passed each other she always says hi."

Hearing her, Iguana nodded, but his focus was on Callie walking out to her vehicle. "Hey, I'll be right back. I need to ask Callie something."

****

Callie was unlocking Sunbird's door when she heard her name being called. Turning around, she saw Iggy jogging over to her and was thankful it was him versus the other man she almost hit with her cart.

Iguana stopped and put a non-threatening distance between them. "I'm glad I caught up with you. I want to thank you again for helping Holly."

"You're welcome, but I didn't do anything that no one else would do." She shrugged acting as though it was no big deal.

Shaking his head, he insisted, "Most people would have passed Holly acting as though they didn't see her."

"Yes, I suppose some would." She gave him an expectant look. "Is there something else on your mind?"

Loving her perception, he cleared his throat and smiled. "Yes. I came over here with a volunteer opportunity for you."

"What is it?"

"I'm teaching a self defense class at The Gym and would like you to help me teach it."

"Wow," she said astonished. "I'm honored, but may I ask, why me?"

"For one, you were great with Holly. You kept a level head in what could have been a stressful situation. I have a hunch you are used to high stress and able to keep calm."

"Okay, go on."

"Two, my instincts tell me you'll be an asset for the women attending."

"Well, thank you. Like, I said, I'm honored."

"You're welcome. Classes start this week. We meet Tuesday, Wednesday and Thursday at 5:30." He handed her a card. "Here's my contact information. Think it over and let me know."

Taking his card Callie said, "Thanks."

"By the way nice truck," he complimented.

She laughed, "Thanks."

"A truck driver needs to be on their toes, but I'm guessing a woman trucker especially does. There are too many bad men out there who think they can take advantage of women." He said this with an air of knowledge as though he knew about her. Before she had time to analyze it, his tone turned sad. "My sister was a victim of brutality."

"Oh, I'm sorry," she sympathized, sensing it was a difficult subject for him and wondered why he shared this with her.

Reading her like a book he explained. "Sorry to reveal so much, but I wanted you to know my 'why' for teaching the class. I want women to learn how to defend themselves. I believe you could help give insight of dangerous scenarios and what kind of signs to look for."

"You don't even know me."

"So far what I do know is you're strong and cautious with integrity. I like that you helped Holly, a stranger.

"Thank you. You're welcome," she said skeptically. Then in a more assured voice she complimented him. "I think what you're doing is honorable."

"Thank you. Think on it and talk it over with your boyfriend."

"Boyfriend?" she said, "Oh, you mean Evan."

"I'm sorry. I just assumed," he said guiltily. He was treading dangerously close with revealing too much; hence telling her about his sister and the boyfriend remark. Conversing with the *smart girl* was dangerous; she was far too easy to talk to! He'll need to be careful of any future conversations they have. *Avoiding Callie would have been easier if I hadn't asked her to help teach self defense classes. What am I thinking?*

"Give me a call if you're interested," he said and began walking away just as his watch alerted him of an incoming message.

Callie heard the sound and frowned. The two quick beeps in the low tone were familiar. She had heard it before...

Oddly, it prompted her to call out to him. "Iggy, I'll help you teach the class."

"Great! See you Tuesday evening!"

"See you then!" Callie waved, feeling important and appreciative at this opportunity of helping others.

Chapter Twenty

At precisely six o'clock, Evan stood on The Baker's front porch. Being here was a mistake. It was the last place he wanted to be. Glancing over his attire he gave a small grimace. He didn't even bother dressing nice or slip into a pair of clean boots. *I could have done better. I would have dressed up if it was Callie.* Callie. He missed her already. So much had happened between him and her since the day he agreed to this date. *I'll just take Janie to supper and then bring her home.*

He rang the doorbell and a few seconds later he was greeted by Mr. Baker.

"Evan. Hi," her dad greeted. "Janie will be down in a few minutes. Please come in."

Evan extended his right hand saying, "If it's all right with you, sir, I'll wait out here. The weather's beautiful."

Mr. Baker met his handshake with a beer as he joined him on the porch. "How about a drink while you wait?"

"Thank you." Evan accepted the drink and the hint that Janie wasn't going to be ready anytime soon. *Ugh,* he thought miserably.

"The breeze has cooled things off this evening. I imagine tomorrow's temperatures will be right back up to hot again," Mr. Baker chit-chatted and continued talking about various things.

Evan did a lot of nodding throwing in "uh-huh" every now and then. Janie appeared at the door. His one and only thought was *finally!*

She had dolled up for their date but in his opinion it had been a wasted effort. Her black mascara eyes made her look deadly, the powder on her face was recklessly put on, and he could tell she had tried covering up the pimple on her cheek with too much pink color. To top it off she wore bright lipstick. He couldn't even describe the color. Was it supposed to be pink, red, or orange? It wouldn't have surprised him if her lips glowed in the dark.

"I'm red-dee," she sang.

"Great, let's go!" Evan ushered her down the steps.

She flitted across the driveway out to his truck, and then helplessly stood beside the passenger door. His mom had educated him to be a gentleman, but there was something irritating about the way she expected him to open her door. *Is the whole evening going to be this way?* While helping her up, he noticed the smell of her too sweet perfume as it invaded his nose. He sneezed, and she blessed him. *Callie's scent doesn't make me sneeze.*

They had hardly made it out of the driveway when she reached over and changed his radio station. He stopped his knee jerk reaction of stomping on the brakes. Last thing he needed was Janie's forehead denting his windshield. Quietly, he changed the station back to country.

"I like this song," he commented, hoping she wouldn't try again, but she did. The song ended and her hand advanced towards the radio.

His stern voice stopped her. "Do not! Change the radio station!" She threw him an annoyed look, and he returned it to her.

At the restaurant he parked the truck near the door.

"You're going to help me get out of this thing, right?"

He bristled. "Do you need help?"

"Yes, please." She batted her eyelashes.

Inside the hostess ushered them to a booth. Evan was relieved, because he didn't have to pull her chair out for her. He sat across the table, and she pouted because he didn't sit next to her. Facing her, he could hide behind the menu. The waitress came and took their drink order promising to be back soon. When she returned Janie wasn't ready to order. His grumbling stomach wasn't going to allow anymore waiting.

"I'll order while you decide," he stated.

Taking her sweet time Janie finally decided. "A grilled chicken sandwich with mayo only, please."

In an attempt to drown out Janie's boring voice *and* story, he checked the online word game he and Callie played to see if she had taken her turn. She hadn't, and he was extremely disappointed. She had avoided playing this afternoon, and he knew it had everything to do with the way they parted after lunch. Yes, he had laughed at her after she jumped on his foot, but deep down it bothered him. They were two jealous people…

Janie interrupted his concentration. "What are you doing?"

"Checking my phone for messages," he replied abruptly.

Agitation was strewn across her round face, and he sighed, settling for small talk.

"So how's your brother doing since he and Callie broke up?" Evan asked, hoping the man was miserable. He hated Simon! Partially because he had dated Callie and mainly because he was an ass!

"Oh, he's fine and glad it's over with *that* girl." Her derisive tone aggravated him.

"Why is he so *fine* with it?" Evan sneered.

Quoting her brother word for word, Janie said, "Simon said 'she had a mind of her own and was too hard headed for him! Callie told him he wasn't worth leaving the road for.' Can you believe that?" Janie mocked. "She has no idea what a great catch my brother is!" she added emphatically.

Evan smiled. "She's got spunk."

"Well with *that* kind of attitude, she'll never find a man in *this* town." Janie's tone digressed. "Not decent ones."

"So any man that dates Callie isn't decent?" Evan challenged.

Her face scrunched with annoyance. "You're trying to trap me into saying my brother isn't decent."

"Well, if the shoe fits."

"It doesn't!" Janie scoffed. Then she realized if she continued defending her brother the evening would end after this meal or worse case scenario: Evan would storm out of the restaurant and ruin her fairy tale image of how this evening was supposed to go. She purposely hadn't brought her wallet tonight so she was penniless. To salvage the evening, she had to swallow her sibling pride and let Evan's comments slide.

"Evan, you're nothing like my brother." In an attempt to flatter him, she slid her fingers across the table onto his arm. "It's no secret you're looking for a soft woman who knows their way around a kitchen and isn't afraid of working up a sweat with house chores or in the bedroom."

What the…! The hand on his arm tightened and her innuendo made his skin crawl. His mind raced with ways of removing her hand without creating a scene. "So you think this is what I need?"

"I know so," she answered confidently. "It's all you've ever said."

Damn! Janie said the same thing that Callie had quoted earlier today. He'd done too great of a job of falsely marketing himself. Everyone, including Callie, believed he wanted a meek woman! And it was so far off from what his heart truly desired!

Janie continued talking. "Most of the girls you've been dating can offer you this, as do I, but I'm different."

She hopped into his side of the booth. Her perfume got in his nose again, and he sneezed.

"Oh, dear, it's the second time you've sneezed. Are you coming down with something?"

His mind shouted…*a bad case of you!*

Rapidly he suggested, "I might be. You may want to move away so you don't get sick."

"Oh, Evan," she gushed. "You are so thoughtful."

She slid back into her seat across the table. He appreciated being able to breathe without the hovering cloud of perfume.

"Seriously, Evan, I am the girl for you. I'm quiet and will stand behind you. Like you, I was raised on a farm. I know how much hard work it takes to keep it all going."

Oh, brother! He succeeded in not rolling his eyes but couldn't help the smirk from developing.

Seeing his quirky smile gave her confidence.

Her voice lowered. "Evan, I read books. I know I can please you in bed." Trying to be sensuous she lifted her brows and was thrilled with his wide-eyed stare. She assumed he was picturing them in bed!

Evan was extremely put off! Having to touch or kiss her made him shudder!

Janie had said all she could without physically throwing her body at him, and she certainly wouldn't do it in the restaurant. She'd have to wait until later when they were alone in his truck.

"Did you have a good day at work?" she asked.

"Yep," he said but did not elaborate because there was no need to. He doubted that she'd actually understand anything about his job at Maslund Trucking. *Callie would.* If he was home now they could be conversing about Maslund business. She'd fully understand it and probably educate him on some things. She'd been working in the trucking industry longer than he had. *I'd love to pick her brain for new ideas.*

Evan listened to Janie ramble on about shoes, the librarian's new hair do, the potluck on Sunday and was he going to be there? He made a mental note to make sure he had plans on Sunday so his family couldn't ambush him. She went on about stuff he didn't care about and his mind drifted.

It's true, I said, I wanted a non-spirited girl. Here one sits across from me and all I can think about is that she is SO Boring! There will be no more pleasing the women in my family! I am taking back my personal life! No more dates! A lonely evening is a lot better than spending time with someone I don't like! Besides, I see enough people during the day to enjoy the quiet of home. AND if I was home right now I'd be with Callie and far, far, far! Away! From Janie!

Their food arrived. Evan doused his burger in ketchup then squirted some on his plate. Without asking, Janie reached across the table stealing one of his fries. He scowled, and she was aware of her mistake, but she refused to be intimidated.

In a passing tone she said, "Oh, please! Don't give me that look! It's not like your going to miss one little fry."

"Yes I am! It was the longest one," he whined.

"Whatever! Quit being so childish," she complained. "It's not a very good example to set for your children."

He stewed. "I don't have any children."

"Eventually, you will." Janie watched him chew his food. Just as he was swallowing she stated, "Together we could."

He choked and managed to cough it out, taking a long drink of his beer. She was still ogling him when he set the drink down. "Please eat," he instructed.

Finishing first, Evan ordered a second beer and watched her eat daintily. It was frustrating! He just wanted to snatch the sandwich out of her hands and shove it into his mouth, eating it so they could leave. His phone made a car horn sound. It was Callie!

Her message read. **Do you mind if I work on the driver's schedule?**

His heart and mind raced over the possibility that she didn't have a date. If he left the restaurant, he and Callie could spend the rest of the evening together. Unless she was using the schedule to pass time waiting for her date to pick her up? No. Not Callie. She'd drive to meet the guy, because she didn't trust other people driving her.

He typed his response. **No, be my guest.**

She replied. **I am your guest.**

He responded. **You don't have to be.**

She replied. **Are you saying you want me to move out?**

He gritted his teeth. **No! I didn't say that. Just the opposite, I want you to think of my house as your house. ☺**

He laid the phone on the table waiting for her to reply but none came. Then an unsettled thought struck him of the reason she was home. *Is her date coming over to the house?* He wanted to ask her if this was case, but he didn't want to sound petty. In the end, jealousy prodded his fingers to type. **Cooking for your date tonight?**

She replied. **What if I am?**

Petty thoughts pressed his lips together. **Who are you cooking for?**

Her response was fast. **You shouldn't worry about who I'm with while you're with Janie Baker!**

He felt the punch of her sarcasm. He should've let it go but his twitching jaw goaded him to re-ask. **So who are you cooking for?**

Eventually, she responded but it had nothing to do with their previous conversation. **An incident occurred at the store this afternoon. I'll tell you more details later when I see you. Long story short, I was asked to help teach a self defense class. I said yes.**

Several questions swarmed through his panicked mind.

He typed. **Who asked you?**

A man named Iggy.

Where?

The Gym.

When?

Starting this week Tuesday, Wednesday and Thursday

What time?

She replied. **5:30.**

Evan was perturbed they couldn't have this conversation in person. *I want to know more about this man named Iggy. I've never heard of him. Where does he live? Why did he ask Callie?*

Keeping his reply brief he typed. **Fine, do it.**

She replied. **I wasn't asking for permission.**

He typed. **I wasn't giving it.**

Observing his smirk, Janie asked sassily. "Who keeps bothering you?"

Evan bit his tongue, stopping himself from shouting, *YOU!* Out loud he said, "Its work. Please finish eating."

While she ate he studied her. She wasn't half bad looking, nor was she half good looking; just not the girl for him. It was time to take her home. He signaled for the waitress to bring the check. Arriving with the bill, Evan paid in cash telling their waitress to keep the change. He didn't pay with a credit card because he didn't want to wait for the receipt. This meant he would have to spend more time with Janie. All he wanted was to go home, see Callie, and be with her. It was better than being with Janie.

Evan helped Janie into the truck as her heavy perfume filled his nose making him sneeze again. Before he closed the door she said, "Oh, I told Charlie we'd be at her party tonight."

"What! Why did you tell her that?" he asked disappointed and annoyed.

"She needed to know how much margarita mix to make." Janie fibbed.

"Bullshit. Everyone knows when the margaritas are gone you switch to beer."

"Well, I want to try the new flavor," she declared and pulled the door shut.

Climbing into the driver's seat, he fired up the engine. Learning nothing from earlier, Janie was changing his radio station again. *What the fuck!*

"What are you doing?" he roared.

"What?" she asked innocently.

"We established this earlier. YOU are not to mess with my radio station."

"I hate country," Janie protested.

"I hate your music," Evan said in disgust.

"Everybody knows the passenger chooses the music."

"Bullshit."

"It's true. My dad lets my mom do it all the time." Her hand moved towards the radio, but he sharply warned, "Don't!"

"But—"

His low voice warned. "We're in my truck. Not your dad's, not yours, or your mom's. Mine! And in my truck the driver chooses the music and nobody else!"

"Well, then let me drive."

He gave her a ridiculous look. "No way in hell! You can't even climb up in the truck without my help. What makes YOU think you can drive it?"

"I saw Callie driving it the other day," she reasoned.

"Because, Callie can handle my truck, and SHE can get in and out of it, ALL BY HER SELF!"

Janie gave him a wounded look, but he didn't budge and added insult to injury by saying, "You are not driving my truck...ever!"

"If we're together you'd have to let me."

Rudely he smashed her hopes. "We're not together. And if I were you, I wouldn't go counting chickens before they're hatched. My truck! My rules! Got it?"

Her perturbed glare met his hard stare.

She backed down and pouted, "You're such a jerk! I can't believe I wanted you!"

Evan bit his tongue holding back another insult. Last thing he wanted was a scolding from his mother about how she taught him to have good manners; knowing his mom would probably hear about this spat through the grapevine.

He turned into Charlie's driveway and threw his truck into reverse parking next to Kellan's. Having his friends here might help move the evening along. He jumped out, catching Janie's maddening stare through the windshield.

He contemplated his choices: Be a gentleman and help her? Remain a jerk and don't help her out? If he didn't help, what if she fell and hurt herself? He'd have to carry her inside or worse take her to the emergency room. Then he'd be obligated to stay with her during the ER visit because his mom had raised him to be a good gentleman.

He grumbled all the way to the passenger door. Janie grabbed his hand and wouldn't let go when he tried yanking it away. Thankfully, his phone beeped again, freeing his hand.

"Not again!" she complained.

"Yes again," he snapped.

She gave him a disapproving frown. Despite the not so perfect evening, she still wanted to hold Evan's hand as they waded through the crowd, especially in front of Francesca Wilmington. Seeing the woman's disheartened look would be divine!

Janie always felt like prey to Francesca; because she always watched her and her dates. Every man she ever went out with was seen with Francesca afterwards, and they never called her again. She had no clue as to why this happened and wished the rivalry could have been friendly but there was nothing friendly about Francesca!

Evan sighed heavily and gave in. "All right, I know you want to parade me through the crowd so let's get this over with."

Enthusiastically, she grabbed his wrist making sure he didn't get lost as they wove through the house saying hi to her friends, a brief hello to Francesca, and she flirted with other men.

Evan finally said, "I've done my duty. Now let go."

She did and it annoyed him that she didn't thank him as they parted ways.

Kellan chuckled when a grumpy Evan sat on the log across from him. "So the date is going well, huh?"

Grimacing, Evan said, "She is so irritating. This is the last time I let my mom set me up, and why on earth did she pick Janie?"

Kellan laughed. "From what I hear, your mom didn't have a choice."

"What?" Evan snapped.

"Yeah," Kellan chided. "According to what Kylee said, rumor has it Janie talked your mom into getting a date with you. It was either listen to Janie gab all day or agree to set you up on a date."

"Poor mom," Evan sympathized. "I would've said anything, too, just to get Janie to go away." Empathizing he thought *after all I did agree to bring her to this party*.

"The date can't be that terrible, can it?" Kellan asked.

"It can and is."

Kellan shook his head. "Evan, you've gotta get over your quirks."

"I like my quirks. They work." He stubbornly stated.

Behind him, Evan heard his brother's laugh. Turning he greeted, "Hey Eric. I haven't seen you in awhile."

Eric patted Evan's back with brotherly affection. "I've been hiding from the women in our family. For some reason they've started focusing on my love life. I believe they're giving up on you."

Evan smiled saying, "Good. They need to give up on me, and I'm sorry you're next. I'll help you out anyway I can."

"Thanks. Oh, and by the way, your date is wasted and mistook me for you, which is easy to do because I am the better looking brother."

Evan smirked and rolled his eyes. "Whatever." Frowning he said, "It didn't take her long to get drunk."

"I think Francesca is pumping drinks into her while she brags about your date," Eric commented.

"Not much to brag about," Evan said dryly.

"Oh, you know girls. They'll make the bad look good when it comes to making other women jealous." Eric laughed his opinion.

Cheerfully, Evan said, "I guess this means I can take her home early unless…" He swung a curious glance at his almost twin brother. "My better looking brother wants to take her? If she's as drunk as you say she is, she won't even know it's you instead of me."

Eric gave him an absurd look. "No. You lie in the bed that mom made for you."

Kellan burst out laughing.

Evan cast his brother a long look saying, "One day I hope to look back on this night and laugh."

Eric teased, "I don't have to look back I'm already laughing." Making a sad face Eric mocked, "Did the girl steal food off your plate?"

Kellan piped in, "Changed the radio station?"

Kylee slid in beside her husband and added, "More than five minutes late?"

Answering them, Evan pointed his finger at Eric then Kellan saying yes and yes! Then pointing his finger at Kylee he fired off his answer, "Seventeen minutes!"

Kylee's face soured. "Oh."

"With friends like you, who needs enemies?" Evan cracked a smile. "I'm glad I can keep you all entertained."

"We are too, brother." Eric slapped him on the back. "Your date is staggering her way over here."

"Shit." Evan stood as Janie approached.

"I'm red-dee!" She slurred versus earlier she had sung the word. Reaching Evan she leaned, and then slumped against him.

"Dude, she just passed out." Eric laughed.

Evan groaned and slung her over his shoulder; carrying her like a grain sack. By the time they got out to his truck Janie was snoring.

Behind him, Kellan said, "I hope she doesn't puke in your truck."

Evan made a bitter face. Janie's perfume lingering in his truck was going to be bad enough; he certainly didn't want her regurgitated supper spewed all over the floor. "Maybe I should put her in the bed of the truck."

Believing him Kylee protested, "Evan, you can't do that!"

"Fine, I won't."

"We'll follow you to Janie's house in case you have problems," Kellan told him then went back and helped Kylee into their truck. His eyes lingered on hers. "I love you, sweet girl."

"I love you, too," she answered.

Evan got Janie home without any incident. Pulling into Janie's driveway Evan waved thanks to Kellan as he drove on. The farm dogs ran to the truck barking ferociously. A light went on in the kitchen. Janie's dad stared out the window and Evan waved while he carried Janie to the door. She hadn't awakened, and he was grateful for it. Mr. Baker held the door open for him, and Evan set her down on the couch.

"Thank you for bringing her home. I hope she wasn't too much trouble." Mr. Baker thanked appreciatively. He always liked Evan. He came from good stock and the fact that he carried his daughter inside verified what a fine young man he was. His daughter's other dates often left her outside on the porch after she passed out.

"She was fine, sir," Evan said. "I hope she's not too sick in the morning."

"Well, I'll put a pail by the couch just in case. Thanks for carrying her inside. She may not appreciate it, but I do."

Her dad walked him out sighing heavily, "Have a good night. Drive safe."

"Thanks, good night." Evan said then warned him, "You probably don't want to mention my name tomorrow."

Her dad chuckled dryly with a shake of his head. "I'm not sure she'll remember what happened tonight."

Evan wasn't so sure Janie would forget how miserable their date had been. Maybe now she would stop pursuing him.

Chapter Twenty One

Evan sped all the way home. Inside the back door he removed his boots. Whistling, he shuffled his socked feet down the hall towards his room but stopped when he saw Callie sitting behind the desk in his office. One hand held a pencil while one finger skimmed over the paper. Her hair was pulled into a ponytail exposing the column he found to be irresistible. Moving closer he recognized the spreadsheets he had brought home from the office. She glanced up with an irresistible smile.

"What'cha doing?" he asked.

"Working on the schedule," she stated softly. "I heard you whistling."

"Good." He grinned. He had hoped it was a nice way of alerting her of his presence without scaring her.

"How was your evening?" she inquired.

"Terrible. Yours?"

She shrugged. "Quiet."

"I would have traded boring babble for quiet," Evan stated.

Callie smiled. She shouldn't have been so pleased that he had a crappy time, but she was and couldn't hide the happiness in her smile.

He chuckled. "Give me five minutes, and I'll tell you everything."

She accepted, and he jogged down the hallway to his room. Shedding his clothes he put them in the hamper and stepped into the shower. He was shampooing his hair when he heard Callie on the other side of the steamed door ask, "Why are you showering?"

"I'm not coming near you drenched in another woman's scent. Aw! I think she marinated in her perfume," he said disgusted, hearing her giggle.

Surprisingly, he didn't mind that she laughed about his torturous date, because the simple truth was, he loved hearing Callie laugh.

He recanted this evening's events. "She wasn't ready when I arrived and made me wait a long time."

"Doesn't she know it's rude to keep a good-looking man waiting?" she said coyly.

"Ugh, tell me about it. Her dad gave me a beer and we talked farming. Wait." He opened the shower door and poked his head out. "You think I'm good-looking?"

His direct stare glued her to where she stood. Bashfully, she said, "Yes."

"Good to know, Callie Cat." His grin teased before closing the door. "She called my truck a *thing*." He hissed the last word. Then he ridiculed what Janie said in a high squeaky voice. "This truck is too high! Oh! I can't get down, help me!"

Callie was rolling in laughter.

"Then Janie couldn't understand why I wouldn't ever let her drive my truck."

Astonished, Callie asked, "Why did she want to drive your truck?"

"So she could change the radio station," he answered dryly.

"Oh. Dear. So she tried changing it?"

"Twice and stole food off my plate."

"Oh. No." Callie winced.

He shut the water off, and she tossed him a towel over the door before he asked for one.

"Thanks," he said appreciatively. "And not just for the towel, for listening and not making me feel as though I have crazy quirks. Well, I do but…"

"It's who you are, and you're welcome."

"Hmm, you're throwing my words back at me." He stepped out with the towel tied around his waist and hopped up on the bathroom counter.

She grinned, enjoying the front row view of the water beads clinging to the muscles on his body. Stepping between his legs she kissed the wet skin, licking the water off his chest. The feel of his steel flesh energized her seduction. She untied the towel and held his cleansed penis in the palm of her hand. Gently, her fingers circled it creating a warm tunnel for it, gingerly stroking and cupping his length feeling it swell into a heftier state.

Her lusting tongue touched his erection.

He moaned.

She licked side to side, up, down, and around.

His fingers grasped her hair.

She sucked his penis, taking him in deep.

He sharply inhaled, releasing his cum as his eyes danced with pleasure.

Immediately following, Evan lavished her with luscious kisses and helped her out of her clothes. Sliding off the counter, he set her on it, announcing it was her turn.

Bending, he kissed her knee and inner thigh on one leg then mimicked his actions on the other leg. She gasped because simultaneously it tickled and revved her senses.

His tongue traveled north towards her southern region. Nearing it, her thighs clamped his head. His sultry laugh was low as his mouth eased

forward and kissed her cunt. His tongue probed deep. Swirly sensations
fluttered through her core.

Her high pitch cry panted his name, and her breasts arched
forward. Tempted by them, he rose and kissed them. She provocatively
begged for more. Aching to feel her wet cunt on his dick he carried her to
the bed. His eyes demanded she take the lead.

She straddled and mounted him, feeding him her breast. His
thumb caressed the nipple that wasn't being sucked, and she moaned her
delight. She controlled their satiated fate; each downward thrust withdrew
satisfied screams.

On the brink of a storming release a passionate roar thundered out
of him. Thrusting upwards he drove excited pleasure into her and felt the
furrowed heat rushing in. Their bodies united and together they
experienced floating bursts of delight as their orgasms sailed through
them.

Callie collapsed into his open arms, and he gently snuggled her
beside him.

Evan nuzzled kisses into her neckline, murmuring, "I missed you
tonight."

She sighed. "Does this mean you're not going out with Janie
again?"

"Never again!" he vowed. "I thought about you all night. I
wanted to see you across the table and listen to you talking. I wanted you
next to me in the truck; riding or driving it, I don't care. I wanted you to
be parading me through the crowd at Charlie's not *her* or any other *her* for
that matter. I just want you, Callie." He expressed endearingly.

Her heart bubbled with love. "Oh, Evan," she sighed. "It's the
sweetest thing anyone's ever said to me."

"Good." He happily smiled.

They fell asleep snuggled in a loving embrace.

The next morning Evan woke Callie up by painting kisses all over
her body.

"Oh," she sighed. "I love –" she abruptly stopped talking, and he
drew his head back.

Her face flamed hot at what she was just about to spontaneously
say, reacting to the natural feel good feeling she was bursting with.
Luckily, her brain stepped in before her heart had a chance to make a fool
of herself.

"Love what?" he asked.

Her eyebrows squinted together, and she dropped into an "uh-oh" I
don't know expression. Saving her and supplying her with an answer,
Evan's orange cat trotted across the bed meowing. "Owen. I love Owen."

He frowned.

She rambled, "Growing up I always wanted pets but my parents were against them. I considered getting a cat to keep me company on the road, but I wasn't sure about traveling with a litter box especially when it had to go number two. Ew," she made a face. "Could you imagine the smell?"

Despite his chuckle regarding the stinky litter box he gave her a long look. "I'm glad you love Owen. He seems to have taken a liking to you. Let's go have breakfast."

She followed him to the bathroom and was disappointed with herself for not voicing her true heart. If she had, they could still be in bed sharing more kisses. If only she had the guts to say that past lovers fulfilled a need, but he stretched it beyond the physical aspect and dove deep reaching her soul emotionally. He was the man she wanted to share her heart with but was too scared to voice it.

"Hey, did you get bacon?" he asked, kissing her bare shoulder.

"Yes, but I didn't know which kind to get so I got an assortment." She kissed his cheek, and he cupped her breast, twirling her in front of him.

In the mirror his hazel eyes caught hers. He whispered, "You're beautiful."

Her eyes briefly flickered amusement then hesitancy.

"I mean it, Callie Cat. Inside and out, you're the most generous woman I know." His sincere expression held truth, and she believed him, trusted him…and loved him.

She closed her eyes and softly thanked him.

"You're welcome." He kissed her good smelling hair.

Her tummy rumbled, ruining the spontaneity of expressing the love in her heart.

She laughed. "Apparently, I am very hungry. If you don't mind, I'll make us some peanut butter and jelly sandwiches. It'll be quicker than eggs."

"All right, sounds good and tonight I'll make us BLT sandwiches."

"Ooh, yummy. A fresh BLT will be a treat," she said enthusiastically.

"Huh?"

"Ordering it at restaurants it often sits in the window too long. The bacon is cold and chewy, yuck!"

He gave her a sympathetic look. "You just needed to order it when Dirk was around. Since the wait staff gives him such elite service."

Callie threw her head back laughing hard at his teasing remark. Between laughs she gasped, "Now why didn't I think of that?"

Evan laughed too, because the happiness radiating her joy was contagious. He followed her into the kitchen and helped get the ingredients out for her to make the sandwiches while she apologized for not knowing how to make eggs.

"I don't care about that. I appreciate you, *wanting* to make me breakfast." He came up behind her and hugged her along with a quick nibble on her neck. She moaned her gratitude and it made him laugh.

"I'm not picky when it comes to eating, Callie. In fact, I could make a meal out of you. This spot," he widened his mouth at the base of her neck, "is mighty sweet. It drives me crazy. I wish I could suckle it all day long."

"Ah," she uttered a pleasing sigh and somehow managed to lift him a completed sandwich.

Resigning he said, "Okay. We'll eat food."

She giggled and loaded the plate with sandwiches while Evan brought a gallon of milk and a glass. "Mind if we share a glass?"

"Not at all," she agreed, pouring the milk.

He took a hearty bite, chewed, swallowed, drank, and then repeated. Done with his first sandwich he looked her straight in the eye and declared, "Callie, this is the best PB and J sandwich I have ever had!"

He took another one.

"Thank you but it isn't hard to make."

"True, yet…" he slightly parted the bread. "The jelly is melded so well with the peanut butter. Amazing, baby girl," he complimented, smacking his lips.

"Thanks and your welcome. Glad you like 'em."

"Love them!" Silently adding *and you!*

"Yesterday when Kylee was here she said I should pack your lunch bag."

He rolled his eyes. "I'm a big boy and can pack it just fine by myself," he remarked dryly.

Callie laughed. "That's what I told her."

"Good. You don't need to start packing my lunch just because Kylee said so." He shook his head. "That's a ridiculous comment."

"I agree but it's good to hear you agree. Oh, while I'm thinking of it, have you heard from Dirk? How are he and Sage?"

"They're good. He says they'll be home soon."

"Do you think they tied the knot while out on the road?" she asked.

He shrugged. "It's possible, but I don't know. Do you think they did?"

She shook her head. "Maybe, I guess I won't be surprised either way."

"And Kellan thought it would be you and Dirk doing the knot tying." Evan let out a big sigh of relief. "I am so glad he was wrong!"

"Me, too," she giggled.

"So are you going to tell me your secret of how you make these wonderful peanut butter and jelly sandwiches?" he smirked.

She snickered jokingly, "I've thought about it, and I'm not ready to give up my secret."

"C'mon," he tried coaxing, but she shook her head.

"I could tickle it out of you." His hand shot forward and his fingers grazed her ribcage. She jumped and squealed, but he managed to keep tickling her.

"Stop it," she gasped laughing.

He caught her wrist and pulled her out of the chair into his lap. Swiftly, before she could protest, his hand ducked under her shirt, rose and pushed the bra away. He fondled one round breast, kneading the nipple, and then moved over to the other one administering the same pleasure. Her breathing became uneven, and her eyes turned ravenous as he lifted her shirt over her head.

"Fair's fair." She helped him out of his shirt and ran her hands over his broad shoulders, down his back and around to his chest.

Having her hands roaming his body was a delight. Unclasping the bra, he kissed her fervently taking away her breath. Then his mouth clamped on one breast, twirling and flicking his tongue across her taut nipple.

He heard a whistle but paid no attention to it but after the third sound Callie asked what it was. He murmured, "It's my brother."

She sat up startled, "What? Here?"

He grinned and held up his phone. "Here."

She breathed a sigh of relief but watched the smile fall off his face after he read the message. "What's wrong?"

He blew out a frustrated breath. "Uh, I almost forgot a very important birthday."

Her eyes questioned.

"Today is my niece's birthday party."

Since he only talked about one niece she guessed, "Macy?"

Evan nodded.

"Shit, you can't miss it." She stressed.

He appreciated her knowledge about the importance of his attendance. Just then an idea popped in. "And neither can you!"

"Oh! No!" she argued. "It's a family thing. I can't tag along."

"You won't be tagging along. You'll be with me."

"Your family won't like it."

He insisted. "Trust me, Callie. They won't mind if you're there."

Uncertainty ran across her face, but then she caved. "You're sure your family won't mind?"

"They won't. I promise, and you'll have fun." Evan gave her a long reassuring kiss. "Feel better?"

She shook her head. "No, I think I need another kiss," she replied wickedly.

He laughed and carried her over to the couch. Wrapping their bodies closer he kissed her until she forgot altogether about the party and focused her sole attention on him, and them.

Chapter Twenty-Two

Janie woke up on the couch feeling strange. She was naked, cold and bewildered. She climbed the stairs to her room and got into bed. Her head pounded thinking back on her and Evan's disastrous date.

How could such a good-looking guy turn out to be so frustrating? She should have listened better to what the other girls had said about his quirks. For example, he didn't have to be so stubborn about his radio station or so whiny claiming she took the longest fry. On their dates, he too, had been preoccupied. The majority of the time he was flipping through his phone. She shouldn't have been so wrapped up in her fantasy thinking he would have been different with her. She would have liked him to focus more on her and converse with her instead of letting her do all the talking.

At the party they went their separate ways, which worked out to her advantage. She was able to brag to Francesca about their date in exaggerated detail. She spun a tall tale about Evan opening doors for her, helping her in the truck, paying attention to her and paying for the meal, leaving out one important detail. She had to beg him to do all of this except the part about paying for the meal. This he automatically did. But Francesca didn't need to know the true details just the faux ones.

Janie rubbed her temple. She had enjoyed Charlie's margarita but she only drank one. So why did her head hurt as though she had gulped three of them? At the party, she had stumbled over to Eric mistaking him for Evan. It was easy to do since the brothers could pass as twins. He had pointed her in the right direction. She remembered swaggering toward Evan but got dizzy and had to sit. Even then it didn't seem possible to be as drunk as she was. Finally she made it over to Evan, declaring she was ready to go home. His face held pure annoyance as she collapsed in his arms. She must have passed out, because she didn't remember anything afterwards.

So why am I naked? She rolled onto her stomach and discovered her breasts were sore. She sat up and held one in her hand. Turning on the light beside the bed she saw their pinkish color. Her memory flashed to a mouth sucking her nipples. Her hand smoothed over her belly and reached down to the exterior of her vagina. This, too, felt sore. She touched the interior walls and made a face. It felt as though she had been bit. Then she saw the bruise on her inner thigh. She gasped trying to remember what had happened. Having no luck, she turned off the light and lay back on the bed feeling even stranger.

In the morning, her dad was singing praises for Evan carrying her inside when so many others had left her on the porch. "Evan was under the impression you wouldn't want to hear his name mentioned today."

"He was right. I am done trying to get his attention." She told her dad. "The girls in town were right about him."

"And what's that?" her dad asked, his forehead wrinkling.

"He doesn't pay attention to his dates; seems preoccupied."

"Hmm," her dad grunted. Of course, his daughter wouldn't be interested in a man he had things in common with. "Well, pumpkin, you'll find your Prince Charming."

Her brother's voice grumbled behind her. "I don't know why in the hell you were interested in Evan Nichols. He's not the man for you, sis," came Simon's bitter reply. "You could do a lot better than him. He's just as bad as Callie."

Mr. Baker kept quiet listening to his children argue-agree about Evan and Callie. It was a made up thing he had created, but he didn't know how else to describe it. With their voices raised it sounded like they were arguing when they were actually agreeing with each other. Most of time, it seemed they were too wrapped up in arguing to realize they were actually agreeing with one another.

He excused himself from the table, leaving the house to let them continue bickering about Evan and Callie. Simon's heart was still soured by Callie's rejection of marrying him. Though Mr. Baker liked the girl he was good with her saying no, because he didn't think she was a good fit for his son. She was too independent. Simon needed a softer girl, reserved, more his equal and Janie needed a man who doted on her, treated her as an equal but wouldn't let her flightiness rule the relationship. He had high hopes when Evan showed up and then they were dashed when he brought her home. He kept encouraging his daughter to keep looking for true love but the more she didn't find it, the more he feared she might not. He would continue praying for his children to find their respected loves and to get them out of the house.

"So Evan brought you home?" Simon asked.

"Yeah, I passed out at the party."

"I guess you and I can't handle Charlie's new margarita flavor."

"I have a killer headache," they simultaneously said.

Janie grimaced. "I only had one drink."

Simon grinned and boasted, "Francesca drove me home."

"What!" Janie shouted. "If she was here that means she saw me passed out on the couch, and she'll know Evan didn't kiss me goodnight," she wailed.

"Sis, she saw Evan carry you to his truck. And what do you care what she thinks anyway?" Simon asked, watching her shrug.

"I don't know. I feel like she's always competing with me. I might have exaggerated a little on the details of how our date was going."

"You'll remember on Sunday how much bragging is the Lord's sin," Simon replied then ignored his own advice when Janie asked, "How long did Francesca stay?"

He proudly hinted, "Awhile."

"Did the two of you, you know?" she inquired.

"What do you think, sis?" he answered vaguely. Keeping the broad grin plastered on his face he let her conjure naughty images of him and Francesca together.

"She's an amazing kisser," he boasted and loved his sister's jaw dropping expression.

"Out of all the men there, I can't believe she picked you to spend the night with," Janie said.

"Neither can I but when opportunity knocks you don't close the door," he trumpeted, wishing he could gloat more about what happened last night, but he kept certain things private. Such as, the blow job he received from his high school sweetheart didn't even come close in comparison to Francesca's. Last night, he was a man experiencing pleasure from a woman. It made him feel *very* important, despite the fact that he had passed out in the middle of his first ever mind blowing orgasm.

During the party, Francesca handed him his second margarita. Halfway through it the alcohol had easily affected him, and he kissed Francesca. She welcomed his interest and gave him the sexiest kiss he'd ever had. On the dance floor, she heightened the thrill when she reached inside his pants and groped his penis and encouraged him to touch her breasts. Feeling her pointed nipples gave him the confidence in accepting her sultry invitation of leaving the party and going back to his place. He suggested her place where they would have more privacy, but she insisted on his house. Lost under her sultry influence he agreed to her demands.

Francesca drove them in her car. While driving she grabbed his hand laying it on her knee saying he could have fun. He wasn't entirely sure what she meant but soon found out after his fingers moved off her knee and on the inside of her leg. She cooed and goaded him to go farther. He did and discovered she wasn't wearing any underwear. Using his forefinger, he circled the edges of her slit as his penis swelled. He couldn't wait to plant himself in her. If his mind hadn't been so foggy he would have asked her to pull the car over for quick sex. He kissed her breast, but she pushed his mouth downward between her thighs. He licked her pussy as her squeals hardened his dick. He was amazed and thankful for her ability to drive while he did this with her.

Arriving at his house, he led Francesca to his room; thankful his parent's bedroom was on the other side of the house. She undressed him, gripped his penis and then lowered her mouth on him! She might as well have been the goddess of love because it was amazing! The last thing he remembered was her sitting on him and feeling himself explode.

When he woke up this morning he was grateful his manhood was still there and was disappointed when Francesca wasn't. It was probably best she snuck out early before his dad woke up. He was a grown man but that didn't mean he wanted to deal with his dad's disapproving frowns.

"Well, I'm glad one of us had an amazing night," Janie said sadly.

"Jealous much," he accused her, but she shook her head. "Nope, I'm glad I know Evan isn't the man for me. Now I can move on."

Throughout the day bits and pieces of the night after Evan brought her home flashed briefly before her. Even before her dad confirmed Evan dropping her off at home, she already knew he wasn't the one who had messed with her. Though he was an ass to her, messing around with women like this wasn't in his nature. *That* wasn't the kind of man he was. However, she was convinced she had been fooled around with but didn't know who or where. One small memory scratched to the surface. She did awaken to a warm breath on her chest. Her blouse had already been unbuttoned and the front clasp of her bra released. She heard her own hot moans and quite possibly heard herself say yes.

"Damn it," she muttered, because she wasn't one hundred percent sure if she had consented to sex or been coerced. She didn't feel violated, but then she didn't feel un-violated. She just hated not knowing or remembering what happened last night! *God! I hope it was safe sex! The last thing I want is to end up pregnant and not know who the father is!*

Throughout the week at various times, Janie sensed she was being watched but couldn't ever verify it. It didn't feel like she was being stalked, but then it didn't feel like she was being admired. It was the strangest sensation she'd ever had. By the end of the week Janie was feeling bold enough to go back to Charlie's wondering and kind of hoping her mystery man would reveal himself.

Chapter Twenty-Three

Kara sashayed her way through kids and parents in one of the party rooms at the local kid's entertainment venue. This birthday party wasn't any different than the rest she had helped cater; the adults' conversed while the kids were wildly excited, dashing in and out of the play area filled with giant inflatable slides.

She set matching pink plates, cups and napkins on the tables. Next she placed cupcakes on the tier stand. They were frosted in two shades of pink; hot and pastel. With an inward sigh, she wondered if her life would ever be settled enough to raise a child. She neatly stacked presents on the floor next to a chair marked *Princess.*

Parents and kids kept filing in wishing the little girl happy birthday and saying hi to her mom. All of a sudden the birthday girl let out a high pitch squeal and ran across the room towards the couple that had just arrived.

"Uncle Evan!" she screamed and jumped into the man's outstretched arms.

He twirled her exclaiming, "Happy Birthday, Macy bug!"

"Thanks, Uncle Evan," she laughed and smiled.

"Hey, kiddo, there's someone I want you to meet." Evan slightly turned his body so his niece could see Callie.

Macy wiggled out of Evan's arms and when her feet were on the floor she stepped closer to Callie as he introduced them.

Callie lowered her face to Macy's eye level observing how the girl's bright eyes honed in on her.

"Macy, your uncle didn't tell me you were as pretty as a princess." Her sincere gushing and genuine smile won over both niece and uncle; Macy's eyes lit up as did Evan's heart.

"Nice to meet you," Callie said, holding her hand out. Macy shook it and Callie said, "May I call you Princess?"

Macy suddenly turned bashful and nodded her head as Callie greeted, "Nice to meet you, Princess Macy."

Evan loved it when Callie curtsied in front of Macy and the five year old ate it up. He was proud of the way Callie made Macy feel as though she was the most precious person in the room. His heart overpowered the rest of him. *She'll make a great mom.* The thought of her sharing a child with any other man knotted his stomach. Callie looked up at him and flashed him a bright smile and his heart was off running again. A possessive arrow shot into him as he wanted to be the man making her a mom!

Macy tugged on Callie's hand and said in a matter-of-fact tone, "You're going to be my new aunt."

Callie blushed and Evan dropped his jaw while people around them snickered. Evan's sister, Macy's mom, came forward and ushered her out the door to go play with her friends. Shaking her head, she laughed, "Goodness, that child. I swear some days I think she's turning fifteen instead of five. Sorry, if she embarrassed you." Holding out her hand she introduced herself. "Hi, Callie, I'm Ellie, Evan's sister."

Callie shook her hand. "Hi, Ellie, nice to meet you, and there's no need to apologize for Macy. She's adorable!"

Ellie poked Evan on the shoulder. "She's a handful! A lot like her uncle."

Evan chastised her. "No, she's a lot like you. I hear pay back is a bitch."

"Just wait your turn. I'm going to sit back and enjoy the show," Ellie teased. Turning to Callie she hugged her hard. "I'm so glad you are okay! We were all worried when you went missing. I know my brother went out of his mind." Even as she said this she wondered *maybe there is some truth to what Macy said about Callie being her new aunt. Children see things differently than adults do.*

"Thank you. It's good to be home."

Evan's heart soared, hearing Callie say this he prayed when she said *home* she really was talking about being with him.

"When are you going back on the road?" Ellie asked conversationally.

Callie shrugged. "I don't know. I haven't decided. I've been enjoying my stay off the road."

Macy came in and grabbed Evan's hand leading him out to the play area. Ellie was relieved. This way she could ask Callie more questions without her brother's annoyed glare.

"Do you think you might not go back?" Ellie asked.

"It has crossed my mind."

"What would you do if you didn't drive the rigs?"

Thoughtfully, Callie said, "I think maybe I'd like to stay and help run the daily operations of Maslund Trucking."

Ellie's eyes twinkled. "I know my brother wouldn't mind if you decided to do this."

Callie down played Ellie's ogling. "In the past he would have."

Ellie shrugged hinting, "It's not the past anymore. I know he thinks very highly of you."

Happily, Ellie noted the easy smile that appeared on Callie's face. It was the same kind of smile that appeared on her brother's face earlier this week when she had remarked this was the happiest she'd ever seen him.

"Well, it's time to eat and get the party started!" Ellie announced.

"I'll go get Macy and Evan," Callie volunteered, returning shortly with Evan carrying Macy on his shoulders.

The children ate peanut butter and jelly sandwiches. Evan snatched three of them: one for him, one for her, and sharing the third with her. Leaning in, he whispered, "These sandwiches do not come close to yours."

She smiled shyly. "Thank you."

Everyone sang Happy Birthday to Macy. After she blew out her number five candle, she chose a chocolate cupcake with hot pink frosting making sure Callie chose her cupcake next. Callie was honored and picked the same cupcake as Macy. Macy gave Callie the sweetest smile. Not only did it melt Callie's heart but Evan's as well. He found himself falling deeper in love with Callie.

The caterer carried a tray of cupcakes through the crowd. When she offered one to Evan, Callie recognized her and said, "Holly!"

Kara looked up and her eyes met a kind familiar face. "Callie. Hi!"

"How are you feeling?" Callie asked in concern.

Kara blushed. "Good. No more mishaps." She shyly glanced at the tall man scrutinizing her. Not in a mean way but with curious worry.

"Evan. This is Holly. Holly, this is Evan my" Callie abruptly stopped, unsure if he wanted her to label him as her boyfriend. In every sense of the word she was ready but since they hadn't personally discussed it she didn't want to overstep boundaries. Fortunately, he pleasantly finished the sentence for her.

"Future boyfriend," he declared, grinning, hearing a rush of hushed voices replaced by a buzz of excited tones of those who had heard him say this.

"Holly's the one I helped in the store yesterday."

Evan nodded, remembering Callie's tale about what happened at the grocery store which led to the stranger asking her to help teach a self defense class. "I hope you're all right," he said.

"Yes, I am. Thank you. It's nice to meet you." She extended her hand, shaking his.

Evan's mom called him from across the room.

Callie was about to walk away but Holly placed a hand on her arm.

"Wait. Could I ask you a personal question?"

"Sure."

"I heard someone say you went missing? Do you mind me asking what happened?" Kara asked.

Callie frowned. She hadn't expected this question.

Sensing her hesitation, Kara said, "Never mind. It's none of my business."

"No. It's okay. I had an unfortunate mishap out on the road."

Kara questioned, "Out on the road?"

After studying Holly's bewildered stare Callie added, "I'm a truck driver for Maslund Trucking, and I was kidnapped."

Kara's heart skipped a beat as she realized Callie was the woman trucker the sister and uncle had been talking about!

Kara couldn't help asking, "How did it happen?"

Callie tossed her head side to side. "I wasn't aware I was being followed until it was too late. I heard an odd noise beneath the tractor rig's carriage so I stopped on the side of the road and…that's when he took me."

Kara openly displayed heartache. "That's horrible!"

Callie sadly nodded. "Yeah."

Kara shuddered remembering the afternoon she was abducted. Like Callie, she didn't know the danger she was in until it was too late.

"Hey, are you okay?" Callie asked. "You look scared."

"Ah, yeah," she fumbled. "I've been in dangerous situations too."

"I'm sorry," Callie empathized. "If you ever need a friend, call me."

"You're offering me friendship? Why? You don't even know me," Kara said astonished.

"Yes and why not? All friends used to be strangers." Callie reasoned.

Kara smiled. "Yeah, true. Thank you."

"You're welcome. Just call me." Callie said.

Kara nodded and said, "Well, I need to get back to work."

"Call me anytime." Callie reminded.

"Yes, thank you." Kara focused her agitated energy on the clean up process. She was eager to be done with this job so she could go home and sort through her thoughts in private.

Callie reached Evan's side and he clasped their hands together. The rest of the party was fun. She enjoyed the conversation with Evan's parents, Eric, and Ellie. They talked about Erin, another sister who couldn't be here due to work travels. She liked his family and was envious of their close-knit relationship. She felt a sense of longing to speak with her brothers and had deep regret for the estranged relationship with her own parents. Evan tugged on her hand. She lifted her eyes to his, and his sparkling gaze made her heart hop.

Throughout the party, Evan had sent his siblings into a tailspin of shock when he shared his cupcake's frosting with Callie, heard him say he was her future boyfriend, and stayed glued to her side publicly holding her hand. His mom, Carol, noted a few changes as well such as, the easy smile on his face when he and Callie's eyes met, she was never far from his view, and his smiled lifted higher every time she laughed or smiled.

Carol had met Callie at Kellan's wedding and instantly liked the spirited young lady. Her cheerful smile had been bright as Evan twirled her across the dance floor. Then Callie had gone missing. The extreme worry Evan had for her, sent him to the verge of being ballistic. Noting his behavior with her today Carol now suspected her son had true feelings for the trucker. She recalled his comment about the right woman being ready for him.

Is Callie the woman he is referring to? I hope not. Carol doubted the spirited young trucker would stay and be with her son. Her heart heavily ached for when the day came and Callie left Evan. Carol cautiously smiled and kindly stated, "Callie, we're all very glad you're home safe and sound."

"Thank you. It's good to be home and safe." She tossed happy eyes at Evan and he beamed a bright smile her way.

Macy opened the last gift, handed it to her mom and announced, "Time to go play!" She ran over to Callie and tugged on her arm begging, "Aunt Callie, come play mosquito ball with me."

"What?" Callie was unsure of the game and gave Evan a baffled look.

He leaned closer, his lips grazed her ear, and his silky voice said, "Its skeet ball, go, I'll be there in a minute."

"Oh, yes, okay." She was flustered by his tickling whisper.

Forty-five minutes later, Macy's smile reached from ear to ear with all of the tickets Callie had won. It was Evan's job to feed the tickets into the machine. The amount of tickets was placed on an in store credit card that could only be used at the gift shop.

"Now it's time for shopping!" Macy clapped her hands together and led them to the game store that was filled with overly priced gimmick toys. With the earnings on her card, Macy was able to purchase three large lollipops and a pink teddy bear she barely got her arms around.

Getting into the truck Callie said, "That was fun and exhausting!"

"It always is." Evan laughed. "She loves this place for the *free* toys." On each hand his first two fingers bent making air quotes when he said free. "It's such a rip off!"

"You were so sweet to pay extra for the bear because she didn't have enough tickets."

"Oh, right!" he laughed. "She plays me for a fool every time!"

Callie laughed hard over his admittance of this. "You're a great uncle!"

"And let's don't forget, in her eyes, you're a great aunt." He grabbed her hand and lifted it to his mouth, kissing it. "Thank you for coming with me today."

"You're welcome. Thanks for asking."

"My family didn't make you feel uncomfortable or unwanted?" He grinned.

She shook her head. "You were right."

"What else was I right about?" he pushed.

"That I would have fun," she mocked.

"We can go home and have more fun?" His blazing eyes drew heat out of her.

"If you promise two things," she bartered, skimming her tongue over her lips.

"What's the first?"

"If you promise to pick up where you left off."

"Where I left off?" he echoed.

"On my ear," she told him, and he grinned.

"Yes, I can." His sultry promise flamed her desire. "What's the second?"

"I want to be your girlfriend," she blatantly announced.

He always adored her direct honesty. "Now or later?"

Her eyes dazzled as she firmly stated, "Now."

Evan pulled her over the console and into his lap. His dark possessive eyes poured into hers, clearly marking her...his. His thumb stroked the velvety skin of her cheek and down the side of her throat, pausing above the shoulder. Then he traced his thumb's path with his mouth. At the base of her neck, his lips engulfed the ridge. His teeth nibbled and drew in her soft flesh. She ardently arched and fire shot into him.

He gritted his teeth and groaned, "Callie, we gotta go."

She pouted her protest.

"If we don't, I'm going to haul you into the backseat." He saw her glance into the rear. "But..." his voice rasped with heavy emotion. "I'd like to take my girlfriend home and make love to her in a bed."

She was swept away. For so long she wanted to be his girl! Flames of passion fluttered in, and sensations swirled everywhere! Her uterus tightened and pooled, aching for him to penetrate the creamy wall he created.

He leaned in giving her a long meaningful kiss. Their tongues plunged, deepening the passion building between them; sharing and tasting their love.

Ending the kiss, her tan tender eyes filled him with warmth, and he softly said, "Callie Cat, let's go home."

Chapter Twenty-Four

Kara flopped on the bed. The birthday party had been fun, but she had no idea how exhausting kids were. They were full of sugar, excitement, and lots of screaming. She laughed because she wasn't sure her hearing would ever be the same again.

Staring at the ceiling she sorted through the day. The most amazing thing to happen was discovering who the woman trucker was! It was Callie! Who helped her in the store! Callie told her she was a truck driver, how the kidnapping happened, and the name of the company she worked for; matching all the information she had heard from the barn conversation.

Kneeling in the closet, she pulled out the "in case of an emergency and had to leave in a hurry" duffel bag. The items she had packed were enough to get by for a few days along with some cash. Picking up the phone, she dialed the number, and waited for Jack's voicemail. Hearing his submarine tone quickened her heart rate and sent silly shivers through her. *Silly indeed, because it's dumb to feel this rush of excitement just by the sound of a voice!* Blaming it on the dry spell of her sex life, she shook off the crazy nerves coursing her veins, took a deep breath and steadied her voice.

"Um, hi, it's me." Her voice rose excitedly as she stated, "I met the woman trucker today, and I'm hoping I can find a way to warn her about the danger she's in. Okay, that's all for now, bye." She ended the call and went to bed.

While Kara slept, Jack listened to the message she left. He noticed the enthusiasm in her voice as she informed him she had met the woman trucker. Looking at his watch he frowned; it was too late to call and instead he sent her a text. His message read: **Please, don't warn her until we talk!** Laying his head on the pillow he prayed she would listen.

****

Kara slept the entire night without any nightmares and woke up Sunday morning fairly refreshed. She checked the emergency phone, read Jack's message, and typed her response: **Ok.**

She showered, dressed, ate breakfast, poured coffee into a stainless steel mug with a spill proof lid and left the house for church. She hadn't had a panic attack since Friday night at the grocery store and was confident she could mix with a larger group of people.

Parking the car, her gaze focused on the tall steeple. It had been awhile since she set foot in a church and wasn't quite sure why she decided to go today, giving credit to the crazy brave force sweeping through her. The pews were full but she found a spot on the outer edge.

During the church service she sang the songs in good harmony and listened to the Pastor's sermon targeting her life.

The congregation dispersed after the last song was sung. People were buzzing with excitement about the potluck right after the service. Kara hadn't planned on staying and was heading for the door when her shoulder was tapped. Turning, she gasped in surprise. "Iggy!"

"You're not staying for the potluck?"

"Um, no."

"Oh, c'mon, what else do you have planned? Surely, you can spare an hour." He persuaded and offered her his arm. "You can keep me company."

"Okay." She smiled and looped her arm through his.

This morning, his assignment led him to church. He hadn't planned on going in, but his curiosity of why the man came here nagged him. Sitting in the back row, he had a good view of people he'd encountered around town. During the greeting several of them came over to shake his hand and invited him to stay for the potluck. Thanking them he made no promises of staying but by the end of the service he felt welcomed enough to stay. Filing out of the sanctuary he saw Holly and decided it would be better to share a meal with a friend in this sea of familiar strangers.

"Great!" Iggy said and maneuvered her through the crowd into an already formed line. "Ooh, we got here just in time."

"You hurried me so we could wait?" She laughed.

"Look at the line behind us. We're in a good spot; guaranteed to get food."

She looked and laughed again.

"You think I'm kidding. I'm not." He smiled.

Iguana saw his assignment walking among the congregation. It appeared his assignment had attended here before because he was knowledgeable of the congregation's dress code of business attire.

Purlieu was the last place Iguana ever expected to follow his assignment to. He was shocked the man had the nerve to come back here. However, the longer he observed, Iguana suspected Purlieu might be the hub of the whole operation! Though his assignment had left town months ago, he had people here continuing the work.

Iguana was close to finding out who in town was associated with the head of operations. He was fairly certain he knew who they all were except one red flag had been thrown into the mix. Before he came to a final conclusion, he needed to rule out the one red flag standing in his way and who currently stood beside him...Holly. He couldn't ignore the fact that she and his assignment kept showing up in the same places. Was it an innocent coincidence or was there a link he was missing?

Facing her, he focused on what she was saying.

"I saw Callie at the birthday party yesterday," she stated.

"Oh?" he said.

"She recognized me from the store and introduced me to Evan."

Iggy grinned sheepishly and said, "I made the mistake of assuming Evan was her boyfriend."

"I don't think you were far off with your assumption, because yesterday at the party he spoke up saying he was her future boyfriend."

Iggy nodded saying nothing.

"Callie's really nice. I like her," Kara commented.

"I asked her to help me teach the self-defense class," Iggy said.

"She'll be good at it. She has this genuine personality everyone loves."

Iggy smiled and said, "I think Callie's one of those all around good-natured people."

"I agree." Kara turned and stared into space. Without meaning to she mumbled her thoughts. "Why would anyone want to hurt her?"

Iggy pounced. "Someone wants to hurt Callie?"

"Somebody did," she said. "Callie told me she was kidnapped."

Iggy's brows rose. "Wow."

"Well, hopefully it's all behind her now," she murmured.

"Unsure, he heard her correctly Iggy asked, "Why wouldn't it be?"

Kara swallowed and gave him a sharp look. "What?"

"Why wouldn't Callie's ordeal be behind her?" he inquired and didn't like the guilt flooding her face.

"People think they're safe and –" she stopped speaking.

Iggy persisted, "And what?"

Kara shook her head and waved her hand. "It's nothing." She swiped the perspiration off her temple. The crowd gathered closer and several perfumes filled her nostrils. The scents shot straight into her brain. Beads of sweat dotted her crown, and she was hot. She heard static and the voices near her seemed to echo just as stars dotted her vision. She gripped Iggy's arm, and her legs felt weak.

The apprehension on Holly's face told him it was something. He wanted to interrogate her, but she swayed and grabbed his arm. Luckily, he caught her upper arms before she crumbled to the floor.

"Whoa. You okay?" he asked, but her starry eyes told him she wasn't. He guided her over to a table and sat her on a chair. "Sit. I'll get our food."

Iggy returned with two plates of food. More than she could possibly eat. He left again and came back with drinks.

"I brought you water. You're sweating."

"Thanks." She wiped her forehead with a napkin.

Sitting down next to her, he handed her the plastic utensils and shot her a worried glance. "You okay?" he asked.

She nodded. "Yeah, I'll be fine."

"What happened?"

She shrugged. "I don't know."

"Yes you do." His eyes probed.

"I'm still tired from yesterday."

"Nope," he said in an aggravated tone. "Try again."

"Okay! Fine! I'll tell you the other reason," she snapped. "The crowd was too close and the too many perfumes made me sick."

This he believed. "There was that so hard to admit," he jested. Then in a softer voice he asked, "So you're exhausted from the party?"

"Yes. There was supposed to be two of us working, but the other girl didn't show up." She made a sour face. "So it was just me."

He sympathized. "That's rough and kids can be draining."

"No kidding! I crashed when I got home."

Iggy pointed to her plate. "You need to eat. Put more meat on your bones. Less you'll swoon."

"Swoon?" She gave him a bizarre look.

"Yeah, swoon." He reiterated. "It happens when you don't eat."

"Not always," she mumbled and stared into his curious eyes. "All the other times I fainted wasn't because I needed to eat."

"So then why did you faint?"

"I have no idea," she said truthfully and became quiet.

"Penny for your thoughts," he drew her out.

"The other day you offered a quarter."

"That's because your thoughts will put me in the poor house." Iggy grinned and she did, too, and this is when he realized that she hardly laughed. He decided to keep their conversation light and airy and the questions he had would wait for another day.

"Are you going to eat the turkey?" he asked.

"No, have it, since you're the one who put it on my plate."

He stabbed the meat with his plastic fork. During the course of the meal they had good conversation. She was introduced to a lot of the congregation, and it surprised her that he knew so many people.

Afterwards, he walked her out to her car. Waving good-bye she realized how much she liked having a friend by her side this afternoon. Not having any friends to confide in or share happy events with was difficult. Iggy was turning into a good friend, but she wasn't able to tell him anything about her past. Wishing she could, she knew if she did it would jeopardize his safety. This was the last thing she wanted, because she had messed up her friendship with Sage; hurting them both. In the end, Sage had forgiven her, but Kara realized she was having a hard time forgiving herself. She had learned her lesson and couldn't risk hurting Iggy. *If anything happened to Iggy because of me, I'd hate myself!*

Kara's bladder nagged her into stopping at a convenience store. Inside, the restroom had three women waiting in line. There was an issue with the plumbing making one stall out of three available. From the irritation on their faces she could tell they'd been waiting a long time. The attendant behind the counter said there was a bathroom outside in the back.

Kara noticed she was the only one taking advantage of the outside restroom and sensed these women knew something she didn't. Stepping into the tiny room the smell of urine hit her nose and now she knew why the other women were willing to wait. She pulled the door trying to latch it. Finally it closed, and she was able to lock it with the dead bolt. The ceramic tile floor was cracked. Some of the white grout had turned black, and she hoped it was dirt and not mold. Hopping from one foot to the other she looked at the stainless steel toilet seat in disdain. With no other choice, she sat.

Finishing up, she washed and dried her hands and slid the lock open but when she turned the door handle it didn't move. She tried again! She pulled and jiggled the handle but it still didn't move! Groaning, she pushed away the panic and forced logical thinking. *I'll call Iggy.* About to dial his number, she heard voices outside the bathroom and quickly realized they were the same voices from the barn! *Crap! I'm stuck here until they leave!* Quietly, she listened to the conversation on the other side of the wall.

****

"Uncle, I saw you this morning five pews back. If you're not careful, people will start recognizing you."

He grunted. "They could care less about me. But, you, Sister, you're popular. You're the one who needs to be careful."

"And your point is?" she sassed.

"I've been following you, and I've seen the places you go. I told you to stay away from that Callie girl."

She snickered. "The places I go are to help the business. As for the other one it's not a big deal."

In a flash, he seized her by the throat, and pushing her, he backed her hard into the outhouse wall. "It will be a big deal if you don't adhere to my orders. Understand me?"

The sister wheezed, "Yes."

He squeezed her throat a little tighter. "Good. Remember I am strong enough to crush you, and I will if I have to."

He released her throat, but his hand moved to her chest, and he kept her pinned as he threatened, "Get your head on straight. I'd rather not run this business without you, but if you continue with this asinine plan of revenge…you're going to force my hand."

"There you go threatening me again!"

"I'm giving you an order!" he spat. "I'm disappointed. It's unlike you to let your pride get in the way of business."

"I hate being humiliated!" she shouted vengefully.

"I don't give a fuck what your reason is. Let it go!"

"*She* needs to pay –"

"No! You need to get over it," he said tightly. "I need you to focus on the load."

"I would, but you haven't told me when it's arriving."

"Soon," he replied.

"I hope you're going to give me a better heads up than *soon*," she snarled.

"Sister, I'll give you a few days notice. Can you work with that?"

"Yes."

"Good. We'll stick with the abandoned barn. It's the most secure place we've got and it's off the beaten path." He laughed wickedly. "I'll be in touch and remember, Sister, heed my warnings about Callie."

She watched him leave. When he was out of earshot, she huffed, "Oh, he is so damn arrogant! Well, I'll show him!"

She gritted her teeth and seethed, "He may be physically stronger, but I have the brains to crush him! He has no idea he's playing right into our hands!" She chuckled evilly, "But he will, and he'll be sorry he didn't listen to me when he had the chance!" she fumed, pounding her fist on the wall behind her.

She was done listening to her uncle. She had her own agenda and it didn't include her uncle being in charge! It was a new generation, and she was going to show her uncle he couldn't control her anymore! The first thing to do was take charge in getting rid of people. She needed help with this and knew exactly who to call; Abel's right hand man. She scrolled through the address book on her cell phone. Finding the name, she pressed it, and then waited for him to answer.

When he did, she purred in his ear, "Humphrey, darling, I need your help getting rid of *someone.* This secret stays between you and me. You can't tell Hank or Abel."

He grunted, "Okay."

"Excellent! I'll be in touch soon with the details." She ended the call, dropped the phone in her purse, and walked to her car, oblivious to the possibility that anyone could have been listening to her conversations.

****

Inside the bathroom, Kara clamped her hands over her mouth. Her stomach riled having heard the sister's purring voice, and her blood ran frigid hearing the uncle's malicious threat and laugh. They were familiar, but she couldn't remember how or where? Terrified, her body trembled. She tried the door again and this time it opened! She ran around the building to her car. Her hands were shaking, but she managed to fasten her seatbelt and keep the steering wheel steady as she drove home; her mind replaying the conversations she just heard.

The uncle warned the sister to stay away from Callie again, and then the sister called Humphrey asking for his help in getting rid of someone. It had to be Callie the sister was referring to.

How can Humphrey be working with such evil people?

Yet her stubborn heart refused to believe he could be as evil as them since his kind rescue stayed fresh in her mind. This was why she was so conflicted when it came to Humphrey.

At home, she ran into the house locking the door behind her. Fear shivered through her again as she headed straight for the emergency duffel bag hidden in her bedroom closet. *I have to tell Jack about this!*

She sat cross legged on the floor holding the emergency phone. This was becoming an unwelcomed habit. She pressed Jack's number and was ready to leave a message, but then she heard his actual voice! Her heart leaped into her throat, trapping the words.

He gruffly asked, "Are you there?"

She stammered, "Uh-uh, y-yeah." She swallowed down her nervous babble. "I-I wasn't expecting you to answer."

"You caught me at a good time."

"Oh-okay," she stammered momentarily forgetting why she was calling. "Um…"

Kara's hesitant tone concerned him. Reading her body language in person would have been a lot easier, but he prided himself on being able to do it via the phone and already knew he wasn't going to like it.

"What's going on?"

"Remember my message about the bad people?" she asked.

"Yes."

"I heard another awful conversation of theirs."

"What! How?" he shouted.

In disdain, she said, "I was stuck inside a disgusting bathroom all because the door wouldn't open."

"Where was this?"

"Outside behind the convenience store," she replied.

"When did this happen?"

"This afternoon, after church," she told him.

"What did you hear them say?"

She sighed then unloaded. "The uncle and sister argued. He was mad with the places she's been to. He told her she needed to focus on the load coming in and said it's going to the abandoned barn but didn't know when it was arriving. Also the woman trucker is in a lot of danger. The sister wants her gone."

"Gone how?" Jack asked.

"Uh, I-I don't know the plan." She cleared her throat. "But I can't sit by and let something bad happen to Callie. I have to warn her! I like her, and I don't want to see her hurt!"

Jack's stomach rolled uneasily. "Callie?"

"The woman trucker who was kidnapped," she said exasperated.

"How do you know her and her name?"

"The uncle said her name to the niece but also Callie helped me with my panic attack, and I spoke with her yesterday while I was at work."

He jumped in. "What panic attack?"

"The one I had at the grocery store the other day. Callie helped me because she's nice and J-sorry," she quickly apologized for almost saying his name. "Nice people don't deserve to be hurt."

"No they don't," he mumbled. "Tell me about your panic attack."

She remarked. "Not much to tell. One minute I was standing and then I was on the floor gasping for air. It's the same thing that happened at the library. I don't know why it happened. Lately, I've been having them off and on."

"What triggers them?"

"I don't know, but I wish I did."

Jack shifted topics. "So Callie's the woman trucker you were talking about in your message?"

"Yes."

"You can't warn her. I don't want you in any danger," he stressed.

"It's too late. I'm already in danger with these conversations I've heard."

He reasoned, "Right now these people don't know anything about you. So let's keep it this way. If you try to warn Callie, in risk of not sounding like a crazy lady, you'll have to say how you know she's in danger. Eventually, word will get out about what you've heard and these people will find you. This can't happen, and I need your help with not letting it happen so please do not warn Callie!"

"But..."

"Tell me where you are. I'll find her and make sure she's safe," he bargained.

Though he couldn't see her, Kara shook her head. "I can't. Dexter warned me of repercussions if I told anyone."

"Even me?"

"Especially you," she informed him.

Interesting, Jack clenched his jaw. An idea popped in. "Tell me four cities within a twenty mile radius of where you are."

Kara named Junction City and four other towns. He didn't like her whereabouts and really hoped Kara had met Callie in Junction City. *Surely, Dexter didn't put Kara in the same town as Iguana's assignment? If he did, it was a risky move and would explain why Dexter doesn't want me to know where she is.*

Jack praised her. "This is helpful, thank you. Don't worry I won't say a word to Dexter about what we've discussed."

"I'm not worried. I haven't spoken with him since he dropped me off here. Are you sure you'll be able to find Callie?"

"Yes." He firmly stated. "Do not contact her or get involved, do you hear me?"

"Yes, I hear you."

In a softer voice he asked, "Where do you work?"

"I work for a caterer."

"Do you like it?"

"Um, I'm not sure. It's okay for now," she said. "Hey, if we're done, I'll let you get back to work."

"Yeah, sure," he agreed nonchalantly.

They hung up, and he moseyed his way back in the compound without suspicion. He retired to the bedroom and climbed into the top bunk pretending sleep when Abel came in. After he heard Abel snoring, he moved to his back with one arm propped behind his head as his thoughts drifted through his phone call with Kara. *Why is she so sure Callie is the trucker who was kidnapped?* The question nagged him, and he had to find out why.

Abel still snored in the bunk below. Not only did Abel make it easy for Jack to sneak away, but the man made himself an easy target to kill.

I wish! Jack screamed in his mind as he snuck out. There were so many nights Jack could've easily killed his crime boss in his sleep but killing him was too simple. He wanted to see the man rot in jail!

Outside, he dialed Kara's number. Her hello was followed by a yawn.

"One more question. How do you know Callie's the kidnapped lady trucker?"

"Yesterday, when we talked, she told me she was a truck driver and had been kidnapped."

On the opposite end of the phone, Jack cringed and was thankful he wasn't facing her. He argued, "Okay but there could be another female trucker who had been kidnapped."

She rolled her eyes at his pathetic attempt of trying to dissuade her and didn't understand why he was. "No, she's the same woman the uncle was referring to."

"How do you know for sure?"

"The uncle said the owners at Maslund Trucking were looking for her, and Callie told me she worked for Maslund Trucking," Kara said victoriously.

Shocked, Jack's jaw dropped. Recovering, he said, "She did, huh?"

"Yes she did," Kara confirmed, sassily.

"Tell me again how you know Callie's going to be harmed?" he inquired.

"I-ah…" Kara contemplated on what to tell him.

"You-ah what?" he persisted.

"After the uncle left, the sister called and spoke to a man on the phone, asking him to help her get rid of Callie," she stated.

An edgy feeling sliced through him. Kara's information was similar to a conversation he recently had. "You heard this today?"

"Yes."

Making sure she was giving him correct information, he re-asked, "They specifically said it was Callie they were getting rid of?"

"Well…" Kara prolonged. "Not in those exact words."

Frustrated, he clutched the air. "What words then?" he asked tightly.

"She asked the man to help her get rid of someone."

"And you just assumed this *someone* was Callie?" He lashed.

"Yes, because the sister doesn't like Callie," Kara defended.

"The man the sister spoke with, did you catch his name?"

She whispered, "It was Humphrey."

What! How in the world had she heard Humphrey's conversation today! It would have been nice believing she hadn't heard it, but Humphrey had only spoken with one female today. Was someone impersonating Humphrey? He had a few hunches of who could, but his quick assessments didn't add up. Fear for Kara lodged in his throat; she knew too much!

She yawned, and he said, "You need to go to sleep." Then he warned, "I need you to be careful."

"I will."

He sternly reiterated, "Really careful."

Jack's extra caution didn't make her feel very safe, but she calmly pushed on wishing him a good night.

Ending the call with Kara, Jack mulled over the possibility of someone posing to be Humphrey. One idea was Abel, but he didn't need to impersonate anyone! All he had to do was find a weak link and make them talk. Second was Iguana, but his friend wouldn't stoop so low. Leading him to Dexter, who would stoop this low, but Jack didn't foresee how it would benefit him.

Which meant he was back to square one; Kara had heard the conversation between Humphrey and the sister. Except, he knew who the sister was and not once, had she ever mentioned the truth about her being Hank's niece!

My God! Eerie shivers waved through him for the golden information he had just discovered. He had a high percentile of where Kara was, and he didn't like it one bit. Dexter said she was safe, but she's not! Questions bounced around in his head. *What is the man thinking? Why doesn't he want me to know where she is?*

Jack's thoughts dragged to the niece. She was the one who requested the *smart girl* be kidnapped and she had Abel help her. Jack wondered where Abel's loyalty laid. Was it with Frank or Hank? What Jack knew of Abel, he suspected his crime boss could be playing both sides and when it came time to choose; Abel would pick the boss with the most power.

His mind rolled back to the conversation Kara heard between Humphrey and the niece. Did the niece want Humphrey's help with getting rid of Callie? If so, Callie was in danger, possibly more so than last time.

****

Jack dialed Iguana's phone number. Hearing his friend's cheerful greeting, Jack said, "Ig, it's good to hear a friendly voice."

"Hey, man, it's good to hear from you. What's up?"

Jack got right to the point. "Were you able to verify Callie's safety?"

"She's safe. Why do you ask?"

Jack said, "I have a witness who has heard conversations about hurting a lady trucker."

"She's doing well. In fact, I asked her to help me teach some self defense classes."

"Ig, you're crazy!"

"True," he snickered. "It's why we make a good team. Is it possible it's a different lady trucker?"

Jack sighed. "I was hoping this was the case, but my witness, she has met her."

Iguana whistled. "Met Callie? This means your witness is near Purlieu?"

"Sounds like it, and I'm having a hard time trusting Dexter's judgment."

"He's a hard one to figure out. Do you need me to keep an eye out for your witness?"

"If you could it would ease my worries," Jack said, gratefully.

"No problem. What does she look like?"

"Shoulder length brunette hair and blue eyes. She's about five eight in height."

"All right, I'll be on the lookout for her. I'll text you when I find her," he promised.

Switching gears, Jack said, "Hey, I've got some information for you."

"What is it?"

"The breeched Memphis load is coming to Purlieu and will be delivered to an abandoned barn. However, I don't know the barn's location or when the load is coming."

Iguana exclaimed, "This is great information! I'll start searching the barns in the area."

"Great! Keep me posted," Jack said.

"I will. One more thing," he began. "You remember the woman I mentioned?"

"Yes. Is hanging out with her helping your cover around town?"

"I think so." Iguana hesitated.

Jack picked up on it, prompting, "But?"

"She's a tad mysterious."

"Aren't all women?" Jack asked.

"True. Except with her it's the things she says, and her mannerism. Every time I say her name, she gives me a dazed look. She enjoys her personal space. If anyone gets too close within her boundaries she turns into a skittish cat. Example, we went out the other night. I walked her to the door, and she was the first woman I've ever met who didn't want a good night kiss. Relief poured out of her after I kissed the back of her hand."

"A woman not looking for romance, does one even exist?" Jack joked.

Iguana stated thoughtfully. "At least for now she isn't which makes her the perfect person to hang with. I'm pretty sure she has ghosts in her closet."

"Well, try not to get too wrapped up in her mysterious past. We can't save everybody." Jack gently reminded him, hating the silence on the other end of the phone.

Iguana cleared his throat. "Sometimes, I wonder if the girl is working with my assignment."

"Really? Why?" Jack asked.

"Often they are in the same places."

"Is it just them in the same place?" Jack inquired.

"No. There's another woman, and she's the one I suspected was the leader here. I want to believe that my assignment and this girl; their paths crossing are purely coincidental. I wasn't sure if I should be taking out the color and focusing on the black and white details."

"Maybe," Jack reasoned then reminded, "But, Ig. The color is what makes you great at your job."

"Yeah, I suppose you're right. Ah, I hate this second guessing. I need a vacation," he griped.

"Yeah, me, too, my friend," Jack agreed. "Don't give up and don't put those blinders on. Keep looking at the color. Hey, I gotta go. I'll check in with you when I can. Good luck."

"Yeah, good luck to you and be careful."

"You, too, brother," Jack mumbled with small affection.

The two men weren't blood related, but when you've fought side by side as the two of them have a certain brotherhood of unity had been formed. He trusted Ig with his life more than any other human being and there was no one better he'd want by his side in a battle than Ig…the man was his brother. A brother he would die for and trust his own life with.

Chapter Twenty-Five

Fingers tightened around Kara's throat, choking her, and she wheezed, possibly her last breath…she gasped and pushed on the heavy body.

"Humphrey," she rasped.

The man grunted. "What did you say, girly?"

Nearby she heard someone say, "Hank, she's Humphrey's."

He loosened his grip but didn't let go of her neck. He licked her cheek, and then swiped his tobacco tasting tongue across her mouth and over her cheeks. He bumped his hard bulge roughly against her pelvic. It made her stomach roll, but she stayed still like a mannequin.

"Girly-girl, it's a damn shame you're not going to market," he grumbled. "You would've brought a pretty thousand." His eyes held vengeful evil.

He punched her hard in the stomach. It took her breath away, and she crumpled in a heap. She wasn't sure how long she lay on the ground in pain, listening to the voices above her. Rough hands picked her up when Hank said it was time to go. She was tossed into the back of a truck with other sobbing girls. At the end of this ride they were unloaded and sorted through again. Some were loaded into more trucks while others weren't.

It was chaotic.

Those that weren't put in trucks were corralled like cattle into a circle. They were on display for the taking as the lawless men chose their unwilling mate and viciously hauled them off kicking and screaming. She, too, was holstered on a hip and flung on a bed…

Kara's subconscious traveled her from the sheds to the middle of a grocery store. Several colorful cans of food lined the shelves. As she was reaching for the can of tomato juice in front of her, malicious eyes vividly appeared, an evil tuba laugh rang in her ears, and a harsh voice sneered, "Girly-girl."

Kara woke up screaming. Though she was drenched with sweat, she pulled the sheet up to her chin. *Girly-girl*, circled in her memory. *Hank, h-he said this to me at the sheds and to someone in the store! His voice is what triggered my panic attack that day. But the voice, the evil laugh belongs to the uncle…* Devastation swooped in and Kara undoubtedly knew Hank was the uncle! *How is this possible?!*

A petrified panic shivered through her making it difficult to breathe. Her breaths became shallow and short. She tried hard to stay calm but couldn't. Unsure of how she did it, she dialed Iggy's number and was thankful he answered. His soothing tone helped her focus on a pulled thread in the blanket. When she was breathing normal again, she apologized for calling.

"No worries," Iggy said. "Are you sure you're okay?" He had been on his way home when she called. Hearing her labored breath, he immediately turned the car around towards her house as he calmly talked to her.

"Yes," she assured him.

"Can you walk?"

Curiously, she answered, "Yes, why?"

"Good. Come open the front door for me."

Inviting him in she said, "You didn't have to come over here."

"Yes, I did. If you had stopped breathing someone had to kick the door down for the paramedics." His firm stance told her he wasn't kidding. He laid his hands on her shoulders asking what happened.

"I had a really bad dream."

He steered her into the bedroom. Lifting the covers he encouraged her to get in. She gave him an uneasy glance. "You're not joining me, are you?"

"I will if you don't get in."

Quickly she hopped into bed. "It's nice of you to come over here and tuck me in."

Covering her, he frowned and sat on the edge of the bed. "Tell me about your dream."

He wasn't surprised when a fearful panic fell into her eyes.

"Holly, I'm here as your friend. I know you trust me since you called me."

She stayed quiet, but he didn't give up. "Listen, I've seen you around town. Majority of the time you're alone, which is okay, but it tells me you don't have many friends. Am I right?"

Her widened eyes said yes, and he continued, "This dream you had was horrific. I just asked about it, and you're scared. C'mon, please tell me. You'll feel better." He coaxed and could tell she was pondering it.

Finally she said, "There are probably some things I can tell you, but there's also things I can't tell you."

He nodded. "Okay. Tell me the things you can."

"Before moving here, I was," she carefully chose her words, "staying in a bad place. The people weren't nice at all. I wouldn't wish my worst enemy to go there." She was struck with a vengeful thought...*maybe Greg.*

Iggy chanced a question. "Tonight's dream was about the bad place?"

She nodded.

"Did this bad place smell good?"

She vigorously shook her head making a putrid face.

He took another shot. "Lately, have you smelled any of these scents?"

Curious caution plagued her. "Maybe, but my panic attack tonight was because of a familiar voice I heard in my dream."

"This voice," he gingerly pursued, "you've heard it in the bad place?"

She nodded.

Iggy boldly continued. "And you've heard it here in town?"

She nodded again.

Holding his breath, he crazily asked, "Is it male or female?"

"Male."

His chest tightened with excitement because she had said so much! "Where in town have you heard it?"

She gave him a hesitant glance before saying, "In the grocery store. I believe his voice is what triggered my panic attack," she stated shyly and rushed to add, "but I didn't know it at the time."

Iggy patted her hand. "I know you didn't. Do you know the man's name?"

"Yes, but I can't tell you. It's too dangerous."

He nodded. "Holly, is it too dangerous for you to know?"

Shrugging, she skirted, "It doesn't matter if it is, because where I was…was a dangerous place."

He didn't pressure her but fear knotted through him.

"Did these people do bad things to you?" he asked.

"Not just me. Other girls too," she sniffed, swallowing tears.

He didn't have the heart to ask what kinds of things. Her misty eyes were enough to break him.

Kara appreciated the friendly comfort of his hand on hers. He was right; she did feel a lot better sharing a part of the secret. She told him he was very insightful. He thanked her, but she wasn't sure if she meant it as a compliment. It was kind of scary how he was able to pull so much information out of her. He was an expert question asker.

"Iggy, thanks for being here for me."

"You're welcome. In case you have another nightmare, I'll be sleeping on the couch in the living room."

"Thank you so much." She smiled.

"This is what friends are for, Holly."

"Well, you're a good one. Good night."

"Night," he wished her, and closed the bedroom door.

Stretching his lean frame on the couch, Iggy gazed at the ceiling while his mind drifted to Holly sleeping in the next room. *Is the voice she heard in the grocery store connected to my assignment? It isn't the first time she's had a panic attack and my assignment was nearby...the library and at church. Is there a connection between my assignment and Holly? But the panic attack at the library and church had been triggered by smells and now tonight she said the grocery store had been because of a man's voice.*

What's going on? What exactly is triggering Holly's panic attacks? Is it my assignment's voice or is it the perfume from the woman he has been following? Could it be both? Or is all of this just coincidental and there's no connection with Holly and the other two?

Iggy hoped it was the latter, because he hated to think Holly could have anything to do with these evil people. For now, he'd keep a keen eye on the mystery laid before him and go from there.

The next morning, Kara saw Iggy's scribbled note next to the coffee pot. *I'll see you later. Call if you need anything.*

It was just as well. She didn't want to answer anymore of Iggy's questions or find clever ways of avoiding them. Besides, this gave her the chance to leave Jack a message about her dream though she wasn't sure of what she should say or how to word it.

Alone in the house, she rehearsed out loud. "Hey Jack. The man who licked me at the sheds is here in Purlieu."

Then it occurred to her that Jack might not have any knowledge of the sheds. *How much does Jack know about me? If he does know about the sheds, does he know about Hank?*

Kara mixed the batter for waffles together, and then poured the liquid into the waffle iron she had purchased at an estate sale in town. She discovered she liked making her own meals and supposed working at the catering company helped with this. Except for the long hours on her feet, she liked her new job helping with food preparation, setting up and decorating for the parties. The last two were her favorites.

Dipping her hands into the soapy water she washed the dishes. The syrup easily disappeared in the warm water along with the coffee stain in the cup. Cooking for one gave her plenty of food. Most of the time she ended up freezing leftovers and using them on a day she didn't want to cook. After cleaning the kitchen, Kara retrieved the burner phone from the duffel bag and rehearsed what she was going to say. Pressing Jack's number, she was connected with his voicemail.

She quickly stated, "In my dream last night, I saw him! I know who he is, and where *our* paths crossed!"

Hours later, Jack called and impatiently demanded, "What are you talking about? Who is he and where have you seen him?"

Irritated by his rude attitude she snapped, "Hi, to you, too!"

"Sorry," he sheepishly apologized. "It's been a rough day."

Kara softened her cranky tone. "I, too, am sorry. I didn't sleep well last night."

"Yes, your dream. Help me understand who it is you saw in your dream," Jack said in a kinder voice.

"I saw the uncle, the man from the conversations I've overheard. Since the barn, his threatening voice and evil laugh were familiar to me, but I didn't know how or where. Then last night I dreamt of the sheds again and this is where I met him face to face!"

"What?" Jack squawked.

"I know you probably aren't aware, of where I was before you and I met in the interrogation room," she speculated.

Jack pinched the bridge of his nose. If Kara had been talking with Humphrey, she could've openly expressed about where she was; since it was Humphrey's cover who had rescued her from the sheds. But currently, he was Jack to her and as far as she knew, Jack didn't know anything about the sheds. This meant he had to be careful with his answers. Cautiously, he said, "I know it wasn't anywhere nice."

"Correct and," Kara stated and continued, "in this awful place called the sheds is where I met the uncle. He was mean and did disgusting things to me…"

Jack didn't want her to go on, but she did, and he had to listen to her recite the physical beatings she received from the uncle. The hand not holding the phone against his ear, clenched into a fist, his nostrils flared, and his eyes shot daggers.

In a weepy voice she finished saying, "He didn't care that he was hurting me."

At this moment, the only wish Jack wanted granted was to be able to touch her through the phone. She needed a comforting hand to hold. Or better, a comforting hug, and if he'd been beside her, he would've have given her one.

"I'm so sorry," he stated with sorrow.

"Thanks," she mumbled and went on to say. "I believe the uncle's voice is what triggered my panic attack in the grocery store, because the words he said to another customer are the same words he said to me at the sheds."

"What did he say?"

She inhaled a shaky breath whispering, "*Girly-girl.*"

The second Kara said this; Jack knew exactly who she was talking about! He gently knocked his fist against his forehead wishing he could tell her that he, as well, knew who the uncle was! Like him, Kara, too, had met the devil, and he hated himself even more because it was his fault. Her quivering voice tormented him, and now, he fully understood why the memories of the uncle haunted her! Listening to the suffering she endured, he guessed this was his punishment for putting her in that damn van, sending her to hell on a coward's debt.

Jack's mind replayed a day in Humphrey's life when Abel said he was introducing him to Hank, the boss man. Prior to the meeting, Jack was extremely thankful he knew nothing of Kara's encounter with Hank. If he had known, it would've been an extremely difficult day for Humphrey, because Jack wasn't sure, he would have been able to keep his emotions hidden while performing his undercover job.

Jack now tried ignoring the panic pricking the back of his neck. *How do I warn Kara of the danger she's in without scaring her?*

Kara's whisper interrupted his thoughts. "Hey, I know if the uncle and sister ever find out about me, it won't be good. But they haven't, and I don't know why they would so…" she trailed off not knowing what else to say.

Jack wryly thought. *Saying, it won't be good is an understatement, but at least she's aware of the danger. For now, all we can do is wait to see what happens. Kara's right. The uncle and sister don't even know who she is, nor do they suspect anyone has been listening to their conversations.*

Taking a deep breath, he cautioned her. "For now, I need you to stay alert. If you sense anything is off kilter –"

"Call you, I know," Kara finished.

"Leave me a message and I'll call or text you when I can," he reminded her.

"Okay," she confirmed.

"So since the grocery store, have you had anymore panic attacks?" he asked and was unprepared for what she was about to say.

"At church, and then after last night's dream I couldn't breathe." She gave a dry laugh. "In the middle of the night, I called…" She abruptly stopped before saying Iggy's name, but Jack caught her pause and sensed her secrecy.

"You called?" he asked suspiciously.

"A friend," she replied lamely.

"Friend, huh," he snarled as his jealousy flared. "So what's your new boyfriend's name?"

"He's not my boyfriend!" she shouted. "He's a friend!"

"Yeah, right," he said sarcastically. His stomach churned thinking about her kissing this *other* man. "Most guys don't come over in the middle of the night for friendship."

Through the phone, his growl intimidated her, and she cringed; thankful she wasn't facing him and since she wasn't, she bravely spatted, "Well, this one does! And if you must know I'm done with men."

Her declaration of no men didn't make him feel better. "Just remember you can't tell your boyfriend anything about your past," he hissed.

"I know!" she declared angrily. "And, I told you, he's not my boyfriend so quit calling him that!"

"You might want to clarify this with him," Jack fired.

His biting tone infuriated her! Silently, she fumed, and refused to voice her frustration on the no win situation. Since Jack had already made up his mind about her friendship with Iggy, she felt there was no need in trying to convince his narrow minded opinion.

Kara's silence depressed him, and it bothered him that she didn't protest more about *not* having a boyfriend. In the end, all he could do was accept the truth and that men were going to be interested in her.

Yawning, Kara said, "If there isn't anything else you need I'm going to hang up and go take a nap."

Not wanting to end the phone call on a sour note, he cleared his throat and in a softer voice he said, "Hey, I'm sorry for snarling. I was out of line."

She was taken aback by his apology. Touched by it, she accepted it. "I forgive you, but you don't have to worry about me. I won't do anything stupid. I'll keep my head low, my eyes sharp and trust my instincts."

He breathed a little easier. "Good girl, you remember."

She heard the smile in his voice and felt giddy.

"Don't hesitate to call about any worries you have." Then he gruffly cautioned, "Be careful."

"You, too, bye," she wished sincerely.

Her genuine concern did all sorts of strange things to Jack's emotions; shaking him senseless. However, until he wrapped up his current assignment and was able to focus on the next case involving Kara, he was going to worry about her.

Ending the call, Kara sighed. She purposely hadn't mentioned the uncle's name to Jack and was thankful he hadn't asked. If he had, she wouldn't have been able to tell him. Saying Hank's name out loud to someone else made it feel more real and scarier. Also, she didn't feel safe saying it in a phone conversation. She would prefer to tell Jack face to face.

Kara put the phone back in the duffel bag. At the time, he had given her the phone; she didn't think she'd ever use it. Now that she had, she was extremely grateful over his thoughtfulness!

If he hadn't, who would she have been able to trust and confide in? It certainly wouldn't have been Agent Dexter because she didn't have the same connection with him as she did with Jack. *Does Jack feel the same connection with me? Is this why he gave me the phone? Or does he give a phone to all his witnesses?* Kara guessed "yes" was the answer to the last question.

Chapter Twenty-Six

Evan parked the truck near the front door of The Gym.

Callie tossed him a frown. "You didn't have to bring me."

He gave her an easy smile. "I know, but I wanted to."

She was smarter as she accused, "You're checking up on Iggy, aren't you?"

"Yes." He nodded then in defense he said, "No one knows his last name!"

"All right, it's a little odd," she agreed, adding, "Glad you're not spying on me."

He opened his door, and she attempted to open hers, but he held her arm saying, "No. Wait."

Through the windshield she watched him walk around to her side. Seconds later he opened the door; offering her his hand.

Taking it she scoffed. "I don't need help getting out."

"No, you don't...but I wanted to." He swung her into his arms.

Setting her feet on the ground he continued holding her. His piercing eyes didn't waver as he whispered, "Callie Cat, just for the record I trust you with all my heart so there's no need for me to spy on you."

Her eyes fluttered into his. Touching his cheek she softly said, "Thank you. It means a lot. I love you."

"How about we grab a bite to eat afterwards?"

"Yes, I'd love to!" she exclaimed.

Sharing her enthusiasm he leaned in and gave her a happy kiss whispering, "I love you, too."

Side by side, hand in hand they walked inside.

Callie introduced the two men. They shook hands; each of them sizing up the other one, Evan more than Iggy.

Iguana observed Evan's reluctance to leave Callie. As Evan left the room, he turned and gave Iggy a cautious glance. Iguana knew better than to assume Evan had left the building. No...he knew those calculating eyes were piercing him from the other side of the large mirrored window.

Iguana began the self defense class by introducing himself then Callie to the six women and two men that were taking the class. They went through the self defense strategies. At the end, the students filed out of the room, and Evan re-entered. Iguana stepped in front of him before he reached Callie.

"Hey, man, I'm not interested in your lady."

Evan gave him a hard look. "Okay. I appreciate your honesty."

He did believe Iggy. All through class Evan didn't see one ounce of interest from Iggy for Callie. He had maintained a safe distance from her, and the other women. He didn't tease or flirt with Callie or the others in class including Holly which made Evan wonder if they were dating. If they are, Evan was impressed with the professionalism Iggy showed.

"Your girl is one of a kind," Iggy stated. "She helped Holly out the other day when so many would have ignored her, and she did it with a level head. She's spirited but wary and careful too. Qualities I respect. I thought she'd be a good example for the others in class."

Evan's eyes held pride. "You got all that in one brief meeting?"

Iggy nodded. "Yes. I've been around the block and have become good at reading people."

Evan liked Iggy. "Thanks for asking her. She's been looking forward to it. Plus, I think it's good for her."

"You're welcome. Thanks for letting her to do it."

Evan chuckled. "She doesn't need my permission."

"Spirited," Iggy laughed.

"That she is," Evan agreed, laughing.

Callie waved to Evan while he talked with Iggy. Her shoulder was tapped, and she turned around and exclaimed, "Holly! You did great in class."

"Thanks, I'm glad you're helping Iggy, and thanks again for helping me."

"Well, if it hadn't been for you, I wouldn't have had this opportunity to help, so thank you." Callie graciously thanked her.

"You're welcome, and I like what you said in class about how danger comes to us when we least expect it. That is so true!"

Callie was shocked by Holly's strong testament. *Was Holly a victim too? Me helping Holly was it a coincidence or an act of fate?*

"Holly, would you like to meet sometime for coffee?" Callie asked.

"Oh, I would love it!"

"Great. Let's meet one day next week."

The women picked a date as the men joined them.

Kara as Holly watched Evan's arm slide possessively around Callie's waist, and his eyes flashed in the same manner, sending the message that Callie was his. Simultaneously, Evan and Callie asked each other. "Are you ready?" They laughed and wished Iggy and Holly a good night before departing.

Kara's eyes followed them out the door, and she hoped one day, she too, could find a loving relationship like theirs. Iggy escorted her to the car. She slid in, fastened her seatbelt, and bid farewell to her friend before driving away. The vehicle in front of her was Evan's truck. She followed them for a little way before they turned into the parking lot of a restaurant. Kara wasn't ready to go home to Holly's house so she kept driving. One of her favorite songs came on the radio. She turned up the volume and sang along and danced in her seat.

Her vehicle crested a hill, and she had a grand view of the surrounding landscape. She saw farming fields scattered with houses, barns and silos here and there, and in the distance was the big lake everyone in town used for recreation. She turned into a grassy driveway with two jutted lines fitting the wheels of a vehicle and guessed at one time it was well used. The path climbed a hill leading to an old deserted homestead with run down barn structures and a dilapidated cement silo. She parked her car behind the overgrown lilac bushes and walked towards a grand old maple tree. She leaned against the sturdy trunk, enjoying the awesome view of the sunset.

While the sun dipped into the horizon she meandered through hip high grass towards the corn field. Intrigued with their height, she stepped between the many stalks. However, she wasn't prepared for the gangly stem leaves hitting her in the face. Dusk settled in making the field darker than when she entered it. She turned, but all she saw was corn and didn't know which way to go! She began panicking and claustrophobia hovered. Remembering how Callie and Iggy helped her, she inhaled a deep breath, slowly exhaled it, and repeated the steps. Closing her eyes, she listened to her surroundings. She heard whippoorwills, an owl hooting…and voices! Carefully and quietly she moved closer. Recognizing the voices she stopped. *Holy shit! It's the uncle and sister again! How do I keep running into them?*

****

"Are you set with the plan?" the uncle asked.

"Yes, you're sending the shipment to the abandoned barn and its set for delivery in three days," the sister verified.

"This new location is the best place we've ever had. It's secluded and no one will suspect a thing."

"You're welcome," she said as though he had thanked her.

"Okay, I'll keep in touch. Three days, Sister, three days." the uncle laughed mirthlessly.

Kara heard a car engine start and then fade away. Thinking they were both gone, she was about to hop out of the field and stopped when she heard the sister's voice say, "Hi, it's me. No. I'm alone. He just left. The plan is still the same. Send Humphrey to help me. I'm going to fuck his one head before I put a bullet in his other one. I appreciate your loyalty, Abel. My uncle has no clue what's in store for him but before he

dies he'll know who breeched Memphis! They all will!" She laughed
evilly.

****

Kara picked the emergency phone up from the bed stand.
Clutching it in her hand, she paced in circles. The information she heard
was dangerous! Jack said to call him with any concerns. Well this was a
major one! No matter what Humphrey had done, she didn't want him to
die! He may have chosen the wrong path but there was some good in him
because he rescued her, and she owed him for that reason alone! She
dialed the number and was disappointed hearing Jack's voice mail.

The words spilled out of her in a rushed, anguished voice. "Oh,
no, no, no…I just heard awful, awful stuff! I don't know why this keeps
happening! I mean it's not like I planned on getting lost in a corn field!
The shipment is arriving in three days and is being sent to the abandoned
barn, but that's not the worst of it! I could be in a lot of danger, especially
if they saw my car and then see me in it! Oh, no! They can't find out
about me! Also, you have to warn Humphrey! He's in really bad
danger…they're going to kill him!"

****

Jack listened to Kara's quivering voice leaving the earth shaking
message. Pressing the phone against his ear, he slipped on a pair of dark
sunglasses and bowed his head shading his reaction. The part about her
lost in a corn field brought a smile but it quickly vanished when he heard
her trembling voice. His jaw dropped when she gave him information
about the shipment! She had no idea how much he needed this! It's what
he and Iguana have needed, and here Kara stumbled upon it!

Then her voice dropped to a bare whisper and her message began
breaking up. The words he heard were "I" and "in danger" followed by a
short pause and then he clearly heard her say, "They saw my car."

Then silence.

Immediately, he called her but there was no answer. In case, she
was sleeping he dialed her number three more times, each time no answer.

He panicked. *Did they find her?! Maybe they didn't find her. With
the crackling phone maybe there were parts of the message he missed.
Yes, this had to be it!*

Glancing at his watch, it was in the middle of the night. *Fuck,
fuck, fuck*! He was left with no other choice than to wait until daylight to
call again. If he knew exactly where she was he would have left his post
to find her. Perhaps the phone was silent while she slept. *I hope!*

Since her rescue she had become a valuable asset to their next case. Losing her would be detrimental to their case and for other reasons he couldn't quite come to grips with. However, he was aware of the increasing concern he had when it came to her safety, and he wasn't ready to lose her in any aspect of his life.

In the morning he called her again. No answer. Throughout the day he called with unhappy results. By nightfall he was agitated and ended up taking his frustration out on one of Abel's new guys by picking a fight with him. Pummeling his fists into the man's gut and face didn't make him any less worried about Kara. Unfortunately, it caught Abel's attention.

"Humphrey, what's up? It's been awhile since I've seen you so worked up. All day you've been pacing and clenching your hands. What gives?"

He started out by apologizing. "Sorry, boss. I feel like a caged animal."

Abel slapped him on the back. "I know how you feel. Lately, I've been feeling like that too."

"Listen, if you're interested I've got a special job that needs your kind of expertise." Abel falsely led, but as predicted his partner's eyes expressed loyal interest.

Abel continued. "You're needed in Purlieu. Wilma called and asked me to send my most trusted man and that's you. Are you up for the task?"

"Yes. Just say when." Jack readily accepted but was leery of the sudden change of plans. He didn't trust Wilma. Many times, he had witnessed her blackmail methods in recruiting allies for Frank. Often she insinuated an uprising was coming and it'd be best to be on Frank's team. Remembering what Abel had told him about the family feud brewing between Frank and Hank, he wondered if the uprising was approaching.

"You leave tomorrow," Abel informed, slapping him on the back. "I hear the shipment is coming very soon. Maybe you can get more information out of Wilma. She seems to like you."

What! Abel knows about the shipment? Why hasn't he told me? Is Abel still legit or am I being played by him, and he has taken sides with Frank? Damn, if it weren't for Kara's knowledge of the shipment, I'd be left in the dark!

"Thanks, boss," he said, sensing the end might be close but didn't know how it would turn out. He'd have to be extraordinarily careful starting with his move to Purlieu.

"No, thank you." Abel fed him more flattering bullshit and wished he could have stuck with the original plan he had for him and Humphrey, but Frank's plan was bigger than his. For now staying loyal to Frank was the better choice. Boy, he sure was going to miss Humphrey. He was the best partner he'd ever had!

****

Evan woke up to Callie gripping his arm and speaking his name. He thought she was awake, but she wasn't. She was in the middle of a nightmare and mumbled familiar words. "Tell Evan I'm sorry."

His hand reached her shoulder; ready to wake her with a gentle shake, but he stopped as she added something new. "You know him?"

He quietly listened as she continued. "I'm so sorry…you couldn't go until it was safe. I wanted to tell him where you were, but I couldn't. It would've jeopardized everything…I'll make sure he finds you. Iguana will protect you."

Evan's eyes widened. He could have kicked himself for waking her up all those other times when she mumbled, "tell Evan I'm sorry."

If he hadn't, they could have found out more information a lot sooner! Frustrated with himself he gritted his teeth. He had assumed Callie had been begging someone to have them tell him she was sorry when this hadn't been the case at all!

She rolled over and continued sleeping. Evan's new thought was *who did she have this conversation with?*

In the distance he heard thunder and hopped out of bed to go close the windows in the dining room. His bare feet padded on the hardwood floor. Lightning crackled and a flash of it briefly brightened the night. Moments later, Callie shrieked and ran down the hallway and collided with him in the foyer.

"Whoa, sweetheart, it's okay."

"Oh, Evan," she sighed with relief. "I was dreaming about- about…"

"You're time in the crate," he said knowingly.

"Yeah," she said dazed.

"You were talking in your sleep. Instead of waking you, I listened." He guided her back to the bedroom. "You said a name I hadn't heard before."

"What name?"

"Iguana," he told her and sat on the bed with his back leaning against the headboard.

She curled into his lap and rested her cheek on his chest. "I remember him. His name is the one I couldn't remember. He protected me until I was found."

"But when we found you, no one else was there."

"He said he had to leave, but help was on its way." She recited.

Evan rubbed her back asking, "What else do you remember?"

Images from the dream flooded her memory. Remembering, she tilted her head back and gave him a confused look. "Humphrey. He said he was sorry he couldn't tell you where I was."

"Humphrey said this to you?" he asked perplexed.

"Yes. He said if he had told you it would have ruined everything he had worked so hard at. He also said he would make sure you…"

"What?"

"You found me." She finished.

His eyes brightened. "Callie! This answers our question as to why Humphrey didn't take your GPS chip, and he let you keep it. My guess is he had a signal jammer blocking us from knowing where you were. When the time was right and it was safe for you to be returned, he released the jammer, helping us locate you."

Her eyes widened with excitement. "Oh! This makes sense."

"Yeah," Evan said in fascination. "The signal is what awakened me."

"What?" she said in disbelief. "Evan, if this is what woke you up, this means you were sleeping in your office?"

"Yes," he said offhandedly. Then realized she didn't know how wrecked he had been when she went missing.

"Evan." She placed her hand on his arm. "Why didn't you go home and sleep?"

"Callie Cat," he mumbled affectionately. "I couldn't leave. What if I left and missed the signal?"

Evan, who had shown her more compassion than any man she'd ever known, just opened the door to her heart. He showed her the lengths and depths he was willing to go for the woman he loved. An insurmountable feeling of joyous love swept over her for the one man her heart truly desired. There was no other man on this earth who would have done this for her. Her heart glittered with gold for the love she had for him.

"I love you, Evan," she cried as tears saturated her cheeks.

"I love you, Callie Cat," he whispered fiercely.

****

Jack called Iguana. "Ig, I'm headed your way, but I'm uneasy about the job they're sending me to help with. I need you to keep a close eye on the *smart girl*. I think she's in danger. I'll explain when I see you." He paused to catch his breath. "Also, I can't get a hold of my witness. The middle of her message was cut off, and of the bits and pieces I did get. It was bad," he stressed.

Iguana heard Jack's anxious agitation. "You've tried calling her?"

"Several times," he said distraught. "No answer. I'm guessing you haven't found her?"

Iguana sensed Jack was at wits end feeling beyond helpless and wished he had better news to give. "Sorry, no. I had a few leads on brunette haired women with blue eyes but they all grew up here and had the yearbook pictures proving it. She must be keeping a low profile."

"Too low," he remarked.

"What happened? Why are you so jumpy?"

"She got lost in a corn field, heard dangerous stuff, and has come in contact with Hank."

Iguana roared, "What! Have you contacted Dexter?"

"No. He'll want to know why and how she contacted me instead of him."

"I don't think he'll care much about the how, but he might question why she trusted you." Iguana pointed out. "How does she fit into this case?"

"She doesn't. She's part of another one." He replied in a clipped tone.

Understanding the severity of the situation Iguana whistled. "Okay, when you get here we'll do an extensive search."

Jack breathed a little easier. "Thanks, man. I'll be there soon."

Chapter Twenty-Seven

Callie had been to Charlie's several times but holding Evan's hand and knowing he was her boyfriend and she his girlfriend was awesome! In the past she'd had this title but with Evan it was different. They weren't afraid to express their love. The kisses were sweeter, casted looks were held longer and there were more fleeting touches.

Since confessing her dysfunctional sleeping habits Evan committed to helping her achieve a normal routine. Most mornings they had breakfast together and on the days they didn't, he made sure she was out of bed before he left the house. Throughout the day they kept in touch through texts, calls, and playing games on their cell phones. Evan used to eat the noon meal with Kylee and Kellan but now came home to be with her before heading to the office. In the evenings, he was home for supper often making it because she didn't know how to cook. She knew how to reheat leftovers in the microwave, make sandwiches, and bake a frozen pizza. She did, however, help with clean up. The time together gave them ample opportunity to talk. It was nice having someone to talk with; telling jokes, sharing fun and fond memories but sharing her regrets and fears was also comforting. Every day she stayed, the less she wanted to leave.

A margarita was handed to Evan. He passed it to Callie and accepted the beer offered to him. They found Kylee and Kellan and conversed with them while The Baker siblings glared at them from across the room. More people came over to say hi; some stayed and talked and others moseyed on. Callie recognized faces but not their names.

After setting their drinks on the table, Evan took her hand and led her to the dance floor. He pulled her close and intimately pressed them together. His grin tilted playfully as his eyes discreetly shared with her, his knowledge of the sexy body beneath her clothes. She teased him by running her tongue across her lower lip. He bent his head and whispered a warning in her ear. His hot breath tickled her skin, and shivers ran down her spine.

She offered. "Let's leave."

His sultry grin said yes. Looking over her shoulder he waved and said hello to friends passing by.

Callie turned to see who he waved to but a permeating smell filled her nose and her vision wavered. She clutched Evan's arm and collapsed.

"Callie!" Evan swiftly caught her in his arms. Cradling her, he carried her through the crowd and outside to the back porch. Sitting down, he looked up in surprise as Iggy joined him, carrying Holly.

Evan gave him an odd glance asking, "I don't suppose she's passed out from the margaritas."

"No." Iggy curtly replied. "Callie?"

Evan shook his head. "Hardly drank her first one." His jaw clenched and his stomach rolled uneasily. How is it two women fainted at the same party same time? It was too coincidental. He took his focus off the other couple and put it back on Callie's mumbling. "Shine the light so I can see her."

"Callie. Callie." Evan stroked her cheek.

She scrunched her face in confusion and lifted a hand to the finger touching her face. It was coarser than the other person who had touched her. This one was warm and gentle versus the cold fingers forcing her chin to move in a direction it didn't want to go.

Opening her eyes she saw Evan. The small smile he gave her was full of worry.

"What…happened?"

Evan shook his head. "You fainted, honey."

She looked up at him in shock and disbelief. "Really?"

His nod confirmed it. He lifted her into a sitting position and Iggy presented himself.

"Iggy," she said in surprise.

"Did you see, smell, eat, or hear something?" Iggy asked her.

"Evan you waved to someone. I was about to turn and see who it was, ugh." She made a sour face. "I smelled something awful." She shivered, and Evan lovingly ran his hand up and down her spine.

Kara woke up in time to see the tender gesture wishing she had a man who cared for her as much as Evan did for Callie.

Callie frantically asked, "Where's the other woman?"

"Holly? Right here." Evan gestured behind him.

Callie looked past his shoulder and gave Holly a fragile smile. Shaking her head, she said, "No. Not her, the other one."

"It's just us, honey." He splayed his fingers over her palm. Turning his head he said, "Holly, why did you faint?"

Remembering who she was, Kara shrugged. She didn't feel comfortable talking to others but Iggy prodded. "It's okay, tell them."

She sighed. "I've been having panic attacks. Certain things set me off."

Callie inquired, "Such as?"

"Ah," she hesitated. "I hear certain words, gruffer tones, um…small spaces or smelling heavy perfumed scents."

Callie narrowed her eyes suspiciously. "Yeah, perfume…that's what I smelled."

Iggy piped in. "You think it was a woman's perfume, not a man's cologne?"

Callie nodded. "Yes."

Iggy inhaled deeply and avoided eye contact with everyone. All the other times Holly had issues, it had been tied to his assignment, but he wasn't at the party. Both women insisted it was a woman's perfume, and he definitely saw a familiar face here tonight! He clenched his hands and swung them behind him. It had to be her! He'd seen her so many times before but had written her off as a link to Holly's attacks. Now, her scent affected Callie too! *What the hell is going on?*

Evan paled as an odd shiver rolled across his shoulders and a prickly sensation like toothpicks poking his skin settled on his neck. Though he was familiar with this oddity; relatively it was a new experience for him, experiencing it one other time…the day Callie was kidnapped. The sensation represented danger. His two best friends, Kellan and Dirk had this same ability, but he never did. However, being friends with them gave him the advantage of it, except for the time they were in the bar fight. Dirk ducked, and he got stabbed with a broken glass bottle. He fingered the spot on his temple. A few inches over, and he would have lost his eye.

Callie felt Evan shiver and saw him touch his scar. She didn't know he had the same warning shivers Dirk had and glided her hand up his arm asking, "Are you ready to go?"

Immediately, he said yes and attempted to pick her up, but she stopped him.

"I can walk. In fact, it'll be better if I do."

Holly and Iggy followed them around the house. Neither of the men wanted to push their way through the large crowd and take a chance on the women fainting again. At Iggy's truck, Evan and Callie said their good-byes and walked towards Evan's truck. Evan helped her into the passenger seat, shut her door then ran around to other side and hopped in. Before putting on his seatbelt he leaned over and kissed Callie.

"I love you," he said smiling.

"I love you," she reciprocated brightly.

He spoke his thoughts. "Isn't it strange you and Holly both fainted?"

She nodded, "Yeah."

"Wasn't Holly at Macy's birthday party?" he asked.

"Yes. She works for the caterer."

He nodded. "And she's the one you helped in the store?"

She nodded her confirmation.

"I wonder what triggered her attack at the store." He mused.

"Huh, yeah, I don't know. Why do you ask?"

He shrugged. "I'm not sure. She's Iggy's girlfriend?"

"I guess so. I see them together a lot."

"As long as he's not interested in you, then it's good." Evan smirked.

"Even if he was interested in me, I'm not interested in him. The man I want is driving me home."

He clasped her hand and held it tight. "I'll drive you anywhere you want to go, unless you want to drive us?" His eyes twinkled.

A bright smile expanded across her face. "No. I'm good. You can drive."

He was speechless. Her statement showed him how much she trusted him! He cleared his throat freeing the emotions stuck in it. Love shined in his eyes when he lifted her hand and tenderly kissed it.

Later in the night, Evan was awakened by Callie sitting on his chest. Her eyes were furious and frightening. She gripped his chin tightly repeating the same words she said after fainting. "Shine the light so I can see her!"

He let her turn his head one way and then the other. The harshness in her eyes lessened, changing to relief.

"Good it's her!" she exclaimed excitedly, and then slapped his cheek so hard it stung. "Thank you, Abel!"

She climbed off his chest and lay beside him again sleeping as though nothing had happened.

Evan's heart thundered. He was stunned and recanted this evening's events. He leaped out of bed in search of pen and paper and found some in the office. He wrote about her fainting, smelling the heavy perfume, adding Holly did, too, the role playing of her dream, and what she said. Recalling, "good it's her" sent chills across his shoulders. While kidnapped she had been visited by another woman. Unfortunately, he had no idea who it could've been. Had she made an enemy throughout these years on the road? Is she still in danger?

Evan suspected deep down in Callie's memory she could describe what the woman looked like. Maybe she'd agree to hypnosis in order to pull the information out of her subconscious.

In the morning, Callie woke up to a sore hand. Immediately, she turned to Evan with panicked eyes. "What happened last night? Why does my hand hurt?"

He smiled. "You slapped me."

"How can you be so happy?" she said devastated.

"It's all right. I'll explain everything over coffee. C'mon."

He filled their mugs then suggested they sit outside. Settled in two lounge chairs Callie gave him an impatient look. "Tell me."

Evan took her hand in his. "Okay, but it isn't as bad as you think it is. Remember the party last night?"

She nodded.

"Do you remember what you said when you were coming around?"

She shook her head.

"You said, 'shine the light so I can see her'."

"So?"

"And you asked, 'where the other woman was'?"

Her tone was flat and full of sarcasm. "Obviously there wasn't one."

Taking a sip of his coffee, he set the cup on the table between them. "But there was in your dream last night."

Her eyes whipped into his. "Really?" she said.

He nodded and told her step by step, word by word, and action by action of what happened in her dream last night.

She gasped. "I can't believe you're not mad at me. Why aren't you?"

"Callie Cat." Sincerity poured from his eyes. "I know you wouldn't deliberately hurt me. If it weren't for the nightmares we wouldn't be having this conversation."

"Why didn't you try to stop me? You know, wake me up."

He shrugged. "I don't know. First I was in shock, unsure of what to do. After I realized you weren't going to hurt me –"

Callie jumped in with "But I slapped you."

He shrugged and continued, "I let you play out the dream, and I'm so glad I did! If I had tried stopping you, I wouldn't have learned so much."

An idea hopped in his brain.

Reading his eyes, she asked, "What?"

"I wonder if we should talk to Iggy."

She gave him a confused look. "Why?"

He shook his head. "I have a feeling he knows something."

Sensing he might be right she guessed, "Something dangerous?"

"Yeah," he said nodding. "How'd you know?"

"Last night I felt you shiver. I didn't know you had them too."

"Never used to until…" Heartache rolled into his eyes.

Finishing his sentence she stated, "I was kidnapped."

He bowed his head and hid his emotions, but she understood his grief and wouldn't let him do it alone. Standing, she coddled him against her chest with her arms wrapped around him. His arms hugged her tight and in her eyes honorary tears surfaced because he was relying on her strength to support him.

Suddenly, she felt the wind storm of his suffering blow into her. He, too, experienced pain from the day she went missing to the day he found her. Then having to helplessly watch her deteriorate each day after bringing her home and never once did she acknowledge it! She did now by brushing her fingers through his hair, striving to give the man she loved the same compassion he's given her.

Evan let the woman he loved console him. She didn't make him feel weak nor did he feel threatened by sharing his pain with Callie. Feeling her understanding of his pain strengthened him, and his love for her!

"Callie Cat, I love you so much." He fiercely stated.

"From sunset to sunset, I love you."

He pulled her into his lap, and together they lovingly held each other.

Chapter Twenty-Eight

Kara was surprised she hadn't heard from Jack. His usual response time was within a few hours; even if it was a short reply texted to her with a capital K, short for okay or a thumb up sign. She worried and wondered if he had tried warning Humphrey of his danger and instead he got hurt or worse, killed! Arriving home after another ten hour shift, she was exhausted physically and emotionally. She drew a bath and then immersed into the deep tub and for awhile the hot water took away her concerns.

Before getting into bed, she checked the emergency phone just in case Jack had contacted her while she was in the tub. She discovered the battery was dead!! The charging cord was loosely connected, and she pushed it in tight and laid it on the nightstand completely unaware of the havocking worry she had created.

In the middle of the night she was awakened by a bee buzzing, but it was the phone vibrating on the nightstand; indicating it was fully charged. There were several messages from Jack; texts and voicemails. Reading them, she cringed. Listening to them, she was devastated hearing his gruff voice.

"Where are you?"

"Call me when you get this message."

"Damn! Send me something so I know you're okay!"

She simply typed. **I'm safe.**

Ten minutes later, the phone rang, and she grumbled a sleepy hello.

"What the hell happened? I've been trying to get a hold of you for days!" Jack roared.

Despite his anger, the deeper timbre of his voice tingled in her stomach. She blushed, thankful he couldn't see it and stammered, "I-I'm s-so-sorry. The battery died, and I didn't know it until tonight."

Jack mumbled a string of obscenities. Then he grunted, "Well, I'm glad the battery was dead and not you."

His abrasive tone contradicted the joyful relief he was feeling.

"Thanks, I think," she said, unsure of how to interpret his curt behavior but if she saw his eyes she would have taken it as a compliment.

"Listen, I can't talk long, but you are okay?" he asked in a kinder voice.

Tears pricked her eyes, but she stayed strong. "I'm good."

Jack suspected she was putting on brave façade for both their sakes and hated that she had to. With everything she's been encountering, she had to be scared! He, too, was scared and it sucked having to listen to her frightened voice. He wished he could give her a reassuring hug and tell her everything was going to be all right.

Kara was about to ask if he had a chance to warn Humphrey but a yawn escaped her, and he said, "You're tired. I'll let you go."

Ending the call, Jack realized he forgot to thank her for letting him know she was safe and sent a text stating this. Her reply was a smiley face. It thrilled him, knowing he shouldn't have been as happy as he was.

Chapter Twenty-Nine

The longer Callie stayed off the road the more she felt Evan's panicked aura. His outer appearance displayed harmony but beyond the layers, his behind the scenes revealed the fear of her leaving him; them.

She tried talking with him about her staying, but he always shook his head and said, "Callie Cat, driving is who you are."

He'd give her a quirky grin and hug her whispering, "I wish you could see that you don't have to choose."

She wished he would just tell her exactly what he meant. Knowing the confusing stare she gave him, crushed him. Why was he so stupid?! She did have to choose! Her choices were stay in Purlieu or be on the road. How did he think their relationship would work with her leaving all the time?! Saying good-bye was never fun!

She liked life off the road. One afternoon Evan came home and found her elbow deep in a stack of paid invoices. Appreciating her initiative, he couldn't help hauling her into the bedroom and showing her his gratitude. The spontaneity of it was enticing, and it was those kinds of moments she will miss having.

The thought of leaving everything they've established thus far depressed her. The truth was she didn't want to go because she loved Evan! Why did he continue questioning her heart? Didn't he know it was his love keeping her here?

****

Evan thought being Callie's boyfriend would have given him a firm rock to stand on but it hadn't. Every day that Callie stayed, was one more day he fell more in love with her and their routine. When she did go, he was going to miss her. A lot! He had become accustomed to sharing everyday stuff with her. He told her stories about growing up in Purlieu and the shenanigans he, his siblings and friends got into. He enjoyed discussing Maslund Trucking business with her, and so much more.

She confided her fear of spiders, worries of not living up to certain expectations; hers, his, and people's, and her apprehension of driving again. This led to the argument they had over and over.

She stated, "If I leave."

He stated, "When you leave."

Evan sensed there was more beneath the surface, but he let the subject lie knowing it was a mistake not to confront it head on.

He brought stacks of papers home from work, intending to finish it throughout the night, but once he walked through the door and saw her smiling face everything else fell to the side.

Being with Callie was his first priority, making her laugh second, and snuggling on the couch watching their favorite TV shows was third. Then carrying her to bed, priceless!

Evan hoped she loved their life, too, so that she'd want to come home to him; them. However each day, she stayed; he sensed the end was coming and feared she'd leave without fully understanding, she was his heart, no matter the distance between them. He had to find a way to express his love before her passive eye rolls, rolled her right out the door without a good-bye.

Words were just words; they weren't going to keep her here forever. He wanted to show her how much he loved her! Buying her a ring wasn't significant enough; it needed to be more expressive. The gift he had in mind would show her how much he loved her!

Stepping through the door, a bell rang above his head, announcing his arrival.

"Hello there," the salesman greeted cheerfully.

Evan assessed the man behind the counter. A salt and pepper beard traced the frame of his round face. His firm handshake, cordial smile, and honorable eyes were welcoming. Immediately, Evan felt at ease with the stranger reminding him of how his dad treated people.

"Good day, Sir," Evan greeted.

"What can I help you with, young man?"

A big grin appeared on Evan's face. "I need a special gift for a very special lady."

"Oh?" the salesman's eyes widened because not many people came in with a special request. Peering into the younger man's eyes, he saw determination and realized this man meant business. His face beamed, and he clasped his hands across his mid section. "Son, it looks like you already have something in mind."

Evan chuckled. "Yes, Sir, I do."

"Hold on. I've got a catalog you can look through." He disappeared into the back and returned with a large hardcover book.

Evan couldn't miss the limp in his walk. Rifling through the pages he made small talk with the salesman and discovered he was a war Veteran wounded on duty. He respectfully thanked him for his service to his country.

"Thank you," the salesman said appreciatively.

Evan found the item he wanted and placed the order making the required down payment. He shook hands with the man and exited the store whistling a happy tune.

****

Cupping her left breast, Evan kissed her shoulder and nuzzled her neck. The sexy whimper she let out was music to his ears as were her satisfying cries five minutes ago when they tangoed through tangled sheets. He had awakened with a hearty appetite, as did she, and offered him the feast he craved.

"I will never get tired of kissing this spot," he declared lovingly.

"Hmm," she murmured, "The same."

"Good, how about every morning," he stated with little question and gave her a deep meaningful kiss that rocked her senseless.

Callie felt his love. It was powerful, overwhelming and a bit intimidating. Hastily, she pushed on his chest. He leaned back with concerning eyes, and she gave the quick excuse of having to pee. Leaving the bed, she fought the urge to run back into his embrace and have him hold her while she sorted through her confusion.

At breakfast, he asked about her plans for the day.

Insanely, she heard domination in his voice. Of course, she was wrong, but it didn't stop her firing off her list in a sassy tone.

Hearing she was having a pedicure, he lifted her foot and set it in his lap. His eyes glittered and his hand slid over her foot, up her shin and down her calf.

"Sexy, lady," he basked brightly.

She loved him and didn't understand why she felt weird. Spontaneously, she jumped into his lap and hugged him hard.

Her lingering hug made him uneasy. "Callie, you okay?"

"Yes. I just feel like giving you an extra hug." She buried her face in his chest.

"Okay. If you need to talk, my day can wait." He offered.

She shook her head and looked him in the eye. "I'm good."

Evan was hesitant about leaving. Something wasn't right, but he couldn't say what. "I will see you later? Yes?"

She forced a smile. "Yes."

He left, but a mile later, he brewed the idea that maybe he should turn around and go home. If he did, he didn't know what to say, though deep down he knew what needed to be said. The subject they had easily hidden in the shadows had surfaced. All of a sudden he felt he was standing on the edge of the cliff. The talk of their future was approaching.

Evan doubted Callie had entertained the idea of having the best of both worlds; him and her career. She needed help seeing this option. In his mind's closet an eerie feeling slithered in that he was running out of time. They needed to talk! Surely, this wasn't the case. Or was it? She had glowed at first light but since then she had become squirrely. His brain raked for clues explaining her withdrawn behavior.

Arriving home at noon, he was disappointed she wasn't staying to eat due to the fact that her nail appointment had been moved to twelve-thirty. Making light of the situation he said, "I can't wait to see the color you pick."

Her eyes narrowed and in a displaced tone she said, "So you can't wait to see the color I choose; but you can wait to see me?"

"And the sassy cloud remains," he huffed, but his heart prompted him to keep her here a few minutes longer. *I can't let her leave on this sour note.*

Evan's grim face worried her. She hated how snotty she felt on the inside and how it was reflecting her outside. There was no point in wishing she could take it back because it was out there. *I need to go before I say something regretful.*

Stepping into her space, Evan cupped her face as his honest, sincere eyes rested on hers. "Callie Cat, without you, my world is dismal. The minute I hear your voice or see your face my world is bright and…"

He paused, making sure she was listening. Seeing her intent stare, he continued in a whispered plea. "I just want time to stop, so we can be us; with our talks, our secrets and so much more."

"Evan," she said teary-eyed. Even after her sassiness he still wanted her.

"Callie." His thumbs caressed her cheeks. "When we are apart, I am counting the hours and minutes until I see you."

She nervously asked, "What if we are apart for days or weeks?"

"Then I'll be counting the days and weeks until you walk into my arms again." He kissed the bridge of her nose.

She believed he would truly treasure her return. He made her feel so important! *Is it fair of me to leave him? What future do we have if I'm gone all the time?*

Callie's apprehension worried him as he drew her closer. He tenderly brushed his lips against hers. His fingers intimately roamed the skin beneath her blouse. Desire coursed his veins, and his tongue sank deeper.

The heated rays of his passion scorched her skin. Callie ached for the fiery release only he could give with the touch of his mouth, hand or cock. She leaned in, and he gripped her ass grinding his arousal against her pussy. She heard a buzz but ignored it as her hand skimmed the waistband of his jeans, unfastening the button.

Then they felt the vibration of her phone in her pocket, reminding them of the nail appointment.

"Callie –" he hesitated then took a chance on expressing what he felt. "You mean a lot to my heart."

Slobbery tears threatened to fall and before they did she threw them into a suffocating hug with her face buried in his neck. She let his strong embrace shelter her. If she continued her driving career there would always be these kinds of moments of never wanting to let go. If she stayed, there would be more commitment to each other. However, she didn't know if she could stay. She really wanted to, but what if she couldn't? It made her want to break into a cleansing cry and never before had she wanted to cry for the sake of it. *What is wrong with me?*

Her phone sounded again.

"Your nails," he piped up. "You have to go. Take my truck."

He gave her the keys and a quick kiss before letting her leave. "Text me when you're heading home."

"Okay."

All afternoon Evan was uneasy with her good-bye. His only assurance of her not taking off is that she was driving his truck. She had hid her face from him after he said the part about how much she meant to him. He might have messed up the delivery but when it came to speaking his true heart, he didn't have any experience with it. He never loved anyone, like he loves Callie. With previous girlfriends he used the word love in description. He loved their hair, eyes, outfits, loved being with them but not that he was **in** love with them.

He prayed the pedicure did some good for her and by this evening she'd be ready for a discussion about their future. The time had come to show Callie he was the man of her dreams and prove to her that she CAN have everything her heart has ever desired!

****

The nail tech applied the oatmeal scrub on Callie's feet and lower legs. The massaging and having soft skin afterwards were her favorite parts of the pedicure. She couldn't wait to glide her hand over the smooth surface. Memories of Evan caressing her leg with kisses appeared in her mind. Is this why he inquired about her appointment today? He was looking forward to kissing her there again? If he was, she wouldn't object. The sexy sensations he had stirred last time had been divine! In fact, Evan was the best lover she ever had! He was generous, paying attention to her likes and dislikes, striving for successful satisfaction for her and him.

She regretted having been bitchy when she left this afternoon. There was no harm with her boyfriend asking her plans today. She shouldn't have overreacted and wondered why she did. She chose his favorite nail color with hopes of it helping with her apology later on.

After Kara picked out her nail color she saw Callie and sat in the chair beside her. "Callie! Hi."

Turning, Callie smiled at her new friend plopping in the chair beside her. "Hi, Holly, how are you?"

Smiling, she said, "Good and you?"

Callie shrugged. "I don't know. I feel a little off today."

"Yeah, I know how that goes." She answered truthfully, wishing she could elaborate.

"Anything you want to talk about?" Callie asked.

"No not really." She shrugged. "What about you?"

Callie sighed. "Evan asked me a question, and I misread his tone and got all huffy. I know now he didn't mean anything by it, and I feel bad for overreacting."

"Sorry." She empathized. "I wish I had advice to give, but I'm not good on giving relationship advice. I have no luck in that department."

"Aren't you and Iggy dating?" Callie curiously asked.

She verbally stumbled. "Uh…well…uh, um, I hadn't thought about us being an item."

"Hmm, I just assumed. I'm sorry, I shouldn't have," Callie apologized.

"No worries. It's just that I came from a really bad relationship, and I'm not ready to start a new one. Iggy's a great guy but the timing isn't right for me. So right now we are friends."

Callie nodded. "He's okay with the friendship?"

"Yep."

Callie nodded again and realized Holly probably didn't see the concern and worry Iggy had for her. Callie had seen his concern for Holly in the grocery store and often in self defense class. Not many men expressed this emotion for another person if they weren't interested in the woman.

"Have you had anymore panic attacks?" Callie asked.

She shook her head and shrugged giving a non-committal answer. "Just when I think I have them under control another one sneaks in."

"Have you figured out the reason why you get them?"

"Not really," she spoke the half truth and then openly admitted, "And they seem to occur in the strangest places."

"Experts say certain things can trigger memories that have happened throughout our life. Some believe the brain is still one of the greatest mysteries scientists have yet to solve," Callie commented.

"Along with outer space," she said, laughing.

Callie laughed, too. "I like the color you picked for your toes."

"Thank you. It reminded me of the ocean."

"I love hearing the waves," Callie gushed.

"Yeah, after being cooped up for so long it was nice smelling the saltiness in the air. I could almost taste it," she said with a bit of melancholy, quickly realizing she had just voiced her thoughts.

"What?" Callie asked in an alerted tone, and Holly's distressed expression greatly concerned her. However, before she could investigate more, Callie heard a familiar voice in the chair beside her. Turning her head, she saw Evan's sister, Ellie, and greeted her with a smile, and then introduced Ellie to Holly.

Ellie leaned over and shook hands with her saying, "Hey, didn't you cater my daughter's birthday party?"

"Yes," she verified.

"Yeah, I thought so." Ellie smiled. "My daughter loves your purple hair! By the way, you did a fabulous job at the party. You kept the kids happy and they listened to you. I was so impressed. If you ever need a work reference let me know, and I'll give you a good one."

"Thank you for saying so," she said shyly, liking the woman, but deep down Kara didn't feel worthy of the Ellie's compliment.

If Callie and Ellie knew anything about the real me and why I'm pretending to be Holly, they wouldn't be so nice. I wish I could tell Callie of the danger she's in but the nail salon isn't the place to have this kind of conversation.

Remembering Jack's warning, about how Callie might think she's crazy. She didn't care; she would risk her sanity if it meant keeping her new friend safe. She leaned back in the massaging chair listening to the other two women talk.

Ellie asked Callie, "Did our mom call you about our sister's birthday?"

Callie shook her head. "When is it?"

"It's in a couple of weeks. My mom wasn't sure if you'd be here but if you are we'd love for you to come."

"Why wouldn't I be here?" Callie curiously asked.

"Mom said you might be gone by then."

"You mean gone on the road?"

"Yes." Ellie nodded. "I told her if you knew in advance you could probably make sure to be back by then."

Ellie's smile was genuine as she added. "We'd love it if you could make it."

Hurt by their mom's assuming statements Callie forced a smile but didn't make any promises. "I'll see what I can do."

Ellie clapped her hands together. "Excellent! If you can make it, Macy will be thrilled!"

The nail tech finished Callie's pedicure and she abruptly announced, "Well, I have errands to run. I'll see you two ladies later."

Callie got up out of the chair before either of them could protest her leaving. The conversation with the ladies was a nice break from her harassing thoughts about whether she should hang up her keys or keep driving.

She liked the adorable life, she and Evan had settled into. It was going to be hard stepping away from their cozy routine; predicting they both were going to have a hard time being separated. Neither heart was going to win. They should have discussed this end result before things started getting so serious and closed in.

Evan wanted to talk this evening. The most dreaded conversation she had been avoiding was now nipping at her heels. She had to face reality. Evan had been right all along! It wasn't IF she went back on the road, it was WHEN. Time was no longer on her side, and she had to be honest with him and say what was in her heart. Unfortunately, she still had two loves; him and Sunbird, and she still couldn't choose which one she loved more.

Callie took a right out of the salon parking lot and drove the half mile to the gas station and pulled up to a pump. Hopping down from the truck she opened her purse and took out her credit card bypassing Evan's. He had insisted she use it for purchases around town and wouldn't take no for an answer. Without arguing she took it but hardly used it. She, too, had pride. Pushing her card into the slot the person at the next pump smiled and wished her a good day. She appreciated the friendly atmosphere of this town versus just being another trucker out on the road. Placing her credit card back in her purse she tossed it through the driver's window and it landed on the front seat. Another familiar voice called out to her. Kylee was fueling her vehicle on the opposite side.

"Hey, hi," Callie greeted.

Kylee pointed to Evan's lifted dually and snickered, "I don't know how you drive that big thing. This one," she threw her thumb over her shoulder, "is just right for me."

Callie laughed, "Kylee. Have you seen Sunbird? Evan's truck *is* small!"

Kylee gave her a thoughtful glance saying, "Huh. I never thought about it like that before."

Kylee's thought process lingered into *and neither has anyone else in town. I now have the answer to everyone's question of why Callie doesn't drive a smaller car!* She remembered hearing the story the first time Callie drove Sunbird through town. Poor Mrs. Patters had thought the sun was falling out of the sky! She would have loved to have seen the shock on the ol' busybody's face!

"Hey, I'm glad I ran into you," Kylee said and reached into her purse. "I have the recipes Evan asked for." She handed Callie a small stack of 3x5 cards.

Callie took them saying, "I'll make sure he gets them."

"They're not for you?"

"No."

"Oh." Kylee gave her a troubled expression. "I thought you asked for them."

Callie shook her head no. "Why would you think that? Did Evan say I did?"

"He didn't. I just thought you were going to cook."

"Why would I?"

Kylee's eyes widened in surprise, and her tone matched. "Why wouldn't you? It's what we women do."

Callie's eyes were blank. "What do you mean it's what we do?"

"Cook," she stated abruptly.

"I don't cook," Callie told her.

"Well, yes, I assumed you didn't when you were driving, but now that you're not, you have access to your own kitchen," Kylee rambled.

Callie stubbornly stated, "It's not *my* kitchen. It's Evan's."

"Well, you know what I mean. You have a kitchen accessible to you. I thought maybe you were going to practice. So you could, you know…" Kylee trailed off.

Callie didn't know. "I could what?" She thought for sure Kylee was going to faint over her aloofness.

Exasperated, Kylee said, "Callie, how do you expect to get a man if you don't cook?"

Callie gave her an absurd look. "I'm expecting him to fall in love with me for the person I am."

Kylee tipped her head. "Sure there's that. But first you have to lure him in."

"You're saying, in order for me to get a man, I have to cook for him?" Callie snidely remarked.

Kylee heckled a laugh. "Yes silly! Every woman knows a way to a man's heart is through his stomach."

Callie scoffed. "That's ridiculous!"

"It's not," Kylee protested.

"It is," Callie argued as she placed the gas nozzle back in its cradle. Shaking her head she ridiculed, "As if that would actually work."

"It does and it has." Kylee's tone was ruffled.

Callie stared at her in disbelief. "And this worked with Kellan? This is how you won his heart?"

"Yes it is!" she said convincingly.

Callie could tell Kylee truly believed this, but it was absurd. However, if there was any truth to it, which there wasn't, but if there was…she could be single for a long time! She had no idea how to cook! Or where to begin!

"Try it. You'll see," Kylee encouraged. "Try the recipe on top. It's easy. It has the key ingredients needed for a meal."

"Which are?"

"Meat, potatoes and vegetable," Kylee informed.

"Aren't potatoes a vegetable?"

"Let me know how it goes," Kylee said before getting in her truck and she in Evan's.

Callie waved bye and set the stack of recipes in the opposite seat. All the way home conversations rotated in her mind. Starting with Mrs. Nichols assuming she'd be on the road to Kylee assuming she had to learn how to cook to get a man! Gosh, if this is what her future held for life here in Purlieu she didn't want it!

Suddenly! She was facing the truth of what she didn't want…she didn't want to take care of a household! Not now not ever! It was one of the reasons she left home all those years ago; rebelling against her parents and why she continued leaving; breaking up with boyfriends. How is it after all these years she was staring down the barrel of another loaded scenario with the one man whom she thought had accepted her for her! Only to find out he did expect her to be somebody she wasn't and never would be!

Which meant there was some truth to what Kylee said about the trail leading to a man's heart is through his stomach. And here she thought Evan really loved her inside and out. He had lied, saying he didn't care that she was a truck driver but deep down he did, because asking Kylee for the recipes proved that he, too, just wanted a woman to take care of him. Feeling betrayed, crushing tears stung her eyes.

She parked the truck in the garage, picked up the recipes and headed inside. Carelessly, she tossed the cards on the counter. They scattered into a messy pile just as Kylee's words rushed into her memory about the top recipe was easy and now she had lost it! Browsing through the pile they all looked hard! It just proved she could read a map and navigate her way through the roads better than she could read and follow a recipe!

She bowed her head into her hands agonizing over her options: stay and pretend to be somebody she's not or leave and stay true to her own self. Her heart cracked knowing the second option was it. *His mom isn't expecting me to stay so why should I?*

Her throat constricted and she sucked in a deep chortled breath. Angry, confused tears glistened in her eyes, but she was too wrought for them to fall. *But, I'm happy here!*
Suffocating images of dirty laundry piled high, kids with snot dripping from their noses, and a wailing cry from their tiny lungs wreaked havoc on her fears. She couldn't be a wife or a mom! She didn't know how to be a good one!

All she was good at was being a great truck driver. It was time to go! After all these years of finding herself, she couldn't lose herself by staying and pretending to be someone she wasn't! She wasn't a homemaker! She was a truck driver!

"Evan will hate me, but he'll just have to understand I have to go." She spoke out loud, unaware that she wasn't alone and jumped when she heard his frantic voice from behind.

"Where are you going?" His demand was rushed.

She twirled viewing his crushed face. "I'm sorry, I have to leave here."

"You mean back on the road," he guessed hotly.

"Yes."

"What? Why?"

"I can't be what you want me to be."

His heart absorbed her scared eyes. "And what is that?" He reached for her, but she backed away as though he was on fire.

"A homemaker," she hissed.

Perplexed he said, "Who says you do?"

"Apparently you are."

"What?" he said confused.

"Yeah!" she roared. "I saw Kylee today and she gave me these." She picked up the recipe cards and shook them in his face.

"What are these?"

"Recipes!" she shrieked. "That you asked her for, for me!" Her eyes blazed into his baffled ones.

She continued in an accusatory tone. "Why did you? Now that I'm not driving, you're expecting me to cook and clean." She took a deep breath. "If I stay—"

"What do you mean *if* you stay?" he bellowed. "I thought you wanted to. I've never pushed you into staying."

She gave him a speechless stare.

"If *you* don't want to stay…then go!" he roared. "I won't stop you *especially* if you don't want to be here!"

"I want to, but I can't!" She started.

He shook his head and waved his finger in front of her. "Oh, that's complete bullshit and you know it."

"Its not!" she protested unable to stop the fear rambling out of her. "I thought you were different, but you're like everybody else. You're trying to change me make me into somebody I'm not!"

He gave her a wounded look. "I've never."

Taking a deep breath, she barreled hurtful words at him. "You're just like my mom. You don't care what I want!"

His pained gaze cut into her. He was devastated hearing her compare him to her mother. A hopeless cloud hovered between them, and she was struck with an infinitive reality. Evan *did* care about her!

What is wrong with me!

Her monstrous behavior caused her severe guilt, and she couldn't bear witness to the disappointment she had caused. It was time to leave on the windstorm she had created. Running out of the house she quickly climbed in Sunbird's cab where she belonged. This had always been her sanctuary and now her bitter tongue drove her to the obvious of – it always will be. She tried life off the road but failed. Now she was going to do what she did best in life; be a truck driver. *Good-bye Purlieu!*

Chapter Thirty

Evan moseyed his way to the back door and caught a glimpse of her scowl through Sunbird's windshield. He didn't run out to stop her. With a sunken heart he leaned his shoulder against the door frame and let her go.

Was this her good-bye?

Fine if it was! He was furious with her jumping accusations and refusal to hear what he had to say! *And what do I have to say?* He stacked the recipes into a neat pile trying to recall when and why he asked Kylee for them. He was fairly sure they had nothing to do with Callie and...

Yes! He snapped his fingers. *My sister asked for them! But then Kylee assumed they were for Callie. And why did this assumption bother her so much?*

Groaning, he rolled his eyes. If only she had had the courage to talk instead of running away!

"Which is what she's good at," he muttered in disdain.

Two hours later she hadn't returned. He had moved past angry into a pissed aggravation about the way she took off. The nagging thought that haunted him all day told him he should have expected this, but he truly intended to capture her apprehension this evening. He was no different than anyone else on earth; always thinking there was more time; another tomorrow. If only she had trusted him. Delay her leaving by a few hours. He was convinced he could have talked her off the fleeing ledge. If he had driven her to the nail salon it might've saved them both a lot of heartache.

Yet...would he just have been prolonging the inevitable?

How many more conversations would they need to have before his comfort level was stable with her not leaving? Is this what their relationship would be like, him trying to convince Callie that their love was worth it?

He never wanted it to be his love keeping her here, because eventually it wouldn't be enough for her to stay. Had they reached this point?

He wanted her to stay not just for him or for her; but for them and their love! The ultimatum he had heard earlier of her saying she was leaving, and he would just have to understand, isn't what he wanted to live with! If he hadn't arrived when he did, she would have done exactly what she promised not to do; leave without saying good-bye, and he wasn't sure if she would have even left him a note!

Another hour passed marking it three hours since Callie drove off. Sinking into the couch he fretted about her return while one question harassed him.

Is she coming back?

He would have felt better if she had taken his truck, but she had taken Sunbird. There was no telling if she'd be back. He could check Sunbird's whereabouts but already he knew the many miles that could be traveled in a three hour stretch. Facing the truth that she was gone would undoubtedly push his cracking heart over the edge.

Distraught tears stung his eyes.

His spirited Cat was spooked and running away again. All because of some stupid recipes! It was heart wrenching because there wasn't a damn thing he could do about it except wait. Wait for her return, but this time he wouldn't be bringing her home; she'd be bringing herself home.

Chapter Thirty-One

In Junction City, Callie parked Sunbird at the supercenter. She had turned into a claustrophobic cat ready to claw her way out of the cab's small enclosure. Her mouth was dry and she was sweating! Needing air she rolled down both sets of windows catching the cross breeze flowing in. She stuck her head out of the driver's window and gulped in fresh air while airing her clinging shirt. A vice gripped her heart squeezing it as if it were an orange. The drive here was unbearable! The walls were too close! She missed the spacious interior of the house where she could move freely. Here she was confined to sit with a tight seatbelt. Tears clouded her vision and fear pricked her skin as she fell into a pit of anxiety. She was hardly an hour from Purlieu! How was she going to be able to drive long distance? Had she lost the ability to drive?

Somehow during this time away from the road she had become stuck between a career she loved and a domestic life she despised. Laughing dryly, she was well aware of the irony of it all.

She climbed down out of Sunbird's cab and headed inside the store. In her hasty flee she hadn't had time to pack. The first aisle she pushed the cart to was bottled water, and then browsed the aisles for plastic ware, paper plates, and napkins. She chose a pre-made deli sandwich, a bag of chips, and yogurt. Yogurt was a staple food for her on the road, but she hadn't touched it one time at Evan's. She hadn't even missed eating it. There were so many other delicious choices at his house, such as, cereal, frozen waffles, and of course the eggs Evan made.

She stared at the flavors of yogurt, unsure what to pick. Her eyes drifted to the egg cartons. She was going to miss having eggs in the morning. No. She was going to miss the man making them. She strolled past the bread remembering all the times she helped make toast. Glancing at the throwaway utensils and paper plates in the cart made her think of the dishes in the dishwasher. She was going to miss the cute tractor mugs, and then there was the laundry. Will Evan miss her folding his clothes? She'll miss smelling the combination of dirt, grass and hay on his farm clothes as she dropped them into the washer. But mostly, she'll miss Evan's scent of vanilla and almond after the shower or the feel of his smooth muscular body against her skin while they made love.

In the shoe department she browsed the boots and then looked down at her sandals. She'll miss showing off her pretty toes after having pedicures. Evan always liked the colors she chose. *Huh, if I hadn't gotten a pedicure today, I wouldn't have discovered the truth about Evan secretly asking Kylee to give me recipes.*

His expectations were so obvious! He wanted her to learn to cook so...*I'll have supper ready for him? Then he'll expect me to clean, run errands, do laundry, and...wait.*

She frowned. *Shit! I'm already doing some of these things! And Evan never asked or expected me to do them. I'm the one who decided it might be a good way to stay awake. Did Evan think cooking might be another way to help me keep busy?*

Her tummy growled. She paid for her purchases and headed towards Sunbird. In the cab, she ate her meal on her lap table, already missing the sturdy oak table and the company of the man who owned it. Again she was faced with choices: Adventure of the road or the adventure of her heart.

Floating in her memory was one of their phone conversations about her finding a man who wouldn't give her ultimatums. She had said a man like that didn't exist, but he was insistent a man like that did exist. She sat up a little straighter.

Had Evan been hinting he's this man? He'd stated many times he has accepted her for the person she is. Up until today she had mostly believed him.

She should have trusted Evan that there was a perfectly good reason for him asking Kylee for the recipes. Maybe he wanted them himself. Callie now realized Kylee hadn't actually **said** anything but insinuated a lot!

If she had been paying better attention to Evan's hidden hints she would have known exactly where his heart laid; with hers. Earlier, he said she meant a lot to his heart but what he meant was, he loved her, and hoped he hadn't scared her. But he had spooked her before this with his innocent comment about kissing her every day. *This is what scared me! It's not fair to Evan for me to be spooked by this kind of loving comment. He had been expressing his heart, and I stomped on it like it was a grape! Shouldn't the man I love, have the right to wish for a future with me? I am a fool for not allowing my heart to love! I shouldn't be so skittish when it comes to making a commitment to the one man I love, because he loves me and all my faults!*

She owed it to Evan, her heart, and their love to go back to Purlieu. She scolded herself for not trusting their love. If she had, then all of Kylee's stupid innuendos of how to win a man's heart wouldn't have shaken her ground. It was time to be an adult and stay instead of running away like a tantrum child. If she had stayed and given Evan the chance to explain, she could have saved them both from this heartache.

She had to go back and listen to his answer about the recipes. Making the decision to head towards Purlieu, her seatbelt didn't feel as

tight as it had when she had left. The tightness in her chest had
diminished and so had the anxiety of being enclosed. Her skin tingled
with dancing thoughts of being in Evan's arms. It made her wonder if
choosing life with Evan in Purlieu was where her new adventure began.

****

Evan woke up when he heard Sunbird's diesel engine outside in
the driveway. A thrilling excitement waved in, but he forced himself to
remain calm, rationalizing she was here to pack up her stuff. He stayed on
the couch waiting, listening for her to come in.

Callie tiptoed through the garage door leading into the house. She
was about to flip the light switch on in the kitchen but stopped. Evan's
feet dangled at the end of the couch. Stepping closer he appeared to be
sleeping. Torn between waking him and letting him sleep she turned away
and missed him opening his eyes.

He cleared his throat, and she yelped her surprise and faced him.
"Sorry, if I woke you."

"Are you here to pick up your things?"

"No."

"You were gone a long time," he mentioned flatly.

"Yes. I'm sorry if I worried you."

"Worrying about you is what I do," he said in defeat.

"I'm sorry," she apologized again, because she didn't know what
else to say. He didn't say anything and she began to ramble.

"Well, the farthest I got was Junction City. The walls were caving
in, making it difficult to breathe. I pulled into the supercenter and
wandered the store for awhile and did a lot of thinking."

She stepped closer. "I overreacted, and I'm sorry."

He grunted and looked at her with hard eyes making it impossible
to interpret what he wanted from her.

"Evan, if you want me to leave."

His hands shot forward. Gripping her hips, he hoisted her over the
back of the couch and roughly sat her on top of his steel body. His
muscular strength dazzled her with a powerful delight.

"No. Stay."

She gave him a wary glance. "You're not mad at me?"

A harsh groan rumbled out of his throat.

She stated, "You are mad."

"Furious! Why did you run?" Evan demanded.

"I was scared," Callie said honestly.

"Of?" he questioned.

"Of becoming something I ran away from years ago."

"Such as, becoming your mother?" he asked.

His analysis was correct and it left her speechless.

He gave a frustrated sigh. "Callie, I think I know you better than you know yourself."

"I think that, too." She diverted her eyes from his, but his disgruntled sigh made her look at him.

"What exactly scares you about it?" he inquired. "Is it the long term commitment with a man? Having children? Being rooted in a house and having no adventure?"

She shook her head. "No, it's not the commitment."

"You've hated the thought of being a homemaker. Why, Callie? Tell me why this scares you so much?"

She took a deep breath. "It means I'll be uptight, unloving, and strict, I'll care about appearances and what people think. I won't love a person for who they are."

The sadness seeping in her eyes was haunting, but he understood her fears. She was still carrying the hurt of her parent's disowning her.

He caressed her cheek with the back of his hand, then cupped it lovingly in his palm, saying, "Callie, honey, I'm so sorry your parents can't love the real you. If I could take the pain of that away from you, I would, but sweetheart your definition of this word isn't you. It's your mother."

Her eyes teetered between believing and disbelief, and he wracked his brain for the right words to help her understand.

"Callie, if you turn into a homemaker would you suddenly not accept me as a farmer? Will you think any less of me?"

She shook her head. "No. That's ridiculous."

"Correct. That's my point. You are you. It doesn't matter if you're behind the wheel of a semi, behind a desk, or behind the counter cooking a meal. You're not going to change who you are."

Her eyes were less cynical but she still asked, "How do you know?"

He grinned. "I know you. You're not going to let it change you, because you're stubborn."

She frowned and was about to protest, but he placed his finger on her lips. "And you're loyal, kind hearted, helpful, and loving. All these fine qualities make one unique girl in the whole world...which is you."

Her glossy eyes expressed how much she truly believed this.

He was thrilled and all he wanted was to carry her into the bedroom and show her how beautiful she was, but they still had a lot to talk about.

"Callie, the recipes weren't for you. They're for my sister."

"Oh my," she said sheepishly. "I'm so embarrassed. I should have stayed and given you a chance to explain. I'm so sorry," she sincerely apologized.

"I forgive you but just so you know I'm not expecting you to cook or clean. I pay Kylee to clean the house, and I can cook pretty damn well myself. I've been doing it for years and you are witness to my good cooking, yeah?"

"Yeah." She nodded.

He rephrased. "Just for the record I don't need you or any other female thinking I need to be cooked for. I know how to take care of myself. Got it?"

"Yes."

"Good. So from now on if anyone else in this town, man or woman, indicates I need a cook, I don't!"

"Well, how do you expect to find a woman?"

His confusing eyes poured into hers. "Explain, please."

"It feels like there is an unwritten rule in this town. In order for a woman to get a man she has to cook for him. A man can cook, but the woman's supposed to take care of the other household stuff."

"What!" He exclaimed but the more he thought about it, it made more sense of what Janie had been hinting she could do for him.

"Something about the way to a man's heart is through his stomach." Callie finished saying.

"That's ridiculous."

Callie shrugged. "Well, that's what I told Kylee, but she assured me this is how she got Kellan."

Evan gave her a preposterous look. "You're kidding, right?"

"She wasn't."

"I'm pretty sure Kellan didn't pick Kylee just because she could cook. I'm sure it didn't hurt but that's not the only reason."

"So you'll be happy with a woman who can't cook?"

He laughed. "Yes."

She frowned. "How do you know?"

His arms wrapped around her shoulders pulling her closer whispering, "Because I'm holding her."

Callie's heart danced. Deep in her belly sensations swirled and somersaulted. Love illuminated in Evan's eyes. "I've loved you for quite some time and it had nothing to do with having any domestic skills and everything to do with your strong, stubborn and fascinating spirit."

"That's good because my stubborn side is still torn between driving and not driving. If this afternoon is any indication of how long distance hauls are going to be, then the choice may have already been made. It still doesn't mean I want to be stuck in this house all day. I guess what I'm trying to say is," she paused to take in a deep breath. "I want to know that the option for driving is available anytime in the future. No matter if I decide now or months from now."

Evan cupped her cheek. "Yes. It is. The option has always been available and always will be. I never wanted you to choose between me and the road."

Her eyes shined excitedly. "Are you saying what I think you're saying?"

He grinned. "I'm saying. You can have me and Sunbird."

Her golden eyes shimmered relief. "You can really let me go?"

Evan chuckled, "I've been doing it for years."

She gave him a willowy look.

He held her face in his hands and absorbed her glossy stare. "All I want is for you to come home to us."

"You're serious about this?"

"Yes," he confirmed emphatically.

"Why?"

"Callie Cat, you're all I've ever wanted. I don't want to live apart from you anymore."

"If I'm on the road we are apart," she reminded him.

His tender eyes swept over hers. He gingerly placed one palm over her heart. "But not here."

"Oh, Evan," she said affectionately. "It's the sweetest thing anyone's ever offered."

"Good!" He triumphantly declared.

"I will come home to us," she promised with a victory kiss.

He scooped her up and carried her through the house.

"One more thing," she said as he deposited her on the bed. "Before we move forward I need to tell you I'm moving out of your guest room."

"Wh-what?" he asked, shakily and was glad he had already let go of her before she delivered her earth shattering news. "What do you mean you're ready to move out? Where are you going?"

Due to his shock, he missed the playfulness in her eyes. She stood on her knees and put her hands on his hips. "I'm moving into your room."

His eyes whipped into hers. "What? Say that again."

She laughed. "Ev,"

He liked the way she shortened his name as it stirred sexy sensations in his short head.

"I'm moving into your room."

"Really?" he asked fascinated.

Callie giggled and nodded.

A cheerful smile appeared on his dashingly handsome face, and he gave her an enthusiastic kiss.

"C'mon, let's get this done right now." Laughter bubbled out of her as he took her hand and led her up the stairs.

An hour later the upstairs had been cleared of Callie's clothes and personal hygiene items and moved into his closet and bathroom; quickly becoming theirs.

Twirling her in his arms, he waltzed her through the closet, through the bathroom and bedroom saying, "Callie, these rooms aren't mine anymore; they're ours."

Evan's sensitivity with establishing things were no longer his but theirs amazed her.

At the edge of the bed, he dipped her low claiming her mouth with his. Lifting her, he laid her on the king mattress and seductively whispered, "This bed isn't mine. It's ours."

His sultry eyes promised many nights filled with lust and love while sexy sensations fluttered her womb. He quickly removed her shirt and bra as his gaze fixated on her luscious breasts. Craving to have one in his mouth, he lowered his face and latched onto one. The soft velvet tip turning taut beneath his tongue was a marvelous feeling as was her begging when she offered him her other breast. Toying with it, the bud hardened and he flicked it between his teeth. Her pleasing hisses tightened his groin.

"Yes, more." She arched her breasts into his mouth.

He obliged, taking turns between them as his hand slid to the waistband of her jeans. He unbuttoned, unzipped, and then removed them along with her lace underwear. His fingers feathered her abdomen before strolling through the patch of hair guarding her fortress. Two fingers forged in fucking her while he suckled her breasts.

She shuddered, and her nails scrapped the skin on his shoulders as waves of ecstasy rippled through her body. She fervently cried his name, and shed her first orgasm on his hand. Leaning forward, she took his focus away from her breasts by connecting her mouth with his. Her hungry tongue dove in capturing his spicy taste.

Leaving her mouth, his teasing tongue harassed *the* spot on her neck driving her into a heated frenzy. Shivers wracked her spine and an aching wetness hung in the depths of her barrier.

The desire brewing between them strengthened.

He stood, removing his garments; eager to taste the places his eyes had roamed and his hands had played. Kneeling beside the bed he kissed the top of her knees, and then gently pushed them apart. He kissed the silky skin of each slender leg and thigh, anxious to feel them circling his back when he drove into her. He continued with his tongue caressing the untouched territories of her belly and outer parts of her legs.

She squirmed and twisted.

"So sexy," he complimented before his tongue ravished her vagina. She wiggled, but he firmly caught her waist; keeping her still.

"Yes," she panted. Her cunt tightened, and he drank the sweet release.

He threw her a satisfied grin. In return, he caught her naughty smile but didn't have time to ponder it, because she swiftly rolled over and shifted her hand onto his cock.

Bending, she fastened her mouth on his enlarged penis and began titillating her tongue on his hefty tip and shaft. She deep throated him. He gasped and parted her curtain of hair so he could watch her hallow him. His praises came out in a fierce grunt as he reached the point of no return.

"I'm coming, baby." He forewarned.

Clutching his ass, she pushed his cock farther into her mouth and let his jagged release slide down her throat.

Laced with yearning he flipped her over onto her back and swiftly entered her. Their fervent bodies soulfully connected as she accepted his deep penetration. His hand gripped and supported her bottom as he lifted her higher.

Her legs entwined his torso pulling him closer, and she matched his rhythmic pace allowing him to take her higher. His thrusts were relentless with the pursuit of obtaining fulfillment for both of them. He needed to feel her core as much as she needed to seize it.

She clung to him while he riveted a powerful orgasm into her, and her body violently shuddered releasing hers. Stars danced in her eyes, and she clung loosely by his neck. His ragged breath filled her ear as he collapsed on her, then next to her. The smell of sex and his glistening body surrounded her. She couldn't move nor did she want to. She just wanted to bathe in their aftermath of their glorious love making. She closed her eyes and he snuggled her closely by his side.

Their eyes met, understanding the unity of love they just shared with the joy of giving and receiving.

In the middle of the night, Callie rolled over to find Evan staring at her.

"Are you watching me sleep?" she asked.

"Yes."

She swept her mouth tenderly with his, sharing the love in her heart with him. Holding her, he caressed the side of her face. "Callie, earlier this evening, you said you didn't feel confident in your ability to do long hauls. Why?"

"I barely made it to Junction City because I felt claustrophobic!"

"Well," he drew out slowly. "I've got an idea and a favor."

"Oh?" she asked curiously.

"Paul's taking paternity leave, and I need a substitute driver for his local route. I would like you to do it."

Her face was covered in pleasant surprise mixed with question. He continued with his sales pitch. "There will be plenty of opportunity for you to stop and take a breather from the cab's small space. I could get one of the new guys to do it, but Paul's route has a lot of our long time clientele, and I don't want them pissed off with any rookie errors."

He paused trying to read her expression, but she kept her poker face intact.

"Will you at least try?" He affectionately skimmed his lips over hers.

Callie felt the tenderness rip through her heart, hating the splitting effect it had on her; torn between herself and him. By not taking the route she would disappoint Evan and herself. She needed to find out if she could drive farther than Junction City. Also, it would be good finding out if driving is still what she wanted to do. Of course, the bottom line was, Evan needed her help and pleasing him is what she wanted.

She finally agreed, "Okay, I'll try it. We'll see what happens."

He covered her hand with his. "Yes, we'll see and remember, you don't have to do this alone. I'm here to help you every step of the way."

She rested her head on his shoulder. "Thank you."

"Lean on me, Callie Cat."

Lightly, she said, "The same as you leaning on me for help with the invoices and scheduling?"

He chuckled. "Yes. It's one of the sweeter things about being in love. We can lean on each other's strengths."

His tender words left her breathless as they reached inside her chest and caressed her heart.

Hugging her to his side, Evan's caring eyes searched hers. "What else is bothering you?"

His concern pulled her in, and she confidently spoke her worried mind. "What if I can't drive again?"

"What if you can?" he challenged.

"What if I don't want to?" she asked.

He mulled her answer, and then said, "What if you want to and you just don't know it?"

She opened her mouth, but he held his hand up. "This is why Paul's route will be good for you. You need to get behind Sunbird's wheel again and see what happens. After you try, we'll have answers."

"Okay, but let's say driving isn't what I want. What will I do for work?"

He sighed. "I believe once you start driving again, you may remember how much you love it. But, if it turns out this is no longer your path, I'll help you find out what is."

Evan's hazel eyes sparkled as his encouraging confidence danced its way into her heart.

"Callie, there's so many choices for you. You can do whatever you want."

"Dirk said, I'd always have a position with Maslund Trucking, and I think that's where I'd want to start."

Evan firmly agreed. "Yes. I'll create a position just for you."

Honored and awed by his statement, she murmured, "Oh, Evan. That is so sweet."

Embarrassed, he took the attention off him by caressing the soft skin on her thigh. His gaze dove affectionately into her tan eyes. "If driving isn't your future, we'll cross the bridge when we get there, but no more worries about what you can't or think you can't do. Okay?"

"Okay." The love careening in his eyes and committal support meant the world to her and her heart. How could she not agree with him?

"No more worries. Things will work out the way they're supposed to," he gently reminded her.

Nodding, she agreed. "I'll just keep my trust in the road."

"Yes. So far it's done a good job of leading you."

"I think it led me to you," Callie said happily.

He gave her a serendipitous kiss. "I agree."

"I love you," she declared lovingly.

"I love you, too, and whatever you decide, you have my love," he said charmingly.

Callie rolled into his side and slung her arm across his abdomen. Having his love was divine, and she was so thankful for coming back tonight instead of running into the empty horizon. It was time to stay, be courageous and stop denying her heart happiness.

Chapter Thirty-Two

Evan lifted her hand off his arm. Her light caresses were arousing. If it hadn't been a ploy to distract him from getting her to work on time, he would've easily succumbed to her charm. It was Callie's first day returning to work. For the next two weeks, she and Sunbird were filling in for Paul and his local route while he took paternity leave.

Dirk's company had a contract with a larger delivery company. The other company picked up loads from the major cities and delivered to Maslund Trucking. The trailers were unloaded, sorted, and then distributed into Maslund trailers to be delivered the next day to the surrounding counties.

This particular job of Callie's required the moving of inventory within a fifty mile radius. At each Maslund warehouse, she'd be delivering and picking up trailers. Her first stop was to a warehouse in Junction City. The trailer she dropped off would be unloaded and dispensed into Maslund's parcel trucks. The new trailer she'll hitch up to will be loaded with the previous day's pick ups that the parcel truck drivers had received on their routes.

"Are you sure you need me to drive? I could stay and work in the office. I'm sure I could find more bills to be paid, or filing that needs to be done, or –"

He placed his finger over her lips. "Callie Cat, you've been a great help to me this last week, but I really need you to take Paul's route. His route has our most loyal, long standing customers. I don't want to jeopardize the relationship with a rookie. Even though we both know everyone needs practice and needs to start somewhere, we also don't want inexperience pissing off these customers."

"Well, thanks for trusting me with it." She smiled.

Chuckling he said, "Callie Cat, you're welcome and thanks for accepting it."

"Okay, but I'm only doing this for you," she huffed.

"Thank you," he said gratefully.

"When I leave today, will you be watching from the window?" She referred to his earlier confessions of always watching from his office.

"Nope, I'll be outside watching my girl go," he proudly stated.

Delighted joy lifted her shy smile. "Your girl, I like it."

He drew her closer. "I do, too." He kissed the top of her nose.

"In the truck yard, I won't display any affection because I don't want others feeling that I'm playing favorites."

Her eyes expressed the tenderness her heart felt. "Thank you. Your respect means a lot."

"You're welcome."

Sliding behind the wheel of his truck he said, "Are you ready?"

She sighed heavily. "As ready as I'll ever be."

An overwhelming urge to touch her grabbed a hold of him. Acting on it, he reached over and pulled her into his lap. Lifting one hand, he turned it over displaying her inner arm. His fingers slid over her palm, wrist, up her forearm to her bicep. Leaning forward, he lightly kissed the pit of her elbow and around the outer edges of it.

The touch of his wet heated breath on her skin shot shivers down her spine. Those shivers spiraled deeper when his teeth lightly nipped and grazed her triceps and shoulders, but she came undone as his mouth dropped onto her neck. Every space in her body tingled and she ached for more than kisses. Sensing this, Evan's hand rounded her knee and thigh. Bypassing her underwear, he entered three digits in her vagina. They penetrated deep, but his middle finger went deeper while the other two swept her outer walls.

The pursuit of his fingers increased, and she gasped, "Yes."

"Come for me," he demanded in her ear.

She quivered, and her high pitched cries echoed through the cab.

Kissing the top of her head, he chuckled and wickedly whispered, "Okay, now I'm ready to take you to work."

Breathlessly, she mumbled, "I love you."

In case she didn't return today, he had to have one more kiss. Gripping the back of her head, Evan captured her mouth with his and felt the heat rising between them.

Callie felt his fiery need in trying to savor her flavor. She moaned, ran her fingers through his silky hair, and entwined her tongue with his.

The thought of this being their last kiss tormented him. If she left- left he didn't know what he would do. His blazing passion turned to fear; she tasted it and sadness struck her.

She opened her mouth to speak, but he placed his finger over it. He didn't want words parting her lips; only kisses. Unfortunately, she persisted speaking and he had to endure words he didn't believe.

"I'll come back," she said.

He believed, she believed this was the truth. Though her eyes held honesty, he still wasn't sure. Especially, since she didn't say *when* she would be back, just that she'd be back. And he didn't dare point this out.

"I know," he said, hiding his fearful thoughts.

Evan truly speculated that within a few hours, she'd call saying the local route was too short, and she was leaving for longer hauls again. He hated thinking this way, but nevertheless he had to prepare himself for *that* scenario.

"I love you." He hugged her tight. Then he abruptly released her and set her in the passenger seat. Fastening his seatbelt, he quickly shifted the truck into drive before he let his heart change his mind and take her back to bed.

"Suddenly, you seem to be in an awful big hurry to get rid of me," she pouted.

"I'm not," he answered sternly. "I don't want you to go, but you need this."

She gave him a confusing glare. "I'm beginning to think you need me, to prove to you, that I don't want to drive anymore."

He shook his head. "No. That isn't it."

"What is it, then?"

"Callie, I need you, to prove to yourself, that you *do* want to drive."

"But –"

He sternly interrupted, "Sweetheart, I need you to understand you can love both Sunbird and I."

She spatted, "You think I don't know that?"

"Oh, I know you don't," he said forcibly. "You've never had me while being behind Sunbird's wheel."

"I had your friendship." She argued, possessed with winning this argument.

"It isn't the same and you'll know what I mean in a few hours."

She opened her mouth to argue, but he tipped his head, nodding for her to gaze out her window. Parking next to Sunbird who was already hooked to a trailer he said, "We're here."

Callie's heart jumped and butterflies sprang in her belly. She was in awe with the sight of her yellow friend sparkling in the sun. Sunbird was washed, waxed and waiting for her. She was magnificent! Callie's eyes dazzled with pride. "She's beautiful!"

He turned sideways and slid his right arm along the seat's ridge. "Yes she is."

Looking at Evan, Callie smiled. "You're talking about me, not her."

He nodded and was rattled when her eyes revealed her fear. He saw that she, too, didn't know what the outcome of the day would bring.

"Do you want me to ride with you today?" he offered.

His invitation melted her heart. "But, you hate driving."

"For you, I would."

His selfless love made her feel weepy; an overpowering determination set in; convincing her she could do this!

"Ev, as tempting as your offer is, I need to do this alone!"

A new spunk flashed in her eyes, and Evan knew she was ready to go. He just prayed it wasn't a forever kind of go. He cupped her cheek. "I love you, and I'm going to miss you."

She touched his bristled jaw. "I love you, and I'll see you when I get back."

Plain as day, she read his haunted eyes. He was afraid she wasn't coming back. Unfortunately, no words could be voiced on this subject, and her actions would have to speak loud. She would have to show him that being in Purlieu with him is where she wanted to be!

"Okay. Be safe. Don't give up." He gave her arm an encouraging squeeze.

The hand on her arm internally heated her, and she gave him a warm smile. She climbed out of the passenger seat and into Sunbird's driver's seat. With mixed emotions she fastened her seatbelt, punched buttons on the dash, and then shifted Sunbird out of park. One hand waved to Evan and the other one wiped a tear. Driving away from him this morning didn't feel as awful as it had the other day. Was Evan right, and she wouldn't be happy with short routes?

Late morning, she became fidgety. On the outskirts of a town she pulled into a park stopping near the baseball diamonds. While eating the lunch she had packed, she strolled around the bases. She missed being home and the freedom it offered. She might have been bored at home but at least she had been able to stand, run and walk whenever she wanted. Having to sit in one spot for hours was so confining! If she was home she could be lounging in the office looking at her picture.

Across the parking lot happy squeals of children caught her attention and the barking of dogs running inside a fenced area. Kids and dogs made families. *Does Evan want a family? Do I?*

By mid-afternoon, she was ready to be home in Evan's arms, so much that she didn't want to finish her route. However, she wasn't a quitter and Evan encouraged her not to give up. Plus, quitting didn't make happy customers. There was no other choice than to move forward!

****

Callie's hesitant smile weighed heavy on Evan's heart. All morning he was agitated by his stubborn pride. Getting her behind the wheel again had seemed like a great idea, but now that she was, he worried about the results. Maybe he shouldn't have been so insistent. He had no other choice than to wait for her return and was tormented with the question of *when*. He stayed in his office with the door locked while pessimism hijacked his optimistic attitude. *Was I wrong for pushing her back on the road?*

Could his heart take the rejection if she came to the conclusion of loving the road more than him? Time will tell, and that's what sucked the most. Having to wait! Hours later, his heart raced when he heard the car horn on his phone. Holding his breath he read her message: **Hey, I'm doing okay, but I miss you.**

He replied: **I miss you, too.**

After reading this message, he released a small sigh of relief. There was a good chance she would return today, but he didn't fully relax until later that afternoon. Staring out the second story window, in the distance, he saw the first speck of yellow coming over the hill. His chest tightened. Relief and happiness trembled through him as his eyes grandly witnessed Callie's return, and her parking Sunbird in the overnight bay!

The same monstrous feeling fell on him now as it had when Agent Dexter called saying they had found Callie alive, and when he carried her from the cargo crate, and when he brought her home.

He soared down the stairwell to the drivers' area on the main floor. He wanted to be the first person Callie saw when she exited the locker room. In the lobby, he paced, thankful that his first day of worrying was behind him. He knew tomorrow would make him a nervous wreck again, but for tonight he was going to enjoy her happy return. He had turned, pacing away from the door and didn't know she had come out until her tired voice spoke his name. Facing her, he saw the mental exhaustion strewn across her pretty face.

"Callie." He gave her an ecstatic smile and loved that she practically jumped into his outstretched arms.

"I'm ready to go home," she said, sagging into him.

"Yes. Let's go." He beamed and hugged her to his side. "Anything special you want for supper?"

She slid her arm along his lower back. Together, side by side they walked out to his truck. "Other than you, no," she murmured, laughing.

He chuckled. "I can make that menu work."

In regards, to her first day back, he had a lot of needling questions. But for now he kept quiet and enjoyed the tranquility of her return.

In the truck, he kissed her hand and held it. "I'm proud of you."

Her eyes expressed sincere thanks.

"I love you, and I'm glad you're here," Evan said sincerely.

At home, his hungry eyes blazed a hot trail over her body. He carried her from the truck to the bedroom dropping their clothes along the way. On the bed, their bodies seared together after being miles apart. The fiery air sizzled and crackled around them. Fear of the unknown had been laid aside as they shared the joy of her return home.

****

Evan accompanied Callie across the truck yard. She lagged two steps behind and he threatened to grab her hand in front of everyone.

"People already suspect we're sleeping together," she mumbled.

"Well, we're not going to flaunt that fact." He reminded her as they approached Sunbird. The truth was he would've liked to kiss her at Sunbird's door, but he wasn't comfortable displaying his vulnerability to the other employees.

"You're sure Linda can handle the paperwork?" she asked again as she did every morning.

He gave her an infuriated eye roll. She opened her mouth for one more protest, but he wouldn't allow it and pointed to Sunbird.

"Yes, I'm sure. Now get up there," he said harshly.

"You don't have to be so bossy," Callie sassed.

"Apparently, I do."

She opened the driver's door and turned, finding him directly behind her. His bitter tone sneered into her ear. "I guess I'll see you later."

Aggravated, she goaded him. "But, you're not going to ask when?"

"No," he said flatly. "It's not my decision. It's yours."

"Are you saying you don't want me to come back?" Her sparing resulted in him throwing her a contempt look.

"Are you telling me you aren't?" he asked icily.

"Uh-no," she stammered. "I was planning to unless you don't want me to. Would you rather I drive off into the sunset?"

"It is what you do," he said in a tortured tone, and then slammed her door shut.

At first she was offended by his battered good-bye but then recalled this morning's crushing kiss that was full of sadness. *How many times do I need to return before he's comfortable with me leaving?* Evan lashing out just now sort of made sense but not entirely. *He's the one who insisted I get behind the wheel again! I've tried telling him I don't want to drive anymore, but he won't listen!*

She despised his driven demeanor on the subject and hated how he was letting his fears dominate an already sensitive departure.

"Ugh, he's such an asshole!" she grumbled, stealing one more glance out the window at him. Despite their savage departure it didn't stop her from admiring his backside. She thought about the glorious body beneath the clothes. The familiarity of her fingers skimming the muscles etched in his shoulders, down his spine and to the ass she loved gripping in the throes of passion. Instantly, her cunt began throbbing, and she groaned because there were too many hours between now and the time she would receive the joy she craved.

Through Sunbird's window, Evan saw her injured gaze and felt it on his back as he walked away. Despite his reasons for no public display of affection, a reassuring kiss would have been very beneficial. He helplessly groaned, knowing how much he fucked up this morning's departure. If she decided to stay away for good he would only have himself to blame.

He wanted to trade his office in for field work. Sitting and thinking in a tractor would have been much better than stewing and pacing in his office. Yet he couldn't bring himself to leave. He personally needed to see Callie return to Maslund Trucking. He pushed down the question he feared the most. If she didn't come back, would he be able to let her go?

Later in the afternoon, Callie returned.

Dropping his rigid body in the chair, he covered his face with his hands. He was extremely thankful she came back, but he needed to apologize for his insecurities. This isn't how he wanted their life to be. He couldn't keep acting like an insane person every time she left. It wasn't fair to either of them. Catching a whiff of her citrus scent, he looked up and saw his beautiful Callie leaning against the door frame. Her sensual body called him, and he rushed over, tangling his arms around her.

Burying his face in the crook of her neck, he frantically whispered, "I'm sorry for my rude behavior this morning. Please forgive me. It won't happen again."

"Oh, Evan, it's okay."

"No, it's not! It's pathetic and my troubled thoughts are not fair to you; either of us. I'm so sorry!"

Without gloating, she accepted his apology, and then said, "I guess we both have insecurities about me getting back on the road."

He sighed heavily. "Yeah, and I wasn't aware of mine until I was faced with you leaving. Every day, you've been saying, you're coming back, but I didn't fully trust you. I…" he trailed off, but she understood and finished his thought.

"You were afraid of me not returning, because I never used to come back on the same day. I leave, I stay on the road for weeks, months and when I do return it's never long. I get it, Ev, but I think together we can work through our fears."

She held out her hand. He clasped it and warm tingles slid through her.

"Yes," he agreed. "We can."

"I'm ready to go home if you are," she said, hugging him.

"Yes, let's go," he said, handing her the keys to his truck.

She stomped her foot on the gas pedal spinning the tires in the gravel. The back end fishtailed, but she easily got it under control and sped down the road.

In an attempt to be stern, Evan arched his brow but in the end his grin won. He said nothing, because he understood her need to drive a little reckless after being cooped up in the big semi rig all day. He also knew she handled his dually like it was a sports car. He laughed heartily, because having her here and happy was a spectacular feeling!

****

Having survived her first week of driving, she headed into the weekend with two days off. By the time Monday morning rolled in, Callie was excited with being able to leave the house for her job. Though, she dreaded the commitment of doing this for two more weeks. Evan had asked if she would fill in for another driver after Paul's route. Of course, she said yes because she loved him.

His happiness was important, despite the fact of living another week in a confined space; fastened by a tight seatbelt, constricting her movement, and followed by hours that dragged on and on! It made her want to scream at the top of her lungs!

The only thing that made it worthwhile was the joy of coming home and collapsing in Evan's arms. She loved talking about the trials and tribulations of their work day. Just like they used to do in their phone conversations except it was much better side by side! She loved being home with Evan, loved cuddling on the couch together eating ice cream and watching TV. Many times she fell asleep in his arms. He'd carry her to bed and the morning alarm happily started their newly established routine all over again. It was an exhilarated feeling!

Friday afternoon, of the second week, Callie's enthusiasm had her bounding up the stairwell two steps at a time. She was officially done with Paul's route! As she approached Evan's office she was surprised that Linda wasn't at her desk. Hearing Evan's voice she quietly stepped inside. He was alone, and she suspected he was talking on the phone. He faced the window but spun around giving her a giant smile. Covering his hand over the phone's mouth piece he hushed loudly, "Lock the door."

She did, and then sat on the sofa removing her boots and socks.

"Yes, Mr. Mayor. All right, I'll see you then. Good-bye." Evan ended the call and set the phone on the desk before he came over and squatted in front of her. "It's so good to see you."

Seeing his joy had smiles shooting across her face. Noticing his tired eyes, she guessed, "Bad day?"

"Not anymore," he whispered with relief. Every time she came back of her own free will showed him it was because she wanted to. For this he would forever be grateful.

She stroked the side of his face. "It's quiet in the office."

He nodded. "Everyone leaves early on Friday afternoons."

"Nice." Her dazzling smile lured him closer, and she saw the daunting desire in his dark irises.

Starving for her, he dropped his mouth, and rolled his tongue with hers. A wanton fever burned between them, and his tongue sank farther into her throat.

He unclasped her bra and removed it. His fingers stroked flawless skin from back to front. One by one, he lifted her breasts into his mouth, turning them into taut buds.

Breathlessly, she uttered his name and arched against his aching body. He removed her pants and panties along with his. Kneeling on the cushions, he scooted her closer to the edge. Lifting her bottom, he raised her surface and entered her fast and deep, satisfying a sexual fantasy of his, of them, like this on the couch.

The jouncing of her breasts heightened the ecstasy as did her high pitched climatic scream. With a reckless growl he drove his release deep in her pinnacle, and then covered her body with his, holding them in a gratified embrace.

"Is tonight when we're going to see the new baby?" she asked.

He nodded. "Yes."

"Before we go, I need to tell you something," she said in a serious voice.

Noting her somber tone, he sat up and set her in his lap. He hated the hesitant aura hovering over her. "Spill it."

Callie's brow squinted. She inhaled a shaky breath and exhaled it slowly. "Getting back on the road was hard but then somewhere along the way I realized you were right." She paused and gave him an uneasy glance. "I do love driving *and* I love you."

Evan's lips spread into a satisfactory smile because he was right. "I knew you would."

He didn't gloat, and she appreciated it.

"It's an awesome feeling isn't it?" he fished.

"Yes, but…" The radiance shone on her face before it bounced off.

"No buts."

Shaking her head she insisted. "I don't think you've thought about how it will be when I'm gone longer than an eight hour day."

"I do think about it all the time but it's all right –"

She interrupted. "How can that be okay? I'll be leaving you!"

"Does it mean you're not coming back?" he asked.

"No," she said insanely. "I…" She frowned contemplating things in her brain. Commitment flew past her and suddenly she understood what it meant! Evan needed more of this from her. More than her reassurance of she'll be back!

Laying her hands on his chest she exclaimed, "Evan! I will be back because I want to!"

Callie's testimony gave him hope.

She began framing out her plan. "Instead of the long months I used to drive, I would like to stay out for a week. The longest I will allow is fourteen days, and I want to stay home for the same number of days."

Evan's excited expression encouraged her to continue. "I also want you to know driving isn't the only thing I want to do. I like working in the office with scheduling, paying invoices, and other tasks. I want to learn it all and want to help in other departments."

"How about teaching at the driver's school?"

"What school?" Callie curiously inquired.

"The one Dirk is starting." Evan chuckled. "We think you would make a great instructor."

"Really?" she asked excited. "Training our drivers correctly from the very start? This would be awesome!"

Her enthusiasm poured into his heart. He was full heartedly in love with her and couldn't wait for the day to come when his special gift was done, and he could offer her everything!

Chapter Thirty-Three

Evan shook hands with Paul and gave Paula a formal hug, whereas Callie gave them both a cheerful hug. Stepping inside their home the scent of powder and baby filled their noses. They were invited to sit, and they cordially sat in separate chairs while Paul sat beside his wife on the couch. The conversation started out with Paul and Callie comparing notes about his route to general questions about the baby.

Evan asked if he could hold the baby. Excitement stayed on his face the whole time he held her. The baby cried when she was transferred from her parent to Evan, but he soon had her quieted with his hushed tones. He was a natural nurturer, and Callie was envious of this ability of his. Seeing a grown man marveling over the helpless babe had Callie's heart racing and stopping all at the same time.

Next it was her turn. Sitting in the rocking chair Callie forced a confident smile that hid the nervy nerves twisting her stomach as Paula placed their daughter in her arms. Callie gaped at the babe in her arms and gently unfolded the pink blanket. Little fingers wrapped her index finger and held on tight. Tears shimmered in Callie's eyes when tiny trusting eyes stared directly into hers taking a hold of her heart. Suddenly, having to choose Evan or Sunbird didn't matter. The grander picture lay right here in her arms! It wasn't just about her, Evan and the road. It was about having a family!

Evan hadn't ever seen Callie so much in awe. Her reaction to holding the infant was fascinating! A small delicate smile brightened her face as she instinctively cooed and ahhed at the baby. In return, the babe responded with little cooing sounds of her own, and he could tell Callie was smitten with the gift she held. All of a sudden he wanted a baby with Callie; her belly swollen with his child! Envisioning this; thoughts of them creating a life and sharing this tiny gift of love swelled excitement through him.

They were quiet on the ride home. Callie stared out the window thinking about motherhood, and Evan focused on the road thinking about fatherhood. For both of them, the minute the newborn was laid in their arms a maternal instinct came over her and he felt the paternal instinct tugging on him.

For the first time ever, Callie entertained thoughts of being a mom and with Evan by her side it wouldn't be scary. Her heart belonged to Evan! She wanted to build a long lasting life with this sweet loving man! Six months ago she was addicted to the road and wanted no part of settling down. Now the idea of sharing a life with Evan wasn't claustrophobic at all!   In fact, it was thrilling and exciting and…adventurous!

Callie broke the silence. "I was nervous when Paula asked me if I wanted to hold the baby."

"You did great," he said proudly, rolling his hand in hers.

"Thank you," she said appreciatively. "It got me thinking about things."

His brow arched inquiringly.

"With the right man, motherhood wouldn't be so bad," she admitted.

Evan sharply inhaled deep emotions. Did she consider him the right man? The certainty displayed in her eyes told him he was. *Yes!*

The rest of the drive home was slow. He couldn't wait to hold her close. The minute they walked into the house, he gave her time to set her purse on the counter, and then he pulled her into his arms.

"Callie, I love you so much!" He nuzzled his lips against her ear.

"I love you," she gushed. "So what's the plan for tonight?"

He chuckled, "I'm going to show you how to make my favorite potato casserole."

She gave him a reluctant look, but he insisted. "It's easy, and you'll love it, I promise."

"I don't know the first thing about following a recipe," she protested.

"Oh, please," he said exasperated. "If you can read road maps you can read a freaking recipe." He laughed, kissing her neck. "I'll show you. It'll be fun."

"Okay," she sighed, giving in.

He told her to open the cream of mushroom soup cans and empty them in the bowl.

Doing this, she asked, "What's next?"

"Green beans," he stated and slid them across the counter in front of her. "Open the cans and drain the liquid with this." He handed her a hand held can strainer. "Then dump the beans in the bowl with the soup."

She did, and he praised her with a kiss. "Remember the meat I browned on the stove?"

She nodded and guessed, "It needs to go in with the beans and soup?"

"You got it. Then we mix it altogether." He handed her a wooden spoon.

She took it and began mixing.

When she was done, he demonstrated how to coat the pan with cooking spray warning, "If you don't use spray the food will stick to it and it'll be hard to wash out." He chuckled, "Believe me I've had to throw a few pans away because I forgot."

Her eyes widened and her lips formed an O shape. Evan leaned in taking advantage of her open mouth. His tongue slid in tangoing with hers. As the kiss ended, she cleared her throat, laughing.

"The next step we have to do is pour the ingredients from the bowl, into the pan and we'll spread it like this." Standing behind her, he placed his hand over hers and rhythmically moved their hands back and forth spreading the mixture evenly in the pan. His other hand methodically moved up and down her side.

Next, he lifted the bag of frozen tater tots, poured them on top and evenly arranged them.

"They don't look appetizing." She commented lazily.

"They will after they cook." He kissed her slender column then moved to open the oven door and placed the dish in the oven. Setting the timer he faced her with a horny gaze.

"C'mon." He took her hand and led her into the bedroom for fun love.

An hour later, the timer buzzed and Evan pulled the casserole out from the oven. "Come see what you made." He called.

"Oh my gosh! Those round potatoes look like hay bales!" she exclaimed.

Evan threw his head back laughing. "All right, then. I'm calling this dish Callie's hay bale casserole."

"Oh! No!" she protested, laughing. "You can't do that."

"Why not? I believe I just did!" He nipped her shoulder, and then spooned a big helping on each of their plates.

Taking a bite he enthused, "Mm, it's delicious!"

He presented her with a forkful, and she ate it. Her eyes lit up at the wonderful taste. "Oh! It is good!"

"And you made it."

"With your help," she said, sharing the credit.

"Some help from me, but you did most of it." His proud eyes locked with hers.

Feeling his pride all the way to her toes, she graciously said, "Thank you. I had a good teacher."

"You know who would love to eat these hay bales?"

Giving up on the answer, she shrugged. "Who?"

"Macy."

Callie laughed.

"You know what else she'd love?"

"No. What?"

"Watching a few of her favorite princess movies with you," he announced.

"Why do I get the feeling you're hinting at something?"

He gave her a rueful grin. "My sister asked if we'd babysit Macy Thursday night."

"Sure. It'll be fun," she said enthusiastically.

"Excellent!" Evan smiled and hugged her.

****

Callie breezed into Evan's office carrying a tall stack of papers. After setting them on the desk, she joyfully shuffled her way towards him and into his arms giving him a kiss.

"Mm, scrumptious," he murmured.

"Speaking of scrumptious," she started saying. "The cupcakes you and Macy made last night were delicious."

He waved his hand in midair as though it was no big deal.

"It was fun watching her. She is such a delight!" Callie smiled.

"Have you had your fill of princess movies?" he inquired.

Callie giggled. "Not yet."

"I'm sorry she keeps calling you her Aunt."

Callie laughed again. "It's okay." She wanted to add, *maybe someday I will be.* Instead she kept this thought to herself. She didn't want to do anything to jeopardize the good between them with an unwanted solicit.

If she could read his mind, she would have heard Evan say *I want to make you Macy's aunt by marrying you.* He coughed, cleared his throat and pointed to the pile. "What's this?"

"Bills needing to be paid," she informed. "My last oil change at the Sullivan's is on top. Due to the circumstances I know why it hasn't been paid, but we need to pay them soon. We shouldn't take advantage of their kindness. Plus, I have a few ideas I'd like to discuss with you and how we could continue a work relationship with them."

"The Sullivan's?" he asked in surprise.

"Yes."

Evan's eyes flashed possessively. "I used to wonder about the low prices they charged us."

Catching his under toned meaning her eyes sliced into him and she huffed, "You think I struck a between the sheets deal with the mechanics?"

"It ran across my mind a time or two," he answered testily. "I was very curious about Kris and Reese. They were taking *really* good care of my best tractor. And evidently they were taking *really* good care of my best driver, too. More than I wanted them to, because you insisted on going there even when it was out of your way."

Seeing his point of view she understood why he jumped to the conclusion she was sleeping with the mechanics and her defenses lessened.

"I felt a whole lot better when I found out Kris is a woman. It was one less man I had to worry about trying to steal your heart." He admitted openly.

She gaped and stated, "You were jealous."

"Hell yes, I was!" he responded emotionally.

She grinned, realizing Evan had no clue about The Sullivan's. Of course, she couldn't blame him. In the beginning, before meeting them, she, too, had misjudged their names and job choice. Most people did.

"So what about Reese?" he asked with a clenched jaw.

She gave him a sly smile. "She isn't my type."

Astonishment fell on his face.

"Callie Cat," he whispered ruefully pulling her close. "You have no idea how many nights these insecurities have kept me awake."

"The same worries I had about you settling down with a nice quiet farm girl."

"Sweetheart," he whispered, caressing the side of her face.

She smiled, because the sharing of their doubts felt good with her heart, strengthening the bond of trust between them.

"Evan, I went from hating you, to looking forward to our phone conversations, to being jealous of all the women I imagined were in your bed, to hoping I could be your woman. Now I am yours!"

"Yes. You're in my heart, Callie Cat."

She skimmed her hand along his bristled jaw and entered his embrace. "There's no other place I want to be."

He kissed her, and she felt his possessive passion shivering through her.

His phone alarm signaled it was time to leave. Sighing, she started backing away, but he wouldn't let her go. "Wait."

His fingers quickly typed a message. When he was done he set the phone on the desk and gave her a playful grin. "There that will buy us some time."

"What will?"

"I told Kellan something came up at the office, and we will be a little late."

She gave him a compelling look, but he shook his head insisting, "I didn't lie." Grinding his hips against her he teased, "Something did come up *and* we are at the office."

She unzipped his pants freeing his aroused penis. Her provocative gaze fed his desires. Only she could satisfy his aching hunger.

"I want to be in you," he confessed jaggedly.

"First be in me here." Licking her lips, she knelt and orally drew him in.

"Yes," he breathlessly moaned, enjoying the way her tongue rolled across his cock. Ready to be in *her*, he guided her onto his hardened length. Together, they moved as one. Together, they shared a frenzied state of desire as undulated passion erupted.
United, they laid in an angel's loving embrace.

****

Evan flipped the light switch off and closed his office door. "First thing tomorrow I'll get a check mailed out to the Sullivan's." He promised.

"I could come in with you and help you write checks for the other bills." She offered.

A delightful smile lifted the corners of his mouth. "I'd like that. Thank you."

"You're welcome. It would be my pleasure."

Hugging her to his side he said, "What else would be your pleasure?"

"Take me home and find out," she teased succulently.

"Dessert at home then," he chuckled lowly.

Callie didn't think there was anything happier than feeling his deep laughter resonating through her, or the love she felt in his embrace followed by promises of further fulfillment of their hearty appetite for sex.

On the way to the restaurant Evan's left hand gripped the steering wheel and his right hand curled with Callie's.

"Tell me about the ideas you have for generating business for Maslund Trucking."

Her face beamed with enthusiasm, and she began with her suggestion of them setting up routine maintenance services with The Sullivan's for Maslund drivers who are passing through Arkansas.

"Sullivan's garage is centrally located. And," she stressed. "It would financially benefit the company and its drivers as well as save time."

Despite the harassing he had given Callie about her relationship with the mechanics, he loved that she made this suggestion, because he'd been mulling this idea for awhile. He'd always been impressed with their low prices and high quality of work.

"What else?"

Next she mentioned, "We could establish an overnight parking lot for truck drivers and for people like Chase and Ivy traveling in their motor homes. With the building of the new highway we could build it near the exit ramp; easily accessible. We could start small and add to it as funds are available."

"What would you add?" he asked.

"Have a bath house, each individual pull through site could have electric and water hook-ups and maybe a picnic table."

Evan could tell she had thought hard about these accommodations. Surmising, all these things are what she had wished for when she was out on the road.

By the time they reached the restaurant he was grinning ear to ear. "I love all your ideas, Callie, and can't wait to mention all of this to Dirk. It's definitely something we can strive for."

"Thanks, Evan." She stated shyly. Having him listen and really value her suggestions made her feel important and proud. His hand tightened around hers, and she gave him a loving smile.

His heart swayed sideways with the cherishing gaze she gave him. He loved her sensible business brain. It was one more reason why he loved her as if he needed any more reasons to love this magnificent woman beside him!

Pulling into a stall, Evan waved to Kellan standing on the sidewalk.

Kellan cocked his head to the side and listened to the music barreling out of Evan's truck through the open windows. *What the?*

In shock, Kellan stepped closer. He didn't know what kind of music was playing on the radio! The one thing he *did* know. It wasn't country! But the duo in the front seat was laughing and didn't seem to notice what was playing. Shaking his head, he and Kylee went inside and got a table. A few minutes later, Evan and Callie joined them.

The foursome sat at a square table with each couple sitting across from each other. During the discussion of what everyone was ordering Callie announced she was having a salad.

Evan insisted she try the pizza. She made a disgusted face saying, "I usually stay away from pizza."

"Callie, this is good food, not sitting around on a warming tray food." He gently reminded her, but her eyes still held reluctance.

"Okay. How about you prove I'm wrong by ordering a cheeseburger and a salad?" he grinned.

She rolled her eyes over his ridiculous bargain, but in the end his persuasive eyes challenged her into it.

"I promise you will not regret it," he stated.

She didn't believe him and waited for their food to arrive to prove him wrong, but she should've known by the playful glint in his eye he had something up his sleeve. When their food arrived, her eyes widened at the toppings mounding the pizza. One topping in particular caught her eye.

"There's bacon on the pizza!"

"Yep," he grinned, watching her swallow her craving.

"Oh. My. Ev," she gushed. "You know exactly how to win the way to my heart."

Callie had stated this innocently, but out of the corner of his eye, Evan saw guilt run across Kylee's face. Evan couldn't help the proud smile that appeared on his face.

Kellan was astonished as Callie reached across the table grabbing chunks of bacon off the pizza, and Evan didn't say anything! Kellan was shocked again when Evan smiled and presented Callie a slice loaded with bacon. *What is going on?*

Callie had somehow maneuvered her way around all of Evan's pet peeves. She had him listening to music other than country, she was able to steal food off his plate, and she had him sharing his food with her.

Then the newlyweds witnessed a shocking incident that probably should have been recorded in the town's history book. It certainly was going to be talked about in the gossip grapevine for months to follow. Callie slid her fries onto Evan's plate! And then! Evan held up the longest French fry and selflessly offered it to her! It didn't matter that she declined it. What mattered is that he didn't keep it for himself!

Unbelievable! Kellan thought. Kylee gave him a knowing smile, and he remembered one of her passing comments. She had hinted there might be love in the air between these two. He had been skeptical, because he had always thought Callie and Dirk were destined to be together. His thoughts reflected backwards to a more recent event when Callie went missing and Evan's smile had vanished.

Before that, he had rarely seen Evan without a happy go lucky grin. Now tonight his friend's smile was the brightest and widest he'd ever seen it. Watching the duo this evening, it looked as though his wife might be right. Though his instincts heavily suspected Evan had already fallen in love with Callie.

What did this mean for their future? Evan often said driving was in Callie's blood and no man could change her. This was true. Callie wasn't the staying in one spot for very long kind of person. If she was a man he would've been dubbing her a rogue.

She was lost now, but Kellan was convinced she'd find her way to the road again, because she wouldn't ever be able to settle down with any man…especially the way Kellan *thought* Evan would want her to.

"Callie. Evan says you've been getting your feet wet again by filling in for some of the local routes," Kellan voiced.

"Yep," she said.

"Does it make you miss the long hauls?"

She swallowed her food then said, "The answer is complicated."

"Is it a time will tell kind of thing?" Kellan asked, viewing Evan's twitching jaw and Kylee's apprehension; knowing they weren't pleased with his interrogation. He didn't care. He was interested in Callie's reaction and was impressed she wasn't uptight as the other two were.

"Yeah, I think it is." Callie gave Kellan a straight forward stare, and he sensed that she truly and honestly didn't know the answer.

Evan understood Kellan's worry, but he still didn't appreciate it.

Callie's eyes shifted between the three sitting at the table with her. "I'm really not sure what my next career step is but filling in with the routes is definitely helping."

Her eyes rested with Evan as she continued. "But I'm confident I won't be alone when I have to cross that bridge."

Evan's heart trumpeted as her statement left Kellan speechless. On the way home he stated how proud he was of her for the way she handled Kellan's questions.

She shrugged. "He's worried about me breaking your heart."

"Well, it's not about him. It's about you and me," Evan stated.

"I know. Thank you." She smiled. "I love you."

"And I love you, Callie Cat."

Chapter Thirty-Four

Kara grabbed her purse and keys, locked the front door and went out to her car. She was starting her busy day with a shopping excursion in Junction City, lunch at her favorite restaurant and then meeting Iggy at The Gym to exercise. With self defense classes done she had made the remark about maybe starting an exercise routine. Iggy volunteered to be her workout buddy. Thinking it was a great idea she accepted but after one day last week and twice this week she wondered why he continued being her partner?

Between the two of them she was definitely the weaker of them. He could run, bike, and walk miles past her. She gave him the opportunity to find a better suited partner, but he graciously stated he enjoyed her company. She thanked him and agreed to meet this afternoon. In another week, she'd give him another chance to quit being her partner.

She impatiently glanced at her watch. The restaurant's parking lot was full and the drive thru line was wrapped halfway around the building. For some bizarre reason she opted to go inside. She had waited awhile and was almost to the front of the line. She was going to be late meeting Iggy and reasoned he'd have to wait because she wasn't leaving town without her favorite meal.

This place served the best spicy chicken sandwich! They had a honey sauce spread on both buns. Lettuce was placed on the bottom bun then the chicken patty, a tomato, and the top bun. Each bite was sweet and spicy as the sauce dripped between the layers. She began craving it the minute she woke up this morning. Yep, Iggy would just have to wait.

Looking down, her toes peeked out from her sandals. The paint on her nails needed a touch up. She'll have to do it herself because *Holly* couldn't afford another pedicure so soon after this last one. This week's luxury was the chicken sandwich.

All of a sudden a chill shivered through Kara as she heard a familiar flirty purr say, "The boys will love you."

Glancing up, the woman in the next row spun and collided with her, and Kara came face to face with the voice she's been hearing in the conversations!

Kara's eyes widened. *It's the sister...the niece! The same woman from the barn, the outhouse and the corn field! But I also know her as...oh! How can this be?*

Instinctively, Kara took a step backwards and so did her memory to a place where she met this woman face to face! Stunned, she remembered what *this* horrible lady had hissed in her ear about being a star in...*Oh! I can't even bring myself to say IT!*

Smiling, the sister tipped into Kara and in a sugary purr, she said, "Oh, honey, you're adorable. I love your purple hair."

The sister swiftly grabbed Kara's chin. "Have you ever thought about modeling? Here's my card, call me if you're interested." The sister released her jaw and called to someone behind her.

Kara didn't bother looking behind her to see where the sister took off to. If she had, she would have would have seen Humphrey. He had seen her and was relieved she didn't turn around. If she had, it would have been a costly mistake for both of them.

Rattled, Kara managed to place her order with the cashier. Feeling unsociable, she ate the food in her car, and drove back to Purlieu while her emotions trickled tears down her cheeks. She was scared, alone, highly concerned, and unsure of what to do. After wallowing, the two little words that had somehow kept her going through the bad times now echoed in her brain. *Be brave!*

Taking a deep breath, she turned into the gym parking lot and grabbed the duffel bag that held her workout clothes. Stepping into the lobby, she gave Iggy a sheepish smile.

"Sorry, I'm late but the restaurant was really busy," she said and hopped into the women's locker room hoping he couldn't see anything else in her eyes.

Iggy sensed something was amiss when she breezed in with a hasty apology. Being late wasn't the problem. She avoided looking at him, and her eyes were puffy; his guess was she'd been crying. *Why?*

She moved past him towards the bikes, saying, "Let's get started."

Following her, Iggy crinkled his forehead. She hated starting with the bikes. He reminded her to stretch. She did but it wasn't thorough. He was happy she began with a slower pace, but by the time she increased to a higher speed, Holly looked as though she was determined to drive the stationary bike off its pedestal. Iggy was thankful they weren't riding on the road. Otherwise, she would've had an accident.

Throughout the rest of their routine Holly's irrational regiment continued. By the end sweat dripped from her hair, and her eyes were jagged with exhaustion. Iggy suspected mental stress played a part in her fatigue. Clearly, she had a problem, and he wished she would confide in him. But she didn't.

In a clipped tone she said, "Hey, thanks. I'm going to go shower. I'll see ya later."

"Yeah, okay," he said defeated, disturbed by her distant behavior.

Iggy thought about waiting for her. Then chose not to and headed for the men's locker room. He had better things to do than to give her another chance to ignore him. In the parking lot, he saw Holly sitting in her car. Hoping she was waiting for him, he started towards her and noticed the agitation strewn across her face when she saw him. He knew now that she hadn't been waiting for him. She hadn't wanted to see him at all, and he would've walked away, but she looked too distressed for him not to offer assistance.

"Holly, hey, everything okay?" he gently asked.

Distraught eyes swung up at him. She frowned. "My car won't start."

"Mind if I take a look?"

She gestured her hand towards the front of the car and pulled on the hood lever, popping it open.

Lifting it, he looked the engine over. Peering around the raised hood he told her to try starting it. She did, and he heard an odd sound. With a hunch of a diagnosis he closed the lid and asked if he could sit in the driver's seat. She got out, and he slid in. He turned the key over halfway waiting for the gauges to move.

"Holly, you're out of gas."

She pinched the bridge of her nose and grunted, "Oh, how could I be so stupid?"

Iggy placed a hand on her shoulder, and she flinched. "It's okay. I've got an empty gas can in the bed of my truck. We'll fill it, come back and put it in the car. It'll be enough for you to get to the station. I'll follow you to make sure you make it there."

"Thank you," she graciously said, accepting his help into the passenger seat of his truck.

"Yeah, sure, no problem," he said, passing it off as no big deal.

"No, I mean it, Iggy. I appreciate you helping me after I gave you the cold shoulder."

"Is everything all right with you?"

She faced him with those darn hesitant eyes he'd seen so many times, and his stomach churned. In an aggravated voice, he guessed, "No, and you can't tell me anything."

Iggy parked the truck and hastily got out. From the back window Kara watched him fill the small gas can. His grim expression had her pondering if maybe she should tell him the truth. After this afternoon's incident she needed help.

"Iggy," she said when he got back in.

"Save it Holly," he sighed. "I know there are things you can't tell me. If you don't want to tell me, it's okay. I respect your privacy. But just so you know if you do decide to tell me. Please know your secrets are safe with me."

"They're dangerous secrets, and I wouldn't ever want to put you in harm's way."

"I'm a grown man I can take care of myself." *Why am I arguing with her? Let it go. Let her be.* He scolded himself and parked next to her car. He untied the can then emptied the liquid into her gas tank. He held the driver's door open for her and closed it when she slid in.

"Have a good night." He wished her.

She fastened her seatbelt, rolled the key in the ignition and listened to the engine roar to life. "Thank you."

Iguana kept his word and followed her to the gas station, but he didn't stop. Instead he waved and drove away with mixed feelings. The longer he knew Holly the more mysterious she seemed to get; the opposite of most people he knew.

****

Iggy couldn't hide his surprise when Holly showed up on his front porch the next morning. His eyes honed in on the dark circles under her eyes and the anguish in them. Swinging the door wide open he threw her a friendly smile. "C'mon in, I'll pour you a cup of coffee."

Stepping in, she apologized for showing up unannounced. He assured her it was all right and forced her wringing hands to grip a cup of coffee. "Careful. It's hot. Don't burn your tongue."

"Thank you." She followed him into the living room and sat opposite of him on the edge of the soft chair. "Are you wondering why I'm here?"

He shrugged. "You'll tell me."

Lifting the cup to her lips she focused on two things; the temperature of the coffee and where to begin the conversation. Taking a deep breath she said, "Iggy, I need your help."

"You have it."

"But it's dangerous." She forewarned.

"What is it?"

She was floored by his immediate willingness of taking on danger. "Someone we know is in trouble."

"We?" he said bewildered. "Who is it?"

"Callie."

Iggy swallowed his held breath. "Tell me why you think this?"

"I don't think. I know," she said vigorously.

"How do you *know*?" he patiently asked.

"I heard a conversation stating it," she said.

"You were eavesdropping," he accused.

"Not intentionally," she fumed. "I never planned for any of this to happen!" She set her cup hard on the table in front of her.

He gave her a sharp look. "Never planned on what to happen?"

Kara knew what she just said was a loaded statement. There was so much she hadn't planned on happening in her life and of course, Iggy knew nothing about any of it, but right now none of that mattered. Callie mattered. Keeping her safe was the main focus, and she worried about Iggy's reaction to the things she was about to reveal.

She sighed heavily. "I never planned on hearing the awful conversations but if I hadn't, I wouldn't know any of the dangers lurking about."

Iggy guessed, "You mean in regards to Callie?"

She nodded. "She's the nicest person I know and doesn't deserve to die."

"What?" he said in surprise. "Someone wants Callie killed?"

"Yes. The sister, she's an evil person." Kara shivered and wrapped her arms around her torso.

Iggy's memory jumped to the day at church. Holly's mumblings *were* about Callie being in trouble. He was trying to process why this was familiar when Holly said, "I know Humphrey is working for bad people but it doesn't mean he deserves to be killed. He –"

Iggy cut her off. "What? Humphrey?" he wheezed.

"Um," she mumbled, realizing he didn't know what she was talking about. "He's the one who helped me get out of the bad place, and I heard the sister say she was going to kill him."

Iguana's heart dropped to his knees. "Kill him?" He stared into space.

She answered, "Yeah, and even though he might be a bad guy, he still helped me and doesn't deserve a bullet to the head."

Iggy gaped over her gory detail. The blood in his veins turned frigid. *Jack was walking into a trap! This is why the meeting place was in a remote location…they wanted an isolated place for the kill spot! I have to warn him!*

"Excuse me, for a minute." Iggy quickly announced, fleeing the room and headed down the hall to the bedroom, dialing Jack's number as he went. Panic filled him when his friend didn't answer. Either, Jack hadn't taken his phone with him; highly unlikely but possible, or the meeting had started, and he was choosing not to respond, and Iggy didn't even want to think about the third option. Swiftly, he typed a one word message and prayed Jack received it in time.

In the meantime, he and Holly needed to talk. Entering the living room, Iggy sat down in the chair across from her. Taking a deep breath, he asked, "Holly, what do you know?"

She gave a dry laugh. "Things I'm not supposed to."

"Tell me," he prompted, and she spilled.

"I'm not supposed to know about the uncle and sister's discussions. I'm also not supposed to know about the shipment of drugs coming in, where it's going, and the sister wanting Callie and Humphrey dead."

Iggy whistled. "Wow!"

She elaborated, "Actually, the uncle wants the sister to leave Callie alone and doesn't even know about the sister's plans for Humphrey."

Iggy heaved a sigh. "How do you know all this?"

"I've heard them say it."

"How and where?" he asked, and her hollow laugh sent chills through him.

"The how is a fluke," she answered. "I was definitely in the wrong place at the wrong time. The day I ran away from you is the first time I heard them. It was in an abandoned barn. The second time was after the church potluck. I stopped at the convenience store to use the restroom. The line for the women's was long so I used the bathroom out the back door. The door handle wouldn't open, and I was stuck inside and this is when I heard them talking again."

"You heard a lot," he remarked.

"The last one I heard was weird."

"Weird, how?" he inquired.

"In all the other conversations, the sister adored Humphrey but not this last time. The man she spoke with, she told him her plan to kill Humphrey."

"Where were you when you heard this?" Iggy asked.

Her face turned a shade of red. "Never mind, it's not important."

Iggy's gut told him it was important. "It could be. Tell me," he persuaded.

"It's embarrassing," she mumbled, but his expectant eyes convinced her. "Ugh, fine!" she huffed. "I was lost in a corn field."

Iggy gave her a dumbfounded look. Kara felt pathetic as he slowly questioned, "You...were lost...in a corn field?"

"Yes."

No way! It can't be! This sounds too much like... Iggy looked at Holly's blonde and purple hair. It wasn't even close to the brunette description he was given. Pieces of conversations flooded his memory. Holly said she wasn't from here and that she came from a bad place. His mind raced…*was it the sheds?* It would make sense if it was, because she connected the man's voice in her dream to the same voice she's heard around town and admitted this voice triggered her panic attack in the store.

Crap! Jack said his witness had come in contact with Hank and Hank was here in town.

Iguana swallowed the shocked lump in his throat. His jaw slightly dropped, but he quickly closed it and maintained a calm exterior; opposite of the internal frantic he was experiencing.

The dots connecting Holly, Hank and Jack's witness was becoming too coincidental for Holly not to be… A knowing peace came over him like the calm before the storm as his heart pounded and echoed in his ears, and he was struck with an *Aha* moment…*This is Jack's witness!*

Chapter Thirty-Five

Jack ignored the vibrating buzz on his wrist. His meeting with Wilma was too important for him to stop and read a message.

Abel had called this morning, saying he needed to meet with her because she had information about the shipment. He was meeting her twenty miles from town at a cabin in the woods.

He was anxious to receive the information. Once he had it, he and Iguana could sort through the pieces each of them had; confident they'd find answers to all the players involved. They were so close to ending this gig he could taste it. His watch buzzed a third time, but he didn't bother looking at it, and waved to Wilma.

She extended her palm in the air but didn't move from the cabin's porch steps. This was different than her usual enthusiastic wave. She also didn't flitter over to him with excitement, and she was alone. Normally, she had at least one bodyguard near her; today no one was with her.

He should have paid better attention to these facts, but his guard was down as he blindly trusted the wrong people.

Feeling the vibration again, he briefly glanced and read the bolded message from Iguana scrolling over the screen: *TROUBLE*

Something was amiss! Otherwise, his friend wouldn't have interrupted this meeting. Suddenly, his instincts kicked into high gear, and he became aware of the quiet surrounding him *and that* Wilma wasn't approaching him!

Swiftly, he dropped to the ground just as he heard a *Pop* and then a whizzing sound above him. A bullet! Aimed at him! *Dear God!*

He heard Wilma screaming. From where he lay he had a clear view of the cabin. She was hunched over and held one hand on her shoulder. He saw the blood oozing down her arm. She'd been shot! His first thought was to go help her, but he was fairly sure he had been the target and didn't want to give the shooter another opportunity to kill him. A black SUV pulled up to the cabin. Two men jumped out and ushered Wilma into the vehicle, and then it took off leaving a cloud of dust and him behind. It irked him that they hadn't even bothered to check on him! Proving his hunch that he *had* been the target! *Son of a bitch!*

He shivered and felt ill. Thoughts of the fate he just escaped swam through his mind. If he hadn't read the message and ducked...the bullet would have collided with the back of his skull, and he'd be dead. *Damn it! What is going on?!*

Three feet to his left he heard a branch crack and the rustling of leaves. Slowly, he removed his gun from its holster. Behind the tree's black bark he saw a flick of orange move and Jack surmised it was the sleeve of a local hunter. The shooter was not a trained professional since he didn't wear clothes camouflaging his body with the scenery versus against it with the bright color. Luckily, for Jack, the man made himself an easy target.

Jack picked up a rock and threw it to the left of the hunter. The man stepped out from the tree, raised his rifle and shot where the rock landed. Jack rolled to his feet and pointed his gun at him.

"Stop where you are, Mister. Slowly put your gun down," Jack commanded fiercely.

The hunter stopped but didn't lower his rifle. Instead he instructed, "You put your gun down."

"I'm not giving you the chance to shoot me again."

The hunter spit a wad of chewing tobacco out the side of his mouth. "Too bad the lady got it instead of you."

"So I was the target and not her."

The hunter cackled. "Yes and I'm going to finish the lady's job." He raised his gun but Jack's draw was faster, and deadlier. The bullet hit the hunter between his eyes before he even had the chance to aim. The man fell to the ground but before Jack approached him, he stayed crouched listening for other signs of danger lurking nearby and was comforted by the sounds of nature stirring again. Out of habit as he walked towards the dead man he kept his gun in the drawn position while the same emotions ran through him. First was guilt for killing another human being. Second was the rationalized thought of one of them was going to die. Third was relief he was still alive.

Jack rummaged through the hunter's pocket and found a phone, keys, and a wallet loaded with cash; obviously half of the payment for the hit job. As most jobs like this the shooter was paid the other half after the job was completed. Careful to not get any fingerprints on the rifle, he put his black gloves on before picking it up along with the rest of the man's belongings. Opening the trunk of the economy car he was driving, he removed part of the carpet. Beneath it was a hidden compartment, and he placed the hunter's personal belongings inside.

Still looking like Humphrey, Jack drove to the roadhouse he had seen on the way out of town and parked in the last row under a tree. He pulled his head through a hooded sweatshirt before going in. Every booth in the restaurant was secluded with tall bench backs and a separate light hanging above the table. Since it was just him, he chose a booth in the back that was designated for two versus four. It was cozy and a good place to sulk.

Setting his phone on the table, he ordered a draft with the waiter. After his drink arrived, he sipped the darker beer, enjoying the slightly bitter taste on his tongue and the coldness on his throat. All the messages were from Iguana and none from Abel, and he worried over the reason why his crime boss wasn't harassing him about the meeting. Had it been Wilma's plan to separate him and Abel, so she could kill both of them? She'll soon discover that Humphrey hadn't died. Jack wondered if Wilma will hire other men to try and kill him.

Damn. His original plan had been to keep Humphrey's appearance while here in Purlieu but now it wasn't safe. Humphrey will need to stay hidden.

Jack left cash on the table for the waiter. About to get up, he heard the couple in the booth behind him laughing and heard the waiter wish them a good day. He remained sitting and waited for them to leave first.

Chapter Thirty-Six

Iggy closed his menu and stared at Holly across the table. *I can't believe Jack's witness has been right under my nose this whole entire time!* He watched her tuck a blonde strand behind her ear as she read the menu. *Geez! The reason I couldn't find her is because she changed her hair color.*

For the past hour since suspecting she was Jack's missing witness, his instincts had convinced him she was. However, he kept his suspicions silent and didn't share them with her. He needed to speak with Jack first. If he was right, together they could talk with her. *Jack*...he still hadn't heard from him and prayed his friend was all right.

The waiter came by taking their order: two cokes and two cheeseburgers. He added bacon and she chose American and pepper jack cheese.

"I can't talk you into the bacon?" he asked.

"No, thank you," she said.

While they waited for their food Iggy brought up a sore subject. "Tell me what happened yesterday and don't say, nothing, because something sparked your edgy behavior."

Though she had confessed her knowledge of some things, Kara felt she still had to be careful answering his questions.

"I saw someone from my past that I hadn't ever expected on seeing again."

Iggy knew there was more. "Elaborate, please."

"I really don't want to," she sighed heavily, but his look demanded more information. Luckily, their food arrived, rescuing her from having to answer.

Iggy asked how she liked the burger.

"It's awesome! It's done just right. It's flavorful and the temperature is still hot. I can see steam rising out of it."

"Yeah," he chuckled. "That part amazes me, too."

"It's the hottest burger in town."

They laughed.

When the waiter brought them the check, Kara snatched it before Iggy had a chance and handed the young man a twenty dollar bill, telling him to keep the change.

"You paying for our meals doesn't get you off the hook of answering my question."

She shrugged and asked, "Are you ready to go?"

"Yep," he answered, standing next to her.

Side by side they started walking towards the door. However, unknowingly, her purse strap got caught on the coat hook hanging on their neighbor's booth. Her purse flung out of her hands and swung backwards hitting the man's thigh before it fell to the floor.

Iggy turned sideways and saw that Holly had gone back to get her purse. He was thankful she had the good sense of zipping it shut before they left the table. Iggy viewed the irritation crossing the other man's face as though it had been done on purpose, and then heard him grunt gruffly. Iggy's jaw hardened as he prepared to fight the agitated man, sensing he wasn't in the mood to be pacified with innocent apologies.

Kara knelt to retrieve her purse and stated how sorry she was. While in the crouched position the boots under the table moved, and she recognized the snake embroidered on them! There was only one man she knew who had boots like these! Rising, strong hands clamped her arms; helping her up. She was powerless against the electricity sizzling through her. Lifting her chin, she came face to face with *Humphrey!*

Jack stared into the bluest of blue, iridescent eyes. To the average person they were blue, but he saw shadows of green, marking them the rarest color of his Sea. It didn't matter she had changed her hair. What mattered were her eyes. They were the most gorgeous set of ovals he had ever seen. When he rescued her from the sheds, it was these eyes that told him she was his brave angel, and she was reciting "be brave". The last two words he had said to her the day he kidnapped her.

"Hum-f..." she uttered and went limp in his arms.

Iguana didn't know which of them was more surprised. He saw more than bewilderment cross Jack's face as Holly fainted. He also didn't miss the gentle way his friend scooped her into his arms and carried her bridal style.

The two men stared at each other. Several questions reamed their minds; none of which could be asked at this particular moment. They had to get her out of the restaurant before she awakened and freaked out.

"Where can I take her?" Jack asked. He was in shock! Kara was the last person he ever expected to see, let alone having her pass out in his arms *and* being with Iguana!

"Out to my truck," Iguana answered.

"Lead the way." Jack's jaw clenched, because his friend's tone was too casual. It was clear the two knew each other. *How well do they?*

Kara started mumbling Humphrey's name.

"Shhh," Jack said, pushing the purple and blonde strands off her face and placed her in the back seat of the truck.

Iguana pushed him aside and lightly placed a cloth over her nose.

"Ah, why did you do that?" Jack winced.

"She was waking up. If she does she'll be hard to reason with. This will keep her asleep for awhile. I'll take her back to my house. Meet me there."

Feeling jealous, Jack grabbed Iguana's arm. "How long have you been sitting on the knowledge of my witness' whereabouts?"

Due to Dexter's secretive behavior, Iguana cut Jack some slack, understanding his friend's suspicions of keeping information from him.

"For the past four hours. Did you get my messages?"

Jack gritted his teeth. "Yes. It's the whole reason I'm standing with you right now."

Witnessing Iguana's relief, Jack knew he was wrong for jumping to conclusions. "Ig, I'm sorry for accusing you –"

Iguana interjected, "It's all right. I understand. We have a lot to discuss."

"Yes."

Three cars over, Iguana saw Callie pointing at them and heard her scream, "It's Humphrey!"

"Hey, leave him alone!" Evan shouted and started coming towards them.

"Go!" Iguana hissed to Jack.

Understanding the severity of the situation, Jack shaded his face by slipping the hood over his head and sprinted off. Within a matter of seconds, his two identities almost jeopardized the mission! It was a good thing Evan hadn't seen his face. After his near miss with death today, he couldn't add anything else to the complicated pile.

There was a chance neither Humphrey nor Jack were safe in Purlieu! He may need to stay behind the scenes for awhile and hoped Ig wouldn't mind digging around for information. He sensed his friend was enjoying the cushier side of spy life; no longer minding the boredom of following his assignment around.

Evan jogged after the man Callie identified as Humphrey but then stopped. Watching the runner retreat he was struck with a sense of familiarity and couldn't help feeling he'd seen him from behind. Looking back at Callie, he gave her a strange glance and wondered who the bearded man was? *Callie identified him as Humphrey, Iggy was having a heated conversation with him, and I've seen him from behind; followed him, yet I've never met Humphrey.*

"Iggy, you okay?" Evan asked.

"Yeah, thanks."

"What did that guy want?" Evan's eyes narrowed suspiciously.

"Homeless man looking for a handout," Iggy said. "Hey, thanks again for your help, but I gotta go."

Evan sensed a brush off as Iggy swiftly got in his truck and shut the door before he had a chance to wish him bye.

****

Jack arrived at Iguana's as himself; he had removed Humphrey's disguise before coming here. Iguana ushered him through the back door. They greeted each other with a short hearty hug.

"Glad to see you alive," Iguana said with relief.

"I wouldn't be if I hadn't seen your message. Thanks for saving my ass." Jack frowned. "It could've been a whole lot worse," he said with a bit of emotion.

"Well, I expect you'll pay me back." Iguana grinned. "C'mon, let's go sit in the sunroom."

Jack followed him through the back of the house to a square room that was lined with windows overlooking the yard. He sat in a swivel rocking chair. It was perfect for his restlessness, because he could move it in a rocking motion and turn sideways.

"Cool, chairs, man," Jack easily commented. "I need some for the house."

"Yeah lounging in a chair like this while gazing at the ocean would be very relaxing." Iguana grinned.

"She's still sleeping?" Jack asked.

Ig nodded.

"Hey," Jack said quietly. "Before she wakes up, I need to tell you, she believes Humphrey and I are two different men. For now we need to keep it that way."

"Got it," Iguana said then inquired, "Is she the one you rescued from the sheds?"

"Yes, Humphrey did."

"So the sheds is the bad place she came from," Iguana remarked.

"She told you about it?" he said in surprise.

Ig shook his head. "Not really. She said a lot of things that didn't make sense. Always told me it was dangerous stuff and didn't want me to get hurt. Of course, she has no idea what I do for a living."

"Crazy, how this is turning out," Jack said.

"Jack, I promise you, I had no idea about Holly's past until this morning."

"I believe you, brother." He narrowed his eyes. "Ig, you know this isn't her real name, right?"

"I should've known Holly Belles was an alias," Iguana said begrudgingly.

Laughter roared out of Jack. "Where on earth did Dexter come up with the name?"

"Not sure. However, it all makes sense as to why she never responded to the name. Good thing she looked both ways before crossing the street. Otherwise, she would've been smacked." Iguana clapped his hands emphasizing the effect.

Jack grimaced. "Thanks for the image."

"Sorry," Iguana muttered. Shaking his head in disbelief he said, "I can't believe she's been under my nose this whole time!"

"Don't beat yourself up. You had a lot on your mind." Jack tried convincing him but wasn't sure he had and asked how they met.

Iguana chuckled. "Well, she won't admit this but she almost ran me over in her car."

Jack's eyes widened. "What?"

Iguana shook his head ruefully. "She pulled over to the side of the road. I ran over and yelled at her. She had been crying, but I was so frustrated with the slow progress of the assignment, and I took it out on her. I felt horrible and worried I might have pushed her over the edge. There was this helpless hopelessness in her eye and it haunted me for weeks. Then I saw her at the library. She fell, and I helped her, and then asked her out."

Jack asked, "How did you know she was my witness?"

"She said Callie was in danger. It sounded familiar, but I didn't put two and two together until she said she got lost in a corn field. Then I knew she was yours."

Jack smirked over the statement of Kara being his. She was, but she wasn't.

Iguana sucked in a deep breath. "Then she mentioned Humphrey and the plan for him to be killed."

They shared a moment of silence; both understanding how the day could have ended.

"Based on the description I gave you," Jack said. "No wonder you couldn't find her. She had changed her hair color."

A third voice entered their conversation. "Who couldn't you find?"

Jack whipped his chair around and peered into Kara's surprised stare.

"Jack. What are you doing here? Where is Humphrey?" she asked sternly.

Her cool tone irritated him. If Humphrey had been sitting here, he was sure she would have given him a warmer welcome. His instincts prompted him to tell her the truth, but when he opened his mouth he said, "I'm helping Humphrey with his undercover assignment."

She rushed on to ask, "Jack, were you able to warn Humphrey of the danger he's in?"

Her frantic concern threw him off. *If she knew I was Humphrey, would she be worried for me?* Giving her a suspicious glance Jack said, "He was warned, but how did you know Humphrey was in danger?"

Confusion flew across her face. "What do you mean? I told you the night I heard it."

"You did? When? The last time we talked you didn't mention it."

She made a sour face. "No not then. The last time we talked you yelled at me because the phone had died."

"I," he started but snapped his mouth shut and let his mind walk backwards. "Was it the night you got lost in the corn field?"

"Yes! Duh! I said it in the message I left."

He raised his voice and defensively said, "All I heard was you were in danger and they found your car, and then I couldn't get a hold of you!"

"No wonder you were so furious." Her eyes widened, and she winced, remembering his domineering tone. "So I'm the one you couldn't find."

"Yes! I asked Iguana to help me find you, but he couldn't because you had changed your hair color." He pointed to her hair. "The description I gave him was your original color."

Her eyes darted between the two men as confusion set in. "Who is Iguana?"

With a rueful grin, Iggy raised his hand. "I am."

Kara's jaw slightly dropped, but for some reason she wasn't surprised. Entering the room she noticed they were in deep discussion and their body language told her they were comfortable with one another.

Finally, she asked, "So how do the two of you know each other?"

"Iguana and I work together."

"You're both Federal Agents?"

"Yes."

"Do you both know Humphrey?"

Jack nodded.

"Iggy, you know my real name is Kara and not Holly?"

He nodded, and her shoulders drooped with relief. "Thank God! I hated keeping my real identity a secret from you. Every time you called me Holly, I just hated it and wanted to scream, it isn't my name!" She gave him a lopsided grin. "But, I'm still going to call you Iggy."

"Iggy's fine. It'll take me awhile to get used to addressing you as Kara. By the way," Iguana extended his right hand saying, "nice to meet you, Kara."

She firmly shook his hand.

Jack spoke up. "The two of you maintaining your covers around town will be beneficial. I'll need to keep a low profile, and Kara you can't mention me to anyone in town. Got it?"

She nodded and directed her question to Iguana. "So, you're working undercover here in town?"

"Yes."

"Are you here for me?"

Iggy grinned. "No."

"Oh, good," she said with relief.

It was Jack's turn for questions. "Is Iguana the guy who came over in the middle of the night?"

"Yes," she said curtly.

Slowly Jack nodded his head and Kara sensed he now believed the truth about her and Iggy being just friends.

"So we're all on board about the conversations she's heard between the man and woman?" Iguana asked.

"Between the uncle and niece," Jack corrected.

Kara added. "The uncle calls her sister."

"And you're in danger, because you know about the conversations." Iggy verified.

Jack and Kara nodded.

Iggy stated, "And you know the uncle from the bad place where Humphrey rescued you?"

Jack didn't mind that Kara had told Iguana about Humphrey's rescue. In fact, he was extremely grateful it was Iguana she had confided in, because there was trust between them. If it was any other man, he would have been jealous of their bond, but since it was his friend, he trusted that Iguana had no feelings for Kara other than friendship. Observing Kara and how she acted with Iguana, he knew she felt the same thing for Iguana; friendship only.

What were the chances of all of this falling into place like it was? Maybe, Dexter knew what he was doing after all.

Iguana questioned. "The uncle's voice has been triggering your panic attacks, and the niece's scent is familiar to you?"

Kara nodded and sat across from them, forming a triangle.

Every time Iguana asked Kara a question, he saw Jack's jaw muscle clench every time. He wasn't done and decided to go out on a limb. "Holly, I mean Kara. Yesterday, who did you see from your past?"

Sorrow filled Jack as he watched Kara wring her hands together and saw fear in her eyes. Sliding off his chair, he knelt in front of her and gently captured her smaller hands in his. "Kara, honey, who did you see?"

She lowered her head and shook it. "No. I can't tell you."

Jack sensed the one person she would tell was Humphrey but it wasn't possible for him to be here. He had to get her to trust him but pushing her wouldn't earn him this right.

"Please don't make me," she pleaded and toppled into Jack's chest.

"Shhh, it's okay." He soothed and lightly rubbed her back.

Pushing away from Jack she sat in the chair again. He handed her a tissue from the box on the table, and she used it to wipe away the tears. His thumb grazed over her knuckles and his caring eyes seemed to absorb her pain.

"Thank you," she said sincerely.

Jack squeezed her hand then sat back in his own chair and changed the subject giving Kara a break from answering questions.

"Ig, I was told the shipment has been delayed until Tuesday. At least that's what I was told before the meeting. Now, after what happened today, I'm hoping this information is still good. If only we could find where the abandoned barn is, we could stakeout the place and monitor the activity."

"Abandoned barn?" Kara said. "I know where it is."

Two sets of eyes whipped into hers.

"What? You do?" Jack asked excitedly.

"Yes."

"Great! You can show us!" Jack exclaimed, ecstatic for another break in the case.

"Sort of," she said hesitantly. "The only way I know how to get there is on foot through my backyard."

Skeptical, Iguana asked, "How do you know this is the place?"

"It's the abandoned barn where I heard their first conversation. The sister suggested the route be delivered there. The uncle agreed because GPS didn't acknowledge the location."

"Oh, this information is grand!" Jack whooped. "Get your shoes on and let's go."

"Now?" she asked incredibly.

"Yes," Jack said enthusiastically.

Chapter Thirty-Seven

Kara led the men through the field behind her house, into the woods and cautioned them about the vine she had tripped over. Coming out of the shady trees into the light she spread her arms announcing, "Here it is!"

Jack stopped her pursuit inside. "Let us check to make sure it's empty."

She thought he was being too protective and rolled her eyes behind his back. "What should I do if there is danger in there?"

"Run back home," Jack answered.

A few minutes later, both men came out saying it was safe.

Inside, Jack gazed up at the high loft. "You were stuck up there?"

"Yep."

"How on earth did you ever get down?"

"All the hay bales you see stacked on the floor used to be up there." She pointed to the loft.

"You threw all those?" Jack asked, stepping beside her.

She nodded.

"Amazing and good thinking," he praised and rubbed the back of her head.

Jack's pride had a wide smile running across her face.

Iguana took a step back, because he hadn't ever seen her smile so bright. Watching the girl he had known as Holly, now Kara, she seemed more alive than before. She was Holly but with a little more zing!

"Looks like the information I got for Tuesday is correct," Jack said. "Two days from now there will be gunmen guarding the perimeter. We'll hardly get within five hundred feet of this place."

"So has Humphrey heard from his boss?" Iguana inquired.

Jack shook his head. "I've been wondering if Wilma got him too."

"You really think that's the case?" Iguana spoke in an unbelievable tone.

Jack gave him a quick hesitant glance. "Yeah. Why wouldn't it be?"

Iguana scrutinized Jack and didn't like what he saw. His friend had too much trust for his crime boss. An eerie shiver passed through him.

"Why, Ig?" Jack cautiously asked again. "What are you thinking?"

Iguana looked over at Kara. She was sitting on a hay bale, gazing at the ceiling and not paying attention to them. Pressing his lips together he suggested, "You don't think there's a chance the boss man could've stabbed Humphrey in the back or turned on him, do you?"

Jack gave him a ridiculous look. "Naw, there's no way," he guffed. "What would be the point?"

"Because he found out who Humphrey is!" Iguana retorted.

Jack shook his head. "Impossible. All tracks have been covered."

"You're sure?"

"Yes. Even if it were true, there's no way in hell Abel would have let someone else kill Humphrey!" Jack said heatedly. "He would've done it himself!"

Ig nodded because he did agree with him on this. "Okay, so let's say Abel –" He was interrupted by Kara's loud gasp.

"That's the man the sister, was talking to on the phone," she jumped up from the bale.

"What are you talking about? What man?" Jack's stomach coiled already sensing her answer. He wasn't stupid. Kara had stayed quiet until Abel's name was mentioned.

"The night I was in the corn field, I heard the sister thanking Abel for his loyalty. She instructed him to send Humphrey to her because she was going to put a bullet in his head." Kara purposely left out the first part of what the sister had said, because it was too raunchy.

Kara continued, "I also heard the sister say to Abel her uncle has no clue what's in store for him, but before he dies he'll know who breeched Memphis." She shivered remembering the sister's lecherous laugh.

"What?" Jack shook his head, because he didn't want to believe Abel had betrayed him. "No, this isn't right."

Spinning on his heel, Jack clamped his hand on the back of his neck and agonized over the new information given.

"I'm sorry, Jack." Iguana offered his empathy.

Kara didn't grasp Iguana's compassion and Jack's devastation for Humphrey's situation. Jack caught Kara's confusion in listening to their discussion. This wasn't the time to let her discover Humphrey's truth, and he steered her curiosity away from figuring it out. Clearing his throat, he said, "I don't believe Humphrey's cover has been compromised but in order to help Humphrey, we need to plan the next step."

"Okay, let's dissect what Kara just said," Iguana suggested.

Jack motioned for Kara to sit on the bale she had been on as he and Iguana each carried a bale and set them down next to hers.

"Are you sure you want me to know any of this?" Kara asked.

Both men nodded and were quite firm with their yeses.

Jack began. "All right, here's what I know. Hank is Frank's uncle. According to Abel, Frank wants to takeover the business."

Iggy said, "I'm guessing Hank isn't aware of his nephew's plans?"

Shaking his head, Jack pointed at Kara. "I don't think so. Especially, with what you heard the sister say, 'before he dies he'll know who betrayed him'."

"So the sister is Frank's sibling?" Kara questioned.

Jack nodded. He had come to the same conclusion. "Yeah, the siblings are steadily building their team. They've even conned and threatened people to join them."

Iguana whistled. "Damn. I never thought my assignment's life would be in danger."

Shocked, Kara asked, "H-Hank's your assignment?"

"Yep."

"He's a dangerous man," she said quietly.

"Yes, he is. I'm sorry you had any kind of contact with him," Iguana sympathized.

"Thanks," she muttered, shivering.

Jack hated the fear filling her eyes. Regret swam through him, and it would stay there until the day he died. Kara would never forgive him for what he did, and why should she? He knew he would never forgive himself.

Iguana spoke solemnly. "The sister must have enticed Abel to join them. Is it possible he had to give up Humphrey as his ally in order to join their team?"

"That would be the only reason Abel let him go. The man's a snake," Jack said in disgust. "After all this time I-ah-he-Humphrey invested." Jack stumbled; almost messing up his undercover identity. "Abel dumps him just like that!" He snapped his fingers loudly. "Unbelievable!"

"So what does the sister have against Humphrey?" Kara asked.

Jack shook his head. "Hell if I know."

"Well, Humphrey's the only person who might know the answer. You'll have to ask him," Kara said innocently.

"I guess so," Jack mumbled and was grateful when Kara yawned. He seized the opportunity of suggesting they head back to her house.

Iguana announced he was going to follow the road and see where it led.

"All right, be careful." Jack warned.

"Will he be okay?" Kara asked as the two of them entered the woods. "I mean, I know he's an agent, but what if one of the bad guys is driving down the road? Won't they be suspicious why a man is out there?"

Jack grinned. "Ig will be okay. He's been in worse spots than a lost man walking down the road. Trust me; he'll come up with a believable cover story."

She glanced sideways at Jack. His whiskered jaw, dark sultry eyes, and muscular build made a rollercoaster fly through her belly. He was tall and moved with a litheness grace. It was nice being by his side versus talking with him over the phone.

"Jack, I can't explain it, but I do trust you."

Taken aback he said, "Really?"

"Yeah," she admitted shyly.

"What about Humphrey?" he asked, kicking himself.

His question threw her off guard, and she made the mistake of looking at him while continuing to walk and tripped on the same stupid vine as before. Helplessly, she fell forward. Jack caught her beneath her armpits and set her feet on the ground, but he didn't remove his hands; they stayed on her.

Heat bolted through them and the air sparked with a sizzling energy.

Kara tried stepping away but a magnetic force kept her there. She found it odd that two men could have this effect on her, yet with Jack it was hotter.

The heated exchange with Kara left Jack powerless. He was stunned by the strong forces pulling him closer; holding her to him. It was better than when he was Humphrey helping her at the restaurant. He was amazed by how much he wanted to shelter her from danger and tell her everything was going to be all right; he'd make sure of it.

A squawking blue jay above on a branch broke their trance.

"Did you hurt your foot?" he asked abruptly.

"No. It's all right." She gave him a small smile.

They continued walking in silence listening to nature. After this morning's near death experience, he was more than happy to enjoy a friendly stroll with a trusting person.

At the edge of the woods, Kara turned and faced him. "Jack, before we met in the interrogation room, I had been in a really bad place, I mean an actual place."

"Yes, the sheds. It's where you encountered Hank," Jack said knowingly.

"You know?" she gasped in surprise.

He nodded and took her hands in his. "Kara," he hushed. "I know Humphrey kidnapped you and why he did. It was because of your ex-boyfriend Greg."

"Yes." She quietly spoke.

He squeezed her hands. "I also know while there, this is where you encountered the sister."

Her eyes misted, and he bravely took another truthful step. "Humphrey said he saw you and the sister talking at the restaurant. He said you looked scared. What did she say to you?"

Kara vigorously shook her head and looked away.

His fingers touched her cheek, and he softly instructed, "Look at me."

Finally, she did, and his pleading eyes prompted her to say, "She liked my purple hair, and said I could be a model. Then she gave me her card in case I was interested."

In his gut, he knew there was more. "Okay, but I don't think this is why you were so frightened. What else?" he prompted.

She tried breaking free from his grasp, but he clamped his hands on her upper arms. "Tell me what she said," he insisted.

"No." She looked down at the ground. "It's not important."

"Yes. It is. Everything you say is important." He rubbed her chin with his thumb and lightly spoke her name, "Kara."

Her rising eyes met his dark stare.

"Please." His soft demand persuaded her to unload pertinent information.

"Jack. She-she's the lady from the sheds!" Tears welled in her eyes.

"The lady?" he repeated, already knowing who she was referring to, but he needed her to say it.

"Yes. The lady from the sheds is the Sister! Her perfume has an awful scent, and I think it's triggered some of my panic attacks! At the sheds, she herded several of us into a special shed. She'd come for us and choose the girls she wanted for her parties. Sometimes girls came back and sometimes they didn't. Of those that returned, they had horrible things to say."

"Were you ever chosen?"

"No. I scooted myself to the back of the shed because…"

He squeezed her hand. "Go on."

"When selecting us, she groped me and said I could be a star in her bed," Kara whispered. "Jack, I'd rather die hungry than to do that!" she said through clenched teeth.

"Then you know her real name, don't you?" he questioned.

"Yes," she replied.

Lifting to her tiptoes, she whispered the lady's name in his ear. Jack pulled her against him and wrapped his arms around her taking this moment to comfort her. There was no way he could let Kara out of his sight. Not now! She was far too precious! Not only as a witness for his next case but this one too! He finally had a witness who could place the sister at the sheds! He hugged her tight because all of a sudden he realized how much danger she was in! It was only a matter of time before the sister realized who Kara was. The sister was smart, and Jack knew despite Kara's hair color change, the sister would remember her face. *I have to get Kara out of town before that happens!*

Chapter Thirty-Eight

The audience clapped enthusiastically at the magician's last magic trick. Next he asked for volunteers. Callie boldly stood up. Evan reluctantly watched her step into the box and the door closed. Then with the wave of the magician's hand and a *Poof,* the door opened and Callie wasn't there. The audience's amazed ooh's and ah murmured through the room. Evan stared breathlessly waiting for the magician to close the door and bring her back, but he didn't. He bowed and curtsied and said, "Thank you, folks, for coming. This concludes our show."

"Bring her back!" Evan shouted, but the magician ignored him as he bowed again and tipped his hat downward…past a long scruffy beard. Lifting his head, his black eyes arrowed into Evan and mocked him.

It was the bearded man! Evan jumped on stage and grabbed his neck. His fingers dug in the man's flesh. "Bring her back! Bring her back right now!"

The bearded man cackled, and Evan shook him watching his head bob back and forth. The beard began slipping. He grabbed it and pulled, trying to see who it was, but the face was blurred.

"Who are you?" Evan asked, but the only answer he received was an evil snicker.

Evan woke up seeing Callie's golden eyes. Anxiously, he asked, "Sweetheart, did I hurt you?"

"I'm all right, but I can't say the same for the pillow." She pointed to the floor, and he saw the flimsy pillowcase lying there.

The pillow was out of the case and had been thrown across the room. Fear slid in at the thought of what he could've done to Callie.

"Thank God it was the pillow and not you," he said adamantly and gently touched her shoulder.

"What were you dreaming about?" she asked.

"We were at a magic show and the magician called for a volunteer for the next act. He picked you and inside the box you went. He spun it around a couple times, said his magic words, opened the door and you were gone, and he wouldn't bring you back."

"Oh. No." She gingerly rubbed his arm. "I heard you yell bring her back. I rolled over and you were fighting with the pillow."

"The magician wore a beard," he said grimly.

Her eyes widened. "The magician was the bearded man?"

He tensed. "The beard was a disguise. I pulled it off, but I couldn't see his face. It was fuzzy, and I keep feeling I should know who it is."

What did his dream mean? She stared at him in awe. "What are you thinking?"

He smiled because she knew the wheels were turning in his head. "Remember, when you told me Humphrey said he wished he could have told me where you were? But if he had, it would've ruined everything he had worked for."

Callie nodded.

Evan continued. "I have been mulling over the part about *he* wished *he* could have told me. I don't understand. I've never met Humphrey."

She agreed. "It is strange. Maybe he was watching you from a distance?"

Evan shrugged. "I think we should talk to Iggy."

Callie questioned, "Why him?"

"This is another thing I've been thinking about." Holding her hand, his thumb caressed the back of it.

Viewing Evan's apprehension, she knew he had something serious to say.

He took a deep breath and said, "I think Iggy is short for Iguana."

Callie's jaw fell in disbelief. Goose bumps waved over her body followed by one big shiver. Trusting Evan's judgment she pieced certain things together and began calculating the similarities between Iggy and Iguana.

Iggy's friendly smile gave her comfort in a sense she could trust him. When she was kidnapped and put in the crate, she trusted Iguana's compassionate promise that he was protecting her, and would get her home safely. "Shit," she whispered. "Then this means Iggy knows Humphrey and probably Jack, too."

"Yeah," Evan agreed and yawned. Inhaling her pretty fragrance, he snuggled her in beside him, whispering, "C'mon, let's go back to sleep."

Callie was envious of his rapid ability of falling asleep. It took her longer because her brain wouldn't rest. Finally she concentrated on his soothing breath lulling her to sweet dreams.

****

Evan and Callie took the sidewalk leading to Iggy's front door. Evan rang the doorbell. While they waited for Iggy to answer the door, Evan gently grasped Callie's hand.

Iggy opened the door and was surprised to see them. He kindly invited them in and asked, "What do I owe the honor of your visit to?"

"Sorry, to bother you so early in the morning, but we have a few questions," Evan said.

"Would you like a cup of coffee while we talk?" Iggy offered.

"Yes, please," Callie accepted graciously.

Iggy led them towards the back of the house into a sunny room and motioned for them to sit on the couch that faced the backyard. "You're in luck. I just finished brewing some. Please have a seat, and I'll bring it out."

Iggy returned shortly with three mugs and a carafe. He poured each of them a cup and then sat down saying, "The questions you have...are they about the other day at the roadhouse?"

Evan answered vaguely, "Some."

"Some? What does that mean?" His questioning eyes were on Evan, but it was Callie who replied.

"Iggy, it means we know you're Iguana, the other man protecting me in the crate when Humphrey wasn't there."

The shock that fell on his face told them this was the last thing he expected to hear. Slowly, Iggy's gaze turned toward Callie. Heaving a sigh he replied, "Yes. I am."

"So, you're a Federal Agent, too?" she asked.

He nodded.

"Are you here watching me?" she inquired.

"You are not my assignment." He firmly stated. "My plan wasn't for our paths to cross, but they did when you helped Holly...and then my big mouth asked you to help with self defense classes."

Evan glared at Iggy and accused, "At the roadhouse, you lied saying you didn't know the man you were talking to, but you do know him, don't you?"

Caught, Iggy answered, "Yes."

Evan continued, "It was Humphrey. Is he here?"

A deep voice from behind answered, "No, he's not."

Evan swiveled and gasped, "Jack!"

The other agent extended his arm, and they shook hands.

Jack smiled. "Good to see, Evan."

Evan said the same, but he wasn't sure if he was glad to see him, because he really wanted to meet Humphrey.

Callie stepped forward and introduced herself. "Agent Jack, hi, I'm Callie. I don't believe we've met."

"Uh, right, nice to meet you," Jack faltered, shaking her hand.

Callie shared a look with Evan. Jack in Iggy's house confirmed their theory about the two men knowing each other.

Jack gave them both a suspicious glance. "What's going on?"

Iggy placed a hand on Jack's shoulder. "They know I'm Iguana."

Startled by the news, Jack cursed under his breath. After the roadhouse parking lot, he knew it was only a matter of time before the couple figured things out, but the timing was inconvenient. Sensing they were here to stay awhile, Jack heaved a tired sigh and plopped in the chair. "All right, let's talk."

Evan led with his first question. "Agent Jack, the day in my office."

During the pause Jack stated, "No need to say agent. Jack is fine."

Evan began again. "Did you know where Callie was when you brought us her phone?"

"Yes," Jack answered.

"Did you give Humphrey the tip to search her boot for the GPS chip?"

Jack's eyes didn't leave Evan's, and he firmly replied, "Yes."

Furious, Evan leaned across the coffee table and grabbed Jack's shirt by the neck. "You son of a...why didn't you say anything?"

Iguana intervened. "Evan, stop."

Jack pushed Iguana's hand away. "No, Ig, I deserve it. He has every right to hate me."

Eye to eye Jack egged Evan on. "Go ahead. Hit me. I know you want to. I won't arrest you. Do it!" Jack yelled.

Callie watched the situation transpire. She knew why Evan wanted to punch Jack, but she didn't know why Jack said he deserved it. She had seen deep sorrow in Jack's eyes and suspected the reason ran deeper than the day in Evan's office when he couldn't tell anyone where she was. Callie fixated on Jack's eyes. They held turmoil and regret. All at once, the similarities sank in, and she absorbed Jack's unique secret!

"Enough!" Iguana shouted angrily and pushed them apart. "Sit down, both of you!"

Evan sat but his stern eyes didn't sway from Jack's. His main purpose for wanting to punch Jack in the face was because he knew about Callie's predicament and didn't say a word to them. This upset Evan the most. Second was the GPS information Jack had given Humphrey. Evan believed if the discussion about Callie's phone hadn't taken place with the agents in the room, Humphrey would've never received information about the GPS chip. They could've saved Callie a lot sooner! However, Humphrey didn't take the chip away. He only discovered where Callie had hidden it, and instead of hurting her, he protected her. Confusion churned in Evan's stomach. For so long, he despised the bearded man but now he viewed him as a hero and his hated desire switched to Jack.

"Why didn't you tell us where Callie was?" Evan asked.

Jack's eyes flickered with pain. "I couldn't."

"Why?"

"If I had, it would have ruined everything."

Stunned, Evan deeply inhaled. "Humphrey said the same thing to Callie."

Jack affirmed. "Yes."

Evan was bewildered. How would he know what Humphrey said to Callie? Unless... *Fuck*. In the parking lot he watched Jack run away! The same man who had exited his office! Oh my God! Jack was...! Goose bumps stormed over his body followed by one big shudder. He raged, "You're Humphrey!"

"I am," Jack admitted.

Evan snarled, "What the hell! You deceived us!"

"I'm so sorry," Jack apologized profusely. "I wished to God I could've told you, but I couldn't. I've worked hard to maintain Humphrey's cover and some of the choices I've made were tough...decisions I'm not proud of but had to be done."

"And Callie was one of them?" Evan asked harshly.

"Unfortunately, yes." The agent firmly stood his ground. "The request came in, and I was caught. If I didn't help, I wouldn't have had any control on how she was treated. So I agreed to help Abel, vowing to myself to make sure she was returned to you unscathed."

Observing Jack's distraught changed Evan's perception. His anger dissipated, and he believed Jack truly didn't want Callie harmed.

Evan extended his hand. "Thank you."

Leery, Jack said, "You're not going to hit me?"

"No. I can't. Now, that I know, you were protecting Callie all along."

Jack pointed to Iggy. "We both were."

Iguana smiled. "I was on board from the start with protecting Callie and getting her home safely. The GPS chip was crucial information. We had used a signal jammer, and we were about to release it when Jack found out she might have the chip in her possession. If we hadn't known about it, the Feds would have stormed in and all hell would've broken loose. Evan, I know you wanted her back sooner, but we needed time to construct a plan for getting her home safely."

"Yeah about that," Evan began. "What was your timeline for leaving her alone and us finding her?"

Jack gave him a questing glance. "Not long. Why? How long was she there?"

"The bottles of water left were bone dry and there was no sign of food. She was disoriented and wouldn't allow any of the rescue crews to take her out. I had to beg them not to drug her before I got there," Evan explained.

Confused, Jack asked, "Wait. What? It shouldn't have taken that long to find her. I figured you'd call Dexter soon after you received the signal."

"I did," Evan verified. "I was ready to go and get her, but Dexter asked me to wait saying, he wanted his team to check it out first, because he didn't want me walking into a terrible situation."

Jack's anger rose while he listened. *Dexter didn't follow any of my instructions! Rescue crews! Why did he get them involved? Ugh! Callie could've died waiting on whatever the hell he was doing!*

"Evan, you were able to get her out, yes?" Jack carefully asked.
"Yes."

Jack looked relieved. "Good."

Iguana cleared his throat. "Hey, Holly's on her way over."

Jack nodded. "Good."

Evan and Callie sensed the agitated energy between the two agents.

"What's going on? Why is she coming?" Callie asked uneasily.

Iguana easily answered, "We will explain once she arrives."

"Also," Jack warned. "Holly can't know I'm Humphrey. No matter what, she has to keep thinking they are two different men."

They promised to keep his secret as the doorbell rang signifying Holly had arrived. The agents left to greet her.

Callie placed her hand on Evan's arm, and he covered it with his. Their soft gazes met and expressed love. The two agents and Holly entered the room. Callie stood and gave her friend a hug while Jack pulled another chair over.

"Callie, hi," Holly said in surprise. "Why are you guys here?"

Kara sank into the chair and glanced at Jack with nervous eyes. Hoping to erase her apprehension, Jack gave her shoulder a reassuring squeeze, and she rewarded him with a shy smile.

Iguana cleared his throat. "Holly, we thought it'd be a good idea for all of us to discuss the danger."

The hair on Evan's neck prickled. "Callie's in danger isn't she?"

Jack nodded. "Yes."

"By the same person who wanted her kidnapped?" Evan inquired.

"Yes," Jack confirmed.

"It's the woman who visited her in the crate, isn't it?" Evan demanded.

Jack looked horrified.

Evan accused, "You know who I'm talking about."

"Yes, but how do you?" Jack's brows furrowed.

"I don't know who she is but the other night Callie dreamed about the incident. I can't shake the feeling that the perfume she and Holly smelled at the party is what triggered the dream," Evan insisted.

Iguana knew which incident Evan referred to. He had a hunch about which woman the scent belonged to, but he had no idea Callie had also come in contact with this woman. Now that he knew, it gave him a broader understanding of the woman's role in her uncle's business."

Iguana looked at Evan. "Are you sure you don't know who the woman is?"

"Yes, I'm sure," Evan said giving him a crazy look. "Why would I?"

"Because she lives here in Purlieu," Iguana stated.

Callie said astonished, "Who is it?"

The two agents started speaking at the same time. Iguana only spoke the first two syllables of the woman's name he knew, but his voice tapered off, letting Jack firmly state the name Wilma.

Evan shook his head. "Um, are you sure you have the right name?"

Jack firmly stated it was correct.

Evan gave him a ridiculous look. "The only Wilma in town that I know of is eighty years old. I don't think it's her you are referring to."

Jack agreed. "Yeah, no, the one I know is much younger, in her late twenties, early thirties."

Evan curiously asked, "What does she look like?"

Jack thought for a moment, determining the best way to describe Wilma. "In high heels she's my height. Without them, I'd say she's as tall as Callie. Her hairstyle is a short bob above her shoulders and the color is strange. It's a blondish white verging on platinum, if that makes any sense. The clothes she wears are fancy, but I've always seen her in short skirts and skimpy blouses and the jewelry she wears is chunky."

Iguana scowled, because the names were different. Wilma wasn't anywhere close to the name he had. Disappointment slid in. He thought for sure they had the same person. Even as he thought this, his gut nagged him that he was still right, though he didn't know how. Then the how revealed itself to him. After Jack described Wilma's appearance, Iguana realized he had just described the woman he knew!

Callie was on the verge of guessing who Jack was describing. The minute he said she had strange color hair Callie was positive of who it was. Hearing it sealed the deal. She sought Evan's hand hoping to feel its warmth but it was cold. Worried, she peered into his disbelieving eyes, and she comprehended he had guessed who it was that Jack was describing. He turned to look at her. His eyes were cold like ice particles.

Kara never heard anyone give this kind of detailed description, but Jack was right. The times Kara had seen the woman, she wore the same kind of outfits that Jack described. Unfortunately, Kara suspected she was the only one in the room who could vouch for the bone chilling eyes that had sexually assessed her. Though it was warm in the sunroom this memory sent shivers down her spine.

Jack observed everyone's reactions. For Kara, he hated the chilling fear that shivered through her, wishing he could take it away and provide her with heartwarming cheer. However, he didn't know if his heart had anything left to give, but if it did, he'd gladly give it all to her.

Then his gaze swung to the other three. Evan's face was haunted while Callie and Iguana's held confusion. All their expressions revealed they knew the woman he described but it wasn't by the same name. If it wasn't Wilma, then what was it?

"So tell me, what name do you know her as?" Jack boldly asked.

In unison, they replied, "Francesca."

Chapter Thirty-Nine

Evan looked at Iggy and clamored, "How do you know Francesca?"

"Uh," Iguana muttered. For a split second he debated about telling a fib or the truth, knowing Dexter wouldn't want the mission jeopardized. But the rest of the seconds that followed reminded him he had too much respect for Evan. Iguana trusted him and everyone else in the room.

"Francesca is related to my assignment," Iguana stated.

"And who would that be?" Evan questioned.

"Her uncle Hank," Iguana replied, bluntly.

The shock registering on Evan's face was beyond belief, acting as if a bucket of icy cold water had been dumped on him. His floundering stare was more than Iguana could bear.

In a dusty voice, Evan rasped, "Hank's back?"

Iguana nodded.

"Fuck, Kellan's gonna hit the roof," Evan said.

"You can't tell him," Iguana warned.

Evan decided he wasn't going to argue about what he couldn't tell his best friend and just nodded his head. All sorts of different things ran through his mind.

Impatiently, Jack cleared his throat. "Before we get too much off the track, can you please tell me why my description of Wilma is the same for this Francesca?"

"They are one," Evan explained.

Jack sulked. "I don't understand."

Evan gave him a long stare as he struggled with the way he was going to explain this strange predicament. Hearing the two names surfaced chilling memories. Inside and out he felt frigid. From the touch of his icicle fingers on his cheek and chin to the blood flowing in his veins.

"Ev, what's going on?" Callie asked concerned.

He turned to look at her and the soft glow in her eyes heated him back to life. He gave her a somber smile. Using a derisive tone, he stated, "Francesca. She's using her dead sister's name."

It was Evan's turn to witness the speechless expressions staring back at him. He took advantage of the wordless space to tell the story.

"The sister's were eighteen months apart. In school they were one grade apart. Wilma was older but not wiser. She was a lot more immature than her baby sister. She lived minute to minute and all for fun. Francesca was more mature, responsible, and goal oriented. Though she was reserved, she often said she wouldn't stay in the shadows of men."

"What happened to Wilma?" Iguana asked.

"In high school, she was killed in a car accident. The driver of the car she was riding in was going too fast around a curve, lost control and hit a tree. Neither of them was wearing a seatbelt and both were killed instantly."

Sad murmurs spread among the group.

"Yeah, awful," Evan empathized and continued. "After her sister died, Francesca left town for the rest of the school year and returned the following year. When she came back, she was a lot different! She was still herself but in a way she was her sister too. It was weird and strange. Francesca had cut her long hair to the bob style of her sister, Wilma's. She dressed the same style as Wilma, she was outgoing, flirty, and demanding but kept the stern regiment and determined ambition for her future plans."

"Wow," Iggy whistled.

Jack's mind was whirling. The minute he heard the part about Francesca not wanting to stay in the shadows of men, it bit him like a wild dog; its teeth sank in and wouldn't let go. *The woman I know as Wilma hints when Frank is in charge she will not be in the shadows. She's also leading Frank's uprising...except there is no Wilma; only Francesca. Then there's the part about the sister saying before her uncle dies he'll know who breeched Memphis. What am I missing?* He thought some more.

Hank is Frank's uncle. Earlier, Iguana, Kara and I suspected Wilma was Frank's sister...meaning Hank is their uncle. His mind repeated *their uncle. Wait!*

He tapped his fingers rapidly on the table as excitement and disbelief erupted inside him. He abruptly stood and placed his hands on his head. *Oh my God, Oh my God that's it that's it!*

The action caught Iguana's attention. "Jack what's wrong?"

"I know who Frank is!" he shouted.

Iguana's brows wrinkled.

Jack paced as he talked. "We've been thinking wrong this whole entire time!" He paused long enough to take a breath and plunged in again. "Frank. He isn't anyone's brother or nephew!"

Iguana gave him a confounded gaze.

"Remember when I said, Hank is Frank's uncle and Frank wants to take over?"

Iguana nodded.

"Think about it Ig," Jack said. "Remember how we suspected Wilma was Frank's sister?"

Iguana gave Jack a peculiar look. "Holy crap," he muttered. "You're telling me Francesca is Frank?"

"Yes!" Jack said enthusiastically.

"Oh my, mother of…" he trailed off as disbelief and shock covered his face.

Evan didn't understand their conversation and asked, "Who is Frank?"

Jack rushed to answer, "Second in command of the human trafficking ring we've been trying to take down! Hank is the leader! You know Dexter came close to busting him awhile back, but he got away. Since then Hank's been operating around the country. We knew the operation was still going strong but didn't know where the main hub was. Until Iguana followed Hank here and it became clear his hometown was the main hub. Frank and his assistant Wilma were in charge of things here in Purlieu."

"Are you saying Francesca has been posing as Wilma?" Evan said in an unbelievable tone.

Jack shrugged. "From what you told us, I guess so."

Evan asked in disbelief. "You think Francesca is this Frank guy? One of the leaders of a major human trafficking ring you all have been trying to take down?"

Evan was hesitant to believe Iggy and Jack's affirming yes. He didn't want to believe something like this existed in Purlieu and someone from their town would participate in something so evil…let alone someone he knew!

"What? How? Huh?" Evan said feeling depleted. He certainly didn't expect an answer anytime soon since they all had the same helpless expression as he.

Kara spoke. "So the sister is using two names?"

Jack nodded.

Pointing to Jack, Kara said, "You know her as Wilma and," she pointed to Callie, Evan and Iggy saying, "The three of you know her as Francesca?"

Everyone nodded.

In her mind, she stated *but I know her as the lady from the sheds.* However, there was no way Kara could say this out loud. It would jeopardize her life here as Holly and put her own life as Kara in extreme danger!

"It's a big confusing mess," Kara murmured.

"Yes, it is." Evan agreed. "What I don't understand is when we started the conversation it sounded like Callie's in danger, but I haven't heard anything clarifying why and how?"

Before the agents could answer, Kara pointed to Callie and revealed, "The Sister, I mean Francesca, wants you gone because you embarrassed her."

"I embarrassed her?" Callie asked perplexed. "How do you know this?"

"I've heard secretive conversations between her and her uncle," Kara said quietly.

Jack confirmed. "It's true. Holly heard them say the trucker lady had been kidnapped. This could mean anyone, but then she heard them say your name."

"What kind of danger am I in?" Callie inquired.

Kara cringed. "She wants you dead."

Callie gasped in horror and Kara continued. "She hated her uncle's decision for letting you go, and the uncle is furious with her and warned her to stay away from you."

Callie shivered, and Evan wound his arm around her. She wracked her brain for the horrible thing she could've done to embarrass Francesca. It had to be earth shattering for Francesca to want to kill her. *What was it?*

Callie faced Evan with high concern. "I'm putting you in danger."

"Shhh," he soothed. "No one's going to hurt you." He reassured and joy swept through him as Callie's eyes reflected the faithful trust she had in him. It was a grand feeling! Something he would cherish forever! He clasped his fingers with hers in a tight mold. Lifting their hands to his mouth, he tenderly kissed her knuckles as his shining eyes expressed love. For a moment, it was just them in the room, the others had faded away. Coming back to reality, Evan reluctantly pulled his gaze from Callie and looked at the others.

Clearing his throat, Evan said, "Holly, these people you've heard talking –"

Jack fiercely interrupted. "Don't have any clue she's been listening and we need to keep it this way."

Kara fearfully gripped Callie's arm. "Please don't tell anyone."

"I won't." Callie assured her.

Evan posed another question. "What else have you heard them say?"

Kara ignored Jack's piercing stare and sternly stated, "Things I can't say."

Evan nodded, sensing none of his questions would be answered. Dropping it, he took another approach as he looked at Jack. "Can you tell me who's responsible for convincing Abel that Sage wasn't the girl he was looking for?"

Jack said, "Humphrey convinced him."

"On behalf of my friend, Dirk, he thanks him *a lot*."

Recognizing Abel's name, fear for her former friend, Sage, gripped Kara. Her brows scrunched in concern, and without thinking she voiced her worry. "Why was Abel after Sage?"

Iguana cleared his throat.

Kara looked up to see Callie giving her an odd look. Immediately, Kara was aware of her error; forgetting Holly wasn't supposed to know Sage. Recovering from her mistake, she curiously asked, "What happened to your friend?"

Callie grimaced. "Sage was kidnapped by the same man who took me."

Kara carefully worded her question. "Why was she taken?"

Callie explained, "Abel had become infatuated with Sage when he helped her with an entanglement she had with a girlfriend while they were having lunch."

Kara winced, remembering the incident well, because she was the girlfriend. She had been infuriated with Sage and attacked her in the middle of the restaurant during the lunch rush hour. So many people had seen her behave so badly, and she had humiliated Sage. This was one of those poor, poor decisions she had made and now was ashamed of; along with all the other bad choices she had made within that time frame. Humphrey had pulled her off Sage and carried her out the back door into the van taking her far away from civilization.

"Did your friend get away?" she asked.

"Yes. My partner and I rescued her in transit on her way to Abel," Callie answered, noticing the relief on Holly's face.

Curiosity prompted Kara to ask, "The man who took you, what's his name?"

"Humphrey," Callie said, hearing Holly's sharp inhale. Her instincts nagged her as she scrutinized her friend's eyes as they flicked with pain. Without hesitation Callie asked, "Holly, have you met Humphrey?"

Before Jack could do anything to distract a tedious situation from unfolding, Kara boldly answered, "Yes, I have."

Callie's eyes never left Holly's face as she questioned, "How?"

"He kidnapped me, too," she truthfully unloaded.

Jack and Iguana gave her a speechless stare. They scrambled trying to put their scattered thoughts into a believable explanation so they could get themselves out of the sticky subject Kara had dropped them in.

Jack's temper simmered beneath the surface. He couldn't believe Kara had been so foolishly careless losing focus on where she was and who was with her; people who needed to believe she was Holly! Now here she was openly discussing her kidnapping with Callie!

"What!" Callie and Evan exclaimed. "What happened?"

"I put my trust in someone who did not have good intentions. In order for that person to get out of a stifling situation they sacrificed me to pay the debt." Kara vaguely stated.

"Oh, Holly, that's horrible!" Callie gasped.

Shrugging, Kara added. "In the end, it all worked out because thanks to Humphrey I am here safe and sound."

Callie smiled. "He did the same thing with me. Made sure I was safe and got back to Evan."

"This proves he's one of the good guys," Kara defended.

Jack's anger fizzled. He was proud of her. There were so many reasons for Kara to hate Humphrey, but she didn't.

"Yes, he is." Callie confirmed.

"Humphrey's like most people; we all wish we could rewind time and change poorly made decisions," Iguana said regretfully.

Viewing the heartache in his eyes, Kara wondered what decisions Iggy wished he could redo.

Silence hung in the air after his statement as though they were mulling over the certain things they could change in the past.

Evan thought of several things he would've done differently with Callie. However, despite not being able to go back in time for a redo, he had to admit things were working out for them. The one thing they could do now was stay ahead of hindsight. Insightfully, he asked, "Do either of you have any ideas of how I might be able to keep Callie out of harm's way?"

The two agents arched their brows and shared a look.

Jack piped up. "How long can you keep her hidden?"

Evan questioned, "How long do you need?"

"A week."

"I can do that."

Callie gave them a ridiculous look and was about to protest when Evan leaned in and squeezed her hand. "Shhh, I'll explain later."

His eyes twinkled mischievously, and hers narrowed with suspicion. Evan then announced the two of them had a long day ahead and needed to get going.

"We'll take care of the threat for you," Jack said. "In the meantime, live like normal," he instructed. "If you see Francesca, please whatever you do, don't confront her!" he forewarned and his eyes pleaded.

Evan and Callie promised they wouldn't confront her and silently hoped they wouldn't see her.

"Please let us know when the threat is over," Evan said as they reached the door.

"We will," Iguana promised.

In the truck, Callie turned to Evan. "Are we really going to lay low?"

"Yes. In fact, I've got a surprise for you and an idea how we can hide." His eyes danced mysteriously.

Her eyes widened with excitement. "What is it?"

He shook his head. "I can't tell you. I'll need to show you."

"Okay, show me." She readily agreed.

He smiled. "Let's go home and shower, get dressed, eat, and then I will."

"Evan!" she whined. "Why can't you just tell me?"

"It's hard to explain but trust me." His eyes twinkled. "You're gonna love it!"

Trusting him, she smiled and simply stated, "Okay."

****

Ninety minutes later, they were back in the truck and headed in the direction of the office.

Callie dared asking, "Where are we going?"

"You'll see in a few minutes."

As they crested the hill, Maslund Trucking came into view. "My surprise is at work?" An uncertain frown creased her face.

"Yes."

The secretive glint in his eyes piqued her curiosity.

"Let's play twenty questions," she suggested.

"Let's not," he hastily replied, parking by the front doors. Since it was the weekend the lot was empty. Unfastening her seatbelt, he lifted her from the passenger seat and onto his lap. He caressed her cheek and gave her a loving gaze. "Callie, you mean the world to me. I love you with all my heart."

There was no need for her to speak because her eyes expressed the true enchantment of the love in her heart, and he felt it as he did with every caress, embrace, and kiss they shared.

Softly, he asked, "Are you ready?"

His tone indicated more, but she didn't know what. However, with all of her heart she knew that as long as she was with Evan she was ready! With an abundant amount of happiness she exclaimed, "Yes!"

Thrilled with her enthusiasm a jovial smile shined across his face. "C'mon, then, let's go."

Keeping her in his arms, he gracefully jumped out of the truck. Her eyes twinkled as she laughed saying, "Are you going to carry me to my surprise?"

"No. I'll let you walk."

He set her feet on the ground. Grabbing her hand he guided her through the front doors, through the lobby and towards the solid door leading outside to the truck yard where the tractor rigs parked. Evan paused and took a deep breath, thankful there weren't any windows in the door. He was overflowing with excitement! He had dreamed of this day for so long when he could offer her everything her heart desired and now that it was here, he was nervous about her reaction.

"Evan." She placed her hand on his arm that was stopping her from going any further. "Is my surprise on the other side of the door?"

"Yes," he said hoarsely.

"You asked if I was ready. Are you ready?" she said.

"Yeah," he whispered. "I've been ready for quite some time."

"Then what are we waiting for?"

"Just a little nervous, that's all," he admitted shyly.

She wondered if he had a big sign on Sunbird that read, will you marry me? It had to be! Why else would he be so bashful to show her?

"Evan, I'm ready," she announced with a cheerful smile.

He inhaled deeply and said, "Okay. I am too."

"Do I need to close my eyes?" She giggled.

"Could you?"

Closing them, she trustingly held out her hand and let him guide her outside.

"Okay." His husky whisper tickled her ear. "Open your eyes."

Chapter Forty

Callie opened her eyes and confusion slid in, because Sunbird was not there! She wasn't sure what she was looking at until Evan said, "Surprise!"

Slowly, she began to understand. After the first initial shock subsided another level sank in as her jaw dropped. Astonished, she stared at her surprise of an extended semi tractor! The sleek smoky gray rig was decked with shiny chrome smokestacks and orange running lights.

She was a beauty!

Callie gravitated towards the new semi tractor. Its virginity sparkled in the sunlight. In awe, she stood beside it and touched it with her hand. She glided her fingertips over the smooth exterior and didn't feel a single scratch or dent.

"She's beautiful!" Callie exclaimed breathlessly.

"Just like you." Evan circled his arm around her waist. "I would have painted her yellow but thought we needed a color of our own. I chose the same color as my truck because it reminds me of the first time you sat in it. You looked like you belonged there. From that day on, no other girl looked as good in my truck as you did. I knew then you had stolen my heart."

His words stole her heart.

Evan clasped his hands behind her. "Callie Cat, I've been patient watching you drive off into the horizon, chasing sunsets, looking for a place to rest your heart. You've agreed to come home to us, but sweetheart you're the one I want to fall asleep with and wake up beside without the use of technology. I want us together; at home and on the road."

"On the road?" she echoed, and her mind reviewed his statement of them needing a color of their own.

"Yes." His smiling eyes were filled with love.

"But you hate driving!"

"I hate being away from you more! I want us together with your schedule. Two weeks on the road, two weeks off give or take."

"Really?" she asked incredibly.

"Yes, really," he confirmed, stroking her hair. "I love you."

"I love you," she cried.

Evan retrieved a small square box from the semi tractor's step. With twinkling eyes, he knelt, lifted the lid, and she gasped when she saw the sparkling diamond ring inside.

"Callie Cat, will you marry me?"

Her gold eyes shimmered with tears. "Yes!" she said excitedly.

Evan stood, and his giant smile reflected extreme happiness. His hands shook as he removed the ring from the box and slid it onto her finger.

Joyful tears streamed down her face. "I love you!" she cried. "This is this is…"

Finishing her sentence he said, "More than you bargained for?"

"Everything I've ever wanted." She sighed happily.

He drew her into his arms. "Callie Cat, you loving me is all I've ever wanted."

Love spiraled through her. Standing on her tiptoes, she snaked her hand behind his head and pulled it down towards her mouth. Their lips wrapped in a loving kiss, and their arms tightly embraced one another. She tasted his promise to love her forever, and he felt the surrender of her fears and the giving of her heart.

After the kiss ended, Evan asked, "Ready to see the inside?"

"Yes!"

"Okay. There are three ways to get in. From the driver's door or passenger's door, or…" he trailed off. "Follow me."

She did, and he showed her the side door located on the passenger side.

"Whoa! This is so cool!" she exclaimed.

Evan held the door open for her. His face radiated a charming smile that made her heart rate quicken. She entered and let her feet carry her up the steps to the main floor. Another moment of awe fell on her as she glanced right to left, ceiling to floor and then turned to gaze at Evan standing directly behind her.

"Wow!" she said enthusiastically and looked around the customized coach again. "What are we going to do with all this room? It's so much bigger than Sunbird!"

To her left, she opened the door and discovered it was the bathroom. In it was a toilet and shower; a curtain separated the two. Across from the bathroom on the other side of the small walkway was the refrigerator, a kitchen table and counter top. Evan lifted part of the counter, revealing a two burner convection stove top.

He chuckled, "Just because we're on the road doesn't mean we don't deserve good eggs."

She giggled, "I'll drive, and you cook."

"Deal," he said, hugging her from behind, and then led her towards the back into the bedroom. A queen size bed was built in on one side and on the opposite wall was a closet with shelves and space to hang clothes.

"This is incredible!" she gushed, trying to absorb all the extra room and wondered if she would ever get used to it. The whole cab was built for two people to live in instead of one, and she loved the idea of them traveling in it.

Smiling, Evan said, "You won't be alone anymore when you drive off into the horizon."

"I never thought I'd find a man who wanted to travel *with* me!" She jumped into his arms, and he twirled her. She laughed because there was room for him to do this whereas, in Sunbird he wouldn't have been able to.

"I wanted to show you how much you mean to me."

"Evan, you have." She placed her palm over his heart. "I love you," she sighed happily and laid her head on his chest.

"I love you." He kissed the top of her head. "In case, you haven't figured it out this is my idea on how to keep you safe."

"You want to stay in here for a week?" she teased.

He chuckled, "Sort of. If you're interested, I've got a load we can go and pick up."

"Yes! I want to!" she replied excitedly. "But on one condition."

"Which is?"

"It's us going."

"Yes, sweetheart, we are going, because this tractor and I are a package deal."

"Sold," she giggled. "When can we leave?"

"Tomorrow morning."

She placed her hand on his cheek. "Everything I've been searching for has been right here in Purlieu. I've been facing the wrong direction this whole time."

"Kind of like I've been in your rearview mirror," he suggested laughing.

"Yes, I should've been looking in the east not the west," she declared.

He smirked. "And everything I want has been in the western wind."

"Evan," she whispered lovingly. "You are my sunrise."

The joy glowing in her eyes was like watching the sun sink into the horizon as both actions warmed his soul and brought him peace. While caressing her cheek, he tenderly said, "Callie Cat, you are my sunset."

Made in the USA
Monee, IL
27 January 2021